D0168563

COWBOY
HEAT
WAVE

KIM REDFORD

sourcebooks
casablanca

Published by Sourcebooks Casablanca, an imprint of Sourcebooks
P.O. Box 4410, Naperville, Illinois 60567-4410
(630) 961-3900
sourcebooks.com

Printed and bound in Canada.
MBP 10 9 8 7 6 5 4 3 2 1

Chapter 1

"I LEFT MY HEART IN WILDCAT BLUFF COUNTY, TEXAS." Audrey Oakes whispered the words that were not her own as she drove deep into that county. Lady Mauve, her great-grandmother, had written the line in her 1933 journal…and those were just a few of the heartfelt words that brought Audrey to Texas so many years later.

She normally loved springtime, but now she had no thought for pleasure. She needed answers and she needed them now.

Lady Mauve's journal described how she'd left behind bootlegger gold when she went from Hallelujah Ranch speakeasy owner to legitimate bar owner in Hot Springs, Arkansas, after Prohibition. Why did she abandon the gold? Maybe it was too heavy to transport. Maybe she planned to come back for it. Maybe it had something to do with revenuers or other law enforcers. Now there was no way to know, since the last pages of the journal had been ripped out.

At most, Audrey had a couple of months to save her grandmother's life. It was a long shot to find buried gold. Maybe it was an impossible shot. But she had to take it. If she hadn't stumbled across her great-grandmother's journal in a dusty trunk while looking for old photographs, she wouldn't even have this chance. Medical procedures were expensive, and in this case, experimental procedures that weren't covered by insurance were impossible to fund.

She'd set out from Hot Springs early that morning with nothing more than general directions for several possible gold locations written in faded lavender ink on yellowed paper to aid in her hunt. She'd counted on things staying much the same in the country-side, but they hadn't.

She certainly didn't expect to find a county dump in what should have been a meadow. She stopped her SUV in the entry and looked at the site. It appeared to cover about two acres and was surrounded by a chain link fence with two eight-foot gates. A faded metal sign stated hours of operation, when an attendant would be on duty, but that time wasn't now.

In Lady Mauve's journal, she warned not to trust anyone in the county, so Audrey decided to be on the safe side. She drove away from the entrance and parked in a small stand of trees so her SUV wouldn't be seen from the highway or too near the dump.

An earlier rain had left the ground muddy, but that didn't stop her. She got out of her vehicle, determined—if at all possible—to find any landscape that still matched the journal's description. She slowly moved around the dump outside the fence. Nothing looked remotely like what she was trying to locate.

Finally, she stopped at the back outside the dump's fence, frustrated, hungry, tired from the long day that had netted her exactly zero. It'd be dark soon. She wanted to get something to eat and find a place to stay in the nearby town of Wildcat Bluff.

As she turned to head back to her SUV, she heard the engine of a big vehicle near the rear of the waste disposal site. What was a truck doing there when the dump was closed? Maybe it was none of her business to investigate—then again, however unlikely, maybe it'd help her piece together information that might lead to the gold's location. In any case, she was curious.

She slowly, quietly made her way to the back of the dump, where she saw a ten-foot drop from the top that allowed trucks to back up and discard their trash loads into containers below. None there now. Instead, she saw a sixteen-foot cattle trailer backed into the lower area that couldn't be seen from above. She crouched down on her knees. She didn't know what was going on, but she didn't figure it was on the legal side of the law...not with the dump closed and the operation out of sight from the road.

She didn't want to be caught spying on the operation, so she stayed still, even when she felt dampness creep into her jeans from the wet ground. Movement on her part might catch somebody's eye, while staying still stood the better chance of keeping her invisible.

Two muscular guys dressed in jeans, shirts, boots, and caps pulled low over their eyes leaped out of the black one-ton cab. They opened the back doors of the cattle trailer, pulled out mobile aluminum panels, and quickly fastened them end-to-end to make a long chute that they extended across the back lane to a pasture fence. They opened a barbwire gate in the fence, repositioned the ends of the chute to butt up to the opening, and leaped outside the chute.

Two cowboys on horseback appeared on the other side of the fence. They quickly drove a line of wild horses—maybe thirty or so—out of the pasture, through the chute, and up a ramp into the thirty-eight-foot semi.

Audrey watched in astonishment at the efficient operation. Nothing had been left to chance. It moved fast, like a well-oiled machine. And they meant business because every one of the guys wore a pistol in a holster on his belt. All went as planned until one of the horses veered away and headed toward her. A cowboy rode after the runaway, jerking off his wide-brimmed hat and waving it to steer the horse back toward the trailer.

She held steady, although she wanted to get up and run away like the horse. Who were these guys? Horse thieves? In this day and age? If so, they knew the dump was empty most of the time without an attendant, so it was the perfect spot for a clandestine operation. Thoughts of old revenuer-bootlegger chases and shoot-outs came to mind.

She and her mom owned the Oakes Rock Shop & Museum on Bathhouse Row. She'd given many tours and sold lots of books on the legendary Roaring Twenties and Prohibition in Hot Springs, which had been a major getaway for bootleggers from as far away as Chicago. It had given her an eye for a particular kind of trouble. Illegal trouble. She suspected that was exactly what she was seeing here and now.

Still, it was none of her business. She wasn't going to get involved, even if this was some type of rustler operation. She had her own agenda and her grandmother's life took precedence before everything else.

She glanced over her shoulder, where her four-wheel-drive SUV was mostly concealed in the trees. She wished she could run over there and quietly start the engine, but it'd make too much noise and might give away her presence. She just needed to sit tight until the horse thieves were gone, then get out of there.

But she ran out of time. The cowboy on horseback glanced up, saw her, looked back, and called to his friends as he drove the runaway up the ramp and into the semi. One of guys slammed the trailer's doors shut on the horses, while the other jogged to the back of the one-ton and began to uncouple it.

She could hardly believe her bad luck. Once that truck was free of the trailer, they could come after her. She leaped up and sprinted for her SUV. She was thankful she'd left it unlocked. She jerked open the door, fell onto the front seat, and locked the door behind her. She pushed the start button, heard the engine turn over, and hit the gas. She bounced over ruts and downed branches, hearing tree limbs scrape the sides of her vehicle as she got out of there as fast as possible. She made the single lane leading out of the dump before she glanced back. Nothing yet. Still, they'd need time to get back up to the main road from the lane below. She hated to think how fast a one-ton, with its powerful engine, could catch her and cause trouble for her much smaller SUV.

She hit Wildcat Road just as the gray of twilight turned to the black of night. No streetlights anywhere, so only her headlights cut a swath of illumination through a tunnel made by long stretches of barbwire fence on either side of the road. She was alone out there—no cars, no people, no nothing, except cattle and horses in pastures. All she needed to do was get to the small town of Wildcat Bluff and find a place to stay for the night. Hopefully, out of sight would be out of mind.

She lost that hope the moment she saw bright headlights coming up fast behind her. They were high, like on a truck, and above her back bumper. Trouble. She'd known it the moment she'd seen those vehicles, cowboys, and horses arrive at the dump. If only she'd been there earlier and missed them. No way to rewind time now. She must get off the road.

She looked back and forth on either side of the highway, searching desperately for a break in the fence lines, a dirt turnoff, an entry to a ranch, or anything that would allow her to leave the road and slip away. So far, she saw nothing except the highway stretching out ahead of her.

She glanced in her rearview mirror. Those headlights were getting closer, fast. She needed to find an exit. A rise in the road was coming up ahead. That was her chance. The driver behind her wouldn't be able to see her once she was up, over, and down the other side. And he'd be looking for her SUV's lights. She wouldn't give him that satisfaction.

She took the hill as fast as safely possible. At the top, she looked to either side, hoping against hope for a break in the fence line. Finally, she saw one. As she went down the other side, she killed her lights…and was immersed in darkness.

She tapped her brakes, jerked her steering wheel to the right, and careened off the main road. She felt her vehicle fishtail as she held tightly to the steering wheel and aimed as best she could in the dark for the break between the two fence posts. She bounced over a cattle guard, scraped one side of her SUV on a post, and slid to the left on the roadbed, with its deep shoulders.

She hit the brakes, felt her harness tighten across her chest, and her SUV came to a stop. But the left front fender listed downward. She was partly in a ditch. No matter. She needed to hurry and get out of there, so she couldn't be seen from the road.

She threw her vehicle into reverse, but she heard the tires spin, spin, spin. Stuck. She hit the steering wheel with the palm of her hand. She tried reverse again. Spin, spin, spin. She was going nowhere. She took her foot off the gas. How deep was the ditch? How thick was the mud? No way to know. She couldn't afford to grind her tires any deeper in an attempt to get free. She didn't dare turn on lights, inside or out, to check her situation.

As she sat there contemplating what to do next, she saw the truck, with its bright headlights, zoom past on the highway. She breathed a sigh of relief. Going too fast, expecting to catch up with her, they hadn't seen her. But she wasn't safe. When they didn't find her, they'd most likely be back. They'd search the sides of the road exactly like she had earlier. No way should she still be here when they retraced their steps.

She gathered her thoughts. Okay, the long day had turned into what was becoming a long, torturous night. She must handle it. Maybe the ghost of Lady Mauve would lead her to safety. Of course, she wouldn't count on it. Roaring Twenties ghosts were part and parcel of Hot Springs, not Wildcat Bluff County. Still, she wouldn't mind a little help.

Worst luck, she couldn't move her SUV. She needed to get away from her vehicle and call for a tow truck. She didn't want to leave anything important behind just in case they saw her SUV and stopped to check on it. She'd placed her laptop in its case and the soft-sided carryall with her clothes on the floor in front of the passenger seat. It was also a good thing she wore comfortable jeans, sweatshirt, and running shoes in navy, a dark color that blended well with the night.

She eased her door ajar, glad she'd set the inside light so it didn't come on when she did. All was quiet outside except for the sounds of nature, like frogs and insects and coyote howls in the distance. She grabbed her purse, computer, and bag. She listened again, but she didn't hear any traffic, so she had a little time to disappear into the darkness.

Fortunately, she was on the opposite side of where her SUV listed into the ditch. She stepped cautiously onto the lane, felt her shoe slide in mud, and stopped to get firmer footing. She looped her purse, computer case, and bag by their straps over her shoulders. After she shut the door, she locked it. She hated to leave her vehicle in such a precarious position, but she hoped it was dark enough that it wouldn't be seen from the highway. She eased her cell phone out of her purse. She wanted to turn on the flashlight, but she didn't dare give away her position.

She glanced around, but saw nothing except dark countryside. She didn't want to wait any longer to call for help. She crouched beside her SUV. She hit a button for the search engine on her phone, but pretty quickly realized she had no service. She tried several more times before accepting the situation. More bad luck. She dropped her phone back in her purse.

She stood up so she could look in both directions. No one-ton yet. Once they passed her going back to the dump, she could hoof it to Wildcat Bluff. It might take all night, but where there was a will, there was a way. Still, she didn't want to be out on a country road alone at night, particularly if she was being hunted…not if she had another choice. She supposed she could walk out across a pasture with her bags, sit down under a tree, and wait for dawn. She might stir up a cow or horse, but probably nothing more dangerous. She thought there must be a ranch house somewhere on this acreage. If she found it, she could possibly get help she could trust there, although that might be miles away, too.

As she contemplated her options, she heard another vehicle engine, but not from Wildcat Road. Bright headlights about the height and size for an ATV washed down the lane and over her. Somebody from the ranch was coming. Friend or foe? This could be the help she needed, but Lady Mauve's journal stressed that nobody could be trusted in Wildcat Bluff County. Did that still hold true all these years later? Time would tell.

She squared her shoulders, adjusted the straps of her bags, and walked away from her SUV to the center of the lane.

The ATV stopped several yards in front of her. Somebody got off the vehicle. A dark silhouette walked toward her in a long-legged stride. Male. Tall. Broad-shouldered. Narrow-hipped. Big man could equal big trouble. What if this ranch was connected, somehow, with the horse thieves, since it was so close by, maybe even shared a property line? But what if it wasn't? Big man could also mean big help.

"Stuck?" the stranger called in a deep voice with the unmistakable Texas accent that invoked hot skin sliding across cool sheets on steamy nights.

She felt that one word slip up and down her spine, making her shiver and wonder at her strong reaction to him.

"Rain will do it." He reached her, a shotgun held easily in one hand at his side.

She looked him over, searching for clues that would tell her about him. He had dark hair worn a little long, to his shoulders. Brown eyes in a tanned face of sharp planes and angles evaluated her right back, as if he didn't trust her any more than she did him. Thirtyish. He was all muscle, clad in typical cowboy clothes of Wranglers, big rodeo buckle, blue-plaid shirt, and jean jacket.

He was obviously a man who knew his way around a ranch, so he had to know horses like the wild ones at the dump. But he was here, not there, so that could mean he wasn't part of the outfit—although he could be the mastermind and stay out of the action. She stopped her thoughts. She wasn't back in the Roaring Twenties in Hot Springs, where most everyone pursued an angle, just as liable to be illegal as legal.

She heard the sound of a big truck growing closer. Rustlers coming back or just a local rancher? She wasn't about to take a chance. "Douse your lights."

"Trouble?"

"Quick."

He flicked his shotgun up with one hand, using nothing more than his strong wrist to lift the weight, so the business end aimed toward the highway instead of the ground.

"They'll see us."

"So? This is my ranch. Nobody's coming here except on my say-so." He glanced at her, then back at the road. "You're a different story."

"I was down at the dump."

He grew still. "Why?"

"I just…just…" She watched as the truck slowed down, lights illuminating her SUV as well as her and the stranger. The vehicle crept past, as if the occupants were getting a good look while debating whether or not to take action. And then, decision made, the one-ton roared away, back toward the dump.

"Friends of yours?"

"I never saw them before tonight." She faced the stranger. "I'm not from around here."

"I can tell by your voice."

"I'm Audrey Oakes. Hot Springs."

He lowered his shotgun, then held out his hand.

She shook it…big, warm, strong. She felt as if he'd touched every bit of her, not just her fingers. She experienced a little thrill at the impact he had on her before she quickly squashed it. She didn't need a good-looking guy on her mind or tempting her body.

"I'm Cole Murphy." He gestured with his head toward the ATV. "Why don't we go up to the house and you can tell me your story?"

"Thank you for the offer, but I don't want to be any trouble. If I can get someplace where I have cell coverage, I'll call a tow truck."

"It's no trouble," he said.

"Still, I don't want to put you out."

"You aren't." He looked at her SUV, then back at her. "Not to worry. We'll tow you out of the ditch, one way or another."

"Thank you."

"You may be more shook up than you realize. I'll get you something hot to drink up at the house." He smiled, eyes crinkling at the corners.

"I'm okay."

"I'm a volunteer firefighter. We're also EMTs."

She felt reassured by that news, although he still needed to earn her trust.

"You're right to be cautious. When we get within cell range, you can call the fire station and check me out."

"Thanks, but—"

"No buts. That's what you'll do. It's the only safe thing for a woman alone at night in a strange place," he said.

"I appreciate the help."

"Anytime." He hesitated as he gave her a harder look. "Did you see something unusual at the dump? Did somebody in that truck follow you from there?"

"I think so."

"In that case, I really want to hear your story."

Chapter 2

COLE MURPHY STARED AT THE STRANDED WOMAN...AND FELT hungry. He'd known something big was coming because he hadn't been able to settle this particular hunger for days, weeks, months. Nothing satisfied him. He'd put it down to the horse thieves that were always a step ahead of him.

Now hunger had a name. Audrey Oakes. She was about five-six, thirtyish. And she was definitely a feast for hungry eyes. He felt a connection that drew him to her stronger than any rope, fancy nylon, or braided leather.

But he was double damned. He couldn't trust one hair on her head. She might very well be connected to the rustler outfit that was making his life hell. Three months ago, he'd discovered twenty of the endangered wild mustangs entrusted to his care by the federal government stolen off his ranch. At the time, he'd been irritated and determined to catch the thieves. Sixty mustangs later, he was a lot more than irritated. He was haunted by the thought of what might be happening to them.

He'd done his best to protect the mustangs by moving them from one pasture to another, but the rustlers still got to them. On a four-thousand-acre ranch, cattle and horses could go missing without being noticed for some time, even with alert cowboys. He was closing one horse thief avenue to the mustangs after another, but he still had to be suspicious of anything out of the ordinary. And Audrey Oakes was way beyond ordinary.

True or not, he needed to hear her story, but he'd be skeptical of every little bit of it. Bottom line, why had she come from the direction of the dump this time of night when it was closed to the public? Why had she careened onto his ranch's narrow back road? Why were the rustlers chasing her? Maybe because she'd caught them in the act or maybe because they were setting up a situation where she needed help on his ranch and that gave her an entry into his world that they could exploit, since he was limiting their ability to rustle his mustangs. On the other hand, she could be legit, meaning he was letting his concerns and frustrations spill onto an innocent woman. Either way, he needed to know more about her.

He took a closer look at her in the bright lights of his ATV. She had eyes the color of lavender. She sported a wild mane of black hair that hung past her shoulders. Pale skin begged to be stroked, caressed, kissed. She was a rare beauty. And he was all in…even if she might be part of the enemy camp.

He took a step toward her, couldn't help himself as his hunger ratcheted up a notch. He wanted her…smell, touch, taste. He caught her scent, sweet and tart. What would her bare skin feel like under his work-roughened hands? Smooth as silk, no doubt. He could almost taste her. Hunger rode him harder. He needed, needed…

"Mr. Murphy, is your gun loaded?" Audrey held up a hand as if to stop him or put distance between them.

"Oh, yeah." He stopped his thoughts in their tracks. What was he doing? He was trying to reassure her that he was there to help.

"I'm not used to weapons."

"On ranches, we're always armed for danger."

She smiled, shrugging one shoulder. "About now, I'd like to be considered dangerous, but as you can see, I'm in a precarious position."

He returned her smile. He liked the fact that she made light of her vulnerability. Strange country. Strange man. Strange situation. And still self-assurance blazed out of her mesmerizing eyes. He liked her sass just about as much as he liked her looks. Yeah, he flat-out liked her. Trouble on two legs, no other way around it… not with a hunger riding him that just wouldn't quit. Suspicion ratcheted up to a razor-sharp edge. Was she naturally self-confident or did she know something he didn't know?

She glanced toward the ranch's entry, as if calculating time and distance in case she needed to quickly get away.

He throttled down his reaction to her, suspicion and all. "Surprised you saw that turnoff. It's narrow. Plus, I didn't Weed-Eat the tall grass."

"I was looking for any opening that would let me off the road." She glanced down at her SUV. "If I hadn't had my lights off, I could've managed the turn just fine."

"You were driving without headlights?"

"Not all the way." She gestured back up the road. "Once I got over that hill, I killed my lights so I couldn't be seen."

"They slowed down to a crawl, so they saw you anyway."

"Yeah." She nodded with a slight shiver.

"We don't need to jaw out here. Let's get up to the house and get you something warm to drink."

He took a step back, encouraging her to follow him. He definitely needed to hear her story. If she truly was *in* trouble, he wanted to help. If she *was* trouble, he needed to know. For now, safety came first, just in case she'd been targeted. He didn't figure anyplace on his ranch except the compound fit that bill any longer.

He glanced up at the motion sensor camera he'd installed on a nearby tree so he could watch this entrance from his computer or phone. He didn't keep the gate closed here. That left it protected by nothing more than a cattle guard to keep livestock inside. He wanted the horse thieves to think they could easily breach this entry, so they would use it and he could catch them on camera. So far, they had been smarter than him. They hadn't come near it. Until now, maybe.

"Did you lock your vehicle?" he asked.

"Yes."

"Good. Let's get out of here." He smiled, trying to appear as friendly and harmless as possible. He figured he could make it with friendly but harmless was a challenge.

"I'll go with you for now, but once we're in cell range, I want to make that call."

"You bet," he said.

"I do appreciate your help."

"Anytime." He glanced toward the open entry to his ranch. Just in case, he didn't want to leave her SUV vulnerable. "Wait a minute."

He walked to the cattle guard, then leaned his shotgun against the fence. He pulled a metal gate from behind the high grass, where he kept it hidden from view. He slid it across the narrow entry, secured it with a length of rusted chain to a fence post, and clamped the Yale lock shut on the chain. Wire cutters could be used on the lock or the chain, but that'd take time and it'd be on camera. For now he'd made it harder to enter the ranch and provided some protection for her vehicle.

He picked up his shotgun and walked back to her.

"Thanks. I feel better with my SUV behind a locked gate."

"So do I." He gestured toward his ATV. "Want me to carry your bag?"

"Thanks. I've got it."

"Just set it in the back of the ATV." He liked her independence just as much as he liked the rest of her.

"Okay."

She turned and headed uphill.

He checked the perimeter again, then followed her. He was all polite cowboy on the outside, but on the inside he was far from polite as he watched the sway of her hips, the length of her stride, and the determined set of her shoulders. She was hot enough to belong on the glossy pages of a magazine, print or online. He wished he could simply enjoy the show. He couldn't. She didn't belong on a ranch in Wildcat Bluff County. Who the hell was she and why was she really here?

When they reached the ATV, she quickly set her big bag in back before she sat down in front. He joined her, nestling his shotgun within easy reach. He was glad he'd driven the bigger four-wheeler with two front seats and an open bed in back to haul stuff, so she had a comfortable way to ride to the house.

He headed toward the compound. He'd feel better about the entire situation once he got them inside the black vertical metal fence with stone pillars that surrounded the heart of the ranch. Nobody was getting in there undetected, not with motion sensor lights, cameras, and dogs. He'd never had anybody attempt to get into the ranch house, but precaution was a deterrent itself.

His headlights cut a narrow yellow swath through the darkness with little light from a new moon. He was familiar with the dark shapes of trees and bushes and buildings up ahead to know that all was as he'd left it.

When he reached the point where he knew there was good cell coverage, he stopped, turned on the inside light, and glanced over at her.

She gave him a questioning look.

"If you'll search for Wildcat Bluff Fire-Rescue on your phone, there's a contact number on the website."

"Thanks." She fiddled with her phone for a bit. "I'll put this on speakerphone, so you can hear what's going on."

"Appreciate it."

She punched a number, then gave him a nod.

"Wildcat Bluff Fire-Rescue. Hedy Murray here," a no-nonsense voice answered.

"Hey there. I'm Audrey Oakes. I'm with Cole, uh…"

"Murphy." He leaned toward the phone. "Hedy, this is Cole."

"What's up?"

"Audrey is here at the ranch. She's from Hot Springs and doesn't know the area around here too well."

"Bottom line," Audrey said, "I turned onto his ranch and managed to get my SUV stuck just beyond his cattle guard."

"Sorry to hear about your trouble," Hedy said. "You're lucky Cole found you. What do you need from us? A tow? A place to stay? Food?"

"Thanks. That's generous." Audrey glanced at Cole with a smile.

"She might be a little shook up," he said.

"I don't think so," Audrey said. "It was just a little—"

"If it's fine with her, I'd like to keep her here overnight to make sure she's okay. I can tow her SUV out in the morning."

"Overnight?" Audrey's eyes widened in surprise. "Really?"

"I'm serious," he said. "There's no need for you to go back out tonight with a tow truck and find a place to stay and something to eat. I've got all that here."

"Not a bad idea," Hedy said. "But, Audrey, if you're not comfortable with that suggestion, just let me know and we'll make other arrangements."

"Where would I sleep?" Audrey asked.

"Guest house." He was glad he had that option to offer, since it'd probably make her more likely to accept his offer.

"Nice place," Hedy said. "If it helps you make a decision, Audrey, I can vouch for Cole. He's a hardworking cowboy and an asset to our community."

"Thank you," Audrey said. "I guess the easiest thing for everybody is for me to stay here till morning."

"Easiest is nothing if you're not comfortable," Hedy said. "If you don't think Cole will mind his manners, just say the word and you're out of there."

"Hedy, when did I not mind my manners?" Cole felt a little affronted at the idea that somebody would question his cowboy manners, instilled in him since birth.

Hedy chuckled. "Better not go there."

Cole gave the phone a dark look before he focused on Audrey's face. "She's funning us both. I'm always a perfect gentleman around the ladies."

Audrey joined Hedy's laughter. "Guess the trick to that is to first find the lady…although I'm sure there are plenty in this county."

Hedy laughed harder. "Audrey, I hope you're going to be around these parts for a bit. I think you'll fit in just fine. I want to meet you."

"I'd like to meet you, too. And I plan to be here for a couple months or so."

"Vacation?" Hedy asked.

"It's personal," Audrey said. "But not private. I'll need some help to accomplish my goal."

"I'm here." Cole realized those words came out in a low growl. If anybody was going to help her, it would be him. When did he get so possessive? It wasn't like him, but he still couldn't stop the feeling.

"When you're ready, come see me at the fire station or at my store—Adelia's Delights—in Old Town. I'll help any way I can, and so will others. That's the way we are in Wildcat Bluff County. We're always ready to lend a helping hand. Don't you agree, Cole?" Hedy said.

"Yes. And that's exactly what I'm doing tonight."

"Thank you both." Audrey gave him a warm smile.

He felt that smile clear to his bone marrow. He just hoped against hope that she was exactly who she claimed to be.

"You're welcome," Hedy said. "Now put the station's number on speed dial so you can reach us quickly anytime."

"I will," Audrey said.

"Now both of you have a good, restful evening," Hedy said. "We can catch up later."

"Will do," Cole said.

"Bye for now. And thank you." Audrey clicked off and looked at him. "What a wonderful, warm woman."

"She's the best," he said. "Are you truly okay about staying here? I didn't mean to put you on the spot, but it suddenly occurred to me it was the best solution for us all."

"I'm fine. And I do appreciate the help."

"Like I said, anytime."

He switched off the inside light, then moved forward again. Soon he reached the compound's entry. A wooden sign supported by rock columns stretched high over the lane. GTT RANCH had been burned into the wood. He stopped, looking, listening, watching for anything unusual in the area.

"What does GTT stand for?" Audrey asked.

"Guess you didn't get Texas history back in school?"

"No." She smiled at him. "That'd be Arkansas history."

"Those histories probably converge as far as GTT goes."

"What do you mean?"

"Back in the late 1800s, folks were leaving home and setting out for the West from back East or places like Arkansas and Missouri. A lot of them scrawled *GTT* on their doors before they left. Anybody who saw those three letters knew another person or family had gone to Texas."

"It was that common?"

"Yep. My family came from Kentucky and settled here. They worked hard and made a go of this ranchland."

"It's beautiful," she said.

"Four thousand acres of pasture, forest, springs, and lakes. Cattle. Horses. Deer. Wildlife."

"That's a lot of land and animals."

"You bet. And now I'm responsible for it." He glanced over to make sure she understood just how far he'd go to protect his family's legacy.

"I thought a great deal rested on my shoulders in Hot

Springs. My mom and I run a store that was founded by my great-grandmother."

"Looks like we both have plenty of heritage behind us."

"Yes." She gestured at the land around them. "But my responsibility is little compared to yours. I don't know how you do all you do here."

"It's what you're raised to know and love. Plus, local cowboys work their hearts out. I bet I'd be all thumbs in your city shop."

"You'd catch on." She glanced over at him.

"Bet you'd be the same here." He snagged her gaze...brown eyes held lavender ones for several heartbeats, as if they were both imaging a world in which she settled onto the ranch and brought new lifeblood to it. GTT.

He jerked his gaze away. He was getting way ahead of himself. She was much more likely to be a danger to the ranch than anything else. He had to keep his head on straight around her, no matter how difficult.

He picked up the remote control, triggered a response, and the gate under the sign slowly slid open. He drove inside the fence, hit a control button, and watched the gate cross the lane until it completely shut off access to the compound. He'd left on lights, mostly on low poles or on the ground, where they didn't cause a major loss of night vision.

He didn't notice any problems as he followed the lane alongside the separate metal fence that surrounded the house and its grounds to the circle drive around a big green post oak. He rounded the circle and drove to the front of the house, which was across the cement courtyard from the empty guesthouse, with the horse barn and other outbuildings set farther back. All the structures were native rock with crimson metal roofs.

A long covered, open carport stretched down the length of the house. It handled four vehicles. He pulled into a slot next to his white with crimson-and-yellow flames pickup. At least he knew those were the colors, since he'd had it specially painted to reflect his work as a volunteer firefighter. Right now, his truck was so muddy from the recent rain that it was hard to tell.

"Pretty place," she said.

"Thanks." As he cut the engine, he glanced over at her. "I added this parking area to keep the vehicles from turning into ovens in the summer."

"Good idea."

"It's not much for looks, but it does the trick." He gestured toward the house. "Anyway, out here is all work area. Relaxation takes place in back. I'll show you later."

"Thanks, but don't go to any extra trouble for me," she said.

"No trouble." He stepped out and grabbed her bag.

She followed him, carrying her laptop case and purse.

He walked out of the carport, turned to the right, and led her to the front door. He heard barking and glanced at the black metal fence that enclosed the house and yard. Two bright-eyed, black-and-white border collies bounded up to the fence, then raced back and forth in excitement.

"Pretty dogs," she said.

"Smart, too. That's Maxwell and Folger."

She chuckled. "Are they the coffee drinkers or is that you?"

"That'd be me and the other cowboys." He joined her laughter. "Seemed like a good idea at the time. We call them Max and Folgie."

He reached into the pocket of his jacket, pulled out two dog treats, and tossed them over the fence. The dogs caught their treats in midair, lay down, and began chewing on the goodies. He walked over and unlocked the hand-carved golden oak front door, reached inside, and turned off the alarm. He glanced back at her with a smile.

"Welcome to my humble abode."

Chapter 3

"NOT HUMBLE AT ALL," AUDREY SAID AS SHE LOOKED AROUND the spacious entry.

Cole leaned his shotgun against a cedar table. An original oil painting of horses racing across a verdant countryside was centered above it.

She could tell by the way he handled the weapon that he was accustomed to having one nearby. She was also aware that he'd been suspicious of her situation from the first. Was this gun-toting standard behavior in the country, or was he anticipating trouble? No way to know yet, but she needed to get the lay of the land as quickly as possible. Hedy may have reassured her about Cole's standing in the community, but he could still have something to do with the horse thieves.

"Take a left into the living room." He set her clothes bag down on the smooth oak floor.

She laid her purse and laptop on top of it, ready to go at a moment's notice. She tamped down her suspicion. She ought to be appreciative of all he was offering her. But between Lady Mauve's warning and the chase from the dump, she was on edge. She simply needed to relax into the situation and take it at face value...for now.

"Let's get you comfortable."

"Oh, this is lovely." She crossed a Saltillo tile floor into a large den, glancing here and there at the Western decor.

"Thanks. Lots of my family added, updated, redecorated, what-have-you over the years until now it's just home."

"It's definitely warm and cozy." She stopped under a soft over-head spotlight set in the thick beam of the cedar-plank ceiling.

"Comfy. That's what I like about it," he said.

She nodded in agreement, but still…it was larger-than-life. Nothing less would do to express her feelings about the ranch, the house, the man. And the term matched the impression she'd gleaned from her great-grandmother's journal. Not gone, not forgotten, still here. She'd grown up with Hot Springs's legend-ary characters and extraordinary events that populated many a book, movie, and television series. She had expected to leave that all behind once she left Bathhouse Row, but she hadn't. Wildcat Bluff County had continued this old heritage as well, but it also held secrets—deep secrets—that she must unlock to save her grandmother.

She glanced at Cole, so solid, so powerful, so in his element. She felt as if she was on the brink of getting caught up in new, and old, drama that threatened to destabilize her well-ordered life. And yet she couldn't turn back or look back. She would continue to follow in Lady Mauve's footsteps.

Cole stared at her as if he hadn't eaten in a week…hungry, oh so very hungry. But for what? He appeared relaxed in the comfort of his own home but at the same time poised on the edge of a sudden burst of energy. Civilization lay uneasily on this man's shoulders. She wouldn't want to be the one to cross him. He reminded her too much of Hot Springs's wild past.

She whirled away from his intense gaze, feeling as if he was igniting a blaze in her, one that was way too combustible. She took several steps into the room and looked around for distraction.

A large fireplace yawned in the center of a long wall com-prised of various sizes of flat rocks. A contemporary oil paint-ing in reds, yellows, and oranges hung above the fireplace. Two red leather armchairs, one with a red-and-yellow-striped throw, had been positioned in front of the fireplace across from a long matching sofa, with a colorful hand-loomed rug in between. One side of the room opened into a large kitchen, while on the other side, sliding glass doors led onto a deep patio with plush outdoor furniture, where steps led down to a big flagstone area flanked by ancient oaks.

"Your home is so special," she said, although it was so much more than that single word. Love over the generations had seeped into the very structure and gleamed from every object that had been selected for it.

"Thanks. I can't take much credit. Mom updated before she and Dad decided to turn the ranch over to me and live the easy life in Florida. I figure that'll wear thin after a while and they'll be back, but for now, I'm taking care of the place."

"Fun in the sun?"

"Yeah. But that's not for me. I've been here all my life," he said.

"Hot Springs for me."

He walked over to stand beside her in front of the fireplace. "I'm content here in the country. How about you and city life?"

"What do you mean?" She felt as if he was pushing for an answer that meant something more than his simple words.

"Life? Content? Here or there?" he asked.

She shrugged, not willing to give herself away by telling him that she hadn't been content since the moment she'd landed on his ranch and met him. Somehow, he made her want more...of what she wasn't exactly sure.

"Sometimes things can come on you pretty fast," he said.

"I enjoy a wonderful life in Hot Springs." There. That ought to satisfy his curiosity and protect her emotions.

He nodded even as his brown eyes appeared skeptical.

She shivered as a chill ran through her. He was observant—maybe too observant to suit her needs.

"Cold? You've been through a lot tonight. It could be hitting you, delayed reaction and all. I can build a fire."

She shivered harder.

"Even better, let's go into the kitchen. I'll make coffee or tea… open a can of soup. What do you want?"

As she contemplated his offer, she felt the stress of the night hit her. She wasn't just cold. She felt weak. And it was so unlike her. She abruptly sat down on the sofa. She just needed a moment to collect herself and then she'd return to her normal in-charge, get-the-job-done self.

"I'm a poor host." He grabbed the colorful throw from a chair and tucked it around her shoulders.

"Thanks." She clutched the edges of the soft fleece with both hands, grateful for the warmth, and pulled it around her body.

"Delayed shock. I'm an EMT. I've seen it before."

She nodded, shivering despite the warmth.

"Don't rush it. You've had a slight shock, but you'll come out of it."

"Thanks," she said.

"Glad I was there to rescue you."

She raised her head and looked at him. A smile played across his full lips, tugging the corners upward. He had such a strong face, all high cheekbones and square jaw in contrast to his sensuous mouth. She imagined touching her lips to his lips, feeling warmth and tenderness. It'd definitely drive away her chill.

"Anyway, I'd much prefer to find *you* in a ditch instead of a muddy cow any day." Humor flashed in his brown eyes.

"Are you comparing me to a cow?" She pretended annoyance, although she knew she was giving herself away by the twitch of her lips at his humor.

"It'd be a compliment. I've got some prize stock on the GTT."

"In that case, it's a good thing I'll spend a night in the guest-house. After that, maybe I'll be considered prize stock."

He chuckled. "You don't need to spend even a single night to be considered prize stock."

She pretended mock annoyance. "Just don't get any ideas about auctioning me off."

"Can't say it wouldn't happen around here." He laughed harder. "Fact of the matter, Wildcat Bluff Fire-Rescue auctioned off bachelor cowboy firefighters for dates at a big charity event."

"You're kidding!"

"Not about something like that," he said.

"Did somebody buy you?"

"Yep." He nodded with a grin.

"Bet the fire station made a bundle," she said.

"Yep." He grinned bigger. "Bought a new booster with it."

"This is quite a county."

"Yep. We're real community-minded."

"Guess I'd better be quiet about being prize stock, just to be on the safe side," she said with a smile.

"Even better. Never volunteer."

"Okay. I'm warned."

"Of course, that might not save you from charity events," he said.

"Somebody around here gets their way?"

"Several somebodies."

"Good thing I'm not going to be around too long," she said.

Suddenly he looked sober. "How long are you planning to be here?"

"I bet you have plans for the guesthouse. I only need it for one night, then I'll find a place to stay in town."

"That's not what I meant."

"No?" she asked.

"It's empty right now. Cowboys are all living in their own homes around the county."

"Good. I wouldn't want to put anybody out."

"You aren't." He glanced toward the kitchen. "Look, we got completely off where I was going. You need something to eat before anything else."

She put her hand over her stomach, realizing she *was* hungry.

"I can heat up a can of soup."

"Really, that's not necessary. I don't want to—"

"Not one more word about imposing on me. Neighbors help neighbors around here...and that extends to those who need a little bit of help."

"Thanks," she said.

"Just take a seat at the bar while I put something together for us. I haven't eaten either. Tomato soup okay? It's not stick-to-your-ribs stuff, but I figure something lighter is better for you."

"Sounds great." She sat down on the leather seat of a wooden stool and leaned her elbows on the granite countertop. Cole's mother had added loving touches when she redid the kitchen, from the stainless appliances to the wooden cabinets.

A comfortable silence fell between them as she watched him open a couple of cans, toss the contents into a saucepan, and set it on the gas stove. While the soup heated, he pulled a box of crackers out of a cabinet, then plucked cheese and grapes from the refrigerator. He placed them all on a bright yellow plate.

"Do you need help?"

"Not a bit. Just relax. I'll have this ready in a jiffy."

When the soup was hot, he poured it into two mugs with the GTT logo. He set those, along with the plate of goodies and a stack of napkins, in front of her.

"Looks delicious."

"Thanks. Anything else?" He glanced around the kitchen, then filled two hand-blown glasses with water.

"This is plenty."

He set the glasses beside the other food before he sat down beside her.

She looked at him as he looked at her. Something passed between them, although she wasn't sure exactly what except that they were sharing an intimate moment that she couldn't have imagined just an hour or so earlier. Yet it was comfortable, as if they'd done it many times.

She arranged her part of the meal in front of her, then stopped to look at him again.

"What is it?" he asked.

"I can't tell you how much I appreciate your generosity."

"Just being neighborly."

"Much more than that. I'm a stranger," she said.

"One in need."

"True. If there ever comes a time, I'll be happy to help you, too."

He hesitated, glanced around the kitchen, then back at her. "There is something."

"Yes?"

"You can tell me what you saw at the dump."

She opened her mouth to tell him exactly what she'd seen, but she quickly closed it and reached for the soup. She took several sips, stalling for time as she thought about the situation. If he worked with the horse thieves, she'd be giving herself away by telling him the truth because the rustlers might not be sure of what all she'd seen from the top of the cliff. She'd be safest not to say much about it.

"The dump?" he prompted.

"I was outside the chain link fence, walking and looking around, when I heard horses and a big truck engine."

"That's it?"

"I guess it's not much of a story," she said.

"What did you think was going on?"

"No idea…except I didn't believe it was normal, so I decided to get out of there."

"They must have seen you and come after you."

"What do you think they'd do if they found me?"

He shook his head, drank from his mug, and then set it down with a snap. "Look, those folks are dangerous. Law enforcement is involved in trying to catch them. I mean federal, state, and local."

"Really?"

"If you saw anything at all that would help, you need to tell them. And me."

She grabbed a cracker and it crumbled in her hand. Now she was really glad she hadn't blurted out the truth. She couldn't afford to get mixed up in an illegal operation that involved the law. She had to stay focused and free to find the gold. A little niggling doubt crept into her mind that made her feel guilty for not helping them, but she shoved it aside. Her grandmother came first.

He drank soup, never taking his eyes off her. "I'm so frustrated and I'm so worried about the stolen horses."

"Worried?"

"Mustangs are endangered because they are overpopulating their limited grazing areas in the West. The federal government has a program to save them by distributing them to large ranches."

"That's what you're doing?" she asked.

"Yes. I have enough good acreage that I received mustangs when I applied for them. They are never to be caught, corralled, broken, ridden, or anything while here. They roam free on the GTT in their pastures."

"That's a noble cause."

"I love animals, particularly horses. I'm glad to help out, but I'm not helping one bit when they get stolen off my ranch. It's serious business," he said.

"Why does somebody want them?"

"They could be trained for riders, but I'd guess they'll be sent to Europe as a food delicacy."

"That's terrible."

"Right," he said.

"And the dump?"

"It shares a boundary line with my ranch. I've tracked the stolen horses there, but that's where I lose them. I can't figure how they're basically disappearing into thin air. That's why I've been working at the dump when I get free time."

She opened her mouth to explain to him exactly how it was being done, then closed it again. Did he really care about horses? Was he really working with the feds to solve the mystery? It could all be the perfect ruse to make money by selling free horses to questionable markets. If she hadn't grown up on gangster tales in Hot Springs, maybe she wouldn't have been so quick to question his motives, but she couldn't overlook his ideal setup. He might need easy money to pay off gambling debts or acquire another piece of land. She hated to think that of him, but she had to be smart about the situation, too.

"I don't mean to be rude, but with everything going on around here, I must ask you something else," he said.

"Okay." She finished off her soup, realizing that he was just as suspicious of her as she was of him.

"What are you doing in Wildcat Bluff County? And why were you at the dump?"

"I suppose it doesn't make much sense from the outside looking in, but I have a very specific reason," she said.

"Tell me."

"My mom and I own a gift shop in Hot Springs. We sell a lot of books about the Roaring Twenties and bootleggers."

He leaned toward her, nodding in encouragement.

"While doing some research, I discovered a connection between Hot Springs bootleggers and Wildcat Bluff County. I decided to write a book about it to sell in our store."

"You think there's enough information for a whole book?"

"That's what I'm here to find out."

"And the dump?" he asked.

"It wasn't a dump back then," she said.

"What led you to it?"

"I found a reference to a general location, so I went there to see what I could find."

"Old liquor bottles? Rusted bottle caps?"

"I didn't know what I might find there. It was just on my list of places to visit," she said.

"Do you plan to interview people? That kind of thing?"

"I hope folks will be kind enough to share family stories from that time period."

"And you'll look around, too."

"Yes…when it's possible," she said.

"How long do you think it'll take?"

"I don't know. Maybe a couple of months."

"Tell you what." He picked up his glass of water and set it back down. "You could stay in the guesthouse while you do your research."

"That's generous."

"Neighborly."

"I'd pay you rent," she said.

"Not necessary."

"Yes, it is." She wondered why he made the offer. Did he want to keep an eye on her? She could keep an eye on him, too, because she realized that she couldn't let what she'd seen at the dump slide. She might not plan to tell anybody about it yet, but eventually she probably would. Besides, she felt sorry for the horses. And if Cole was innocent, he might need her help to save the horses and catch the thieves.

"I want to keep you safe."

"Safe?" she asked.

"Think about it. The rustlers saw your license plate. From there, they could get your name and address. By now they may know who you are. You could still be in danger."

She hadn't thought of that. She felt chilled again.

"Just in case they come looking for you, my ranch compound is the safest place for you."

"But why would they go to the trouble of finding me? I didn't see enough to identify anyone or anything that would be truly useful." And that was true. She couldn't pick out a face or name names, so she really couldn't be much help to Cole or the law.

"They won't know that for sure. I'd like you to stay here, where you're safe, at least until we catch the thieves."

She looked into Cole's sincere brown eyes. What if he was part of the rustler outfit and this was their way of keeping tabs on her? Maybe they'd alerted him at the house before he ever came down to find her. Still, he was a well-respected part of the community. Was she better off to stay or go?

"Maybe you'll remember something you saw that didn't seem important at the time. We could go back to the dump and retrace your steps."

She nodded, even as her mind raced with alternatives. What would Lady Mauve do? Audrey squared her shoulders. Her great-grandmother would take a chance on finding the gold…and probably the mustang rustlers as well. She wouldn't pass up a golden opportunity like this one to be at the heart of the action to right a wrong and save a life.

"You'll stay?" he asked.

She smiled, liking him despite all her doubts. "Let's go see this guesthouse of yours."

Chapter 4

COLE UNLOCKED THE FRONT DOOR TO HIS GUESTHOUSE under an activated motion sensor light. For some reason, it felt like the most natural thing in the world for him to be holding Audrey's carryall with her clothes and other intimate items. He wasn't sure what had gotten into him. He didn't normally invite strangers to stay on his ranch compound, particularly when he had horse thieves striking all over the place. If she wasn't working with the rustlers, she could draw them here. He didn't need extra trouble or worry or commitments.

And yet, why did he feel this compelling need to protect her? He wouldn't trust anybody else to do it either. No rational answer came to mind. Above all, he wanted her to be exactly who she said she was. But he didn't believe it—not entirely. Something deceptive lurked in the depths of those crystalline lavender eyes. He just hoped like hell it wasn't something that would hurt either of them...or the horses.

He opened the door, punched off the alarm, flipped on the overhead lights, and gestured for her to enter. He shut and locked the door behind them, taking no chances on safety, although that might have gone right out the window the moment he invited her inside.

He watched as she glanced around and tried to see the place through her eyes. *Cozy* was the only word he had for the den with its hardwood floor, stone walls, and vaulted ceiling with cedar beams. A brown leather sofa and matching recliner along with hand-carved cedar tables took up most of the space. A breakfast bar with leather-trimmed wooden stools separated the den from the kitchen with its sparkling stainless steel appliances and granite countertops.

"Oh, this is delightful." Audrey walked deeper into the room, then glanced back. "Are you sure you want me to stay here?"

"Only you." If he could've taken the words back the moment he said them, he would've. He meant them, but he shouldn't mean them and she shouldn't know he meant them.

"I can't imagine a more wonderful place to stay while I'm in the county."

"There's only one bedroom and bath," he said.

"That's all I need."

"Guess we should've made it bigger when we converted a section of the horse barn years ago."

"It's perfect." She smiled, revealing her pleasure.

He realized he was on the verge of apologizing because he wasn't offering her a bigger, better place to stay. He clamped his lips together, walked across the room, and opened the door to the bedroom. He flipped a switch and the ceiling fan, with its array of lights, showcased the king-size bed and its colorful pillows and turquoise spread with brown barbwire embroidery around the top edge.

"What a beautiful room."

When she slipped past him, he felt the sensation like the lightest brush of a delicate feather as he caught her tantalizing scent. He went rigid all over. He tracked her as she walked around the room, letting her fingertips trail over the top of the dresser, pause on the desk with matching chair, and finally linger on the bedspread. No way to stop his need now. He followed her, imagining the covers tossed back, clothes thrown to the side, and two bodies entwined on the big bed.

"Think you can be comfortable here?" he said in a voice gone deep and gravelly with suppressed emotion.

"Much more than comfortable. Happy."

"Happy." He felt the soft look she gave him go straight to his heart and lodge there. He wanted nothing more than to share her happiness.

"Yes." She followed a line of barbwire embroidery with a fingertip. She adjusted the straps of her purse and computer case on her shoulder, then picked up a turquoise pillow in the shape of a cowboy hat. She hugged it to her chest as she smiled at him.

He wanted to be that pillow in the worst way. Yet all he could do was stand there and stare at her beauty under the spotlight. He ought to do or say something to break the spell, but he didn't want to break it. He wanted the moment to go on forever.

She gave the pillow a squeeze and set it back on the bed.

What would it feel like to be squeezed by her? He might go as squishy as the pillow. He smiled at the thought. If nothing else, she was giving him a renewed appreciation for the decor of the place. To get his mind off her, he opened the closet door wide, stepped into it, and set her bag on top of the built-in drawers.

She peeked around his shoulders. "Terrific! Wish I had this much room at home. My house is older, so the closets are small. I'm just glad I have closets at all. Did you know that once upon a time the government taxed every room in a structure, so nobody built closets?"

"Guess that's why you find those big armoires in antique stores."

She grinned at him with a teasing light in her eyes. "Do a lot of antiques shopping, do you?"

He laughed, shaking his head. "Mom. She's the shopper. I'm the muscle."

"Along with the eye candy." Audrey put a hand over her mouth. "Excuse me, I didn't mean to get personal."

"Thanks. I'll take a compliment any way I can get it."

"Still…"

"Mom insisted on a big bath as well as a big closet. She said men might not care much about them, but women sure do." He eased the conversation away from the personal to save her from the embarrassment, but he was pleased to know she liked his looks.

"That's so true."

"Why don't you set your bags down on the desk and take a look in the bathroom."

"Guess I might as well settle in." She glanced into the closet where he'd set her carryall, then she slipped her computer bag off her shoulder and laid it flat on the desk. She started to set her handbag down, but it tipped to the side and stuff fell out of it.

"Women carry a lot." He knelt on the floor to pick up the debris.

"Normally I use a small purse, but I wanted to bring a lot with me for the road trip."

"Understandable." He handed her a tube of lipstick, granola bar, bottle of water, and several tissues.

She plopped them all back in her purse.

"What's this?" He gently picked up an old-fashioned-looking notebook with a faded, ragged purple cloth cover that appeared well used by loving hands. He stood up and started to open it.

She quickly but gently took the journal away from him. "It's... it's—"

"If it's none of my business, say so. I'm just curious. It looks old and interesting."

"It is both." She pressed the notebook over her heart with both hands.

"I'd like to hear its story."

"You might have heard about a woman called Lady Mauve who lived here during Prohibition times."

"Heard about her? We're ground zero right here in Wildcat Bluff County for her doings back in that era," he said.

"I caught it on the news."

"It's settled down now, but when her underground speakeasy

was found intact on Hallelujah Ranch, Cowboy Heart-to-Heart Corral, that new dating site, launched from there."

"I saw the pictures online." Audrey cocked her head to one side.

"Pictures." He cast his mind backward in time to the one photo of Lady Mauve dressed as a sassy flapper that had been used for promotion. "If you bobbed your hair, you'd look a lot like her. You do anyway."

"So I've been told," Audrey said. "Black hair. Lavender eyes. Pale skin." She smiled. "No way for colors to show up in the old photos unless they were hand-tinted."

"Are you telling me…"

"I'm her great-granddaughter."

"And that's how you came by…"

"Lady Mauve's journal," she said.

"Why didn't you come forward when the Hallelujah Ranch speakeasy discovery was in all the news?"

"I only recently found her journal and decided to write a book about her life and times, if I could get enough information. As far as the speakeasy and all, I didn't want to be part of that circus. My mother and I live a quiet life just the way it's been handed down to us."

"Unlike Lady Mauve during her heyday?"

"After Prohibition, she wanted nothing more than to live and work in peace and happiness."

"Makes sense. I guess a lot of folks felt that way back then," he said.

"They lived through a tumultuous time, particularly if they were running illegal liquor and hosting folks in speakeasies."

"But it was exciting, too. Life might have seemed dull after the wildness of that era."

"For some folks, I'd guess so. Lady Mauve was a different story."

"She was special, wasn't she?" he said.

"Yes."

"Are you going to put the journal in your book?"

"Maybe parts of it. I haven't decided exactly how I'm going to construct the book yet. I suppose it'll depend on the information I find here."

"I wish you'd told me from the get-go. There are lots of people who'll want to meet you and help you. Best of all might be Jake the Farmer."

"That's good news. Who is Jake?" she asked.

"He's our resident centenarian."

"Over a hundred years old?"

"Right. He lived during Lady Mauve's reign in our county, so he'd know things nobody else knows."

"Reign? Isn't that overstating her importance?"

"No, I don't think it is. From what we've all been told, she was the mover and shaker in Wildcat Bluff County, from her speakeasy on Hallelujah Ranch to the pivotal town of Destiny on the bootlegger run. She hired, fired, controlled, inspired...and was loved by everyone."

"Wow. I hadn't heard it put that way," she said.

"You ought to be proud to be her great-granddaughter."

"I am."

"Somebody should throw you a party, as in the prodigal great-granddaughter of Lady Mauve returns to her family roots...or something like that."

"I think you're giving us way too much credit. Besides, I don't want to get caught up in a media whirlwind."

"We're talking about the county's legendary hero."

"Don't you mean antihero? After all, she worked outside the law."

"Prohibition hurt folks more than helped them. Their heroes were those who brought fun and glamour and happiness to their lives," he said.

"I can see your point. Still..."

"You need to talk with Jake."

"I do want to meet him. He sounds like a wonderful resource," she said.

"Jake will want to meet you, too. He's sharp as a tack and still works in his garden."

"That's great. But let's don't tell him my connection to Lady Mauve, at least not up front," she said.

"Okay. But he may figure it out pretty quick. He's that sharp."

"We can see how it goes."

"If you really want to meet Jake, I can set it up and take you to his farm. No need to mention your connection to Lady Mauve."

"I don't want to put you out any more," she said.

"I'd like nothing better than to be part of your hunt for information."

"Thanks."

"Besides, Lady Mauve is still a big mystery. She simply disappeared at the end of Prohibition. There's lots of speculation about where she went and what happened to her. And now, you turn up here."

"From Hot Springs."

"With her journal," he said.

"True."

"It's big news for Wildcat Bluff County."

"If it is, I really don't want to be the center of Lady Mauve speculation. I thought I'd just quietly conduct a little research for my book."

He shook his head. "I doubt that's possible."

"Can't we keep it secret?"

"How?" he asked.

"I don't have to tell anyone else that I'm Lady Mauve's great-granddaughter."

"You look like her."

"Lots of people look similar. It's only a single photo taken a long time ago."

He sighed. "Do you really want me to keep your secret?"

"For now...at least."

"You'll eventually need to come clean."

"I don't want a lot of undue attention," she said.

"I see your point. It could get in the way of your investigation. Folks might be calling you up with all sorts of speculations, half-remembered stories from their grandparents, and you would attract media hounds and news reporters who want to cash in on the Lady Mauve story."

"When it comes time to promote the book, lots of interest would be good, but right now—"

"Got your point." He glanced around the room, then back at her. "Do you want my help?"

"Yes."

"You've got it. And I'm glad for anything that'll take my mind off those horse thieves...not that anything really can because it's my job to hunt them down and stop them. But still, your story is positive."

"I'll help you however I can to save the mustangs," she said.

"Thanks. Not sure how you can do it, but you never know."

"Likewise. Not sure how you can help me, but you never know."

He chuckled. "We're quite a pair, aren't we?"

"Caught up in worlds larger than our own."

"Right." He looked at her more closely, brown eyes questioning. "We just want to take care of our worlds without interference, don't we?"

"Yes. But sometimes we get involved in situations beyond our control."

"And then all we can do is our best to fix what is broken."

"That's exactly right."

"I'm glad you shared your story with me."

"It doesn't have an end yet," she said.

"I'll do my best to help you make it a happy one."

"Thanks."

"I won't push you, but I'd like to read Lady Mauve's journal someday. From everything we know about her, she was a brilliant woman known for beauty and kindness."

"I wish I'd known her," she said.

"Everybody who hears about her wishes the same thing."

"I just hope I can live up to her legacy."

"You're making a good start by coming here."

She patted the journal that she still held over her heart. "I know what she said about her life. Now I want to know what others said about it."

"The actual truth is probably somewhere in between."

"You mean that sometimes we lie to ourselves just to get through the night."

"And day."

"I'm sure her journal is *her* truth."

"And her legacy is *our* truth," he said.

"Maybe I can find a way to combine them."

"One thing, I'm really starting to want to read this book."

"Am I assured of at least one sale?"

"Make it two. If you'll sign the copies, I'll send one to my parents," he said.

"Done."

"Glad that's settled." He grinned at her. "How did we get from me showing you the place to settling Lady Mauve's legacy?"

"Just lucky, I guess." She returned his grin.

"Bathroom. Take a gander."

"My pleasure." She walked over, peeked in the open door, and moaned in delight.

"That good, huh?" He looked over her shoulder. His mom had done it up right. Shower, whirlpool bath, double sinks, fluffy turquoise towels, basket of soap, scents, and bubble bath. "Do you want me to show you how to use anything in there?"

"Thanks. I'll figure it out. For now, is there food in the kitchen?"

"Soup didn't stay with you?"

"I'd be a poor host if I didn't offer you something."

"Not to worry. Mom will have stocked it. Use whatever suits you." He stepped back. "You've had a long day and you need to unpack. I'll get out of your hair."

"I didn't mean to drive you away."

"You're not." He pulled his cell phone out of his pocket. "If you're comfortable with it, why don't we exchange numbers? That way, if anything comes up, you can call me."

"Good idea." She moved past him and tugged her phone out of her purse. "Okay. What's your number?"

He quickly told her.

She entered the digits, then sent him a text message.

"Got it."

When she received his reply—*Sleep well*—she smiled at him. "I'm glad to know you're there in case of trouble, along with other first responders at the fire station."

"We are. You should be safe here, but keep your door locked at all times." He walked out of the bedroom.

She followed him into the den. "Thanks again."

"You bet. Night." He opened the front door, stepped outside, and heard the door lock click into place behind him.

Chapter 5

AUDREY TOOK A DEEP BREATH, TURNED AROUND, AND LEANED back against the front door. What a day. It felt like a week or even a month since she'd left Hot Springs that morning…from one world into another. She hadn't expected to stir up a hornet's nest or meet a hot guy almost the moment she set foot in Wildcat Bluff County. How could she have anticipated it? Nothing was going as she'd planned when she'd come up with her idea. Absolutely nothing.

Lady Mauve must have adjusted her plans on the fly because she'd never know when a revenuer would burst through her speak-easy door or a bootlegger would drink all the hooch instead of delivering it. Of course, Lady Mauve would've adapted with lookouts and teetotalers. Audrey just needed to turn her mind in the right direction to deal with what she'd encountered today.

But first things first. She was hungry now that the shock of the day was wearing off and she was accepting her newfound situation. Bottom line, it could be worse, much worse.

She set her phone on top of the bar, walked into the kitchen, opened the refrigerator, and looked inside. Not much perishable, of course. She could remedy that tomorrow. For tonight, she wanted comfort food. She peeked into the freezer. Glory be and thanks to Cole's mom's foresight, she snatched a frozen dinner— mac and cheese—out of the freezer. It'd be ready in a jiffy.

She watched the container spin around inside the microwave for the allotted time, then plopped it on a paper plate out of a cabinet, grabbed a spoon, and sat down at the bar. She sighed in relief as she took a big bite. Maybe life wasn't completely out of her control after all. If she could satisfy her hunger, she could surely find the bootlegger gold. Besides, a little food in the tummy always gave her self-confidence a boost.

She finished off the mac and cheese pronto, tossed the container in the trashcan, and turned her mind back to the business at hand. She wished she could consult Lady Mauve, and she could in a way through the journal, but for here and now, she had the next best thing. Mom. Now was as good a time as any to update and consult.

She picked up her phone and walked into her new bedroom. She sighed in contentment at the comfort that surrounded her. After she snuggled into the soft cushions of the chair, she pulled up FaceTime on her phone and smiled at the face so similar to her own that popped up when her mother answered. Vivian a.k.a. Mom.

"Audrey! At last. I was worried sick when I didn't hear from you for hours."

"Hey, Mom. Regret I worried you, but I'm all safe and sound here in Wildcat Bluff County."

"That's a relief."

"How's everything at the store?"

"Fine. You left your end of it in good shape. Claudine is working out just fine."

"Great."

"You're the one who took off for the Wild West," Vivian said.

"Texas."

"Just as I said."

Audrey laughed, nodding at her mother to let her know she was pretty much in agreement with that statement.

"Texans."

Audrey laughed harder, thinking about what she'd found in Texas.

"What's so funny?"

"Got to laugh. You just wouldn't believe what I stepped into the moment I set foot on Texas soil."

"You're not in danger, are you?" Vivian asked.

"Not at the moment."

"I don't like the sound of that."

"Nothing is as simple as it seemed in Hot Springs."

"You thought it was simple. I never did."

"True." Audrey turned sober. "How is Mimi?"

"Stable. She's getting the best care a nursing home can provide, but still…she's weak."

"I'll find the gold as fast as I can, but things are complicated here. So far, the landscape isn't even the same as the journal."

"I'm not surprised. It's going on a hundred years since Lady Mauve cut a wide swath through that countryside," Vivian said.

"But I'd hoped—"

"Me, too. If that's not the reality, then we make the most of the hand we've been dealt. That's what the Oakes women have done since Lady Mauve."

"True." Audrey rethought laying her problems in her mother's lap. She was right. Oakes women always rose to the occasion, no matter how dire or strange. For now she didn't really know enough about the horse rustlers or Cole's possible involvement to make an informed decision. Until she got more facts, the best thing she could do was keep a sharp eye out for the situation and be ready to pivot if it heated up.

"Now, tell me what's going on."

"I met a man." Audrey knew that would make her mother happy, since she worried that Audrey would follow the path of the women in their family in never finding a loving life partner.

"Oh! The first day? How? Where? Who?"

"Mom!" Audrey chuckled at her mother's excitement.

"Don't tell me y'all were just filling up at the same gas station."

"Actually, he came to my rescue." She decided to edit the truth. It wouldn't be a lie, and it wouldn't upset her mother either.

"A knight in shining armor." Vivian sighed. "Was he on horseback? I take back anything I ever said that might be misconstrued as negative about Texans."

"Misconstrued, ha! Anyway, it rained earlier in the day."

"Slick roads. You didn't get hurt, did you?"

"No. But I took a turn too quick and ended up in the ditch on his ranch."

"Rancher?" Vivian asked.

"He's a nice guy. In fact, he's a volunteer cowboy firefighter, a first responder in this county. I spoke with a woman at the fire station to check him out before I agreed to stay at his ranch while I am here."

"Wait a minute. Back up. Did you say you're staying with him at his ranch?"

"Yes."

"Audrey, that's not like you to move in with a guy on first acquaintance, or even long-term acquaintance."

"I'm in his guesthouse...not his bedroom."

"Oh. Do you feel safe?" Vivian's eyes darkened in concern.

"Yes, I do feel safe with him. And I told you I spoke with—"

"I know. But he's a man, a cowboy, a guy. Did I say male?"

"Several times."

"I suppose he's tall, dark, and handsome."

Audrey laughed again. "As a matter of fact, he is."

"By the sound of your voice and the look on your face, I feel as if I'm already losing you to a stranger...and a Texan at that."

"No chance of losing me and you know it. Anyway, how often have you thrown a man at me over the years?"

"I'm always looking out for your best interests," Vivian said.

"I know. Mom, he's kind of a great guy, but I don't know him very well, so there's little chance of this growing into anything."

"You never know."

"Yeah, I do. I'm completely focused on finding that gold. Mimi's got my total attention."

"Did you tell him about writing the book?" Vivian asked.

"Yes."

"Did he buy it?"

"Yes," Audrey said.

"Perfect. Did it bother you to lie to him?"

"Now that I'm here, I'm not sure it's a complete lie anymore."

"Really?"

"I'm getting kind of interested in telling Lady Mauve's story as it started here in Wildcat Bluff County," Audrey said.

"Combine it with Hot Springs' heritage and it'll sell in our store."

"Online, too."

"That's exciting," Vivian said.

"Lady Mauve's journal is so intriguing and such a slice of history written from a distinct viewpoint that it'd almost be a shame not to share it."

"Audrey, I'm proud of you. You didn't have to take this chance in life. Now you're even talking about writing a book. As long as you're safe, I'll do anything to support you."

"You always have. And you know I'll do anything to save Mimi."

"We all will."

"Mimi's always been so strong and vital and active. It came on her so suddenly. A wasting disease. What does that even mean?"

"I don't think the doctors know. I really think they just want to experiment on her with their fancy drugs and surgery and stuff."

"They do want to help her."

"But I'm not at all sure they know how," Vivian said.

"It's either let her go or let them try experimental stuff on her."

"I can't imagine either choice."

"We'll do whatever it takes. Once we have the gold, then we'll have the money to make choices."

"Yes, you're right." Vivian's lavender eyes filled with tears. "We must both be strong. There has to be a way out of it for her."

"And us."

"Yes." Vivian blinked away tears. "Now, what do you need from me? Food. Money. Clothes. Anything. You name it and I can send it to you."

"Right now I have everything I need. I'm fortunate to be in this lovely place." Audrey panned her phone around the room so her mother could see the den and kitchen.

"That's wonderful." Vivian smiled. "It's so much better than a motel room. You're very lucky. Maybe Lady Mauve is watching over you."

"Maybe so. I feel perfectly safe inside a fenced compound on a four-thousand-acre ranch. You don't need to worry about me."

"I'm your mother. I'll always worry about you. However, for now I'm reassured you've selected a good and safe place to stay. And a little eye candy never hurt anybody."

"So true." Audrey grinned. "We'll save Mimi. Just you wait and see."

"When I visit her tomorrow, I'll tell her about your adventure in Lady Mauve's old stomping ground. She'll be excited to hear about it."

"I hope so."

"Lady Mauve is the only parent she ever knew. She never met her dad or was told anything about him."

"Nothing at all?"

"Nothing...except that he was the love her life," Vivian said.

"He was my great-grandfather. Your grandfather. Wouldn't it have been wonderful to know even his name, some little thing about him like he parted his hair in the middle or was a sharp dresser or—"

"Yes." Vivian's eyes filled with tears again. "And wouldn't Mimi have loved knowing her father?"

"Wouldn't we all have loved knowing our fathers?"

"I'm sorry. I really regret I didn't choose a man who would hang around and help raise you. But how was I to know he was a rolling stone who would take off the moment he found out I was pregnant?"

"It's not your fault. You've always been two parents rolled into one."

"Thank you," Vivian said.

"Look, let's just accept that Oakes women go for the fast-talkin', sharp-dressin', good-lookin' guys…"

"Who don't hang around long."

"Right. For now, we need to keep our focus on Mimi."

Vivian nodded in agreement. "I'll keep everything rocking along here. If you need anything, call or text me. And for sure keep me updated so I can share your journey with Mimi."

"It'll be almost like Lady Mauve's diary, won't it?"

"Yes." Vivian chuckled. "One thing for sure, Oakes women have always lived exciting lives. We have interesting experiences to share and write about."

"Now that I'm in Wildcat Bluff County, that's turning out to be truer than ever."

"Just stay safe and don't work too hard."

"Same to you."

"Guess we ought to go and get our sleep."

"You're right. Mom, I love you."

"Love you, too."

When the connection was severed, Audrey was left with a blank screen and an empty house. She felt the distance widen between her and her loved ones. She missed them. She glanced around her new surroundings. Lucky to be here, true. But definitely on the lonely side, too.

She felt restless. She stood up, walked back and forth across the den several times, and stopped in front of the recliner. She wanted to get on with it. But she couldn't, not at this time of night. She picked up her phone and carried it into the bedroom, then unzipped her laptop case and set up her computer on the desk. She pulled a phone cord out of her purse and left her cell charging. Last, she set the journal on her nightstand, so she could reread sections as she needed them. Lady Mauve, even if only available in her journal, was a familiar presence.

She might as well unpack and get ready for bed, although she didn't feel sleepy. Too big a day. Too strange a place. Too much energy zinging through her. Thoughts of a good-looking cowboy nearby didn't help either.

Now that she was here, she wished she'd brought more clothes. A couple pairs of jeans, a few tops, pj's, and underwear didn't really cut it. She'd probably need to buy more or Mom could send more. She hung up the jeans and put the rest into drawers before she set out an extra pair of running shoes. At least she'd thought to throw in a casual dress and heels just in case.

She grabbed her pj's and headed for the bathroom. Luxury at its finest. Shower or bath? She felt too impatient for a bath, so she grabbed a washcloth, bar of soap, and shampoo. When she felt the sting of hot water against her back, she moaned in pleasure. She loved the rain shower head and the scent of lavender as she soaped all over. Soon she felt clean, refreshed, and ready to slip between soft sheets. Sleep finally sounded good.

After she toweled dry and put on her pj's, she tossed all the throw pillows to one side, pulled back the covers, and snuggled into the big bed. She lay there a moment, enjoying the pleasure of relaxing after a strenuous day. She yawned as she reached over to turn off the lamp on the nightstand. Everybody's day probably started early in the country, so she should get her sleep in early. She noticed the journal, with its faded lavender cover and fascinating contents.

"Good night, Lady Mauve. Please help me find the bootlegger gold so we can save your daughter's life."

She switched off the light. Quiet. She hadn't realized how quiet it would be in the countryside compared to the constant background noise of the city. Coyotes howled in the distance. An owl hooted in a nearby tree. A dog barked. Maybe not so quiet after all.

And then a new sound invaded her room. She sat up, startled, and looked toward her cell phone. It chirped again. But that was wrong. No one would be calling her now, not here. Unless… Oh no, Mimi.

She threw back the covers, snapped on the light, leaped out of bed, and grabbed the phone, jerking it off the cord. "Yes. I'm here. What is it?"

"Audrey?" a deep male voice with a Texas accent said.

She blinked, felt her brain scramble to connect the dots, and came up with Cole. Not Mom. Mimi okay.

"Audrey, did I wake you?"

"Yes. I mean, no. I'd just gotten into bed."

"Bed?"

"Yes." That simple piece of furniture suddenly took on a great deal more meaning with just the way he said it. She walked back, plumped up the pillows, and slipped under the covers.

"You had a bath?" he asked in a voice gone all growly.

"Shower. Wonderful soap, towels, everything."

"Did the room get steamy from the heat?"

"A little bit."

"Did you bring a robe? I don't think Mom left one."

"That's okay. I brought pj's."

"You're wearing those now?"

"Uh…" She glanced down at the purple silky fabric that caressed her curves, or at least maybe that's the way he would have described it. For her, they were just a comfortable necessity. She glanced toward the closet. Was she going to start seeing her clothes through his eyes? No. Absolutely not.

"Did you take them off?"

"No. They're purple."

"Like your eyes?"

"Darker." What was he getting at? Why were they having this conversation? And why did she feel titillated by it?

"Silky?"

"Yes." And then she knew she was in trouble. "Are you in bed, too?"

"Right."

"Pj's?" she asked.

"No. I can't sleep in anything."

She felt her breath catch in her throat. He was naked. He was naked in bed. He was naked in bed with her on the phone.

"Too hot."

"Hot?"

"Yes. You know how it is."

She didn't before, but she did now. She threw off the covers to try and cool down. "Cooler now?"

"Should be, but I'm not."

"Turn up the AC?"

"I wish it'd help." He gave a low chuckle, as if amused by himself.

She felt that sound vibrate up and down her spine, twine in and around her body, create enough heat to set off a fire alarm.

"Guess you're wondering why I called."

Startled, she sat up in bed. "Are the rustlers back? Did they get into the compound? Are the dogs okay?"

He chuckled again. "I don't think they're after the dogs."

"Good."

"And they didn't get into the compound."

"Good."

"I called to check on you."

"Good. I mean thanks. I'm fine," she said.

"Did you find everything you needed for the night?"

"Mac and cheese in the freezer for dinner."

"Comfort food. That sounds like Mom."

"It hit the spot."

"I'm glad," he said.

"I really can't thank you enough for coming to my rescue."

"Guess I can't thank you enough for letting me come to your rescue."

She laughed at his teasing words as she leaned back against her pillows. "I'll pay you back somehow."

"I'll let you."

"Will you?"

"Yes. I just need to think of what I'd like as payback."

"I'm afraid I won't make much of a ranch hand," she said.

"Plenty of cowboys for that job."

"Maybe I could take you to dinner or something like that? I mean, besides the rent for the guesthouse," she said.

"I'll take something."

"What?"

"We'll decide on *something* later." He chuckled in that low-throated way again. "Right now, you probably need to get some sleep."

"You, too."

"Not sure how much sleep I'll get tonight."

"Really?"

"I'm thinking the color lavender just might keep me awake. For now…night." And he was gone.

Lavender? Did he mean like her eyes or her pj's or Lady Mauve's journal? One thing for sure, she didn't feel so alone anymore.

Chapter 6

COLE UNLOCKED THE GATES INTO THE WILDCAT BLUFF WASTE disposal station early the next morning. He didn't expect to find much from the night before because a cold rain had descended on the area just after dawn and soaked everything again. Luck continued to be on the side of the mustang rustlers. Maybe they'd get careless. Maybe their luck would run out. Maybe the wild horses would break free from their captivity. But he couldn't count on any of that. He could only count on himself…and the law.

He kicked a rock out of his way as he walked past one of the waste ponds, checking the ground for tracks. Unfortunately, the rain had done its job and washed away any evidence that might have been left. Mud caked the bottoms of his boots. He pulled his cowboy hat down lower on his head against the cold wind that belonged in winter, not spring. He buttoned his jean jacket to ward off the chill. Even the weather was against him.

All the trouble that kept piling up simply made him more determined than ever to catch the thieves, bring them to justice, and save the horses. And now Audrey had been thrown into the mix. Last thing he needed was a distracting woman on his ranch. But it was best she was where he could keep an eye on her…and how he wanted to keep an eye on her.

He kicked another rock in frustration. What were the odds that Lady Mauve's great-granddaughter would show up in the middle of the mustang heists? What were the odds she'd careen onto his ranch? What were the odds she was going to be sticking her nose into anything and everything in the quest to write her book? If she didn't look so much like her ancestor in the old photo, he'd question the story about her ancestry.

If he couldn't question that fact, he could sure question everything else about her. No, he couldn't. Not after that midnight phone call. He'd just had to go there, hadn't he? He'd thought about her in that big bed all alone just across the way from him. Was she naked or in a gown or pj's? Did she smell of the lavender soap his mom had put in the bathroom? Maybe she was even waiting for him to come and kiss her good night. True or not, he liked all of those scenarios a whole lot better than the one where she was on the phone with the thieves, setting up their next heist once she got inside information from him.

He shoved his fists into the pockets of his jean jacket as he eyeballed the area. Best keep his mind on facts, not fantasies. Trouble was, Audrey was shaping up to be a mind-blowing fantasy. He wanted nothing more than for her to be telling the truth, but he still doubted it.

He sucked in a deep breath of clean, cold, fresh air to clear his mind. If he was going to ride this horse to the finish line and win, he had to get his head screwed on tight and think straight.

As he kicked another rock out of the way, he heard a vehicle pull up outside the fence. The dump was closed today, but that didn't mean he wasn't going to have an important visitor. He walked over to the entry gates and opened one.

Sheriff Calhoun met him there. The sheriff wore his trademark tan police uniform with a holstered revolver on one hip, equipment belt, black cowboy boots, and a beige Stetson.

"Morning," the sheriff said.

"Bit chilly, isn't it?" Cole replied.

"Don't you know it." Sheriff Calhoun walked into the dump. "I've got news."

"Figured as much."

"I didn't want to discuss this over the phone."

"Yep." Sheriff Calhoun's sharp brown eyes missed nothing as he looked around the dump.

"Last night mustangs were loaded up and hauled out of here."

"How do you know?"

"We've got a sort-of eyewitness."

"Sort of?"

Cole paced away, then turned back, feeling the frustration ride him again. "Stranger turned up at the ranch last night. She cut it too close getting off Wildcat Road and got stuck in the mud. She thought she was being chased by a one-ton from here."

"Who is she? What'd she see? Why was she at the dump? And where is she now?"

"She says her name is Audrey Oakes."

"Okay," Sheriff Calhoun said.

"But more to the point, she says she is the great-granddaughter of Lady Mauve."

"You're kidding me."

"Nope."

"Is she for real?"

"All I know is she looks a lot like that old photo of Lady Mauve."

"Don't that beat all." Sheriff Calhoun raised his hat, ran a hand thoughtfully through his thick, dark hair, and put his Stetson back in place.

"She says she's researching a book about Lady Mauve and her connection to Wildcat Bluff County back during Prohibition days."

"That'd be interesting."

"She plans to interview people."

"If true, it all sounds reasonable. But you're not buying it for some reason. Spit it out," Sheriff Calhoun said.

"It seems too convenient that she arrives in the middle of the mustang heists with a perfect cover story. And the rustlers chase her from the dump to my ranch where I rescue her. What if she's working with them?"

"Wait a minute. Back up here. You're jumping to a big conclusion."

"I know it…and I hope I'm wrong," Cole said.

"First, what did she see? It's not just me that needs to know to move this investigation along. Feds, too."

"She says she only heard horses and a big truck engine."

"Semi, most likely," Sheriff Calhoun said.

"Right."

"But they saw her and didn't want to take a chance on what she might or might not have seen."

"My thinking exactly," Cole said.

"No, not exactly. You suspect she's working with them."

"Yes."

"Okay. I'll grant you it's a suspicious situation, but that doesn't mean she's one of the rustlers."

"I hope she's who she says she is," Cole said.

"Where is she now?"

"On the ranch."

"Your place?" Sheriff Calhoun asked.

"I suggested she stay in the guesthouse. That way I can keep an eye on her."

"And you figure she can keep an eye on you."

"Works both ways," Cole said.

"If you want me to talk with her, I'm not going to do it. That's a sure way of setting off alarm bells for the rustlers, if she's thrown in with them."

"I agree. I thought maybe you could check her out. She's from Hot Springs. She says she owns a store there with her mother."

"Sure. I can do that." Sheriff Calhoun looked out across the dump. "Look, I don't want to get the great-granddaughter of Lady Mauve crosswise with the feds. If she's on the up-and-up, she's an asset to our community."

"And if she's not?"

"We'll catch her and the others in the end. It's just a matter of time."

"I'm afraid we're running out of time for the horses," Cole said.

"I'll let you know if I discover anything that contradicts her story."

"Thanks."

"You've got her in the perfect place to watch her."

"Yeah. I thought I might volunteer to help her with her book research, like take her to see Jake the Farmer."

"Good idea." Sheriff Calhoun turned toward the gates. "But be careful. If she's not working with them, she could be vulnerable. And that means you, too."

"Rustlers won't get into the compound."

"You can't stay there all the time. Neither can she," Sheriff Calhoun said.

"I'm always armed."

"Stay alert, too." Sheriff Calhoun held out his hand. "And keep me posted."

"Will do." Cole shook the sheriff's hand, then watched him leave.

He stood there until the patrol car was out of sight, wondering if he'd done the right thing. Should he have alerted the local police, which could easily run all the way to the Bureau of Land Management and the U.S. Marshals? He'd hate to see Audrey targeted by both sides of the law. On the other hand, if the rustlers came after her, she might very well need law enforcement. And for sure the mustangs needed it.

He walked over to the gates, locked them, and got into his pickup. What was done was done. He'd had no choice. Now he would continue his own investigation. And if it was at all possible, he'd clear Audrey's name *and* rescue the mustangs.

He hit Wildcat Road thinking ahead. He had checked Audrey's SUV before he went to the dump. It was exactly where they'd left it last night. Only one wheel went into the ditch, so it'd be easy enough to pull out. He had a chain in back, but he'd go to the compound and get her first. That way she could take her SUV to the guesthouse.

He drove slowly past the narrow entrance, saw her vehicle, pulled inside the compound, and parked in front of her place. As he got out, he heard Max and Folgie bark greetings, but he didn't have time to go see them.

He rang the doorbell, impatient now that he was here and so close to visiting her again. Maybe in the bright light of day she wouldn't have the same effect on him as last night.

Audrey opened the door and smiled at him. She wore a red long-sleeve T-shirt, faded jeans, and sneakers.

He couldn't have been more wrong. She looked good enough to eat…and he hadn't had breakfast.

"You're up and around early." She held up a cup of coffee. "Want some?"

"You know it."

"Come into the kitchen. I'll pour you a cup."

"Thanks." He followed her inside, but he'd about have followed her anywhere.

When she sashayed into the kitchen, he sat down at the bar to watch her. He could tell she'd quickly made herself at home by the way she grabbed a mug from the upper cabinet and poured coffee from the carafe. Cozy. No other word for it.

She set the mug down in front of him. "Did you eat yet?"

"What if I said I hadn't?"

"That's okay. Are you hungry?"

"Yes." He didn't want to admit it, not even to himself, but he was beyond hungry into famished.

"How about toast and jam? That's all I found for breakfast."

"Sounds good."

She turned back, bustled around a bit, and presented him with a plate of toast cut diagonally. She set a knife, fork, spoon, and napkin in front of him. Last, she opened a jar of blackberry jam and put it beside everything else.

"Thanks." He slathered jam over every piece of toast and chowed down, stopping only to sip coffee.

"You *were* hungry."

He nodded, not about to stop and chat in the middle of his meal.

"You fed me last night and now I've returned the favor."

"Thanks."

"I'll pick up fresh food in Wildcat Bluff."

He swallowed the last bite of toast, then downed his coffee.

"I suppose there are some nice places to shop there."

"There are a couple of regular grocery stores and a store that specializes in organic."

"Perfect," she said.

"Do you need a guide?"

"I think I can find my way around a store." She gave him a narrow-eyed look. "I'm a woman. I shop."

He grinned, liking her sass. "Sounds like my mom. Now, take me to a hardware store and you might never see me again."

She grinned back at him before she turned to wash up.

He handed her the jam, watched her screw the lid back on tight and place the jar in the refrigerator. He'd just eaten, but simply being with her made him hungry all over again.

"If you're going to shop or do anything else on your own, you'll need your vehicle."

"I was thinking the same thing."

"Do you want to help me pull it out of the ditch?"

"Right now?" she asked.

"Can't think of a better time."

"Okay. I'll grab my purse and let's do it."

While she went in the bedroom, he stepped outside and opened both doors of his truck.

He heard her shut the front door and glanced up. She'd thrown on a warm purple jacket that highlighted her eyes. In her happiness, she sort of danced over to his truck and planted herself in the passenger seat. He sat down beside her. He liked being in an enclosed space with her. Somehow, it was sexy as hell.

And then he pulled his mind back to the matter at hand. It wouldn't do to be so distracted just because she was sitting beside him or because he was saving her SUV. He backed up, drove out of the compound while carefully avoiding hungry thoughts.

When they reached her vehicle, he stopped and looked over at her.

"It's not as bad as it looked at night," she said.

"Not bad at all."

"How are you going to do it?"

"I've got a chain that I'll wrap around your axle, then I'll gently tug you out of there."

"What do you want me to do?" she asked.

"Get in the driver's seat, turn on the engine, and steer while I pull you out. It shouldn't require much from you. I just want to make sure we get you safely back on the lane."

"Okay." She hopped out of the truck, ran over to her SUV, climbed inside, and left the door open.

He turned his truck around, got out, grabbed the heavy chain from the pickup bed, then walked over to her SUV. He had to get down on his back in the mud and slide under her vehicle to secure the chain. It was messy work, but necessary to get the job done. When he was satisfied the chain would hold and not damage her SUV, he pushed out, knocked mud off his backside, and walked over to her.

"Do you want me to turn on the engine now?"

"Yes. Put it in neutral."

"Okay," she said.

When he heard her door shut and the motor turn over, he

walked back to his truck and got inside. He eased his pickup forward, feeling the weight of the SUV drag on his truck. He was glad he had the powerful engine of a one-ton, although he'd hauled much heavier loads than her lightweight SUV. It was no problem at all to slowly pull her vehicle out of the ditch and onto the center of the lane. All done, he cut his engine and stepped outside.

He started toward her, but about halfway there, he stopped and simply stood still because she'd gotten out and come to meet him. It felt like the most natural thing in the world to be taking care of a problem with her.

She gave him a big grin and held up her hand for a high five.

He gave it to her, but he wanted so much more…at least a hug.

"We make a great team."

"You took the words right out of my mouth," he said.

"I can't thank you enough." She smiled. "The chain is a neat trick. It's so much better than a big old tow truck."

"Quicker, too."

"You're right handy."

"Thanks. I do my best." He gestured toward her vehicle. "Let me get my chain and let's go home."

"Home?" She cocked her head to one side.

"The compound."

"That's home to you."

"And home to you…for now," he said.

"True. And it's lovely there."

"I'm glad you like it." He realized they were standing close together. Not the way strangers naturally kept distance between them when they talked—the way friends or lovers instinctively stood close when they communicated. And neither of them was moving away from the other.

"Yes…yes, I do." She glanced away, as if she'd just realized their closeness and was surprised by it.

"I'd better get that chain."

"Yes, you'd better."

Still, he didn't move. She didn't either. It felt as if they were bound together by something far stronger than an iron chain.

And he didn't want to break it.

Chapter 7

AUDREY PARKED IN FRONT OF HER NEW HOME, ACROSS THE cement courtyard from Cole's house. Home sweet home. She really was lucky he'd been generous enough to let her stay there. And he'd even towed her car out of the ditch. Life was definitely looking up in Wildcat Bluff County. No wonder Lady Mauve had loved it so much. And yet she'd left. Why? It wasn't in her journal. It hadn't been conveyed to her daughter. Maybe that was another mystery Audrey could solve while she was here.

She got out, checked the mud she'd spun and splattered all over the blue paint. Tires were a caked mess. She needed to get to a car wash, but all in good time. She couldn't make that a priority, not with so much else to be done.

Cole stopped his truck beside her and swung down to the ground. "How did your vehicle ride? Any problems with that tire?"

"Funny you should ask. I was worried about the mud. You went straight to the mechanics."

"You can't afford to have trouble with your transportation, not in the country."

"Far as I could tell, it's the same as ever," she said.

"Good. We can clean your SUV later with the power washer."

"I can go to a car wash."

"Don't bother. We'll do a better job here."

"Okay." She was beginning to wonder how she'd ever lived without a man as handy as him.

"What do you want to do today?"

"Please don't let me interfere with your normal schedule."

"I told my ramrod I'd be out of pocket today. I'm free to introduce you around…if that's what you'd like."

"But—"

"In a tight-knit community like this one, you'll get a lot better reception if you don't walk in on folks cold."

"I hadn't thought about that. I guess you're right," she said.

"Once a few people understand who you are and why you're here, then the word will spread around the county. I don't doubt most everybody will be interested and helpful if possible."

"In that case, I'm happy to accept your kind offer. Maybe I can buy you lunch."

"Good idea. I'll take you up on it. I know just the place to go. From there, the word about you will spread fast," he said.

"I hope it'll be positive word."

"Lady Mauve is the key. She's a legendary figure in this county and homegrown. Got to be positive."

"I'll do my best to fit in."

"Be yourself and you'll do fine."

"I'd better change clothes," she said.

"Keep the jeans. If you want, you can change tops."

"It's a little chilly today. I think I'll put on that lavender sweater I brought with me."

"Whatever you think is best."

"Come on inside while I change."

She unlocked the door and stepped across the threshold. He was right behind her. She wasn't sure how it had happened so fast, but the two of them inside her new place seemed perfectly normal. She just shook her head at the way life could change on a dime.

She left him in the den while she went into her bedroom. She found the sweater in a drawer and was glad she'd brought it. Lightweight cotton with long sleeves was perfect for a day like today. Plus the sweater was dressier than a tee for meeting and greeting. She wanted to look her best. She ran a brush through her medium-length dark hair, put on a little makeup, selected a pair of gold hoops for her ears, and decided she was good to go.

"Wish me luck." She pressed her fingertips to the faded cover of Lady Mauve's journal, then grabbed her purse and rejoined Cole.

"Snagged these from the fridge. Hope you don't mind." He held up two bottles of water. "We might need them later."

"Thanks. And I don't mind a bit. They're yours anyway."

He smiled. "Yours now."

"I'll buy some more at the store and replenish the supply."

"If it suits you, that's fine."

"It suits me."

"Come on. Let's get on the road."

She locked the door behind them, then sat down in the shotgun seat of his truck.

He gave her a quick smile. "I think the place to start is Jake the Farmer."

"If he really knew Lady Mauve, he's bound to have some insider information. That's exciting for me…and the book."

"I called him. Landline, mind you. I gave him basic info. He's at home and waiting for us."

"Let's go!" She returned Cole's smile with a grin. Bootlegger gold, here she came.

He drove them to Wildcat Road, turned toward Wildcat Bluff, and punched the gas on the big engine so the pickup growled as it gained speed.

"Jake lives in a 1920s farmhouse. Friends and neighbors make sure he has everything he needs, but otherwise, he manages life on his own. He's outlived all his contemporaries, so his friends start twenty years younger and go down from there. He's a popular guy with all ages."

"I look forward to meeting him."

"No AC in his house. He says he can't stand the cold air blowing on him. It wasn't all that long ago that he finally let us completely update his farmhouse with electricity, running water, and an indoor bathroom."

"He really didn't want to leave the twentieth century, did he?"

"More like the nineteenth." He chuckled. "I suspect he still uses his old outhouse now and again. They grew them tough back then, so he didn't need or want luxury…or what he considers luxury."

"I can't wait to meet him."

"He's over a hundred years old. That can't help but make a person special, but he's much more than that. You'll see when you meet him."

Cole turned onto a dirt road and drove past neat rows of farmland with green shoots sprouting everywhere.

"Does he still farm?"

"Not as much as he used to. Other folks take care of that for him now. He still manages a big garden near his house."

"I'm impressed."

"We all are," Cole said.

"He never married? No children?"

"Rumor has it a broken heart kept him from ever walking down the aisle, but that could just be a myth to explain his solitary life."

"He's a romantic figure, isn't he?"

"Guess you could say that. For sure, he's bigger than life."

Audrey glanced at Cole. Jake wasn't the only one bigger than life around here. Maybe the old saying *Everything is bigger in Texas* contained a grain of truth.

Cole followed the road to a house painted bright white with a center-peaked, gray-shingle roof that extended over a deep, cozy porch. Jake the Farmer stood up from a wooden swing with green cushions and left it swinging back and forth on its chains as he walked past two rocking chairs with green-and-white-striped cushions.

As Cole parked on the circle drive, Jake walked down the three stairs off the porch and stood there, hands relaxed at his sides.

Audrey had her first good look at the centenarian. He appeared much younger than his actual age. She thought it must be the difference between chronological age and biological age. He was all deeply tanned skin stretched taut over a strong bone structure with prominent cheekbones. Long silver hair had been pulled back into a single plait. He gave the impression of reaching to the sky with his slender body that still appeared supple.

Jake walked over and opened her door. "Welcome to Oakes Farm."

Audrey froze at the sound of her last name. "Oakes?"

"Yes, indeed." He held out his hand to help her down from the pickup in time-honored gentlemanly fashion.

She took his hand, felt the roughness of a working man's skin and something else…a connection that she had no name for.

"Good to see you." Cole broke the moment as he walked around the truck and joined them.

Jake chuckled. "Folks have been saying that for nigh on thirty years. Can't say I blame them. Surprise myself sometimes, too, that I'm still on top of the good earth, not under it."

Cole laughed. "It'd take a lot more than age to get a fine man like you down."

Audrey smiled as she stepped down beside Jake, who was a few inches taller than her.

Jake kept holding her hand, gently but almost possessively, as he turned his face toward her.

She felt caught by surprise. He was blind…milky-white eyes that must have been full of color at one time.

"It's why I don't stray too far from home," Jake said. "I know my home and land like the back of my hand, so it's no problem living here."

"I was just surprised."

"Understandable. I forget about my lack of vision most of the time. I wasn't always this way, but it's been a long time since the accident."

"Most folks forget, too," Cole said. "If you'd worn your sunglasses, she wouldn't have known."

"I wanted Audrey to know." Jake smiled, patted her hand, and let go. "Come on up to the porch and sit a spell."

"Thank you," she said. "And thanks so much for seeing me."

"A man, particularly an ancient man, should never pass up the opportunity to spend time with a lovely woman." He turned toward the house.

"You sound like a romantic." She walked beside him as they took the steps together.

"Sit with me on the swing. It'll be like the springtime of my life again." He hesitated at the door. "Sweet tea?"

"No, thanks. We don't want to put you out," Cole said.

"No bother."

"Thank you, but we just had breakfast," she said.

"Okay."

Audrey settled onto a soft cushion beside Jake while Cole sat down in a nearby rocker. As Jake pushed the swing with one foot, she experienced the oddest sensation that they had been together in this very swing many times. But of course it was impossible.

"Wildcat Bluff County has always been a romantic part of Texas," Jake said. "It's built into our blood and bones here."

"And just to prove it, a dating site called Cowboy Heart-to-Heart Corral launched from Lady Mauve's speakeasy on Hallelujah Ranch," Cole said.

"I heard about it on the news." She hesitated, not sure if now was the right time to get deeper into why she was here.

"I know about it," Jake said. "And I hear it's doing real well."

"That's what I hear, too," Cole replied.

"The woman who launched the site came to see me. She wanted to know about Lady Mauve. I told her the plain truth. She was a beautiful lady with beautiful tastes. That's why the speakeasy is still such a treasure. Wish I could see it…again. But those days are over."

"You could still go there," Cole said.

Jake shook his head. "Let our ghosts dance to their own music. I don't wish to intrude upon them."

"I hope you won't feel that way about why I'm—"

"Lady Mauve never did anything by half," Jake interrupted her. "She never entered a room she didn't own. She never started a business she didn't expand. From bootleg to speakeasy was an easy step for her."

"She was a remarkable woman," Cole said.

"When she went, she left a cold trail," Jake continued. "But if I know her, and I did very well, she'd have preserved her legacy for the right person at the right time to find and share."

"Like the speakeasy?" Cole asked.

"Yes, the speakeasy." Jake turned toward Audrey and sunlight bathed him in a golden glow. "Like a message in a bottle, has more of her legacy now washed up on shore?"

"Yes." Audrey hadn't meant to tell anyone, but now that she was here with Jake it just seemed right. "I found her journal, but I'm not sharing that information with anyone else yet."

"Personal. Yes, I understand. I'll respect your wishes."

"Thank you."

Jake smiled as a melancholy expression passed over his face. "And so, after all these years, she sent you to me. I wonder how she could possibly have guessed I'd still be here, waiting and watching."

"She couldn't know." Audrey returned his smile, even realizing he wouldn't see it. Maybe he could sense her pleasure in his company. "I think she just wanted to record her thoughts."

Jake chuckled. "Like I said, she never did anything by half. If she left a journal to be found, then she meant for those words to be known."

"I guess she could've hoped for it."

"Mauve never lived on hope." Jake nodded toward the wide expanse of the fertile green land of the farm. "She believed in tilling the soil until it yielded the crop she'd planted deep in the ground."

"That's a good way to be."

"The best." He turned toward her again. "What do you think about your last name and the name of my farm being the same?"

"Oakes." She looked at him, wishing she could see into the depths of his eyes for the secrets she felt sure were there. "I'm surprised."

"Oakes was kind of a joke between Mauve and me. It meant we'd both put down deep roots and we'd live as long as the mighty oaks on this farm."

"You knew her very well, then?"

"Yes. Where did you find her journal?"

"Hot Springs." She knew he meant more, as in did she buy an old trunk and discover it, had it been in her family, was it given to her? If she gave that detail, she would reveal her connection to Lady Mauve. And still, she trusted him not to push for more at this time.

"So near and yet so far." Jake appeared sad for a moment before he cleared his expression. "I never knew where she went...but then nobody did. That was her choice. I hope she was happy with it."

"I suppose she was." But Audrey wasn't so sure about that fact anymore.

"We don't want to take up too much of your time today," Cole said.

"Garden is calling to me." Jake smiled. "But I always enjoy visitors, particularly special ones."

"Cole told you why I'm in the county, didn't he?" Audrey asked.

"Yes, he did."

"I hope you'll help me with my book. I think I'll include sections of Lady Mauve's journal in it."

Jake held out his hand, palm turned up. "My dear Audrey

Oakes, it will be my pleasure to bring Lady Mauve alive on the pages of your book, along with other characters and events that made that brief time in history so spectacular. I think you'll be surprised at what I have to offer."

"Thank you." She clasped his hand, then let it go and stood up. She didn't want to tire him or ask too much of him so soon. Still, she didn't want to leave him after just meeting him. He appeared solid and yet life at his age could be fragile.

Jake got to his feet, too. "I'd very much like to hold Mauve's journal. Maybe you would even be so kind as to read sections of it to me."

"Yes, of course. I'd be honored to share her words with you. I mean, you actually knew her." Audrey felt touched, even a little teary, at his request. It was such a simple one for all he had just agreed to do for her.

"You'll come back right away?" Jake asked, appearing a little forlorn at the expectation of her departure. "I have a great deal to share with you."

"Very soon." She held back a hug, although that was her instinct. She couldn't wait to get back to him for so many reasons.

"Audrey's going to be talking to other people in the county, too," Cole said.

"Good." Jake smiled at her. "You'll enjoy getting to know the folks around here. And they're sure to feel the same about you."

She didn't want to leave him alone on his porch. She didn't want to leave Oakes Farm at all. But he was a stranger and she couldn't impose on him any more on such short acquaintance. They would have time to share what they knew about Lady Mauve because nothing could keep her away. And so she quickly walked down the steps and to the truck, hearing Cole right behind.

She opened the door and looked back. Jake stood on the edge of the porch with his hand raised in farewell.

Cole got into his side of the truck and shut the door.

"Goodbye," she called. "I'll see you soon."

She quickly sat down in the passenger seat and Cole drove away, leaving a trail of dust back to the farmhouse.

"What do you think of Jake?" Cole asked as he turned onto Wildcat Road.

"He's a wonderful person. Can you imagine having him in your life as your father, grandfather…"

"Great-grandfather?"

"It'd be terrific," she said.

"Too bad Jake never had children," Cole said.

"Yeah." She watched, unseeing, as the countryside flew past. "I think he was in love with Lady Mauve. What do you think?"

"Maybe. Most likely all the men were. From what I've heard, she was all in for her fancy lawyer."

"Lawyer?"

"Yeah."

"Wonder what happened to him," she said.

"No idea."

"There's a lot we don't know, isn't there?"

"Yes. But Jake can be a big help."

"I'm anxious to spend more time with him. He may even have clues to what Lady Mauve means in some of the journal sections that don't really make sense to me. Like Oakes, for example. I had no idea it was a made-up name that meant longevity to her."

"That had to be a surprise."

"I may be in for a lot of surprises in Wildcat Bluff County."

"Could be." Cole glanced over at her with a smile. "I'm taking you to the Chuckwagon Café for an early lunch. I think you'll be surprised how good the food is there. They even serve award-winning pies."

"Sounds wonderful. I'm hungry. That toast didn't stay with me long."

"Me either," Cole said.

"Do you think he's lonely?"

"Jake?"

"Yes. No family and all," she said.

"I doubt he's lonely. He's an independent cuss with all the friends in the world."

"That's good. I'm glad to hear it. Still…"

"I know, but he's lived a long, happy life."

"True."

"For now, why don't we turn our minds to the café. It's a county meeting place. Once I introduce you there, word about you will spread fast."

"What should I expect? Will they give me the cold shoulder or welcome me with open arms?"

"Neither. They'll be interested in you and give you a chance to prove yourself."

"Okay." She tossed back her hair. "Bring on the Chuckwagon Café."

Chapter 8

AUDREY TOOK IN THE SCENERY AS COLE DROVE DOWN Wildcat Road. They passed signs over ranch entrances with cows from black and red Angus to white-faced Hereford to humpbacked Brahmin. Mares with newborn colts frolicking at their sides grazed in pastures with blue ponds and green trees. Springtime had sprung in North Texas, with its rolling hills, clusters of trees, and an abundance of healthy animals.

"We're coming up on Old Town in Wildcat Bluff," Cole said. "It's the original part of town that draws tourists and locals alike."

He slowed down as he turned onto Main Street, a wide stretch of the road with buildings along one side.

She lowered her window so she could get a better view of the row of one- and two-story buildings built of stone and brick and nestled behind a white portico that covered a long boardwalk. Sunlight glinted off store windows. She felt as if she'd stepped back in time into an Old West town like the ones she'd seen in tintype photographs.

The Wildcat Bluff Hotel anchored one end of the street. It was an impressive two-story structure of red brick with a grand entrance of cream keystones and a second-floor balcony enclosed with a stone balustrade supported by five columns. Next door, the Lone Star Saloon had the old batwing-style doors.

"I can hardly believe it," she said. "Everything looks as fresh as if it were built yesterday."

"Wildcat Bluff takes pride in its heritage."

"Is that an original saloon?"

"Yep. It's served food and drink since the 1880s. Live country music on weekends."

"I'm impressed."

"We're proud of our town and like to share it." He pointed toward a store. "That's Gene's Boot Hospital. If you need clothes or shoes or belts or something, that's the place to shop. Thingamajigs offers office supplies, cameras, video equipment, stuff like that."

"Both could turn out to be handy."

He drove past other stores where pickups were nosed in along the curb. He found an empty spot, pulled in, and parked between two other trucks. He glanced over at her with a smile.

"Ready to become a part of Wildcat Bluff?"

"Ready as I'll ever be." She tucked the strap of her purse over a shoulder, opened her door, and stepped down.

"Got to do this right." He joined her on the boardwalk and held out his elbow.

"You mean, 'when in Old Town, step back in time'?" She wrapped her fingers around his arm, felt his muscles tighten under her fingertips, and experienced a little thrill at their closeness as they began an old-fashioned promenade.

"You got it."

She paused in front of Adelia's Delights, with its display of glass bluebirds in the window. "Those are made in Arkansas!"

"They're beautiful." He turned to look at her. "Like a lot that comes out of Arkansas."

She smiled, knowing he was giving her a compliment and enjoying it. She looked back at the display. A tortoiseshell cat lay twined among the delicate bluebirds. The kitty looked so perfect she might have been a stuffed animal until she turned her head to look in their direction.

"What a pretty cat," she said.

"You talked with Hedy at the station. That's her gift store and that's Rosie, Queen of Adelia's. She's one of the best Hemingway mousers in town."

"Do you mean she's a polydactyl?"

"Right. Extra dewclaws like the descendants of Hemingway's cats at his former home in Key West."

"Somebody must have brought cats out west over a hundred years ago," she said thoughtfully.

"They were worth their weight in gold at lots of places. They kept out vermin." He chuckled. "Plenty of fights over cat-stealing."

"Hard to imagine now."

"Not so hard around here. Folks still prize their cats."

"I'm glad."

As they continued, she caught the scent of lavender, rose, and frankincense, so she stopped in front of a store with MORNING'S GLORY painted in purple and green on a front display window. Inside, she saw bath products, paintings, and other items produced by local artisans.

"Morning Glory really supports the community with her store," he said, looking in the window.

"I can't wait to shop there."

"You'll enjoy it. And wait till you meet MG. She's an original flower child and will help you any way she can."

"That's good to know."

At the end of the street, a carved wooden sign painted in red and white that hung from hooks above the boardwalk read CHUCKWAGON CAFÉ. Red-and-white-checked curtains filled the lower half of the windows.

"Here you go. Best food in town." Cole opened the door and ringing bells announced their arrival.

Audrey stepped inside and took a look around. The long room had high ceilings covered in pressed-tin tiles and smooth oak floors. Wagon-wheel chandeliers—old lantern-type globes attached to the outer spokes of horizontally hanging wooden wheels—cast soft light over round tables covered in red-and-white-checked tablecloths. The spindle, barrel-back captain's chairs pulled up to the tables were full of folks. A tiger oak bar with enough dings and scratches to look original stretched across the back of the room with battered oak barstools in front and a cash register on one end. A window behind the bar revealed a kitchen updated with chrome appliances.

"Cole, as I live and breathe, whoever have you brought us?" A petite, silver-haired woman wearing a frilly pink apron over a denim blouse and skirt walked up to them with a smile and big plastic-covered menus in one hand.

"I'd like you to meet Audrey Oakes. She's staying in my guest-house while she's in the county."

"Pleased to meet you. Call me Granny, like most folks do, or Lula Belle if you want to get fancy."

"I'm not much on fancy," Audrey said. "I'm delighted to meet you. Cole tells me y'all have the best food in town."

"Don't pay him no never mind." Granny leaned forward. "Between the two of us, I slip him a few bucks under the table to say flattering things."

Cole laughed. "Not likely. Food here is too good to need it."

Audrey smiled. So far she liked everyone she'd met. She particularly liked their senses of humor.

"Granny is head of the Steele clan. They own this place and a couple of Steele Trap Ranches," Cole said.

"I wouldn't say that head thing too loud." Granny chuckled. "Those wild ones of mine think they're the cat's pajamas. Not me."

"She means her grandson Slade, granddaughter Sydney, and great-granddaughter Storm."

"Storm Steele?" Audrey's eyes widened. "Do you mean the Storm of *Fernando the bull and his beloved cow Daisy Sue* fame?"

"She'd be the one." Granny shook her head. "Can't keep up with that young'un no way, no how."

"Not true." Cole laughed. "They're all chips off the old block."

Granny looked proud for a moment, then tapped the menus. "Figure you came in here to chow down, not gab."

"Both," Cole said.

"Really?" Granny looked from one to the other, blue eyes brightening with interest.

"When you get a chance, will you sit down with us?" Cole asked.

"You know it." Granny glanced around at the tables with diners, then back at them. "Get something in your bellies, then we'll talk."

"Thanks," Cole said.

"Anytime."

Granny led them over to a table that seated four in a back corner of the establishment that afforded a little privacy. She set down the menus, gave Audrey a wink, and quickly walked away.

Cole pulled out a chair and seated Audrey, then sat down in one so that both had their backs to the wall.

She handed him a menu and opened hers. Lots of choices. She glanced over at him. "I could be all day reading this."

He chuckled. "Most people know what they want before they ever get here."

"Are you going to take pity on me and make recommendations or am I going to make you wait while I read the entire menu?"

"Go ahead and take a look. You've got choices like fried catfish, fried chicken, chicken-fried steak, hamburgers, chili, and fresh pies and cakes for dessert. Best barbeque in Texas. Oh yeah, if you don't want fried, they also grill fish, chicken, and steak."

"Oh my. That all sounds delicious." She glanced up and down and across the two inner pages, then flipped to the back.

"I didn't mention breakfast. Ham and eggs. Bacon and eggs. Hash brown potatoes. Buttermilk biscuits with real butter and homemade jellies. Coffee strong enough to keep you going all day."

"Say no more or I'll never be able to make a decision."

He chuckled as Granny dropped off two glasses of water and sets of silverware wrapped in napkins.

"Made up your minds yet?" she asked.

"I'm going simple today. Barbeque brisket sandwich with fries and coleslaw. Sweet tea," Cole said.

"I'll take the same thing. But I can tell you right now, I'll be eating my way through your menu while I'm in the county." Audrey closed her menu, picked up Cole's, and handed them to Granny.

Granny chuckled. "That'd suit me just fine. Back in a jiff."

Audrey watched her walk back to the kitchen with a spring in her step, chatting with customers along the way.

"So far so good?" Cole asked.

"It's wonderful here. Granny is terrific. Jake is wonderful. And you're...you're..."

"Yes?" He grinned at her, eyes alight with mischief. "Surely I get a fine descriptive, too."

"You do. Let's see...magnificent."

"Not bad."

"Ha. That's good. You just want more."

"Always." And he gave her a look with his warm brown eyes that promised more in so many different ways.

Granny picked that moment to set two glasses on the table, then she hurried away.

Audrey took a big gulp of iced tea to cool down. Cole had a way of heating her up that just wouldn't quit.

A little later, Granny arrived with a tray and set it down on their table. She slid a big plate loaded down with goodies in front of each of them, then stepped back.

"Thank you," Audrey said.

"Enjoy. In a minute, I'll let someone else take over my station and come visit with you. I'm not normally running all over the place, but an employee called in sick so I'm subbing."

"And you're doing a good job of it," Cole said.

"After all these years, ought to." She grabbed the tray and was gone.

"If Granny could bottle her energy and sell it, she'd make a fortune," he said.

"You're right." Audrey focused on her plate of food. "This looks delicious."

"Dig in."

And she did.

She couldn't have been happier with the tender brisket, the sweet-hot barbeque sauce, the crusty-on-the-outside-while-soft-in-the-middle fries, and crisp, not-too-sweet coleslaw. When she finished the last bite, feeling way too full but completely satisfied, she leaned back in her chair and glanced at her companion.

"Was I right or was I right?" He wiped a smear of ketchup away from his lips with his napkin.

"I could've gotten that for you."

He paused in midmotion. "With what?"

She paused, too, as she realized both of them were thinking the same thing at the same moment. She pursed her lips, then realized what she'd unconsciously done. She grabbed her glass of tea and took a big drink.

"You can clean my mouth anytime any way you want to do it."

She almost choked as she swallowed and quickly set down her glass.

"If you'll let me do the same with you."

"Delicious food."

He just grinned and tossed his napkin on the table.

"Granny will be back soon. What are we going to tell her?"

"The truth."

She hesitated, mind reeling back over fact and fiction. She had to keep her story straight. And yet, now that she was here in Lady Mauve's old stomping ground, she kept getting drawn into Wildcat Bluff's reality, not the old reality of Hot Springs. She had to keep her priorities straight or she'd never find the bootlegger gold.

"Okay, folks, spill it." Granny took the chair beside Audrey. "I got a sneakin' suspicion this is gonna be good."

"It's pretty much out of the blue," Cole said.

"My favorite kind of good." Granny leaned toward Audrey. "Do you need more tea to wet your whistle?"

"Thanks. I'm good."

"How'd you meet Cole?"

"She turned off and got stuck on my ranch last night."

"Quick work." Granny grinned, fanning her face as if they were too hot to handle.

He just shook his head. "You know I'm trying to catch those mustang rustlers."

"Everybody knows it."

"Audrey was out at the dump and got chased by them."

Granny turned serious. "What'd you see?"

"Not much. I heard horses and a big engine." Audrey began to wonder if it'd be easier to come clean instead of trying to hide the truth. Still, she had a story and she'd better stick to it.

"But they thought you saw more than you did." Granny looked from one to the other.

"That's what we decided," he said. "That's why she's staying at my ranch. Safer."

Granny nodded thoughtfully. "But, Audrey, why were you at the dump at night?"

"Dusk." She took a deep breath. "Anyway, I'm here from Hot Springs."

"Love those old bathhouses," Granny said.

"My mom and I run a gift shop on Bathhouse Row. We thought it'd be a good idea for me to write a book about the bootlegger connection between Wildcat Bluff County and Hot Springs."

"Well, I'll be hornswoggled." Granny grinned. "For real?"

"We think it'd sell well."

"Not only in Hot Springs. It'd sell like hotcakes in Wildcat Bluff, too," Granny said. "Hedy would carry it in her store. Morning Glory would love to showcase it, too. I'm sure they'd do a book signing and everything. Our local DJs would surely feature you on KWCB."

Cole chuckled. "You sound a lot like Storm when she gets up a head of steam to promote Fernando and Daisy Sue."

Granny joined his laughter. "Guess the acorn doesn't fall too far from the tree."

"How is she doing?" Cole asked.

"Lordy, that girl is all het up about the Wildcat Bluff County Spring Stock Show."

"Who isn't?" Cole asked. "Wish I could show a mustang there, but those horses are wild and meant to be kept wild."

"Best not mess with a good government program like that one," Granny said.

"Right."

"What's the stock show?" Audrey asked.

"Folks from all around the county will be entering their animals to compete for awards. Kids are particularly encouraged to enter horses, cows, goats, pigs, chickens that they've raised by hand."

"That sounds great. I wonder if it might fit into my book."

"No doubt," Granny said. "You're going to include photos, aren't you?"

"Guess I'd better." Audrey liked the support she was getting for the book that was supposed to be a cover story. It was starting to take on a life of its own…and she liked it.

"Good," Granny said. "But back to Storm."

"It wouldn't have to do with Little Fernando and Margarita, would it?"

"You know it." Granny looked at Audrey. "As the twins of Fernando and Daisy Sue, they're celebrities in their own right. Storm made sure of that fact. They're about a year old and she plans to enter them in the stock show."

"They're sure to win," Cole said.

"I hope so." Granny cocked her head to one side. "You never know. There are a lot of great black Angus bloodlines in this county."

"I guess I'd better put a chapter in the book about Steele Trap Ranch being home of the famous Fernando and Daisy Sue."

"If you don't want an earful from Storm, you'd better make it a good one," Granny said, eyes alight with humor.

"How old is she now?" Cole asked.

"Nine going on ninety." Granny winked at Audrey. "Guess I don't need to bring you up to speed on the Fernando and Daisy Sue love story."

"I've seen the website, heard their stories on the news, and been caught up in their drama like lots of folks," Audrey said.

"We'd never have gotten national coverage if a sharp television reporter out of Dallas hadn't taken a liking to Storm and Wildcat Bluff. Bless her heart. She's covered all our major events for some time."

"She might even interview you about your book," Cole said.

"It's just a book. I doubt it'll garner that much interest. And it's not even written yet."

"All in good time," Granny said. "It's bound to be connected to Hallelujah Ranch's speakeasy and that got quite a bit of publicity. Maybe you could insert more background information that would give the story legs again."

"Good idea," Audrey said. "That's what I'd like to do."

"You ought to talk with Jake the Farmer." Granny nodded to Cole. "He was alive during that time. I think he knows a lot more than he's ever said about Lady Mauve and all those shenanigans. If anybody can get it out of him, I bet it's Audrey here."

"As a matter of fact," she said, "I just met him."

Granny gave her a sharp look. "How'd it go?"

"He agreed to be interviewed for the book."

"Terrific," Granny said. "Spring is looking to be full of fun surprises."

"Best of all will be when Sheriff Calhoun and I catch the rustlers," Cole said.

Granny turned serious. "Let me know if I can be of any help."

Cole nodded in agreement.

"And, Audrey, I'm no spring chicken. I'm happy to share anything I remember or heard back in the day. Just let me know."

"Thanks so much for your generosity...and the delicious food."

"Anytime on both."

As Granny stood up, the front door burst open. A little girl with wild ginger hair and big hazel eyes raced into the café. She wore a rhinestone-studded, long-sleeve T-shirt in bright green, jeans, and turquoise boots. She threw herself into her great-grandmother's arms, tears running down her cheeks.

"Granny...they're going to try to take Fernando away! They say he doesn't belong with me on Steele Trap Ranch."

Chapter 9

COLE WATCHED AS GRANNY PICKED UP STORM, SET HER great-granddaughter on her lap, and hugged her tight. She slowly rocked back and forth, not saying a word as she gave comfort. He felt sick at heart. Surely no local rancher would be cruel enough to break a little girl's heart.

He glanced up as he heard the thud of boots hit the wood floor hard. Sydney Steele, Storm's mother, strode across the café with a look of fury on her face. She was strawberry blond, tall, strong—obviously a cowgirl from birth—and looked determined to right a wrong. She wore a red-and-white-striped pearl-snap shirt with jeans and red boots. On her heels came Slade Steele, blond and blue-eyed, tall, muscular, and furious. He dressed much like his sister in a green-plaid snap shirt with jeans and black boots.

Sydney sat down at the table. Slade pulled a chair out from a nearby table, turned it around, positioned it near Granny and Storm, and sat down, his arms folded across the chair back.

Granny looked up from where she cuddled Storm. "Update."

"Lawyers involved," Slade said.

"Better get Nocona Jones on the horn," Granny said. "Nobody messes with her."

"If not for all the publicity making Fernando so valuable—" Sydney said.

"Beyond his hot sperm," Slade said.

"Right," Sydney said, agreeing. "We never would have heard word one about this situation."

"Looks like somebody wants to make money off Storm's hard work," Granny said.

"Plenty of shenanigans in the cattle business," Slade said.

"But to take from a nine-year-old girl…" Sydney reached over and stroked Storm's long hair.

"Not to mention how Fernando, Daisy Sue, and their twins are the center of her life. And a lot of other people's lives, too." Slade thumped his bootheels on the floor. "It's cruel."

"No end to cruelty in this world," Granny said, "but we don't usually see too much of it in Wildcat Bluff County."

"Outsiders." Sydney leaned back, glanced up, and did a double-take when she saw Audrey. "Speaking of outsiders…"

"Audrey Oakes," Cole said.

"Who is she? What is she doing here?" Slade asked.

"And does she have anything to do with our current misery?" Sydney drilled Audrey with sharp blue eyes.

"I just got here yesterday from Hot Springs. I'm not lawyered up or anything."

"Of course that's what you'd say." Sydney frowned at Cole. "Are you vouching for her?"

"He doesn't have to," Audrey said. "I can vouch for myself. You know, innocent until proven guilty."

"Sydney didn't mean to insult you." Granny held up a hand as if to separate the two women. "She's on edge."

"I apologize. I was rude," Sydney said. "Granny is right. I'm on edge, but it's much more serious than that."

"That's okay," Audrey said. "And I regret your trouble."

"Thanks." Sydney cocked her head to one side as she looked closely at Audrey. "You remind me of someone. Can't think just who. Granny, don't you agree?"

"Now that you mention it, yes. I'm not sure either. Maybe it'll come to us later."

"Maybe so," Cole interrupted. "For now, we want to hear all

about what's going on with Fernando. But first, let's get introductions out of the way. Audrey is here to research a book about the bootlegger connection between Wildcat Bluff County and Hot Springs. She's staying in my guesthouse."

"Oakes," Slade said. "Any relationship to Jake's Oakes Farm?"

"No," Audrey said. "I just met him today. Great guy."

"Slade, Sydney, and Storm." Cole pointed to each member of the Steele family as he said their names.

"I'm pleased to meet all of you," Audrey said.

"Okay." Slade gave her a nod, then turned toward Cole. "If you want to take her and go, that's okay. Otherwise, you're both sworn to secrecy about what you're going to hear."

"If you want me to go, I'm happy to go. If you think I can help—Audrey, too—we'll stay."

Slade glanced at Sydney and Granny. They both nodded. "Guess we want you to stay. You're a good, trustworthy rancher. Plus, you're fighting to save your mustangs from rustlers. We've supported you. Now we need you to support us."

"You got it." Cole dreaded to hear what they were going to say. Fernando was larger than life in their county. And the big bull was the basis of Storm's entire world. If there was anything he could do to help, he'd definitely do it. He sat up straighter, bracing himself for what was to come next.

"You know the old Zane Ranch?" Slade asked.

"Sure do. Biggest outfit around here, but run by outsiders since the old man died." Cole wondered where this was going.

"It's had one worthless foreman after another," Sydney said. "Absentee ownership never works out worth a damn."

"May not even be the foreman. Most likely, the owners just want to skim profits from their own ranch with no thought to land and animals." Cole understood that viewpoint only too well. It was why he made a point to know his ranch and take good care of it.

"Could be," Slade replied. "One way or another, Zane cattle don't get the best care."

"But that's not the point." Granny stroked Storm's long hair.

Storm sat up straight and glared around the group. "Fernando belongs on Steele Trap Ranch. I found him. I saved him. I raised him." Tears filled her eyes and ran down her cheeks. "What would we do without him? Think about Daisy Sue. They'd be heartbroken without each other. And the twins!"

Cole felt his gut clench. He had an idea where this was going... and he couldn't think of an upside.

"I don't understand," Audrey said. "I'll be the first to admit I know little about cattle operations, but how can there be a question that Fernando doesn't belong with Storm on Steele Trap Ranch?"

"He belongs with us, yes." Granny gave a big sigh.

"Big ranch like the Zane with thousands of acres is susceptible to cattle losses. It can take time for cowboys to even figure out they're missing part of a herd," Slade said.

"Audrey, I doubt you would know this, but a certain percentage of the largest ranch's stock is made up of so many strays that are kept for their own use," Sydney said. "It's just an accepted way of doing business."

"I didn't even know I was missing mustangs at first." Cole leaned back in his chair, wanting to get away from what was coming but knowing there was no way to do it. Still, Audrey needed to know more details about ranches because it might impact her book, so he was glad she was getting firsthand information.

"Newborn calves are vulnerable to coyotes, weather, ground conditions, particularly if they get separated from their mothers," Slade said.

"I'm Fernando's mom." Storm raised her chin in defiance. "He doesn't know any other."

Cole couldn't stand the suspense any longer. "He doesn't have a brand. Does he have an ear tattoo?"

"Yes." Granny gave a sharp nod of her head. "Not every ranch uses them because they're just more trouble. You know it and I know it."

"Yeah. My ranch uses them." Cole groaned. "I suppose the numbers lead straight to Zane Ranch."

"Yes." Granny pulled Storm tighter to her chest.

Storm sat up again. "I saved him. There was this big storm. Afterward, I was out looking around and found this little wet, scared calf. What I was I going to do? Leave him out there alone? Coyotes would have come at nightfall."

"You saved his life," Cole said.

"Whatever ranch he came from would've figured he was lost," Sydney said. "Everybody knows a scared calf can run through ten fences and get separated from the herd. Cows can even float downstream and end up far from their homes. If Storm hadn't found him, he would've been dead. We thought he'd have been written off as a loss."

"By the time he grew up, we'd put a lot of time and money into him. We decided to sell his sperm and list him as unregistered," Slade said. "I mean, a good bull is a good bull. Ranchers will pay what you want, no questions asked."

"If Fernando weren't famous, I doubt we'd ever have heard from Zane Ranch," Granny said.

"How did they put it together?" Cole asked.

"New foreman. Ned Atkins." Sydney looked pained. "From what I hear, he's going back over the books line by line. He's looking to make a name for himself and collect a big bonus."

"We know Fernando was weighed and measured at birth with recorded information about his sires. That's standard," Slade said.

"All Atkins had to do was check the system." Cole thought about the situation a moment. "But how did he connect Fernando with one particular lost calf? You know they've lost a lot over the years."

Slade nodded. "That's a real good question."

"Who comes in contact with Fernando?" Cole asked.

"He's been out in a pasture," Sydney said. "And he's friendly with people."

"Trespasser? Bought-off cowboy?" Cole tapped his fingertips on the tabletop in frustration.

"We're missing something," Sydney said. "Who had the idea that Fernando might be the missing calf and then went about proving it?"

"That's right," Granny said. "I'm guessing somebody knew a calf showed up on our ranch. Neighbor, most likely."

"Atkins is new around here," Slade said. "Maybe he connected the dots first. Maybe not. One thing for sure, he's running the show now."

"I hate to say it." Cole shuddered at another idea. "But what about the twins?"

"That mean ol' man can't have them." Storm clenched her fists. "I'll fight him. No...I'll take all four and we'll run away to the Dakotas. We'll hide out there. I'll set up a fund-me account and fans will be sure to donate to support us in our quest for freedom. Anyway, nobody can own them. They're free cattle. I promised them that...I did." She burst into tears and buried her face against Granny's shoulder.

Cole felt even sicker. Was no animal safe anymore? He couldn't help but compare the Steele problem with his own stolen mustangs. They had to find a way to save them all.

"We're not living in the Old West." Granny patted Storm's back. "And we're sure not living in a Western novel where wrongs most likely get righted. I'm afraid you can't just take off for the Dakotas. Those states are a lot more settled now than in the old days and the law can find you."

Storm raised her head, frowning. "Okay. We're back to fists. We fight."

Granny smiled. "That's my girl. You bet we're going to fight."

"And win." Storm wiped her eyes with the back of a small hand.

"Right." Granny glanced at Cole. "You've got a pretty big ranch."

"Four thousand acres."

"Livestock can get lost there."

"You bet."

"If a few cattle managed to break through fences and wander over there, you'd never know, would you?"

Cole grinned, feeling better about the situation. "Never. And the cowboys wouldn't know either. They're too busy with GTT cattle and keeping an eye on the mustangs."

Granny grinned, too. "Mind you, we're not taking the law into our own hands. Code of the West, we understand. This is code of the ranchers. What is normal practice for all of us. We just want to make sure a few famous cattle don't go missing on Steele Trap while we battle this situation out in court or behind the scenes."

"Smart move," Cole said.

"Thanks." Sydney patted her daughter's back. "So far we're keeping this below the radar, but we can't keep it there forever. When it hits our local grapevine, it'll get into the news fast. We want to have all our ducks in a row before that happens."

"I won't say a word about it." Cole realized he was now sitting on two big secrets—Fernando's ownership and Lady Mauve's family. He had thought catching the rustlers was trouble enough. Now life had gotten even more complicated.

"Me either," Audrey said.

Cole glanced around the group. "Just let me know what you need when you need it."

"Thanks," Granny said. "We hope we won't need you, but it's best to have a plan in place ahead of time. Our first order of business is getting Nocona Jones brought up to speed so she can tackle this situation from the legal end."

"She's the best lawyer in the county," Cole said.

"In the state...maybe all the states." Storm gave the group a big grin. "And she's personal friends with Fernando."

"Can't beat that." Cole grinned back at her.

"Guess that brings us all up to speed," Granny said. "We best get back to work. We can't let some tomfoolery break our stride."

"You bet." Cole stood up and held out a hand to Audrey. He figured now was a good time to make their exit and let the Steele family have a little time to themselves...or as much as possible in the café, although their little corner provided quite a bit of privacy.

When he felt Audrey's fingers clasp his own, she got to her feet beside him.

"It's been a pleasure meeting all of you," she said. "I regret to hear about your troubles. If I can be of any help, please let me know. I'll be out and about talking with folks as I research my book. Maybe I'll hear something."

"Good idea." Granny smiled. "Keep your ears open. You just never know what you might run across."

"I will."

"Later," Cole said.

He walked with Audrey away from the table, across the long length of the café, and out the front door. Once there, he couldn't resist giving her a little reassuring hug. Maybe he needed one himself. Spring was shaping up to be a doozy. He might need a scorecard for all the players.

"If Fernando wasn't a famous bull and worth a lot more money than just an ordinary bull, Zane Ranch would never have come after him. Right?" Audrey asked.

"Not a chance." He walked with her down the boardwalk, noticing that the sun didn't seem quite as bright or the day quite as pretty after what they'd learned from the Steele family.

"If it's common practice to keep strays, then I don't see how, legally, that ranch can take him."

"That's the problem. Common versus legal. I honestly don't

know if there's a precedent for this type of thing or if it's up for grabs."

Audrey stopped in front of his truck and put her hands on her hips. "Well, they can't just come, load up Fernando, and take him away. Can they?"

He stopped, too. "I don't know, but I sure wouldn't take a chance on it."

"That's why GTT might be getting four visitors someday."

"Right." He opened her door. "Strays are one thing. Rustling is another and not to be tolerated. Atkins is bucking unwritten rancher law. When this all comes out, and it will, he's bound to be the most unpopular cowboy in the county...particularly if the trouble he's causing keeps Storm from entering Fernando's twins in the spring stock show."

"Well, he ought to be a lot more than unpopular."

"If he gets a pocketful of cash out of the deal, I doubt he'll care."

"That's just plain sad." She stepped up into the cab.

He shut the door, walked around to his side, and sat down beside her. He started the engine, but sat there a moment looking at the Chuckwagon Café sign. Kindhearted people ought to be left alone, but he knew good and well life didn't always work out that way.

He backed out and headed down Main Street, trying to turn his mind to his own business. He had enough to plow through without adding an additional worry. But he *would* worry about Storm and Fernando and Daisy Sue and the twins. He glanced over at Audrey. Added her to the list. He didn't want to see any of them harmed by circumstances beyond their control.

"Don't worry too much about the Steele family. They're strong and resilient. Granny will never let her great-granddaughter be hurt by some outsider coming in here and looking to make a fast buck on—"

"Fernando the Wonder Bull."

"Storm may be only nine years old, but I wouldn't want to go up against her and what she loves and protects."

"I hope I learn something that helps when I'm out and about."

"You never know."

"Right."

"Before we get out of town, do you want to pick up stuff at the grocery store?" he asked.

"Thank you, but I've already taken up too much of your day."

"If you need something, let me know. We can stop."

"No, please. I just want to go home. After learning about Fernando, I don't feel much like shopping."

"I hear you. We can always come back later."

He headed down Wildcat Road toward the GTT. He wanted to get her safely back inside the compound. It'd been a big day already, and he needed to do some ranch work. Maybe she could make some notes for her books or something. Rest might not be a bad idea either.

As he came upon the narrow ranch entrance, he noticed black smoke spiraling up from the ground. It wasn't too high yet, but it was definitely a fire. He immediately went on alert. He'd wait to call Hedy at the station. He wanted to know what they were dealing with before she sent a booster or called in more firefighters. If it was controllable, he could probably handle it on his own. He tromped down on the accelerator to get there faster.

"Is that a fire?" She pointed at the dirt turnoff where she'd gotten stuck.

"Looks like it."

"On your ranch?"

"Looks more like it all the time."

He pulled off the road and parked on the gravel slope. His ranch gate yawned open. Somebody had cut the chain. He looked up into the tree. Somebody had yanked down the camera and made off with the video evidence. And that same somebody had started a fire. Fortunately, the ground was still wet and the grass damp from the morning's rain, or the blaze would be racing across his pasture. As it was, the fire struggled to take hold.

"Audrey, I need the fire extinguisher and my jacket on the floorboard."

"Are you going to fight this fire yourself?"

"Yes. I don't think I need to call in a rig."

"Then I'm helping you." She gave him a determined stare.

"I've got some towels in back."

He liked her can-do attitude. He opened his door and the stench of burning grass hit him. About the only good thing he could think about the situation was that they'd gotten there so soon after the start of the fire.

And then he had another thought. It made him catch his breath. Only two people had known they were going to lunch in Wildcat Bluff and would be gone for a while. He sure hadn't been the one to call horse rustlers to alert them about the camera. He sure hadn't been the one to tell them to cover their tracks with a fire. He sure hadn't been the one to draw out the meeting with Jake.

Just when he'd begun to trust Audrey Oakes, all his original suspicions came hurtling back.

Chapter 10

Audrey struck the hot flames with two towels on one edge of the fire. Smoke swirled up and around her. She coughed to clear her lungs. Heat radiated up from the ground. She could feel it through the soles of her shoes. She tried to keep her hands from getting burned while she fought the blaze, but still she might have blisters on her fingers later. No help for it. She would heal, but if the fire got away from them, it could do untold damage.

Now she had a better appreciation for firefighters. They put their lives and bodies on the line every time they were called out… and never complained about what it cost them. They were dedicated to their communities. Here and now, she could do no less.

She raised both towels over her head and came down hard again, smothering as she beat, beat, beat. She glanced across the blackened area at Cole. He tossed aside one empty canister and started on a second one as he sprayed the perimeter to contain the flames. A finger of fire leaped up and tried to make a break for it across the ditch beside the lane. He quickly pivoted and aimed a long stream of spray that doused the blaze until it subsided into black ashes.

As far as she could tell, they were making good progress. They wouldn't need help. They made a good team.

Team. She froze. What if this was a setup for the team of horse rustlers? It'd convince her that Cole was to be trusted, not one of them. He'd let the sheriff know, so the law would be on his side again. And the video evidence was gone and any incriminating footprints or tire tracks were extinguished in the fire. Oh, surely not. Please let it not be so. She'd just begun to trust Cole and want to work with him.

On the other hand, what if this was a message from the rustlers warning her, as well as Cole, to stand down, keep their mouths shut, and let them have the mustangs? Otherwise, they could and would escalate and cause a great deal of damage to the ranch and livestock. She felt chilled, despite the fire's heat, at the thought they might be vulnerable. If that were the case, they should stand together against the rustlers.

And yet Lady Mauve's words came back to haunt her. *Trust no one in Wildcat Bluff County.* That'd definitely include horse thieves. Everyone else she'd met she liked and instinctively trusted, but should she? She supposed it came down to *trust but verify*. She must wait to make final judgments.

"Good job," Cole called.

"You're sure?"

"Yes."

She let her arms fall limply to her sides, muscles burning from the unusual activity as she gulped in air filled with the scent of charred grass. The towels were sadly blackened with holes here and there from burning embers. And yet she still clutched them just in case she needed to leap into action again. It was a good thing she was in fairly decent shape because Wildcat Bluff County was turning out to be demanding in so many different ways.

"Are you okay?" he asked.

"Yes." She flexed her stiff fingers.

"Let's finish putting out the fire."

She nodded as she raised the towels again.

"There's not that much left." He smiled at her. "I just want to make sure we don't leave any embers that could start another blaze."

"I'm with you on that one."

"I can get most of it with the last of this can. If you'll make sure nothing escapes my notice, we can be done and head up to the house."

"All right."

But she didn't let him do all the work. She walked toward the center, crunching over grass and charcoal where downed twigs had burned up. She beat at the last gasping flames as he sprayed chemicals here and there, putting out the final hot spots. She kicked out, checking for anything under the top layer of black crust. When she couldn't see any more problems, she glanced up and caught him watching her. He gave her a cool smile and a hot look.

"Thanks." He didn't say more but he continued to give her a thoughtful perusal with his brown eyes.

"Anytime."

"You didn't have to help."

"I wanted to. I was here and you needed it."

"You're not all city, are you?" he asked.

"Guess I'm adapting to country pretty fast."

"Maybe you're more experienced than you've let on."

"What do you mean?" She couldn't imagine what he was thinking about her, but she didn't think it was good. She'd helped, hadn't she? What more could it mean than putting out a fire?

"I mean you're willing to get your hands dirty. Not a lot of shopkeepers would or could do it."

"If that's a compliment, I'll accept it."

"Yeah," he said. "Let's get up to the house. I need to call the sheriff and get him or a deputy out here."

"What about the gate?"

"I'll get another length of chain. It won't stop the rustlers, but at least it'll deter them. That's the best I can do at the moment."

"New camera, too?"

"Yep. And new location for it."

"Good."

"Come on." He slipped the strap of one canister over his shoulder, then picked up the other can.

She crunched across blackened grass with him to the truck, glad they'd caught the fire in time no matter the circumstances.

He held out his hand. "I'll take the towels."

"They're ruined." She handed them to him.

"That's okay. Lost plenty before this fire." He tossed them in the bed of the pickup and placed his empty fire extinguishers on the floorboard of the back seat.

"Just in case, I'll start carrying a couple of towels in my vehicle." She settled into the passenger seat.

"Always a good idea." He sat down beside her.

He drove up the lane at his usual pace, not too fast, not too slow, but she could see his tension by the way he gripped the steering wheel. He was not nearly as casual as he pretended to be. She hoped it was because he was worried about the rustlers, not because he was working with them.

When he came to the entry gate outside the compound, he stopped and pulled out his cell. He glanced over at her. "This can't wait. I'll put the calls on speakerphone."

She nodded in reply.

He selected a number.

"Wildcat Bluff Fire-Rescue. Hedy here."

"Hedy, it's Cole."

"Trouble?"

"Yep."

"Need a rig?" Hedy asked.

"No. Audrey and I took care of it."

"How bad?"

"We caught it early."

"Good."

"Somebody cut the chain on the gate at the small entrance to the ranch. They stole my camera and set a fire. I smelled accelerant…probably gasoline. Good thing the ground and grass were damp."

"Still, this isn't good," Hedy said.

"Tell me about it. I'm about to call Sheriff Calhoun."

"Want me to coordinate with him and send out somebody to take samples?"

"Yes. Let me know when and I'll meet y'all down there."

"Will do." Hedy hesitated. "And, Cole, be careful."

"You know it. Thanks."

He punched another phone entry.

"Wildcat Bluff Sheriff's Department. Sheriff Calhoun."

"Sheriff, this is Cole."

"Trouble?"

"Somebody hit that narrow entrance to the ranch. They cut the chain, stole the camera, and set a fire."

"Rustlers?"

"Maybe. But why?" Cole asked.

"No telling. Is the fire out?"

"Yes. Audrey and I were coming back from town and caught it early."

"Lucky," Sheriff Calhoun said.

"Yes. Hedy is going to send somebody out to take samples."

"I'll coordinate with her and be there to check out the scene."

"Thanks. I'll meet you."

"See you soon."

Cole clicked off and glanced at Audrey. "You're out of it from here on."

"But—"

"No buts. I'm taking you back to the guesthouse while I finish up this sorry business."

"Can I help?"

"You've done enough. I want you safe. I'm sure you've got plenty of your own stuff to do, but I wish you'd do them in your place till we get this sorted out today."

"Okay." She wasn't going to argue with him. However it played out, she wanted to be on the sidelines, watching, not interacting… at least until she knew more about the situation.

He hit the remote control and the compound gates slid open, and he drove through and shut them behind him. He abruptly stopped his truck and glanced at her again.

"Look, if you don't feel safe here anymore, you can move somewhere else. Won't hurt my feelings none."

"I admit the fire is unsettling, but I'm probably safer here than anywhere else."

"I hope so." He started forward again.

She didn't say it, but she had to wonder if he'd decided it was better for the operation to have her gone from the ranch. Maybe she was meeting too many people, making too many new friends that she could go to if she saw more that made her suspicious. She didn't want to go, no matter the rustlers. She liked it here. She liked the guesthouse. She liked Cole, no matter what. She was best off here, at the heart of the trouble…and her research.

He parked in front of her place and turned to her. "When I'm not here, listen for the dogs. They'll bark an early alert of intruders or trouble."

"Okay."

He hesitated, still looking at her. "I don't like to leave you here alone, but I've got to take care of business. And I need to meet the sheriff later at the gate."

"I'll be fine. Don't worry about me."

"Can't help but worry. Still, stay inside and you'll be okay. I'll call and check on you. And if anything comes up, don't hesitate to call or text. I may be out of cell range, but I'll eventually get your message."

"Thanks." She opened her door but felt a hand on her shoulder stopping her from leaving the cab. It felt strong and protective.

"I'm serious. Anything at all, please contact me."

She glanced back with a smile. "I will." And then she was out the door and headed toward her new home.

She opened the door and stepped inside, but still he didn't go, as if not wanting to leave her. She gave a little wave and closed the door. Only then did she hear him pull away.

She untied her sooty sneakers and dropped them to the floor, so she didn't track debris across the floor. She leaned back against the door and took a deep breath. What a morning. Before that, it'd been *what an evening*. She needed time to let things settle into place. She was getting hit with so much so fast, she felt as if her head was spinning. And yet she couldn't allow herself to become overwhelmed. She must focus on what was most important, what she was doing here in the first place, what saved a life, what didn't.

She set her purse down on top of the bar, washed her hands at the sink, and checked for signs of burns. Her palms were hot, but she didn't see any blisters. She grabbed a bottle of water out of the refrigerator, sat down on a stool, and rolled the cold bottle back and forth across her palms. Felt good.

She took another deep breath. She must get focused on her own goals. So much was going on in the county, she could hardly think about why she'd come in the first place. That had to change. She'd call Mom. If anything would do the trick, that'd be it. She wanted to share what she'd experienced and learned anyway. Plus, most important, check in about Mimi's health.

She picked up her phone and carried it, along with her bottle of water, over to the recliner and put her feet up. She pulled up FaceTime.

"Audrey, are you all right?" Vivian asked, looking and sounding concerned, as well as a little harried. "It's the afternoon. I thought you'd be out and about."

"Everything gets started early in the country."

"Still...did you run into trouble?"

"I'm beginning to think there's nothing *but* trouble in this county."

"That doesn't sound good," Vivian said.

"It's interesting anyway."

"Hang on. Let me go back to my office for some privacy."

"Slow day?"

"So far. You know how it goes. When it picks up, it'll be a rush all at once," Vivian said.

"It's as if everybody gets the same memo at the same moment."

"So true." A door slammed shut. "Now let me sit down. I've been on my feet all day."

"Feel good?"

"Wonderful." Vivian smiled as she smoothed down her perfectly coiffed dark hair.

"How's Mimi?"

"She's better."

"That's great news. But how? I mean..."

"I know what you mean. She's taken more interest in her food. She actually complained about it," Vivian said.

"Terrific. She had enough energy and interest to complain."

"Absolutely. And she can hardly wait to hear about your next adventure in Wildcat Bluff."

Audrey chuckled.

"What?"

"There appears to be no end of them."

"Did you actually get a lead on the gold? This fast?"

"No, but, Mom, wait a minute, back up," Audrey said.

"To what?"

"You said Mimi is really interested in what I'm learning here."

"Yes. She wanted to sit up in bed to hear your report," Vivian said.

"She sat up?"

"I propped some pillows behind her and her eyes were alert... almost sparkling lavender like they used to be."

"If that's the case, she needs a report every day." Audrey felt her heart lift with happiness. Maybe hearing about Lady Mauve's old stomping ground was almost as good as bootlegger gold for Mimi.

"I think the same thing."

"You could take her a small delicacy to eat while she listens to the stories. Maybe she'll even put on a little weight."

"I'll do it. Something from her favorite bakery," Vivian said.

"Mild but fattening."

"Cheesecake."

"Perfect." Audrey smiled at her mother, feeling as if they were finally able to do something. And they'd always enjoyed being coconspirators on projects—saving Mimi's life was their biggest, most important project yet.

"Now, bring me up to date."

"Let's see. I met Jake the Farmer, lunched at the Chuckwagon Café, found out a ranch is suing to take Fernando the Wonder Bull away from the Steele Trap Ranch, fought a fire that mustang rustlers most likely started, and Cole left me here so he could meet the sheriff to collect evidence at the fire site."

Vivian's eyes grew wide as she pressed her palms to her cheeks and started to laugh, shoulders shaking with mirth.

"And there's still the evening yet to come."

Vivian laughed harder.

"You think I'm making this up, don't you?"

Vivian caught her breath, eyes bright with tears. "No. It's just… oh my, what a place. Not much time for your search, is there?"

"I'm beginning to think Lady Mauve was just the tip of the iceberg."

"Rustlers? Fire? You aren't in danger, are you?"

"Cole says I'm in the safest place possible on his fenced compound with two smart dogs on patrol. And he's armed, too."

"Good. If it gets too dangerous, you come straight home. You're making my life look…"

"Sane and sensible," Audrey said.

"Dull."

"Dull obviously won't do for Mimi."

"Do you think Lady Mauve's daughter needs a little excitement in her life?"

"Like mother, like daughter."

"Exactly."

"We'll make this story like a novel." Audrey felt her chest grow warm with tenderness for her grandmother. "Mimi can't go anywhere as long as the story continues. And maybe she'll get stronger, too."

"Kind of like that old tale where the heroine stays alive one more day after she tells a new story each night."

"Yes."

"Does Mimi know about Fernando the Wonder Bull, the love of his life Daisy Sue, and their twins, Little Fernando and Margarita?"

"I doubt it. I don't know all that much about them," Vivian said.

"Bet she'd like the ongoing saga. Nine-year-old Storm Steele is the mover and shaker of all the publicity and love for this cattle family. There's a website and social media. Why don't you try sharing it with Mimi?"

"Okay. She might find in interesting."

"I can keep you updated on it."

"Tell me about Jake the Farmer."

"Oh, Mom, he's a centenarian and he actually knew Lady Mauve."

"That's extraordinary. What till Mimi hears about him. Did you learn much from him?"

"Just met him. Great guy. Beautiful farm."

"Maybe you could get photos or videos and send them. Mimi would love it," Vivian said.

"I'll see if I can. One thing. He never married. I wonder if he loved Lady Mauve and could never settle for anyone else."

"That's so romantic, but not realistic."

"I know. Still…"

"As exciting as all this is, we must remember your real purpose there," Vivian said.

"I'll definitely start searching for sites tomorrow. But my best bets may come from talking to folks around here."

"True. You've already made great connections." Vivian leaned toward her phone, appearing mischievous. "You didn't update me on the mysterious Cole. Sounds to me like you're spending a lot of time with him."

"I am, but it's not personal. It's just the way things worked out."

"Well, you never know."

"Matchmaker."

"I'm not very good at it, but I do try."

"Mom, I'm keeping you from work. I can give you more details tonight when you get home."

"That'd be great. For now, just stay safe. It's your biggest priority."

"I'm fine. Give Mimi my love."

"I will. Love you."

"Love you, too."

Audrey set down her phone and leaned back in her chair, missing her family, missing her old routine, missing what she'd always thought would be her entire life. And yet…she felt excitement building for the new, not the old.

She heard her phone chirp and picked it up. Cole calling—definitely the new and definitely the exciting.

"Hey there," she said.

"How are you doing?" he asked.

"Okay."

"Really?"

"Yes, I am."

"I didn't mean to put you through so much today. It's not always like that around here."

"I'm beginning to think there's never a dull moment in Wildcat Bluff County," she said.

"Maybe not dull, but we do have our calmer moments."

"Sounds good."

"Look, to make up for wrangling you around so much, I thought this weekend I could grill a couple of steaks and we could relax outdoors on the patio. Are you interested?"

"Sounds great. What can I bring?"

"Just yourself. That's more than enough. I'll let you know when. I've got to go now. I'm meeting the sheriff at the gate."

"Good luck."

"Thanks. Later." And he was gone.

She smiled a secret little smile. Never a dull moment certainly was the truth…particularly when you were living just across the courtyard from a dazzling cowboy firefighter.

Chapter 11

A WEEK LATER, AUDREY TROMPED OUTSIDE THE DUMP'S CHAIN link fence. She'd chosen to come here late in the afternoon, when there was little chance anybody would see her. She didn't want a run-in with either side of the law or any person casually stopping by. If she wasn't careful, her cover story could wear thin, although more and more she wanted to write that book and make it a reality.

She'd bought boots at Gene's Boot Hospital because rain continued to plague her search. A new parka kept her warm, and she carried her phone, billfold, and a small trowel in its deep pockets. She was as ready as she could be to find something, anything, to help. A steel-gray sky with thick clouds appeared ready to dump on her at any moment, so she'd better hurry. Yet she moved cautiously as she stepped on slippery grass and across downed twigs and limbs. The last thing she needed was to fall, get hurt, and have to be carried out by Wildcat Bluff Fire-Rescue.

She'd gone back over Lady Mauve's journal for leads, but most of the sites were behind fences, on private property. She wasn't sure there was a way to get to them, so they were on a back burner for now. Destiny was high on her list of accessible sites. The small town afforded her the good excuse of shopping or eating or even getting gas. She hoped she could snag an invitation to visit Lady Mauve's old speakeasy on Hallelujah Ranch. Maybe Cole could help her with that one.

For today, she was focused on the dump site again. She walked back over to the post oak where she'd been standing when she'd heard the rustlers. Today, it was quiet—or quiet like in the country, with birds and insects and other sounds of nature. She placed her hand against the rough bark of the tree. She felt sure something was here, had to be here, but what and where?

She thought back to Lady Mauve's words in her journal. *Wire binds but can twist, twine, rust. Legacy can crumble, dissipate, disappear. What I carry lasts forever.*

Audrey didn't understand the words any more in remembering them than the first time she'd read them. And yet gold had to be the key. It never tarnished and always held great value. But carry? Those words were written beside the drawing of an oak tree in a grove. This was the prime location. Surely Lady Mauve meant she'd carried the bootlegger gold here, or perhaps to another place, and buried it.

If it came to that, Audrey might need to buy a metal detector to carry around, but if anyone saw it, they'd surely draw a conclusion she didn't want them to about her.

She circled the tree again, sliding her palm over the bark until she felt a sharp pain. She jerked back. A small bead of blood welled up in the center of her palm. She grabbed a tissue out of her pocket and clasped it in her hand to stanch the flow, although it was only a trickle.

Puzzled, she looked more closely at this section of the tree. Something glinted, even in the gray light of the day. Wire protruded from the bark. She'd heard trees could eat almost anything in their way as they grew from small saplings to sturdy elders. She carefully felt the wire with a fingertip and followed it around the circumference of the oak. She felt the sharp edge that slightly protruded outward. She took her trowel out of her pocket and chipped at the bark around the wire edge. Pieces fell to the ground and left a slight wound, revealing wire that had been shaped by someone many years ago.

Audrey caught her breath. A message? She couldn't be sure. The metal was rusted yet still intact, but she thought there were probably two letters twined within a small heart. She wished she could tell which letters of the alphabet, but they were broken in places. If she removed the wire, she'd destroy it. She took several shots with her phone camera. Later, she would study the photos. Enhancement might make the letters more legible. If she could figure out the message, she might be well on her way to the legendary gold.

A little nick in her skin was a small price to pay for her first real clue. If she hadn't felt it, she'd never have noticed the wire. She'd just put a little antibiotic cream on it when she got home. Until then, she was fine. More than fine. She felt ready to celebrate. She could hardly wait to send the photos to Mom and Mimi. Maybe they'd have a better idea about what it meant or exactly what it was.

She whirled around and almost ran into Cole. She suppressed a scream as she backpedaled into the tree.

"What are you doing here?" He appeared thunderous, more angry than the sky above.

"I could ask the same of you."

"If you'll recall, I work here. I watch over the place."

"I came back for some research," she said.

"Sure."

"Why else would I be here?"

"Right," he said.

"I don't know what you're getting at."

"Did you find anything?"

She would've told him. She would've been thrilled to share her discovery with him at this exciting moment. She would've liked his input. But she couldn't, not now, not when he appeared to be accusing her of trespassing on dump property or something more sinister.

"Well, did you?"

"If I'm not supposed to be here, I'll leave. But I was under the impression this was public property...as in a county waste disposal center."

He jerked off his cowboy hat and ran a hand through his thick dark hair in agitation. "It's not that. I was surprised."

"So?"

"Okay. I apologize if I came on too strong."

"I'm done. I'm leaving. You can have the place all to yourself."

"Wait." He clamped his hat back on his head.

She had her spine against the tree and she didn't like her position, but she didn't back down. She raised her chin. "What?"

"You're still coming to the cookout tonight, aren't you?"

"No." She felt vindicated to reject him, even if it felt more like a loss than a win.

"Audrey, don't be that way. I apologized for my behavior."

"You didn't apologize for accusing me of trespassing."

"Okay. I apologize for that, too."

She shrugged, not by any means mollified. Words were easy. Actions always spoke the truth.

"Look, we keep getting off on the wrong foot. I'm trying, but I'm under a lot of pressure due to the horse thieves."

"I understand." She stepped to the side and away from him. "I can move out."

"Don't you dare." He followed her, dogging her footsteps toward her SUV. "It's not safe."

"They haven't been back. They haven't hunted me down. They're probably long gone." She reached her vehicle and opened the door.

"We don't know anything for sure, except we shouldn't be at each other's throats. I'm throwing those steaks on the grill by seven. I hope you'll be there. Max and Folgie hope you won't because they'll get your portion."

Just the thought of the dogs made her feel like relenting and letting go of her irritation. She was overreacting and knew it, but she was just so frustrated…not just with the gold but with him, too. She realized a little too late what their frustration and irritation implied about their relationship. They were going to be on edge around each other until…until they ended up in bed. And she wasn't going there. She couldn't—wouldn't—go there with a guy who was mostly a stranger and one she couldn't trust at that. She needed to stay away from him.

"Think about it. Cool off. I'll see you about seven."

She got in her SUV, shut the door, and drove away. Surely she was strong enough to stay away from him. But did she really want to?

She felt uneasy, as if life was sneaking up on her and giving her no choices about her future. She needed and wanted a friend. Mom and Mimi were physically too far away. Jake flashed into her mind. Yes, he'd become her friend. She needed down-to-earth. She needed practical. She needed a longer view of life. Jake had all of that and more.

Without conscious thought, she realized she'd already made the decision and turned toward Oakes Farm. It felt good…like going home.

She parked in front of the farmhouse and noticed her tension begin to drain away. Jake wasn't on the porch, but he opened the front door and stepped outside. She was so glad to see him. She quickly got out and hurried to the steps.

"Audrey, I'm glad you stopped by," Jake said.

She no longer questioned that he knew her without seeing her. It was his gift of sensing the world around him. She set her foot on the bottom step.

"Wait." He picked up his long wooden staff from where he kept it propped next to the front door. "I'll join you. Let's go to the garden."

She moved back, wanting to help him down the steps but knowing he didn't need it or want it.

"I'm fine," he said as if reading her thoughts. He grasped the wooden handrail in one hand as he carefully stepped down to the ground.

"I know you're okay. It's just—"

"Appreciate your concern. If I ever let myself be mollycoddled, I'll go down fast. Plus I need the exercise."

"It's a beautiful place to walk."

"The best." He turned toward the garden just turning green with new growth.

She walked beside him, breathing in the clean, spring-scented air and feeling peace settle over her.

"That's better." He turned his head toward her, then back toward the garden. "You were agitated when you arrived here."

"Yes." She didn't even question how he knew. They simply got each other. They had from the first.

"Want to tell me about it?"

"No…yes…I'm not sure I even know."

"Do you see any weeds around the new corn plants?"

"Yes."

"Will you pluck them so they don't impede the growth of what is valuable to us, what nourishes us?"

"Yes." She bent over and started plucking green weeds and tossing them into a pile at one side.

"Good." He stood quietly, face turned up to the sun. "The trick in life is to know what is valuable and what is not."

"Do you mean like weeds and corn?"

"Exactly." He held a hand up toward the sky. "Sunlight nourishes all. We grow strong in the rays of the sun."

"You're right." She felt the warmth of the sun on her back and it felt good, like the soothing touch of her mother's hand when she was a child.

"Weeds grow fast," he said. "Some people want fast. They pluck the weeds of life that bring little nourishment and so they pluck and pluck and pluck as their desperation to find fulfillment grows. Other folks have more patience. They plant. They nurture. They protect. Only when their plants grow to maturity do they pluck that which gives life-sustaining nourishment."

"You're wise."

He chuckled. "I'm old. If I haven't gained a little wisdom over the years, I doubt I would still be here."

She smiled, knowing she'd done just the right thing in coming to him. She stood up, reached out, and tentatively clasped his hand, hoping he wouldn't reject her action.

He squeezed her hand in return. "Let your wisdom grow from your experience in life."

"I will. Thank you." She held his hand for a moment, and then let go. "I've felt so out of my depth since I came to Wildcat Bluff County."

"It's not the depth," he said. "It's the breadth. Maybe it's both. In any case, you're enlarging your world, and sometimes that can feel so unfamiliar, maybe even dangerous, that you want to rush back to the protective womb."

"But that's no way to gain wisdom, is it?"

"And it's no way to live life to the fullest."

"Are you thinking about Lady Mauve?" she asked.

"Always. Particularly right now. She always challenged herself and those around her. If she felt fear, she confronted it, moved through it, and owned it. That's how she did so much and how she inspired others."

Audrey took a deep breath, feeling her heart, her entire being, expand with hope and happiness. If she followed in the footsteps of her great-grandmother, she would be all right. She couldn't let fear of the unknown stop her. Mimi depended on her. She straightened her shoulders, feeling lighter and stronger.

Jake leaned down and stroked the vibrant green leaves of a young corn plant. "I hope you'll be here to enjoy the fruit of my labor."

"If at all possible, I'll help you harvest."

He turned his face toward her. "I'll count on it."

"Good." She stepped back. "I need to go now."

"You'll come back soon?"

"Every day."

"I'll look for you."

"Do you want help back to the house?"

He chuckled, shaking his head. "Thanks, but no. This is my world and I know it well."

"You really helped me today."

"Good. When you need me, I'll always be here for you."

"Thank you. Do you need anything? I can pick up stuff at the store and bring it to you tomorrow."

"I'm okay, but I appreciate the offer."

"How about I bring you something tasty from the Chuckwagon?"

He grinned. "Now that's an offer I won't turn down."

"Barbeque? Chicken-fried steak? Or...?"

"You pick. Anything from there is delicious."

"I'll bet you want pie," she said.

"You know it."

"Flavor?"

"Whatever Granny recommends," he said.

"You got it. I'll bring treats tomorrow."

"Great."

"Guess I getter go." She didn't want to leave him, but he'd inspired her to get back to her quest and ease into the life that was beckoning her. Still, she hesitated to step out of the garden.

"Go." He laughed. "I want to hear all about what you do today tomorrow. And I want my Chuckwagon."

"You got it."

She hurried to her vehicle, then hesitated and looked back at him standing in the garden with his tall staff in one hand and his feet planted firmly on the ground. If she hadn't come to Wildcat Bluff, she'd never have met him…and her life would be so much poorer for it.

With Jake's words of wisdom ringing in her ears, she drove straight back to the ranch. She wanted to share him with her mother, but they were miles apart. Still, they could be connected through her.

She walked inside her cabin, sat down on the recliner in the den, and called home.

"Hello, dearest." Vivian answered her phone. "Let's chat, but I need to leave soon."

"Where are you going?" Audrey sat up straight. "When did you ever go out much after work?"

"I'm going to the range."

"Where?"

"Target practice."

"As in guns?" Audrey asked.

"Yes. My sweet new little Sig needs to be loosened up."

"You? Armed?"

"Dear, we live in perilous times. It pays to be cautious."

"Wish you'd told me that before I got here."

"We should've done it years ago. I probably wouldn't have thought of it except, well…you know, Gerald is former military and he says it's best to be prepared for the unexpected."

"Gerald?" Audrey stared hard at her mother's face, feeling as if she'd morphed into somebody else. "Who is Gerald? When and where did you meet him? What do you know about him? And—"

"Slow down. I met him at Mimi's nursing home. He's a nice man. I guess we sort of bonded over our mothers and being alone in life."

"You've got me."

"I know, dear. I'm talking about a life companion."

"You gave up on guys years ago," Audrey said even as she sensed

Jake's words of wisdom ringing true. *Plant. Nurture. Grow. Harvest.* Maybe her mother was nourishing herself in a new way.

"I'm rethinking my position and I think you should, too."

"What? Where is Mom? Who are you?" Audrey laughed as she teased her mother.

Vivian chuckled, lavender eyes lighting up with humor. "Dear heart, I know this must come as a shock to you."

"You've always tried to find somebody for me."

"It's me this time." Vivian sighed. "Gerald's special. He's just flat-out a wonderful man who's lived a fascinating life and he's so good to me, so concerned about me. I feel the same about him. Dear heart, I like him. I really do."

Audrey leaned back in her chair. "In other words, he's the opposite of my dad."

"The father you never knew."

"True. If Gerald makes you happy—"

"He does," Vivian said.

"I'm glad for you."

"Thank you."

"Mom, I have news, too," Audrey said.

"Quickly, dear."

"First, how is Mimi?"

"I can hardly believe it. She ate three bites of cheesecake today. And she sat up even higher in bed. She's getting stronger. She'll want the latest news, particularly about Jake."

"I visit him every day. I don't stay long. I don't want to tire him. We're just…I don't know…friends, I guess. I can't imagine a day he's not in. And he's so very wise," Audrey said.

"That's wonderful. You can enjoy someone like him in your life. And I'm sure he appreciates your visits as much as you do."

"I'd love for you two to meet each other."

"Maybe we can someday," Vivian said.

"Soon, I hope. We share Lady Mauve. That means a lot to me."

"Me, too. And Mimi."

"On another note, I found something important today. But in the middle of it, Cole discovered I was at the dump again and was quite rude," Audrey said.

"Rude?"

"Yes. And then he had the nerve to think I'd still come to his place this evening for him to cook steaks. I guess I'm still sort of steamed about it, although I probably shouldn't be."

Vivian grinned, nodding her head. "He likes you."

"Well, I like him, too. But still, I'm in the midst of saving Mimi's life."

"That doesn't mean your life is on hold, nor mine either."

"There's so much to do. And I don't trust Cole completely," Audrey said.

"Are you afraid to trust a man because your father left before you were born? Does that make you think all guys are untrustworthy?"

"Me? What about you? We've always been fine. Just the three of us. Only now, Mimi…"

"Audrey, dear heart, no matter what we want, we can't keep our loved ones with us forever. There is a time to hold on and a time to let go."

"I'm not letting go of Mimi anytime soon…or Jake either for that matter. I'll save her. I swear it."

"We both will. What I'm trying to say is that if you get the chance at love, it's the most precious thing in the world. I'm beginning to believe that is Lady Mauve's gift to us," Vivian said.

"Love?"

"Yes." Vivian's eyes filled with tears. "Whatever you do, don't turn your back on love. I have this chance with Gerald. Is it scary? Yes, a little. But we're strong women. We can take a chance on our hearts being broken or our hearts being healed. Isn't it worth a chance?"

"Mom?"

"Yes?"

"You never talked like this before. We were always complete. We didn't need anyone else," Audrey said.

"We are still complete. We don't need anyone else. And yet… to be with, well, a mate, to laugh with them, to share triumphs and sorrows, to know they're there for you, to know you're there for them…I want it. I'm willing to take a chance on it."

Audrey put a hand over her heart, feeling the deep emotions cascade over her. "I don't want to lose you."

"You can't. We're tightly bound. But I want more for me. I want more for you. I want love in our lives. And I'll tell you this…from the moment you mentioned Cole Murphy, I saw your eyes light up in a way I've never seen before in your entire life."

"Well, I do like him," Audrey said.

"Give him a chance. Give yourself a chance."

"Are you saying I should go to his house tonight?" Audrey asked.

"Absolutely. Wear something sexy."

"I don't have anything sexy. And I wouldn't wear it anyway."

"Is this the first time y'all've had a chance to be alone, just together, without any crisis to deal with?" Vivian asked.

"Maybe."

"Make the most of it." Vivian smiled tenderly. "You've worked hard all your life. You deserve a few hours of pleasure. Take them. Make the most of them."

"Okay, Mom. I'll go."

"Just as well. Cowboy firefighter that he is, he'd probably come and roust you from your lonely lair anyway."

Audrey chuckled, easily imagining just such a scene. "Well, I really don't want the dogs to get my steak."

Vivian laughed. "That's the best reason of all to go."

"I think so, too. And I'm thrilled for you. You deserve as much happiness as you can get from life."

"So do you. Now, what did you find today?"

"It seems almost anticlimactic after your big news."

"Mimi will want to know about it."

"It's not much, but I found something in that hundred-year-old-plus post oak. I'll forward the photo. Maybe it'll make sense to you. It's kind of hard to make out, but it looks like… No, I'll let you and Mimi tell me what you think it represents and if it's of benefit to us."

"Will do." Vivian pressed a kiss to her palm and blew it toward Audrey. "Must run. Love you."

"Love you, too." Audrey caught the kiss and touched her palm over her heart as her mother's face disappeared from the screen.

Maybe there really was enough love to go around to all the special people in your life. Still, that wasn't her main concern right now. Mimi depended on her staying on track to save her life. Especially because of Jake's age, she wanted to spend every possible moment with him and share those moments with Mimi. And then there was her mother's new life.

Gerald. A vet? What war? It was just sort of unfathomable. Gun-toting Mom? Vivian and Gerald like Bonnie and Clyde? What century was Audrey living in anyway? Wildcat Bluff just kept blending the past with the present, between mustang rustlers, speakeasies, bootlegger gold, and a centenarian who'd lived through it all. Maybe life made more sense to Jake than to her at the moment. She valued his take on the world. Cole had enlarged her world, too. She felt as if everything in her life was up for grabs now. She just needed to nurture her garden and all would be well.

She walked into her bedroom and threw open the closet door. Sexy? Not even there. She needed something comfortable and warm enough for a cool spring night. Still, she wanted to please Cole. And look her best.

By the time seven rolled around, she'd taken a shower, dried her hair, put on a little makeup, and donned a soft red sweater, jeans, jean jacket, and red ballet slippers, since she wouldn't walk far. Definitely comfortable and perfect for an evening outdoors.

Cole met her at the outside gate that led into the backyard. He'd spiffed up, too, in pressed jeans, blue shirt, and boots. She wished he didn't look sexy, but he did…and more delectable than sizzling steak.

"Glad you could make it," he said.

"I figured you'd come and get me if I didn't."

"I would've. I don't want to eat alone."

"I'd like to try the steak," she said.

"It's the best our county has to offer."

"Guess that's saying something in cattle country."

"Yep."

He pushed open the gate. "I put Folgie and Max in the barn with chew toys. Last thing we need is to fight them off all evening to protect our food."

"Thanks." She chuckled at that image.

She walked into the backyard, which was a beautiful oasis. A round flagstone patio had been built at the back of the house. It contained a table with six chairs, a fire pit for heat in the winter, a hammock hanging from two old oaks, and to one side green artificial turf marked a three-hole miniature golf course on a raised bed surrounded by natural bricks. She particularly liked the sound of running water in the four-sided fountain made of natural stone. In the distance, she could see the beautiful vista of green grass, verdant trees, and cattle.

"Cole, this is absolutely stunning."

"Thanks. Glad you like it." He smiled as he glanced around the area. "Mom and Dad—with a little help from me—did all the design and work."

"It's well worth it."

"I think so, too," he said.

"That's a fancy grill."

"Yeah. Mom wanted an outdoor kitchen and she got it. We've had lots of good food out here."

"I can well imagine."

He gestured toward the grill. "It's already hot. Baked potatoes are wrapped in foil in the coals. They're ready to go. I can throw on the steaks anytime you want. How do you like yours cooked?"

"Well done."

He chuckled. "Okay. Yours goes on first."

"Can I help you with something?"

"Sure. Fridge is right there. If you'll pull out the lazy Susan, it's got the sour cream, bacon bits, and chives. Salt, pepper, and hot sauce are already on the table."

"You're quite the cook."

"Nothing like my mom, but I do my best."

"Do you want me to set the table, too?" she asked.

"Thanks. Use the red bandanna placemats and napkins. If you want to get our drinks, there's sweet tea and ice in the fridge."

"I'm happy to help. You throw on the steaks while I get everything else set up."

He gave her a big grin, then went to work.

She set about her tasks, marveling at how well organized and efficient he'd been in preparing their meal. He'd also put a lot of time and effort into it. If she'd known he was going to this much trouble, she'd never have considered turning him down. She had better manners and appreciation for others than that. She could only blame it on being edgy, just like him.

Pretty quickly, she smelled the delicious aroma of cooking meat. She could hardly wait to eat. She hadn't realized how hungry she was or how she'd missed this type of family gathering. He wasn't family, of course, but the entire setting was definitely a family atmosphere. And the other thing—they were comfortable putting a meal together, as if they'd done it many times before.

He glanced over at her, as if he'd heard her thoughts, and nodded in agreement or self-satisfaction.

And in that moment, she knew exactly what her mother meant. No longer alone. Somebody who got you like you got them.

Chapter 12

As Cole cooked steaks, he heard Folgie and Max howling in the barn. They could smell the meat and wanted it. He'd saved them choice bites for later. Share and share alike with his dog friends or they'd guilt him into it anyway. He smiled at how happy the dogs would be when he tossed chunks of meat into the air and they leaped up to snap it between sharp teeth. But that was after Audrey went home. For now, it was all about the two of them...and making amends for his earlier behavior.

He picked two potatoes out of the ashes with stainless steel tongs and placed them on Mom's favorite turquoise plates. He filled the rest of each plate with a big slab of prime steak. It'd be tender and tasty. Audrey would go home with a full stomach and good thoughts about him. At least, that was the plan.

He set a steaming plate on the placemat in front of her, then eased onto the chair across from her with his own full plate.

"This looks wonderful." She cut open her potato, pulled back the foil, and started adding condiments.

"It better be." He didn't bother with his potato. He went straight for the good stuff. He used a steak knife to slice through the tender meat, speared it with his fork, and put it into his mouth. He moaned at the explosion of fine taste. He definitely had a winner on his hands.

"That good, huh?" She chuckled as she took a bite of potato.

"Yeah, that good." He sliced off another bite.

"I'd better try it." She followed his earlier actions and soon moaned just the way he had at the taste.

"Am I good or am I good?" He grinned, satisfied that the meal had turned out so well.

"When it comes to steak, you're obviously the best."

"That's not the only thing I'm the best at." He gave her another grin, knowing his gaze was conveying a message that had nothing to do with food.

She stopped, fork in midair, eyes wide.

He felt a little burst of satisfaction that she'd gotten his message. They could make a good team in a lot of ways outside of cooking meals or fighting fires. He'd wanted her in his life since the first moment he'd met her…and every moment since that time. He wanted to enjoy her company, get to know her better, let her get to know him. He wanted her to come into his world, but first he had to open the door. Could he set aside his distrust enough to take a chance?

Maybe he'd already taken that first step…more like several steps. She sat across the table from him eating food he'd prepared for her. She lived in his guest cabin in comfort. She stayed behind his compound fence in safety. If he'd trusted only his mind, he'd never be at this point with her. Somehow or other, he'd trusted his gut all the way. And now he wanted to take the next big step.

He listened to the silence around them as they ate, totally concentrated on their food, or so it would look to an outsider. No doubt he could cook a mean steak and enjoy it, but tonight most of his enjoyment came from the fascinating woman sitting across the table from him.

Lady Mauve's great-granddaughter. How could that even be true? And yet, from all he'd heard and seen, Audrey had the look, the presence, the self-assurance, and the drive of that once-upon-a-time speakeasy proprietor. Everyone had loved Lady Mauve. Everyone who met Audrey loved her, too. Maybe he should start calling her Lady Audrey. It did have a certain ring to it.

He smiled at the thought as he cleaned the last food from his plate and leaned back in his chair to watch her. The warm rays of a setting sun gave a rosy glow to her porcelain skin. She almost looked like she belonged in another era. She would've been perfect to model for an Erté painting of a woman clothed in a long gossamer gown.

Audrey pushed her plate back, shaking her head. "Wish I could finish your delicious food, but I just don't have room for it all."

"Not to worry. I know two cow dogs who'll be more than happy to eat what you leave, potato and all."

She chuckled. "Starving, are they?"

"If I didn't know better, I'd think they were by the way they act."

"Dogs."

"Yeah. Can't live with them…"

"Can't live without them."

He smiled when she completed his sentence, almost as if she completed him in every way. He took a deep breath. He needed to slow down. His gut reaction was running away with him again. Whatever happened to mind over matter?

"They're making a pretty big racket in the barn."

"I did my best to distract them. I hoped out of sight would be out of mind. But they can smell up to miles away, particularly if it's a tasty treat like steak."

She laughed. "Now I feel guilty."

"Don't. They work guilt like pros."

"I could take my leftovers to them."

"No. I set aside pieces for them. They'll get fed later."

He stood up. He had to get her mind off the dogs. If he let them out and they bounded in here, he'd never get her attention back on him. Folgie and Max were gluttons for attention, particularly for the adoration of women. They'd pull so many antics that he might as well slink off into oblivion.

"You're sure?"

"Later." He hoped he didn't sound gruff, but much more about the dogs and he was going to take her inside where she couldn't hear them.

"Okay."

"Dessert?"

"I'm so full."

"You don't want to miss fresh apple pie with cheddar cheese from Chuckwagon Café. Slade makes it. He's won lots of awards for his pies."

"The Steele family is so talented."

"Yeah." He didn't want her thinking about Slade Steele any more than the dogs. Come to it, he wanted her thinking only about him. Jealous? He might as well admit he was getting there… or was already there.

He removed two precut pieces of pie out of the fridge, warmed them in the microwave, and set them on the table. He had to admit the pie looked good.

"Yummy." She pulled one of the turquoise plates toward her.

He sat down and claimed the other.

She cut a piece of pie with her fork, slid it into her mouth, and smiled in satisfaction.

He wanted to see a lot more of that look on her face. And he wanted to put it there…but not with food. Still, the pie was good. She was even better. And he was well on his way to not caring if she was the biggest rustler in the world. Maybe if he was good enough, she'd give him back his horses. He couldn't keep from chuckling at how far gone he was after just a couple of meals with Lady Audrey. Yeah, lady. She might be all lovely manners at the table, but he'd bet he could persuade her to cowgirl it up in bed. She could ride him all night long and he'd just ask for more.

"Cole, are you all right? You look a little flushed. Did the pie go down wrong?" Audrey leaned forward, concern in her lavender eyes.

He laughed outright. Flushed? Yeah, right. And it had nothing to do with sugar in the pie. It had everything to do with the sweet thing across the table. He'd bet Lady Mauve had guys standing in line to bootleg for her. They'd have been willing to run revenuer traps, make the mash, guard the speakeasy, anything at all. He froze at his thoughts. What if Audrey truly was cast in her great-grandmother's image? Bootlegger to horse rustler. What if Lady Audrey was the mastermind?

He went from hot to cold in an instant. And then he scoffed at his reasoning. He was letting his mind take over again. He'd trusted his gut so far. Was now the time to change?

He forked a piece of pie into his mouth, trying to turn Audrey from rustler back to writer. It wasn't easy.

"If you're not feeling well, I could go home. Dinner has been wonderful. You could feed the dogs."

He pushed his plate away, no longer hungry. He had to do something. He couldn't let this fester.

She stood up and started stacking the plates.

"I'll do that later."

"Now is as good a time as any. You did all the work. Let me clean up. I'll take these to the kitchen. Do you have a tray?"

He got to his feet. Now look what he'd done. He couldn't seem to stay on an even keel with her. If he'd stop thinking about rustlers, they'd be fine…or at least she wouldn't be about to head out the door. What the hell? Did he actually like the idea of her being an outlaw like Lady Mauve, living life on the edge, just one step ahead of the law? Lady Mauve had been portrayed as glamorous, exciting, a savior of the little people. But stolen horses were an entirely different matter.

"The tray?"

He pointed toward the countertop beside the grill, mind still digging him deeper. If Audrey ran a bootlegger enterprise and speakeasy, would he make hooch for her, raise cattle for her, cook for her, protect her?

He watched as she picked up the tray and carefully set everything on it. She moved gracefully, as if cleaning off a tabletop was part of a dance routine. He wanted to dance with her. He'd hold her close. He'd smell her hair. He'd feel her curves. He had no doubt they'd move together like they were born to it.

Bottom line, yes, he'd have bootlegged for her back during the Depression, when everyone lived on a razor's edge and were one day away from starvation. And just like Lady Mauve, they'd have saved their friends and family.

But that was then and this was now. He needed to get his mind out of fantasy and back to reality. That meant keeping Audrey here long enough to share some quality time that didn't include dogs or rustlers or fires or any of the Steele clan.

Mind made up, he got to his feet and reached for the tray.

She pulled it toward her. "Take the leftovers for the dogs. The rest is going with me."

"I told you I don't want you cleaning up."

"And I told you I was going to do it. Either take those leftovers or they're going down the garbage disposal."

He smiled, liking the fire in her lavender eyes. "You'd let Folgie and Max starve just to get your way."

"Hah!" She smiled back at him as she balanced the tray against one hip while she picked up the piece of steak and set it on the countertop. "There. Those dogs can't ever say I didn't do something for them."

He chuckled as he snatched the last of the potato and plopped it down beside the steak. "Same can be said for me."

"Fine." She wheeled around, took the steps up to the covered patio, got the sliding door open, and disappeared into the house.

He glanced around, feeling as if he'd missed something important but clueless about what it was. Guess when she made up her mind to do something, she did it. He grabbed the placemats, put them away, and headed after her.

What he found in the kitchen totally surprised him—she was up to her elbows in sudsy water. She'd filled the sink and was hand-washing the dishes with a determined tilt to her chin.

"You're my guest," he said. "I don't want you doing—"

"I don't like using a dishwasher for so few items."

"You can let them build up."

"Not tonight."

"Okay." He wasn't going to get into an argument over washing dishes.

"You can dry."

"Fine." As he grabbed a dish towel, he wondered how his romantic evening had turned into kitchen duty. Audrey could easily mastermind anything, about like Lady Mauve.

As she washed and he dried, he realized how comfortable they were together in such a domestic setting. It seemed perfectly nat-ural...and almost a prelude to something even more intimate. He felt desire rise in him. He wanted to up the intimacy that had been building between them. But how? Did he throw caution to the wind? If so, how would she respond? She'd given every indication that she liked him.

He set the dish towel on the countertop and moved closer to her. She glanced up with a questioning look in her eyes. And in that instant, he saw her eyes change to mirror the desire he felt. He moved closer still, reached out, and cupped her chin. She gave him a little smile. Encouraged, he leaned forward and pressed his lips to her mouth in the lightest of kisses. She gently, almost tenta-tively, returned his kiss. He raised his head to see her expression. Her lavender eyes had darkened to near purple.

She smiled again, and then placed her palms, dripping sudsy water, on either side of his face.

He scarcely noticed she'd left water running on one side of the double sink. He had his mind on more important matters. He wrapped her in his arms, kissing her again, only this time with the passion that was blazing its way through him. He wanted her to know how he felt about her. It was high time. And if she was anything like her ancestor Lady Mauve, she'd take what she wanted from him...and he'd be happy, more than happy, to give it.

He kissed her with all the longing he'd stored up from the moment they'd met, tracing her lips with his tongue, delving deep into her moist mouth, tasting the sweetness of apple pie. And all the while, he pressed their bodies closer together. He wouldn't be surprised if steam was rising from the heat they were generating together.

Now that he'd tasted her, touched her—and she'd returned his kisses—he wanted to carry her upstairs to his king-size bed. Nothing less would do.

"Audrey..." he said urgently.

"Yes?"

"Let's get out of here and—" He heard water splash against the floor. He glanced down. Water cascaded over the edge of the sink.

"Oh no." She turned off the faucet. "Hope you have a good mop."

Chapter 13

By the time Audrey mopped up the soapy, watery mess with Cole, she knew their kissing time was gone. A wet floor simply wasn't romantic. Yet she still felt singed around the edges. She had to remind herself that she wasn't looking for a relationship. She was supposed to be researching a book. He was supposed to be hunting down rustlers. And yet it'd felt so good to kiss him that she wanted to do it all over again.

He glanced around the kitchen. "Let's set the mops on the patio where they can dry."

"Suits me." She forced her thoughts back to the practical and followed him to the sliding doors.

He opened the door with a soft whoosh.

Two big dogs leaped into the dining room, pink tongues hanging out as they grinned in happiness and ran into the kitchen where they slid across the wet floor, leaving muddy tracks.

She just stood there, too stunned to move.

Cole dropped his mop and leaped into action. He ran into the kitchen and tried to grab collars, but Max and Folgie thought it was terrific fun and raced ahead of him, slipping and sliding and distributing mud everywhere.

She finally walked to the edge of the kitchen with her mop still in hand. She stared at the floor—her just cleaned floor—and then up at Cole chasing the dogs around and around the room. The dogs were barking. Cole was growling. And she started laughing.

Cole stopped to stare at her.

Max and Folgie stopped and stared at her.

She stared right back...and laughed harder.

Finally Cole joined her laughter. "Best get these bad boys outside." He grabbed Max's and Folgie's collars and guided them toward the sliding door.

They barked and tap-danced around his feet, trying to get back to the kitchen.

"Audrey, come with us. They think we're playing and they don't want to leave you out of the fun. Otherwise, it'll be hard to get them outdoors."

"Let's see." She rubbed her chin with a fingertip as if trying to make up her mind. "Clean a muddy floor or romp around outside. Tough choice." She dramatically leaned her mop handle against the bar. "Guess I'll choose the great outdoors. You get the floor."

"Thanks. You're too kind."

"Come on, boys!" She clapped her hands together and hurried to the open door. She paused long enough to look back.

Cole let go of the collars and the dogs ran toward her.

She barely got out the door ahead of them. They raced down the stairs, around the fountain, back up the stairs to bark at her, and chased each other up and down and around the trees before coming back to lie down in front of her, tongues hanging out as they panted in happiness.

"You encouraged them." Cole stepped outside, flipped on outside lights, and leaned both mops against the stone wall.

"Didn't take much." She glanced at the mops. "Are those a message that we need to mop again?"

"Forget the kitchen floor."

"It'll dry muddy."

"I might try throwing food on it and letting the dogs lick it clean later. They made the mess, so they should clean it up, shouldn't they?"

She laughed, shaking her head. "Really, we could take another go at it."

"Forget about it. I'll deal with it another time."

"But—"

"You're my guest. No more floors. Let's have some fun."

"I didn't want to mop again anyway."

"Smart." He chuckled as he stopped beside her, reached down, and rubbed the heads of Folgie and Max. "Troublemakers."

"Bet you didn't feed them."

"S-t-e-a-k is in the fridge."

"They know the word?"

"Ha. They taught it to me," he said.

"Can we feed them now?"

"Guess we'd better. That's why they're here."

"How did they get out of the barn?" she asked.

"Folgie has learned to open the lock with his teeth. I should've been more careful."

"Smart dog."

"Yeah. They're border collies. They're working dogs. That means they're smart, high energy, and bred to herd. They'll herd sheep, cats, each other, even me."

She laughed. "So they came inside to herd us outside?"

"No doubt. Besides, we left them out of the fun and food. That's not acceptable border collie behavior."

"In other words, we were the bad dogs?"

"Yeah. Guess we might as well admit it."

"Not me." She patted each dog on the top of his head. "I'm going to feed them. That means I'm the good dog."

"Okay. I'll play bad dog to your good dog." He walked over to the outdoor kitchen. "Just remember, they'll never forget you gave them steak."

"They'll love me forever?" she asked.

"More like they'll slobber on you forever."

"See me, expect food."

"Yep."

She laughed again. She hadn't known she'd have so much fun. Dinner and small talk could hardly compare to what she was experiencing with Cole. One thing she was coming to know about Wildcat Bluff County—the unexpected was the expected. And she liked it.

"Come on. Let's see how high they can jump," he said.

She followed him to the fridge, where he pulled out a plate with bite-size pieces of steak all ready for the dogs.

"Make them work for it," he said.

"How?" She got a good grip on the plate when he handed it to her because the dogs were excited by the smell and were leaping up and down around her.

"Toss a piece into the air."

"Okay."

"But let's go out on the lawn. You can throw away from you so they don't knock into you. And it'll give them more room to maneuver."

"Is this sort of like playing Frisbee?" she asked.

"Yes…except more serious. Wait. I'm not sure anything is more important than a game of Frisbee with them, unless it's herding."

"They're kind of serious dogs, aren't they?"

"Playful, too."

She followed him out to the short green lawn, dogs romping around her all the way. If she wasn't careful, all those paws and her feet could get tripped up and she'd go down with the plate of steak. She was already wet. Grass stains would just about complete her perfect country look.

"Go ahead, toss a piece," Cole said as he came up to stand beside her.

She felt his solid presence supporting her, encouraging her. It was just feeding the dogs, but she felt as if his support could extend to other areas in life, just as hers could to him, as it had always done with her mother and grandmother.

"If you make them wait much longer…"

She picked up a piece and tossed it well above the dogs.

Max leaped up, twisting his body in midair as he snagged the steak and gulped it down, not bothering to chew.

She quickly threw another piece above Folgie's head. He performed the same moves as Max and scarfed down his treat in the blink of an eye.

"What'd I tell you?" Cole leaned closer, brushing shoulders with her.

Both dogs barked, sat down, and raised a paw.

She chuckled at their antics. "Did you teach them that clever move that no human can resist?"

"Yep. I told you they're smart…probably smarter than the two of us put together."

"Glad they're patient with us."

"When it comes to steak, they're infinitely patient."

She tossed another piece, then another.

Folgie and Max leaped into action, grabbed their treats, and came back for more.

"What are we going to do when I run out of steak?"

"Frisbee. That…or let them herd you."

"I'll go with Frisbee."

"Finish up. When I put the plate away, they'll know that's it for now."

"Okay." She threw out one piece, then the last one right after it.

While Max and Folgie leaped after the steak, Cole took the plate from her and put it out of sight in a cabinet.

She looked over at him and smiled to herself. They were quite a pair. So far, nothing had stopped them, or even slowed them down, from enjoying life and each other.

"Watch this." He zinged a bright yellow Frisbee up and out over the lawn.

Folgie and Max saw it and took off, strong legs eating up the distance fast. Max shouldered Folgie out of the way, leaped into the air, and grabbed the Frisbee. He trotted back to Cole, long tail wagging. He gently set the Frisbee at Cole's feet and stepped back, brown eyes bright with anticipation.

"Makes me wish I had four legs," she said. "That's impressive."

"Bet they pity us because we only have two legs." He threw the Frisbee farther this time.

Folgie was still out there, so he leaped into the air, snapped the yellow disc between his teeth, and trotted back. He set the Frisbee down at Cole's feet, then stepped back.

"They're adorable," she said.

"What?" He gave her a mock frown. "Why don't you try fierce, loyal, smart, clever—"

"Adorable. I think that encompasses all those words."

"Just don't let them hear you say it."

She chuckled. "I'll whisper it then."

"Not helpful…not with a dog's hearing ability."

"True." She sighed in contentment. "Cole, thanks for this evening. It must be the first time I've relaxed since arriving in this county."

He turned to look at her, expression serious. "That rough?"

"You've been there for a lot of it."

He nodded.

"Don't things ever settle down around here?"

"I'm not sure what you mean by settle down. You're in the country. There's so much to do to keep things running, rough or smooth, that you just put one foot in front of the other and hope for the best."

"That's not encouraging."

"It's not for the faint of heart." He threw the Frisbee again. "You learn to depend on yourself and your friends, neighbors, and family."

"I've always done that with my mother and grandmother."

"I mean fix-it stuff or even dangerous stuff, where somebody's got your back and you've got theirs."

"Like the Steele family knew they could turn to you for help with Fernando?"

"Right. And I know I can count on them if I get in a bind."

"Like with the mustangs."

"That's with the law, but still, folks are keeping an eye out for the problem and will let me know if they see or hear anything that will help."

"Good." She opened her mouth, then shut it. She wanted to be one of those friends who helped him in a time of need. She even had the information to do it. But still she hesitated, remembering her entire trust issue with him. She'd just kind of forgotten it, or set it aside, during the pleasure of the evening. She wanted to trust him, but Mimi's life depended on her being cautious. And so she remained silent about what she'd seen at the dump. Come to think of it, what was she even doing here having fun anyway?

"And that's why everyone is willing to help you," he said.

"I appreciate it." She felt even worse about holding out…still, she had to put Mimi first.

"Everyone realizes you appreciate their help."

She took a deep breath. She was getting in too deep here. "Thank you for a lovely evening, but I need to go."

"What?" He moved in close to her. "Was it something I said?"

"No."

"I thought we could have wine or play golf or more Frisbee."

"Need to go."

"Audrey, talk to me. Something's going on you're not telling me about. If it's trouble, let me help."

"I…I…"

He wrapped his arms around her and pulled her close.

She could feel the strong beat of his heart, feel the strength of his muscles, feel the warmth of his hands stroking her back, soothing her…maybe even soothing them both because she'd put this wall up between them.

"Everybody has trouble now and again," he said. "You're strong. I know it. Everybody who meets you knows. It doesn't mean you're weak if you need to lean on somebody else for a little while until you get your feet back under you."

She took a slow breath to steady herself because his words were going deep, along with his presence. She inhaled his essence, as if she was pulling his strength, his fortitude, into her. And along with it came the scent of sage, citrus, and musk. It was a heady combination.

"Lean on me, please." His voice had gone deeper, slower, the cadence almost hypnotic.

And she did lean into him, wrapping her arms around his waist as she allowed herself this moment while she gathered her internal forces to plunge back into the fray.

"You can trust me. I'm rock solid. Anybody around here will tell you that truth."

She felt the dogs press their warm bodies against the back of her legs, as if they too were offering her strength and support. She felt wrapped in a cocoon of blessings…and it felt so good.

"Audrey, I'm not a man for casual stuff, if that's what you're thinking." He set his hands on her shoulders and tilted her back so he could look into her eyes.

She nodded, trying to grasp words but they'd fled her.

"I like you. I've liked you from the first. You're brave, bold, and you have the makings of a fine cowgirl."

She couldn't keep from smiling at his highest tribute to a woman.

"I believe everything you've told me about the store and the book. I saw the journal." Pain flashed in his brown eyes. "But you're holding something back. It's got a hold on you. Let me help you with it. I won't judge you. I'll just help you get out of it."

She felt chilled at his words. Did he know about the bootlegger gold? Would he try to use her to get to it? The journal. She should never have showed it to him. The rustlers. Thieves wanted easy marks. Free horses. Free gold. What could be better? She swallowed hard. Oh, how she wanted to believe him, how she wanted what he offered her, how she wanted this glimpse of happiness to be real. But Lady Mauve's words came back to haunt her...*trust no one*. And Mimi depended on her to be strong, like her great-grandmother.

She rose up on her tiptoes and pressed a soft kiss to his lips.

"You'll let me help?" he asked. "You'll let us explore...whatever this is between us?"

She gave him a final hug and stepped back, negotiating away from the dogs as well. "Secrets..."

"Should be shared."

"You have them, too."

Pain ran through his brown eyes again. "I'm up against a wall. I must protect the mustangs at all costs."

She nodded. "Maybe our time just isn't right."

"Don't say that. We can work through...around...blow up, if necessary, whatever stands between us."

She took another step back. "It was a lovely evening. I'll never forget it."

"I'll never let you forget it."

"I really need to make progress on the book."

He shuttered his gaze. "Okay. I'm patient. I'm here for you."

"Thank you. But—"

"It's the book. Okay. I can go with that for now. Give me time to set it up and I'll take you to Destiny."

"I can go alone."

"No. I'm still not sure you're safe from the rustlers," he said.

"But—"

"It's not just the town you'll want to experience. You need to meet the Buick Brigade."

"What's that?"

"It's who. They are the four matriarchs who know everything that goes on in this county. If they perceive wrongs need to be righted, they'll be set right. Births. Deaths. Marriages. Businesses. They watch over it all. And they're the daughters of the movers and shakers during Lady Mauve's reign. They have stories handed down by their families. If they like you and believe your cause to be valid, they'll help you. If not, they'll be really polite and show you the door."

"Formidable."

"Yes. Loved and respected, too." He smiled, but it held a hint of sadness. "If you won't accept my help, maybe you'll accept it from them."

"I've already accepted so much help from you. I really don't want to push it more."

"You're not pushing. I'm offering."

"Thank you."

"The Buick Brigade?" he asked.

"I'd like very much to meet them."

"Good. I'll let you know when I set up a visit with them."

"See how much you're helping me? You also introduced me to Jake and he is a treasure. I need to do something to repay you."

"I'm glad I can help. You owe me nothing…except maybe your smiles."

She smiled as his reward. "Really, I do need to go."

"I don't want to let you go."

"But you will."

"Yes…but only because I know we'll be together again soon."

"Next time, I'll cook." She glanced down at the dogs. "Guess it better be something that'll appeal to our canine friends."

"That's always a good idea with Max and Folgie."

She turned toward the gate, then looked back. "The floor?"

"That was the dogs' fault."

142   KIM REDFORD

"But they won't fix it."

"I will." He smiled with eyes gone deep chocolate. "Come on, I'll walk you home."

"It's just across the courtyard."

"Yeah…but there's an incentive."

"What?"

"I might sneak a good-night kiss."

Chapter 14

A WEEK LATER, AUDREY SAT BESIDE COLE IN HIS BIG ONE-TON as he drove toward Destiny. She'd had a few days alone to reorganize her thoughts and feelings. No doubt Cole was real fine. No doubt he was interested in her just like she was him. Yet, all told, they should simply be friends. She didn't really believe that would satisfy them, but it seemed the logical course considering their situations.

She'd moved on with her search for bootlegger gold, not that it'd done her much good. She'd driven around the countryside, getting the lay of the land that had changed little since Lady Mauve's days. She'd made her way to Sure-Shot, the small Western town that had once been situated on an old cattle drive trail from Texas to Kansas. She'd picked up groceries in Wildcat Bluff. She'd bought a few more items at Gene's Boot Hospital in Old Town. She was definitely getting a sense of the county that allowed her to feel more at home all the time.

And yet Mimi remained foremost on her mind. Mom had printed out the oak tree wire message and given it to her grandmother, to see if she could decipher its meaning. By all accounts, Mimi was excited about being part of Audrey's research trip to Wildcat Bluff. She was also eating better, talking more, and in general taking more interest in life, an absolute added benefit to the entire venture. In fact, Mimi was anxious to come to Wildcat Bluff just as soon as she'd built up her strength. She wanted to meet Jake and follow in her mother's footsteps. Audrey was thrilled with this news, but she also remained cautious about her grandmother's health.

Jake was also in Audrey's thoughts. By now, she almost felt as close to him as she did Mimi. Somehow, he just seemed part of her family. She visited him every day, although today she'd made the Buick Brigade her first priority. She needed to make better progress on locating the gold and writing the book.

She glanced over at Cole. Big, strong, rugged, determined to help her any way he could. Was it just being a good neighbor, dedication to the county, deeply personal, or—and she hoped this wasn't true—keeping an eye on her for the rustlers? *Time will tell* was the only thing she could settle on.

"You're awfully quiet today," Cole said.

"My mind is whirling with this and that, to-dos and to-don'ts."

"To-don'ts?" He chuckled as he kept his strong hands wrapped around the steering wheel.

"You know. Everything is on the to-do list until it falls off, onto the to-don't list."

"How does it fall off?"

"Turns out not to be workable or is a waste of time or…"

"Why don't you just toss the to-don't list and forget about it?" he asked.

"You never know. It might come back to haunt me. I don't care for surprises."

He reached over and squeezed her hand. "For somebody who doesn't like surprises, you've had about nothing else since you got here."

"True." She squeezed his hand in return, noticing the little hot zing up her arm from his touch.

"Some surprises are good. Like you." He threaded their fingers together for a brief moment, then placed his hand back on the steering wheel.

"You're right. Most everything in Wildcat Bluff County has been a good surprise."

"That include me?"

"You know it," she said.

"No, I don't know it. You ran out on me the other night and have gone your way ever since."

"I kissed you nighty-night, didn't I?"

"Yeah. But did you really mean it?"

"Couldn't you tell?"

He glanced over at her with a smile lighting up his dark eyes. "Pretty hot, wasn't it?"

She returned his smile. "Yeah." And that was exactly how a woman fell off a road paved with good intentions.

He jerked his truck back from the edge of Wildcat Road, chuckling. "Better keep my eyes on the road. You're too distracting for safety."

She laughed. "Better keep our minds on the matter at hand, too."

"Destiny is coming up. You'll enjoy it."

After a while, he drove up a rise and crested the top of a cliff overlooking the muddy Red River as it made its way east toward Louisiana before eventually joining the Mississippi River, heading south to the Gulf of Mexico. To the west, buildings rose above the flat-topped mesa.

"There wasn't ever a ferry at Destiny like there was at Wildcat Bluff," he said.

"Why not?"

"It's too high above the river. You'll notice there aren't many trees…at least not since the first settlers arrived and created the town."

"They didn't like trees?"

"They used the lumber to build their homes."

"And they wanted a pretty vista." She pointed across the river at the tree-lined, red-tinted earth of Oklahoma.

"Right. And it looks as if they didn't want anybody to sneak up on them, so they created a clear field to return fire if necessary."

"Defensive, then?"

"By now, it's anybody's guess, but that's an accepted reason," he said.

"And the Buick Brigade?"

"Story is that four businessmen—their ancestors—came with plenty of money and a desire to keep an eye on each other, and anyone else who came to town, from their front porches."

He turned west and followed the two-lane highway. "You'll notice the road up here doesn't end in the town. That's probably defensive, too."

"Guess they were protective of their privacy."

"And safety."

"Did they have outlaw shootouts here like in Wildcat Bluff?"

"And Sure-Shot." He pointed toward the town. "No. Destiny has always presented a genteel face to the world."

"But it's like they were anticipating trouble."

"Figure they didn't want any surprises."

He rolled into town and eased his truck to the side of the street. "Here's Destiny."

Four three-story Victorian mansions stood side by side on large lots on the south side of Main Street. A small dovecote built as a replica of each house had been set on a tall pole at the front corner of the homes. A single-story carriage house and former stable had been built behind each house.

The painted ladies came in four colors with accent trim. The first on the block was pale yellow with gold. The second was fuchsia with purple. The third was white with navy. The fourth was aqua with green. They all had wraparound porches, octagonal turret rooms, multipeaked roofs, distinctive ornamental trims, and wide entry staircases with elaborately carved handrails. Each home had a unique, whimsical design, from a steamboat with keyhole windows to gingerbread fantasyland to multicolored stained glass to jewel-cut fascia.

On the other side of the street, single-story buildings with Western false fronts painted white promoted businesses on hand-carved, hand-painted signs that hung above the continuous board-walk under a connecting portico—Destiny Books and Coffee Parlor, Destiny Sweetheart Café, Destiny Mercantile, Destiny Feed and Fashion Emporium, Destiny Junk and Antiques, and Destiny Chocolatier.

On either side of the businesses, twelve small, single-story farmhouses with peaked roofs spread out, six to each side. Each house had been painted a different pastel color and gleamed like a long rainbow in the sunlight. All had matching gray slate roofs. And the front lawns were enclosed with white picket fences. A few pickups were nosed into the parking spaces in front of the business buildings.

"It's almost as if time forgot this town," Audrey said. "It could almost be an oil painting from the late 1890s. Those house are definitely Queen Victoria era designs. And it's all so perfectly maintained, you'd never know the buildings were over a hundred years old."

"I'm glad you like it. Each lady of the Buick Brigade lives in one of the painted ladies."

He made a U-turn, drove back down the street, and parked in front of the Victorian house painted fuchsia. Four women stood on the portico beneath a gingerbread-laced edge of roof.

"That's Doris's house," he said. "In case you wonder, and no one has ever asked because that would be considered rude, the ladies are close to ninety if they're a day. They've been friends all their lives, and they've all outlived one or more husbands."

"Can't wait to meet them."

"They're also tough. Meet you at the door with a shotgun cra-dled in their arms kind of tough. But fair. Kind. Smart. And they love Wildcat Bluff County with the kind of devotion and protec-tion that a mother gives her children."

"I like their attitude."

"Let's introduce you." He got out, walked around the front of his truck, and opened the passenger door.

When she stepped down, he held out his arm in the formal way a Victorian gentleman would've done. She was glad she'd dressed up just a bit in lavender blouse and slacks, black flats, and gold earrings for this special occasion.

"When in Destiny…" She slipped her hand around his arm, remembering their walk in Wildcat Bluff's Old Town.

"That's right. Ladies and gentlemen are the order of the day."

He led her up the sidewalk, mounted the staircase with her, and stopped in front of the four ladies. They stood erect, as if they'd practiced walking with books on their heads at a young age and never lost the knack.

"We're so happy you're here. I'm Doris," one of the women said with a toss of her silver shoulder-length hair.

"We appreciate the invitation," Cole said. "I'd like to introduce Audrey Oakes."

Doris beamed, her brown eyes lively. "Thank you so much for joining us today. These are my dear friends, Louise, Blondel, and Ada." She indicated each one with a graceful gesture of her hand. They ranged from short to tall, slim to plump, hair dark to platinum, with clothing that ranged from trim pants to full skirt.

"I'm so happy to meet all of you." Audrey smiled at the group.

"Please join us in my parlor for tea," Doris said.

"Thank you," Audrey replied.

She followed the ladies into a cool, shadowy hallway of walnut panels. A worn, faded Aubusson runner covered an oak floor. They turned through an open doorway and emerged into a brighter room. Lace curtains over floor-to-ceiling windows had tied-back maroon velvet drapes. The parlor was crowded with delicate furniture, gewgaws on every surface, and colorful scarves and tablecloths covered almost everything.

Doris and Ada sat across from Blondel and Louise on matching Queen Anne love seats made of gilded wood with maroon velvet upholstery. A small table between the two settees held a tray with a china teapot in a violet flower pattern and six matching teacups with saucers, plus a plate stacked high with misshapen cookies.

"Please sit." Blondel indicated two chairs that were left empty on either end of the table with a wave of a long-fingered hand that displayed several sparkling diamond-and-gold rings.

"Yes, please," Doris said.

Audrey took one of the chairs while Cole sat down on the other. She noticed he eased his large frame carefully onto the fragile-looking chair. She hoped it didn't break under the weight of his muscles. He probably hoped the same thing.

"Isn't she just lovely?" Ada put a fingertip to her plump chin as she looked at Audrey from head to toe.

"Absolutely." Louise patted her platinum helmet of teased and sprayed hair.

"Stunning," Blondel said.

"Never in my wildest imagination did I expect to see the spitting image of Lady Mauve walk through my front door." Doris clasped her hands together.

"But how…" Audrey glanced at Cole, who looked surprised, then around at the Buick Brigade.

"Photographs, my dear," Blondel said.

"Yes, indeed. We have photos, as well as clothes, from that time period. Our parents were deep into Lady Mauve's business," Louise said.

"Not that they allowed us to know much," Doris said.

"But we were quite adept at listening at keyholes outside closed doors," Ada said.

"It was delicious fun." Doris smiled at her friends, blue eyes dancing with humor.

"Did Cole tell you I'm researching a book about Wildcat Bluff County as it's connected to Hot Springs during Prohibition?"

"Yes indeed. We're very excited by the idea," Louise said. "But we didn't know…"

"Absolutely didn't realize…" Doris said.

"We had no idea that…" Blondel said.

"You're a descendant of Lady Mauve," Ada said.

"I'm not telling a lot of people yet." Audrey smiled at the group. "I'm her great-granddaughter."

"Fabulous," Blondel said.

"Please tell us what happened to her after she left Wildcat Bluff." Louise leaned forward.

"I will, but first I'd like to know more about her life here."

"We'll happily share information," Ada said.

"There was traffic—fast cars, fast men, fast women—on the roads between Destiny and Hallelujah Ranch during Prohibition from the Roaring Twenties into the thirties and the Depression era," Doris said.

"Moonshine." Ada gave a sharp nod. "People were not to be denied their pleasures."

"And there was great profit to be made, if not caught by the revenuers." Louise glanced around the group, patting her hair again.

"Why Destiny? And Hallelujah Ranch?" Audrey asked.

"Location," Blondel said. "Neither place can be caught by surprise."

"They came to Destiny from the bigger towns," Ada said. "The pretty flappers and their fancy men, all gussied up and out for fun."

"Lady Mauve's Hallelujah speakeasy at Big Rock had quite the reputation as the best blind tiger in several counties," Ada said. "Music, liquor, dance."

"But Hallelujah isn't in Destiny, is it?" Audrey asked.

"Oh, no." Blondel smiled. "That was Lady Mauve all over again."

"She was just so smart," Louise said.

"I don't understand the connection." Audrey looked around the group, hoping for a better explanation.

"Destiny is where partygoers lost their tails, if there were any," Ada said. "They lunched or had ice cream or shopped in town, where they received the current password and directions to Hallelujah Ranch."

"Pigeons were faster than Model T Fords. They were used between Destiny and Hallelujah to alert the speakeasy if revenuers were on their way," Doris said.

"Those were all Lady Mauve's ideas," Blondel said. "She was so clever that her blind tiger was never raided and her moonshiners never caught."

"That says a lot." Audrey was more impressed than ever by her ancestor. "And nobody ever knew what happened to her?"

"A mystery," Ada said.

"Do you mean that at the end of Prohibition, Lady Mauve simply closed up shop and drove away for parts unknown?" Audrey asked.

"Not unknown to her," Ada said.

"But why leave when she had friends and business here?" Audrey asked.

"You would know that better than us," Doris said.

"Maybe she planned to come back, but something happened and she couldn't make it." Blondel looked at Audrey for an explanation.

"Love," Doris said.

"Certainly," Louise said.

"Love?" Audrey asked.

"Why else would a woman pull up roots and disappear?" Ada said.

"She fell in love and went with him." Blondel looked at Audrey with a hopeful expression on her face.

Audrey shook her head.

"Lady Mauve ruled the roost at Hallelujah," Doris said. "She kept schedules. She granted jobs. She maintained quality control. She hired muscle. And she retained the best lawyer money could buy to keep everyone as safe as possible."

"She rarely left Hallelujah," Ada said. "All came to her."

"She loved beauty. She left behind that beautiful speakeasy, as well as a long string of pink pearls and a gorgeous silver set." Blondel looked to Audrey again. "Surely she planned to return."

"We always thought love was her downfall." Ada gave Audrey a sad look.

"True," Louise said. "He was a charming, handsome scoundrel, that lawyer of hers."

"And jealous," Ada said.

"Well, she was a legendary beauty. Irish. Porcelain skin. Violet eyes. Black hair," Blondel said.

"And everyone loved her because she was powerful, provocative, and protective." Ada smiled pensively, as if remembering someone she'd known well.

"Well, not everyone loved her," Blondel said.

"He did love her," Louise said. "He loved her too well. Jealousy and moonshine didn't sit well with him."

"The lawyer?" Audrey asked, hearing all this old history for the first time.

"None other," Ada said. "At least that's the story as we pieced it together."

"But nobody knows for sure." Doris appeared thoughtful. "One day Prohibition was over. Bootleggers were over. Revenuers were over. Lady Mauve was gone."

"And they took all the excitement with them," Blondel said.

Ada looked straight at Audrey. "Only it's all come alive again. First the speakeasy was found and reopened. Now you're here."

"Tell us, please, that Lady Mauve lived out the rest of her days with the man of her heart," Blondel said.

"I hate to disappoint you." Audrey glanced at Cole, then back at the ladies. "She went to Hot Springs and went legit. Prohibition was over, so she opened a popular bar and restaurant that supported local musical talent."

"But what about her beloved?" Ada asked.

"As far as I know, there was never a man who stayed in her life. She had a daughter. My mother had a daughter. And here I am."

"But…but who is your grandmother's father?" Doris asked.

"That is something I'd very much like to know." Audrey shook her head. "I suspect he was a man she met in Hot Springs who didn't stick around when she became pregnant."

"But all the men here loved her," Blondel said.

"Maybe she didn't mix business with pleasure." Audrey wished she had a different, better ending to her great-grandmother's story, but she didn't.

"That's very disappointing," Louise said.

"Devastating," Doris said.

"Heartbreaking," Blondel said.

"On that sad note, we definitely need tea and cookies to lift our spirits," Ada said.

"But I believe she lived a happy life." Audrey felt a need to defend her great-grandmother's choice.

"Of course, dear," Blondel said.

"But without love…" Ada said.

"She did quite well," Louise said.

"Yes, indeed." Doris picked up the teapot, poured liquid into all the cups, and handed them around the group.

Ada raised the plate of cookies and held it out.

Audrey selected one, but she eyed it a little skeptically due to its misshapen form.

Cole picked up a cookie and took a big bite. "Delicious as always." He chuckled. "Let me guess. You used the Texas cookie cutter…or maybe this one is the cowboy boot."

Ada grinned, only lifting a shoulder in response.

"She makes the best sugar cookies in the county," Cole said. "But she keeps us guessing about the shapes."

"Mystery is a vital part of life," Ada said. "Maybe we were better off imagining Lady Mauve living a life of love and leisure."

"You're right. She loved beauty," Audrey said. "She created a magnificent watering hole for the beautiful people. Actors. Dancers. Singers. Musicians. Artists. They all came to her."

"Like folks came to her speakeasy," Blondel said.

"Yes," Audrey replied. "I believe she shared her love of beauty with many people, rather than a single man."

"That does sound like her, doesn't it?" Doris glanced at her friends.

They all nodded in unison.

"We look forward to sharing more with you," Doris said.

"And I'll be happy to tell you details about her life in Hot Springs," Audrey said.

"But first, you must visit Jake the Farmer," Blondel said.

"He knew her well," Ada said.

"So he will have the best memories of all," Louise said.

"I've met him and I've been visiting with him for several weeks." Audrey nodded at the group.

"Excellent," Ada said.

Doris raised her cup of tea in a toast. The other three quickly followed by raising their cups. Smiles brightened their eyes.

"To our very own Lady Audrey."

Chapter 15

COLE DROVE BACK INTO THE COMPOUND, WATCHED THE GATE close behind him, and started toward the house. Audrey was quiet beside him. She hadn't had too much to say since they'd left Destiny. Maybe she was mulling over all she'd learned or making a mental list of questions for Jake or thinking about inviting him inside her home for a cup of coffee, but no more tea, thank you very much.

Still, she seemed too quiet. He was, too, for that matter, but his mind was on the mustangs and how to keep them safe. He'd asked the cowboys to keep rotating them in pastures and keep a closer eye on them. So far that appeared to be working because they hadn't been hit again. There were no leads from any branch of law enforcement and that was most discouraging of all. Still, no one would give up searching for the missing mustangs and the rustlers.

"Do you think I really look that much like Lady Mauve?" Audrey broke the silence.

"There's definitely a resemblance in the one photo I saw. The Buick Brigade have more pictures, so I'd trust their opinion. Does it bother you?"

"No." She glanced over at him with a little frown. "It's just… Lady Mauve's legacy is larger than life. I didn't get that impression from her journal. She just seemed kind and maybe a little sad."

"Outer and inner images can be different, don't you think?"

"Yes."

"What's bothering you?" he asked.

"I'm proud to be her great-granddaughter and look like her. But how can I ever live up to her reputation? Won't folks around here always be disappointed when they compare me to her?"

He hit his brakes and turned to stare at her. "Audrey, no one—and I mean not a single person—could ever be disappointed in you."

"I'm not larger than life."

"You don't need to be to be loved by others."

"I'm not the bedrock of a community."

"You don't need to be to contribute to others," he said.

"I'm not supporting artists like she did."

"You don't need to do all of that in the same way, if you need to do it at all. Let me remind you that you're researching and writing a book. That makes you larger than life, bedrock of our community, and a supporter of the arts."

She reached over and cupped his cheek, giving him a tender smile. "Thank you. Was I having a dark night of the soul?"

"We all do on occasion."

"Do you? I can't imagine it," she said.

"For me right now, it's the mustangs. They depend on me to keep them safe. I've let them down. No matter what I do, the rustlers keep finding a way to get at them."

She pressed her fingertips against his lips to silence him, then cupped his cheek again. "You're doing all you can do. Nobody can expect more…not even you. We'll get them. I'll help any way I can."

"You?" Had he completely misjudged her from the first? She sounded so sincere. And her momentary lack of self-confidence about being compared to her great-grandmother gave him a glimpse into her character. Writer, not rustler.

"I'll be out and about talking with folks. Let's hope I hear something useful."

"Let's hope." He covered her hand with his own, then slid her fingers back to his mouth and gently kissed each fingertip.

"More than hope. We'll get them." She stroked his cheek before she turned back toward their houses. "Guess we'd best get on with it. Folgie and Max will know we're here. They'll expect treats at the very least."

"Good thing I left them in the patio area instead of letting them roam free in the compound or they'd be all over us by now."

"In that case, they deserve double treats."

"They'll surely think so." He hit the gas, rounded the tree into the courtyard, and pulled up in front of the guesthouse.

He immediately sensed something was wrong. Folgie and Max barked alarms from the gate leading into the patio. What was on Audrey's front door? And her SUV… He looked more closely. The windows were cracked all the way around. He felt a knot in his stomach explode into an acid burn.

He jerked his phone out of his pocket, not waiting a second to contact the sheriff.

"Sheriff Calhoun here. Cole, what's up? More missing mustangs?"

"I hope not." But now that Cole thought about it, maybe Audrey's SUV damage was a diversion from bigger matters.

"What is it?"

"Intruders got inside the compound and damaged property."

"How did they get in?"

"Don't know. Just got here. Need to look around," Cole said.

"Don't mess with anything. I'll get there soon."

"Thanks." Cole disconnected, slipped his phone back in his pocket, and glanced at Audrey.

"I can't believe what I'm seeing. Are my SUV windows actually cracked?"

"Looks like it."

"That's crazy. How could it happen?"

"Intruders. Maybe rustlers," Cole said.

"They got in here?"

"I don't know how...but I'll get that problem solved pronto."

She opened her door. "I want a better look at the damage."

"Wait." He pulled his SIG Sauer out from under the seat, checked the safety, and started to step outside.

"Why?" she asked.

"You'll be safer here while I check out the place."

"I'm going with you." She gave him a fierce look. "Lady Mauve wouldn't have hung back in the face of trouble. I'm not going to either."

"Okay." He liked her grit, but he still worried about her. "If there's a problem, you'll go right back to the truck, won't you?"

"Yes."

If push came to shove, he didn't know if she'd actually do it, but he hoped so.

"I said yes." She smiled. "And I'll drag you with me."

He returned her smile, liking the fact that she wanted him out of danger, too, even though sometimes it wasn't possible.

He stepped out of his truck, SIG held at his side, pointed downward. He heard her feet hit the pavement, too. He walked over to her SUV, then slowly circled it. Sure enough, the safety glass of every single window had been cracked, but not with blows from a hammer or something hard and heavy. Real cute. They'd taped firecrackers to the glass, then lit them. The explosions had caused the windows to crack. He looked down. Tires were okay, far as he could tell. They could've slashed the tires, but those would have been an easy, quick fix in town. Windows would probably need to be ordered before installation. It'd take a while and keep her out of action longer...or so they'd probably thought.

"Cole, I don't understand." She pointed at the damage. "Who did this? Why did they do it?"

"I hate to say it, but I figure it's the rustlers, sending you a message to stay quiet."

He put an arm around her shoulders and tugged her against

his chest in comfort. No mistaking the pain and confusion in her voice. Maybe she was putting on an act to gain his sympathy, but he didn't think so. What would be the point? She was living here. She had access to comings and goings on the ranch. She could already transmit intel. No, she was genuinely upset.

He hugged her tighter. He felt the dual sensations of relief and happiness—not about her vehicle or the compound, but about her authenticity. She was keeping something from him, but as long as it didn't involve the rustlers, they could deal with it later.

Folgie and Max kept barking their alarms, anxious to be let out and catch the intruders' trail. He'd let them do it in a moment.

"When we catch those rustlers, they're going to pay for the damage to my SUV," she said.

"You bet."

"Do you think they did anything else?"

"Don't know. For sure, you're not going to get in it and turn over the engine."

"Do you mean it might explode or something?" she asked.

"I doubt they set explosives."

"Firecrackers are explosives."

"Yeah. But maybe that's the extent of their message," he said.

"Hope so."

"Let's check your front door." He quickly walked over with her on his heels. It didn't take long to see the problem. Somebody had spray-painted a message in red paint on the turquoise door.

"No snitching," Audrey read out loud.

"Like I thought, they believe you saw something and don't want you to talk." He glanced at her, but she looked away from him. Again, he got the impression she knew more than she'd said.

"Maybe I'd better move out. I don't want to put you, the dogs, your ranch in jeopardy."

"We were already in danger."

"Still…I'd better find a place in town," she said.

"And endanger somebody there?"

"I hadn't thought of that."

"Think about it." He looked from the guesthouse to the main house. "Better yet, move into my home."

"What?"

"You'll be safer. It'll be easier for me to guard one house than two. Plus the dogs are there."

"Are you certain I'm still in danger or that I can put others in danger?" she asked.

"I'm not certain about anything." He pointed at her vehicle and the door. "That's a warning. If they get worried again about you talking about what you saw, they might escalate. My mustangs must be really important to them."

"I'm sorry about your door. I'll pay to have the spray paint removed or get the words painted over."

"It's no big deal. Your safety is most important."

"And yours."

"Once Sheriff Calhoun collects evidence, we'll move your stuff into a guest bedroom," he said, then hesitated, realizing he was being high-handed even with the best of intentions. "I mean, if it's okay with you."

She looked all around, then back at him. "I don't want to be so much trouble. I just want to do what I came here to do without hassles."

"I just want to run my ranch without hassles, too. Sometimes it doesn't work out that way."

"True. Still…"

"I'm offering you a place to stay with me. Will you do it?" he asked.

"Yes. And thank you. You're being more than kind. You're being…"

"Neighborly?"

"Much more than that, I think," she said.

"Look, the rustlers aren't just my problem. If they branch out into cattle, they become a big Wildcat Bluff problem. What helps us helps everyone."

"Makes sense. I just wish I weren't caught up in it."

"Me, too." He felt a sense of urgency to check the compound fence. He needed to know how the intruders had gained entrance. "Let's let Folgie and Max out and walk the perimeter."

"Okay." She glanced down at her feet. "I need to change shoes. These flats won't do. I need sneakers."

"Are you good with going inside? I don't hear the alarm, so I don't think they breached the security system."

"I'm fine. Let me get my key." She ran back to his truck, returned with her purse, pulled out a set of keys, and opened the door.

"I'll go in first and check the place." He quickly shouldered open the door and stepped inside. Nothing looked out of the ordinary, but he looked in the kitchen, bedroom, and bath before he was satisfied all was as it should be. He quickly rejoined her.

"All okay?" she asked.

"Looks good."

"I'll just be a minute."

He took the time while she was gone to look, listen, and sense the compound. Far as he could tell, the intruders were long gone. If they'd been watching the place, they would've seen him leave with Audrey. They could've made short work of their vandalism and been gone. He'd bet they came in through a pasture to the compound fence on foot so they didn't get caught on security cameras at the entries. They wouldn't have needed to carry much, little weight for fireworks, lighter, and can of spray paint. Good thing he'd confined the dogs or they might have been taken out. That made him mad all over again, but he choked back his anger. He needed to be cool and calm to see this attack on his ranch through to a satisfactory end. And he'd get there, one way or another.

When Audrey returned, she'd changed to jeans, a long-sleeve tee, and running shoes. She slipped her phone in a pocket, locked the door, tucked her keys in a different pocket, and nodded that she was ready to go.

He approved the fact that she didn't waste time on appearance, although she looked great as always. They needed to get a move on. He started past his truck, then stopped. He needed to think like the rustlers. They'd used fire at the ranch entry. They'd used fire to set the firecrackers. No fire that he could see from here, but still, he decided to be on the safe side. He jerked open a pickup door and grabbed a fire extinguisher. He slung it by its strap over one shoulder. Now he was ready to see what he could see.

He took long strides, with Audrey right by his side. He stopped at the gate where Folgie and Max waited for them, jumping up and down, clawing at the fence in their eagerness to get out. He unlocked the gate and swung it open.

The two dogs bounded out, gave Cole and Audrey the sniff test, appeared satisfied with their discoveries, and took off due north toward Destiny.

"We can't keep up with them," she said.

"No matter. They'll come back to us. Like trackers, they'll range out ahead and bring back news."

"So we follow them?"

"That direction, but I'll make a sweep of the entire perimeter. The compound fence isn't that large," he said.

"It's a good fence."

"Yes. Still, it's ornamental, too. Six-foot vertical black metal bars are meant more to keep out four-footed predators than two-footed ones. I'm surprised those rustlers had the nerve to get in this close."

"And show their hand so clearly," she said.

"Yep. They'd have been better off to stay out in the pastures." He took long strides toward the section of fence where both dogs had their noses to the ground. They were sniffing and pawing at the dirt while whining low in their throats.

"Looks like they went right to something," she said.

"They picked up the intruders' scent when they were at your SUV. They'll never forget it. Plus the rustlers left an air trail for them to follow."

"Ranch dogs are a lot more than for company, aren't they?"

"You bet. They're vital working dogs. And they're usually a good deterrent to interlopers. It doesn't make good sense for the rustlers to have taken a chance coming up here and causing damage." He stopped in his tracks.

"What is it?" She stopped, too.

"Forgot. Had it on my mind the moment I saw your vehicle." He jerked his phone out of his pocket and hit a button to connect with his head honcho. He hoped Russ was at the cattle barn and in cell range. Phone rang several times.

Russ picked up. "Hey, boss."

"Need you to check the mustangs. Bet we've been hit again."

"Hell no!"

"I'd guess it happened last night," Cole said.

"Nobody's been out that way today."

"Better take a head count and take it now."

"Will do," Russ said.

"Call me ASAP. I'm at the compound. We were hit here, too."

"Hell no!"

"Yep."

"How bad?" Russ asked.

"Nuisance more than anything. I think it was two-pronged. Scare tactic that would also distract us so we'd be chasing a cold trail."

"Pretty lady okay?" Russ asked.

"Yeah. She's been with me."

"Best keep an eye on her."

"I'm on it. And Sheriff Calhoun is on his way."

"Good man. I'm out of here," Russ said.

Cole clicked off his phone and pocketed it. He felt his gut churn. Not only could he not keep the rustlers off his ranch, he couldn't even keep them out of his compound. Something had to give…and it wasn't going to be him.

"So…maybe you think it's not about me after all?" Audrey said.

He glanced at her. "That's not what I meant. It's very much about you. Like I said, two-pronged, I'd bet. Get you in control. Get more mustangs. I may be wrong about the horses. We'll have to wait and see."

"But if so…by now they're long gone."

"Yes."

"Makes me sick," she said.

"You and me both." He started forward again. The can felt heavy hanging from his shoulder. Lot of good it'd do. All the fire-fighter training in the world wouldn't help him save the horses. But he couldn't feel defeated—not now. Not ever. He trudged onward, watching the dogs, thinking about the mustangs, wishing he'd done something sooner or different for another outcome.

When he reached Max and Folgie, he immediately saw the trouble. Rustlers had dug under the metal fence, then they'd piled dry winter leaves and knee-high dry grass over the hole to conceal it. Just beyond the fence, tall spring grass rose high in the pasture. If not for the dogs digging at the site, he might have walked right by the breach. The rustlers had done a good job getting into and out of the compound, but they'd also known they had plenty of time with the dogs confined at the house and him gone to Destiny.

He knelt down to look at the pile of leaves…and heard a hiss, a click, and saw a flash of light as a firework exploded, sending brilliant color in a whoosh into the air and sparks outward into the dry debris. A red-orange blaze erupted and sent fingers of fire toward the pasture. Timer set to go off now? Had to be. He felt adrenaline kick in like it always did when he was confronted by a fire. If this got away, it'd be an out-of-control wildfire in no time flat. He had to stop it and stop it now.

"Audrey, grab the dogs and get back." He leaped to his feet as he jerked the canister off his shoulder.

"Come here, Max and Folgie. Good doggies. Come to me," she called.

"Thanks." He didn't look around to check on them. No time. He aimed the nozzle of his can.

"I've got them," she said. "You get back, too."

"Can't."

"Do you want me to call Wildcat Bluff Fire-Rescue?"

"Give me a minute. Let's see what I can do with one can."

"Do you have another fire extinguisher in the truck?" she asked.

"Yes."

"I can run back and get it. I'll put the dogs where they're safe in the patio area. I can get the towels out of my SUV and help."

"For now, stay back. Wait."

Containment was his first priority. The metal fence wouldn't burn, so that was good. But the dry leaves were going up fast. He sprayed in an arc outside the fire where it had already blackened a wide area and sent white smoke spiraling up into the sky. If the rustlers were watching for their handiwork, they would see the smoke and think they'd won this round. Not true. Folgie and Max had saved the day. He just needed to complete their good scout work…if the chemicals held out. If not, Audrey could run and get him the other can to finish containment.

"Cole, I hate to wait. I can be back in a jiffy," she said.

"Guess you'd better go. I've about got the fire completely circled with foam. To be on the safe side, I'd better cover it all."

"Okay…but get back and stay safe while I'm gone. If anything happened to you, I'd…"

"Go. I'm fine. I've fought a few fires before and we're winning this one," he said.

"No need to call for a booster?"

"I've got it." He stepped back, watching the center of the fire start to die out as it reached its fuel limit.

"Cole, we're going now."

He glanced over his shoulder…and smiled at the sight.

Audrey stood tall, with hands on the collars of Max and Folgie. All three looked ready, willing, and able to take on anything that might endanger GTT Ranch.

Warmth enveloped him…and it had nothing to do with the fire.

Chapter 16

AUDREY RAN BACK TOWARD THE FIRE, LUGGING THE HEAVY fire extinguisher over one shoulder by its strap and carrying two towels in one hand. It'd taken extra time to get Max and Folgie to stay behind a closed gate. They'd wanted to continue to help, but they were safer out of the way. She'd worried about Cole during the entire process.

Finally, she could see him again. She slowed to a trot, then a walk. He was just fine…more than fine. In lieu of towels, he'd taken off his shirt to beat at what was left of the fire. She hadn't seen him naked from the waist up until now. He was muscled from hard labor, starting at his wrists, moving all the way up to his shoulders and across his back. Sweat glistened on his taut, tanned skin in the sunlight.

She caught her breath. He was simply gorgeous—not only in body, but in mind and spirit as well. She'd come to know him so much better in the last couple of weeks, a time that seemed longer and yet not long at all. Time appeared to stand still when she was with him, or maybe it had something to do with the specialness of Wildcat Bluff County.

In any case, her initial distrust of him was dissipating fast, particularly after everything that had happened at the ranch today. His dedication to helping all creatures great and small, from wild mustangs to fighting fires to a stranger in need like her, was the antithesis of a rustler who looted from others.

She needed to trust Cole. She wanted to trust him. She believed—finally—that she was ready to trust him.

"I'm back," she said.

He glanced over his shoulder, face darkened with soot, and smiled, eyes lighting up with pleasure.

She slipped the strap off her shoulder and held the canister out to him.

"Thanks." He tossed her the shirt and took the can.

"Towels?"

"Don't think we'll need them." He pulled the pin, aimed the nozzle, and sprayed chemical over the blackened area.

She hung the towels around her neck and let them drape down. She shook out his shirt, sending soot and debris flying, along with his musky scent.

She brushed the soft fabric with the palm of her hand, imagining doing the same thing to the contours of his chest. His shirt would never be the same, not with all the holes, from pinpricks to dime size, but then she didn't much think her heart would ever be the same again either. She could now well understand how Lady Mauve had "left her heart in Wildcat Bluff County." When it was time to go, Audrey might very well do the same thing.

Would she regret it? No. Happiness could never be regretted, no matter the final outcome. She was sure her great-grandmother had felt the same way. Maybe that was why she'd picked up a thread of sadness in Lady Mauve's journal. Happy but sad at the same time. And yet she'd made enough good memories to last a lifetime.

Audrey would do her best to make her grandmother happy in whatever months or years she had left to enjoy life. That was her original goal. And it still was. If she lost her heart in the process, it was a small price to pay. And yet she wanted her own happiness, too. She clutched Cole's shirt in her hands and pressed it to her heart.

He finished off the can and turned to her.

She tried to smile, but her thoughts were overriding her reaction to their current situation.

"We saved the ranch again," he said.

"I'm glad, but I feel like it's somehow my fault."

"The rustlers were already working my ranch before you came to the county," he said.

"Still, they followed me that night."

"Audrey, are you all right?" He set the empty canister beside the other can, then walked over to her.

She held out his shirt, not wanting to give it back but knowing that was the right thing, the only thing, to do.

"Seriously, has this all been too much for you? I mean, you aren't used to this type of life. You're city. Not country." He took his shirt, slipped his arms into the sleeves, but left it hanging open in front to reveal a big rodeo buckle on a thick leather belt looped through the narrow waistband of his jeans.

"No. It's just…just…"

"We need to take care of you."

"I'm okay. You're the one with all the trouble on your ranch," she said.

"Yeah. But *your* trouble happened on *my* ranch."

"Not your fault. Is the fire completely out?"

"It's still hot, but no embers. Sheriff Calhoun needs to collect evidence from several sites when he gets here."

"We're waiting for him?" she asked.

"Yes. And for news about the mustangs."

"Do we wait here?"

"If you like, we can go to the house. I don't see why we can't go ahead and move your stuff. We'll be careful with the door and not disturb the evidence, although I doubt there will be much to help. Still, we need to go through the process with the sheriff."

"Okay," she said.

"And we'll get your SUV towed to a good place I know in Wildcat Bluff to get your windows replaced. I hate what that'll cost you. It happened on my property, so let me pay for it."

"Absolutely not. You're already doing too much for me."

"At least you can borrow a loaner from me, so your research doesn't get slowed down."

"Okay. I'll accept that from you," she said.

"Do you drive a four-on-the-floor stick shift? I'll understand if you don't because most people don't get trained on it anymore."

She smiled, nodding. "As a matter of fact, that suits me just fine."

He grinned. "Great. I've got this vintage Jeep that'll get you around the countryside and back into rough country if you need it."

"It sounds like fun to drive, too."

"You'll like it."

"Okay."

He nudged the ashes of the fire with the toe of his boot. "We've done all we can here."

"I'm so glad we caught the blaze in time."

"Me, too." He picked up the canisters and slung them by their straps over his shoulders. "Let's get back to the house."

She walked beside him, feeling as if she should do something more, knowing she could do something more...but when was the right time?

When they reached her SUV, she cringed at the sight. She'd clamped down on her emotions, but she really wanted to rant about the destruction. It was so personal, so premeditated, so cruel that the rustlers must be stopped at all costs before they caused even more harm. She'd have that talk with Cole at the first opportunity.

"If you'll pack up your stuff, I'll help you carry it to the house," he said. "I need to get up there now. I want to reassure the dogs and check in with the sheriff. I haven't heard from my head honcho about the mustangs. I don't take that as a good sign. If it looked like they were all present and accounted for, he'd have gotten right back to me. Bet they're counting heads now."

"You think you've lost more, don't you?"

"I'm trying to stay positive, but it's not looking good."

"Go. Take care of business. I'll move myself. I don't have much to carry over," she said.

"You're sure?"

"Yes. And yes, I'll be careful not to touch anything on the door. I'll just unlock, step over the entry, pack, move, and lock up behind me."

"Okay." He looked steadily at her. "If you see or hear anything out of the ordinary, don't hesitate to call me." He patted the phone in the pocket of his jeans. "Phone's always with me."

"Same here." She mimicked his action.

Still, he didn't move.

She didn't either. She realized they didn't want to separate, particularly during a time of crisis. One of them had to make the first move. She jerked the keys out of her pocket and unlocked her front door.

"Be careful."

"You, too," she said.

He turned and took long strides toward his house.

She walked into the guesthouse and carefully shut the door behind her. She glanced around, regretting the upcoming move. This place had come to feel like home. No more. Not with the rustlers getting bolder by the day. She was grateful to Cole, more than grateful, but she wouldn't go there now.

She headed for the kitchen, then stopped. She'd leave her food and supplies. He'd have plenty in his house. If he didn't, they'd bring hers over later or shop for more in town. She needed to focus on essentials.

She walked into the bedroom and straight to Lady Mauve's journal. How many times had her great-grandmother been caught up in a crisis that needed immediate action to solve the problem? It'd probably been more times than she could count. Audrey had grown up in a stable world, a protective environment created by her ancestors. The rustlers threatened to destroy that world. She had no intention of letting them do it.

She picked up the journal, pulled her phone out of her pocket, and sat down on the bed. She needed family right now. She didn't have long, but long enough. She punched up FaceTime.

"Dear heart, what's going on?" Vivian's face, so similar to Audrey's own, came on the screen.

"Mom, I just needed to connect a moment."

"Are you hurt?"

"No," she said.

"Good. Anything else can be managed."

She smiled. She'd been right to call. Mom could always put things into perspective.

"It's him, isn't it?"

"I'm moving in with him."

Vivian's lavender eyes opened wide. "Already?"

"It's for safety. I don't have time to go into it all now, but there's been a break-in at the ranch."

"Oh no! Maybe you need to move into town or even come home."

"I think I'll be safest at his house in a guest bedroom. I can still keep up my search for the gold," she said.

"I don't like it."

"I don't either, but it's where I am. You wouldn't give up easy, would you?"

"You're right. It's not in our Oakes bloodline to back down."

"Exactly," she said.

"But you must take precautions and stay safe."

"I will. I am."

"Good," Vivian said.

"I've got to go soon, but before I do, I want to ask about Mimi."

A smile transported Vivian's face from worried to happy. "She ate a whole piece of cheesecake yesterday. I think she's putting on weight. I suggested I push her outside in a wheelchair to enjoy the sun. She's thinking about it. Most of all, she wants to get to Wildcat Bluff and meet Jake. I think she's going to make it...soon."

"That's wonderful...amazing...stupendous."

"All that and more. It's you, Audrey. And Jake. I'm sure of it. She's getting more interested in life again. She loves your reports from Wildcat Bluff. And she never lets go of that printout of the wire message. It's stained and creased now, but it's as if it's become her lifeline."

"I'm so glad I've been of help, but it's not nearly enough."

"It's a good start. And she thinks your photo is of two initials entwined with that heart. Remember, that's what lovers used to do in the old days—maybe still do. They carved the first initial of their names within the outline of a heart onto the bark of a tree."

"If that's so, then our two went one better. They made their message out of steel wire to last forever," Audrey said.

"And you found it. She's intrigued with the mystery and she's trying to figure out the initials."

"Lady Mauve's journal sent me to that tree. Do you suppose she had a secret lover?"

"Wouldn't that be delicious?" Vivian asked.

"She couldn't have been lonely, not her."

"Maybe she was too busy taking care of her community for love."

"Could be..." Audrey stroked the cover of Lady Mauve's journal. "But I hope not."

Vivian nodded, then shook her head. "Your great-grandmother is not our concern today. You are. Now what can I do to help?"

"Just being there for me."

"I'm always here for you."

"I know. Thank you. Now I need to go pack and move," she said.

"You'll call later?"

"You know it."

"Love you." And Vivian was gone.

Audrey sat there a moment, phone in one hand and journal in the other. Links to her past, present, and future. She needed to look at the bigger picture. She would continue her hunt for the gold, but the community of Wildcat Bluff was in danger. She needed to be like Lady Mauve and do what she could to keep it strong and viable.

She took a deep breath and stood up. No time to lose. Cole needed her. Wildcat Bluff needed the information that only she had to help stop the rustlers from taking over and destroying lives.

She packed up in record time, haphazardly tossing stuff into her bag because she knew she'd be removing it again soon. She slipped her laptop into its case, gently eased the journal into her purse, and looked around the room. She'd already made her bed, but she'd wash the sheets later. For now, it was as good as it got when time was of the essence.

She flipped straps over her shoulders, turned out lights, and stepped back outside. She carefully locked the door, then headed across the courtyard. She gave her SUV a determined look, knowing she'd get it repaired as soon as possible. The rustlers weren't going to stop her or even slow her down.

At Cole's front door, she hesitated, then squared her shoulders, opened the door, and walked right inside. If she was going to live here, she was going to make herself at home.

"Cole?" she called from the entryway.

"In here."

She set down her bags, then followed the sound of his voice into the living room. He sat on the sofa in front of the fireplace looking dejected. He still wore his sooty shirt and dusty boots. He hadn't changed a thing.

"What is it?" She sat down beside him.

He glanced at her, checking her over as if she might have been in an accident. "Glad you're here."

"You got news?"

"Mustangs. Twenty more gone." He leaned his head back against the sofa and shut his eyes.

"I'm so sorry." She wanted to help him because he was in a world of hurt. She understood. She felt that way about Mimi.

"Yeah." He sat up and ran both hands through his hair. "Sheriff's on his way. He was on the other side of the county. Said he'd send a deputy except he wanted to personally see to this one."

"Good."

"Won't make one damn bit of difference. Somehow or other I just can't get a break on the mustangs," he said.

"Cole, I—"

"Put your stuff in the downstairs bedroom. It's got its own bathroom. You ought to be comfortable there. I'm in the master suite upstairs. If you prefer more space, I can move out. I don't care. I just want you to be happy here."

"Thank you. I'm sure it'll be fine."

"I need to get cleaned up, but I feel too tired to move."

"You ought to eat," she said.

"Not hungry. This whole mess is weighing on me."

"I understand. I'm going through it with you."

He glanced over at her. "I need a hug. Does that sound too pathetic?"

"No. I just called my mom for a verbal hug. You and me…we deserve a big hug." She scooted over.

He embraced her. She wrapped her arms around him. And they simply held each other for a long, long moment. She felt comforted by his warmth and strength.

Finally, he sighed and let her go. "Thanks. I needed that."

"I did, too." She smiled. "Now, run upstairs, take a shower, change clothes, and come back down here."

"Telling me what to do already, are you?" He grinned, brown eyes lighting up with humor.

"Looks like somebody's got to, so it might as well be me."

"Do I stink?"

"You smell like smoke," she said.

"That'll happen fighting a fire."

"While you get cleaned up, I'll make sandwiches. Do you have fixings?"

"Bread in the pantry. Sliced smoked beef and turkey in the fridge."

"Perfect," she said.

He rose to his feet and held out his hand, palm open.

She clasped it, and he helped her stand up. And then she was enveloped in another big hug, this one full-body contact. And it felt good, like coming home after a long, hard journey.

He lifted his head and pressed a soft kiss to her lips. "I really am glad you're here...in the house with me."

"I'm glad, too." She smiled. "Now hurry up. I'm hungry."

"I feel like I could eat, too." But he still didn't let her go. "You'll be here when I get back, won't you?"

"Yes."

"You could put your things in the bedroom."

"I will," she said.

"I called about your SUV windows. They'll send a tow truck out later and take your vehicle back to their shop for repair."

"Thank you." And still he didn't let her go.

"Least I could do."

She rose up on tiptoes and gently kissed him. "Now go before I have to lead you up there."

"I wouldn't mind that one bit."

She smiled as he finally stepped back, turned, and left the room. She heard him lock the front door before he headed upstairs. She needed him, but he needed her, too...if they were going to get out of this mess.

She crossed the living room, not admiring its beauty this time although it was as lovely as before, because her mind was on taking care of business. She walked into the kitchen. He'd made the floor shine. It was clean enough they might very well be able to eat off it. She smiled as she remembered they'd shared their first kiss in this room, then she dismissed the thought. She had to get everything ready for him before he came back downstairs. When it came to showers and clothes, men were quick-change artists.

She found bread, meat, and condiments as well as plates, napkins, glasses, and silverware. She set it all on top of the bar, then made sweet tea in a pitcher and set it beside the food. Dessert? Sure enough, she found the last two pieces of a lemon chess pie from the Chuckwagon Café. She set those on plates and added them to the meal. Satisfied, she looked it over. Perfect.

Maybe she had just enough time to set her stuff in the downstairs guest bedroom. She hurried into the entryway, grabbed her bags, and followed the hall to the back of the house. She flipped on a light and stepped into a pale lemon-yellow room with a gold-and-purple comforter on the king-size bed. Contemporary furniture filled the light and airy room. Floor-to-ceiling drapes had been pulled back to reveal sliding glass doors that led onto the patio above the outdoor kitchen, dining table, and gurgling fountain. Max and Folgie lounged on the green lawn. If she'd been happy in the guesthouse, she was ecstatic here. But she had no time to appreciate it further. First things first.

She set Lady Mauve's journal on the nightstand nearest the door before she went into the bathroom. Luxurious. Pale yellow had been continued here in the towels and marble countertops. Vanity lights. Double sinks. Shower. Whirlpool bath. She could hang out and be content in this room alone. But still there was no time.

She washed her hands using lavender liquid soap and dried them on a fluffy hand towel. She glanced in the mirror and pushed her hair back from her face. Sighed that she looked like it'd been a long day, then shrugged. That was the least of her worries.

She quickly retraced her steps back to the kitchen. Cole stood there, watching, waiting for her. A shower and change of clothes had done wonders for him. He appeared refreshed and ready to take on the next challenge.

"Find your room?" he asked.

"Yes. It's lovely. Thank you so much."

"Food looks great. Thanks."

She gestured toward it, realizing they'd become stilted with each other after their emotional sharing earlier. Maybe he wasn't exactly sure where to go from here. She wasn't sure either, so she simply walked over and wrapped her arms around his neck. He immediately pulled her close. They shared another long moment of togetherness.

She leaned back, then stepped back. She needed a little distance from him now. "Cole, I..."

"What is it?"

She realized he'd become sensitive to her moods, anticipating where she was going almost before she knew herself.

"Folgie and Max. Did something happen—"

"No. I saw them out back. They're fine."

"Then what is it?" he asked.

"I have something to tell you, but let's eat first."

"Just lost my appetite. Tell me now."

She walked across the room from him, then turned to look into his brown eyes. "Remember when I told you I didn't see the rustlers?"

"Oh hell...you've been holding back!"

Chapter 17

Audrey looked away from Cole's intense gaze. Anger. She hadn't counted on that emotion. She'd thought he'd be grateful. He ought to be grateful for the information she was about to share. Instead... Oh well.

"I thought you were the horse thieves' mastermind," she said.

"You what?"

"I did."

"How could you think that? My horses are being stolen. Fires were set on my ranch. Now your vehicle has been vandalized. How could you possibly think I'd do that to myself?"

"If you were the mastermind, it'd be a good cover," she said.

"But I asked you to stay here. I was protecting you."

"In case I saw something, you could keep an eye on me."

He just shook his head, sat down at the bar, and poured a glass of tea. He drank half of it, watching her all the while.

"Think about it. I arrive in Wildcat Bluff County, see what I saw, get chased, get rescued, get put in a guesthouse, all in the blink of an eye. And Lady Mauve wrote in her journal not to trust anybody in this county."

"Of course she'd write that. She was running an illegal speakeasy and selling illegal hooch. She'd trust nobody except those closest to her, and maybe not even those folks. Revenuers would always have been after her."

"I hadn't thought about it that way. I just knew to be careful and suspicious," she said.

"When did you change your mind about me?"

"I wanted to believe you right from the start. Why else would I have stayed so close to you?"

He opened his mouth to say something, then shut it again.

"And your ranch is a good place to branch out and do my research."

"Now do you believe I'm not behind the horse thieves?"

"Yes."

"Why the change of heart?" he asked.

"It's been coming on all along, particularly as I got to know you better. Today was over the top. You just wouldn't have done it."

"Thanks." He finished off the tea and set the glass down with a snap. "You need to tell me what you saw, but I'm not sure now I can believe you."

"What?"

He gave a short laugh, but it was without humor. "What the hell were you doing out at the dump in the first place? Are you even writing a book? If you can't come clean about one thing, how can I believe you about another?"

She took a deep breath. This conversation was going south fast. She thought she could just tell him about the horses and be done with it. Maybe it'd help. Maybe it wouldn't. But she'd have a clear conscience.

"See? You're thinking about what new cockamamie story to tell me now," he said.

"No. It's just that I thought this would be simple."

"When has anything been simple since you careened onto my ranch?"

"Actually...nothing."

He poured another glass of tea but sipped it this time. "I suppose the only way to get you to tell all is if I do it first."

"What do you mean?"

He set down the glass, looked all around the room and back at her. "I thought you were the horse thieves' mastermind."

"Me?" She laughed but it wasn't a funny feeling, more one born of disbelief and frustration. "I wouldn't know the first thing about loading up horses in a big semi and hauling them somewhere to do something with them."

"Semi, huh?"

She nodded, having just given away her big news.

"Looks like you've quite a bit to tell me."

"I'd say the same thing about you," she said.

"It was damn suspicious you coming from the dump at night with the rustlers on your tail and just happening to crash land, of all places, on the very ranch where the horse thieves were making their heists."

She thought about that for a moment. "Guess it could look that way if you were of a suspicious mind."

"I've been of a suspicious mind since the moment they first stole my horses."

"Let me get this straight. You wanted me to stay on your ranch so you could keep an eye on the boss of the horse thieves?"

"And on the off chance you were innocent and in trouble, I wanted to keep you safe," he said.

"Thanks."

"You're welcome."

She rubbed her forehead, trying to make sense of it all.

"Sorry I haven't done a better job of keeping you safe."

"I'm okay."

"Your SUV is a little worse for wear," he said.

"Fixable."

She looked at him. He looked at her. She saw his lips twitch. She felt her mouth twitch. And at the same moment, they started to laugh, shaking their heads as they stared at each other in amazement.

Finally, she caught her breath. "Guess I should thank you for the compliment. You thought I was a whole lot smarter and craftier than I could ever imagine."

"Thanks, I guess. As a simple, hardworking cowboy, I never thought I'd be mistaken for a horse thief mastermind."

She chuckled, then grew serious. "Let's don't tell anybody."

"Never. We'd be the laughingstocks of the county. We'd never hear the end of it. Of course, everybody would love it."

"You bet. That kind of gossip is irresistible. I'd be the smart Lady Mauve's dumb great-granddaughter."

"And they'd think I lost my wits the moment I met you," he said.

"Really?"

"Are you kidding? Damn straight. As the Buick Brigade said, you're the spitting image of Lady Mauve. From all accounts, everybody loved her."

"Love?"

He hesitated a long moment, brown eyes hooded as if hiding a secret. "Yeah, love."

"Well, they won't think that about you and me. We've been bickering almost from the moment we met."

"Not all the time."

"A lot of it," she said.

"Need I remind you...the kitchen kiss?"

"That was sort of an accident."

"Was it?"

"Well...it was unexpected," she said.

He glanced around at the counter behind her, then stalked over. He picked her up around the waist and set her on top, wedging in between her legs. "Would you call this unexpected?"

"Yes." She put her hands on his shoulders, not sure if her action was to hold him back or draw him forward. She felt her heart rate increase in expectation of his next move...or hers.

"An accident?"

"No," she said.

"We'd been building toward that kiss from the time we met and you know it. How could it have been an accident?"

"I don't care about semantics." She felt hot all over. She resisted the urge to clamp her legs around his waist, but the desire was growing stronger by the moment.

"Do you care about this?" And he kissed her.

She felt that kiss destroy the last resistance she might have considered erecting between them. She wanted him. She'd wanted him from the first moment she'd seen him. And she'd wanted him more with each passing day. Now she had him…or he had her… or they had each other.

All the misunderstandings, the conflicts, the confusion evaporated into thin air as they deepened the kiss. He pulled her closer. She tugged him against her. He ran his hands up and down her back. She stroked his broad shoulders and felt the muscles play against her palms. He broke the kiss and nuzzled one side of her neck and then the other, rubbing his face against her sensitive skin as if he was marking her with his scent.

She nibbled his jawline as she found her way back to his lips, where she continued to taste him, toy with him, take pleasure in him. And he returned that pleasure by delving deep into her mouth, driving her higher and higher. She wrapped her legs around his waist and felt his hardness press into her. She moaned as his hands left her back and cupped her breasts, upping the delicious sensations to almost unbearable heights.

"Audrey, do you care? Tell me you care," he hissed against her hair.

"I care…"

"I can't wait any longer." He pressed urgent kisses against her temple. "I've been waiting for you since the moment we met."

"Here? Now?"

"It'll be quick, I know. I can't help it."

"Quick is good." She squeezed him with her thighs, thinking all gone, feeling in ascendancy.

He clasped her waist with one hand while he used the thumb

and forefinger of the other to quickly unbutton her jeans and lower the zipper.

She caught her breath. He was so fast and strong. It took two hands for her to make the same movement. She was glad she was wearing a wisp of a thong, so there was practically nothing between them.

He stroked her bare stomach with long, strong fingers. "Your skin is so soft and smooth."

She moaned again, knowing she'd never see a countertop the same way again. She also now knew how to heat up a kitchen without ever turning on the oven. The only ingredient she needed was Cole Murphy.

"Now?" he said on a ragged breath.

"Yes, I…"

But the rest of her words were cut off before she ever spoke them by the shrill ring of his cell phone.

He glanced down at his pocket, then back at her with a this-can't-be-happening expression on his face.

"Better answer it." She barely got the sentence out.

He eased back from her but just enough to jerk his phone out of his pocket. "Cole here." He sounded gruff.

"Sheriff Calhoun. You okay?"

"Yep. What's up?"

"Got hung up, but I'll be there soon."

"Thanks." Cole clicked off and tossed his phone on the countertop.

"I heard the conversation," she said.

"Hell of a time to call."

"Yes."

"You deserve better than a quickie anyway." He zipped up her jeans and buttoned them, then stepped away from her.

She felt chilled at the loss of his heat.

"And there's food to eat." He backed up but kept his gaze on her.

She slipped off the counter and moved forward, stalking him.

"We got sidetracked."

She closed in on him.

"You need to tell me what you saw before the sheriff gets here."

"I don't want food. I don't want to talk with the sheriff." She placed her palms flat against his broad chest. "I want you."

He groaned as he leaned down and pressed a kiss to her forehead. "I want you, too. And you know it. If you want to torture me, you're doing it."

"I want to please you."

"Later. I'll do whatever you want."

"Promise?" she asked.

"Yes."

She pressed a fingertip to his lips and received a kiss in response. When had she gotten so bold? Was it Wildcat Bluff County? Was it Lady Mauve's influence? Was it the power of Cole Murphy?

"Come on." He clasped her hand. "Let's eat while we can."

She squeezed his hand, then sat down at the bar.

"What do you want? Turkey or beef?" He set two slices of bread on two plates.

"Turkey."

"Mustard or mayonnaise?" He picked up a knife.

"Mayonnaise."

"Sorry I didn't have tomatoes or lettuce. Should've been pickles in the fridge." He spread mayonnaise on all four slices of bread before he placed turkey on hers and beef on his. He cut the sandwiches in half, then slid a plate over to her.

"This is fine. Thank you." She took a big bite.

He followed her example.

They ate silently for a while, as if filling the empty places in their stomachs would fill the empty space between them.

After he'd eaten half his sandwich, he looked at her. "Good?"

"Wonderful. Thank you." She smiled. "Really, thank you for everything."

"Wish I could've finished what we started." He glanced over at the countertop.

"For another thank-you?" She chuckled, teasing him to ease the tension.

"I'll let you thank me later."

"Do you have in mind just how you'd like me to thank you?"

"I'm working on a list."

She laughed. "Would that be a to-do list?"

"It's sure not a to-don't list."

She laughed harder.

He joined her laughter, then quickly finished off the rest of his sandwich.

She pushed her plate over to him, and he polished hers off.

"That was good," he said.

"Pie, too."

He slid a plate over to her, then dug into his own pie.

"Delicious." She savored the creamy lemon flavor.

"They know their pies at the Chuckwagon."

"I wonder how it's going with Fernando. Have you heard anything about that lawsuit or whatever it is to gain control of him?" she asked.

"Far as I know, it's an ongoing situation. They haven't contacted me, so I'm not involved in it...yet."

"Such a shame. I really feel for Storm and the rest of the Steele family. After all this time, I wonder what set off that ranch to come after Fernando."

"Never know about some stuff. We just have to be prepared for the unpredictable," he said.

"I guess it's like me coming to Wildcat Bluff. It seemed so cut and dried in Hot Springs. Simple even."

"Simple always makes me leery because too many times it turns out to be complicated."

"Yeah."

"Let's get a glass of tea and go to the living room. I want to hear your story and we might as well be comfortable there," he said.

When they were settled on the sofa, she took a deep breath and smiled at him, wanting to ease the earlier tension.

"I'll be grateful for anything you can tell me that will help us catch those horse thieves," he said.

"I probably should show you, but first I'll tell you." She took a sip of tea. "You know the dump well, don't you?"

"Yes."

"You know how it drops off in back?"

"Yes."

"That's where they put a semitrailer."

"You're kidding me." He stared at her in astonishment. "That's smart, real smart. Their activity couldn't be seen from the road."

"And cowboys on horseback drove mustangs out of a pasture across the lane in back, up a chute, and into the semi attached to a one-ton."

Cole looked off into the distance, as if he was visualizing the scene. "So that's how they're doing it. Simple."

"I don't know who owns that property, but I assume it's being used by the rustlers to hold the horses until they're transported."

"That's GTT land."

"Really?" she said.

"Guess I've made it too easy for them. No wonder they thought they could come into my compound and cause trouble."

"Easy?"

"They're not driving those horses off my ranch straight into a transport. I've been thinking about this all wrong. They're keeping them on GTT land until it's convenient to move them," he said.

"But how could they be sure you wouldn't find them?"

"Four thousand acres is a lot of ground for cowboys to cover. Animals can get lost in that amount of space...like Fernando. Plus I follow governmental guidelines, and the mustangs must roam free," he said.

"It's more complicated than I realized."

"And simpler. Now that I know how they're doing it."

"I hope what I saw helps."

"Helps? It's huge. I mean, now that we know how they're doing it, we have a good chance of catching them," he said.

"Good. I regret I couldn't tell you sooner."

"That's over and done with." He set his glass on the coffee table, then plucked her tea out of her hand and set it down, too.

"What?"

"You deserve a big kiss."

She leaned toward him and pressed her lips to his. "That what you had in mind?"

"Good but not nearly good enough." He kissed her with all the passion he'd stored up from earlier.

When she came up for breath, she smiled at him. "Do you think we have time before—"

"Not one more word about it. I'm hanging on by my fingernails here."

"You kissed me."

"Couldn't resist it." He suddenly frowned, stood up, and paced over to the fireplace. He looked back. "I just realized we have a big problem."

"What?"

"You've withheld information. Not just from me. But from the law. I'm talking federal as well as state and county. The feds take those mustangs very seriously."

"Okay. I'll just tell them what I know and that's that," she said.

"No, it's not." He paced back and forth. "You saw that happen about two weeks ago. How do you explain not telling them until now?"

"Amnesia?"

"Not funny."

"I don't know. I guess I don't have to tell them at all," she said.

"Of course you have to tell them." He paced faster. "The rustlers struck again last night. It didn't rain. There might be tire tracks, hoofprints, boot marks."

"That's better than when I saw them. It was raining, so nothing was left to incriminate them."

"They're really getting bold." He ran a hand through his hair. "I hate to say this, but we could move up the date when you saw them and say that you were out there last night. That way we could go to the dump and maybe get proof that's where they're staging their operation," he said.

"No. You can't lie to the law. I won't let you. It's my problem."

"We won't lie. We'll stick to your original story...only we'll add to it. You were out there again last night, and describe what you originally saw. That's why we got hit today. Makes more sense anyway."

She cocked her head to one side. She noticed he was saying "we" and she appreciated it, but she didn't want him to get into trouble.

"We'll share what you saw. Everyone will be grateful and thrilled to move this case along."

"Okay, I guess. Still—"

He looked at her more closely. "What were you doing out there, anyway?"

"Remember, the book?" she said.

"And why would you go back?"

"The book."

He sat down beside her. "If we're going to get through this together, I need the truth. Please."

She clasped her hands together in her lap. Mimi. She couldn't betray her grandmother in her hour of need, but she couldn't abandon the horses to some terrible fate either. She was caught between a rock and a hard place. She needed to trust him and take a chance.

"Is it so terrible? Is writing a book even real?" he asked.

"Lady Mauve's diary mentions bootlegger gold."

"Gold." He grinned, appearing relieved at the news.

"What?"

"Did you think it was a secret?"

"Yes," she said.

"You thought if anybody found out about it, they'd beat you to the gold?"

"Yes."

"Audrey, everybody in the county—and beyond—knows the legend of Hallelujah Ranch's bootlegger gold. In fact, just a few months ago, two yahoos from Hot Springs were here causing all kinds of trouble trying to dig it up."

"Did they get it?" she asked.

"No. As far as anybody knows, the gold doesn't exist. It's just a legend."

She slumped forward, defeat riding her hard.

"Were you counting on it that much?"

"Yes."

"Why?" he asked.

She clamped her lips together. She didn't want to talk about Mimi. Couldn't. The pain was too great...and too personal.

"Audrey?"

She raised her head, not about to be stopped just because others didn't believe in the gold. She did believe in it. She *must* believe in it. Besides, she had Lady Mauve's journal. Nobody else had that information. And she wasn't about to share it.

"Are you okay?"

"I'm just disappointed," she said.

"Don't be. It's a fun legend, that's all." He leaned toward her. "You're still going to stay and write the book, aren't you?"

She smiled at him, although she felt deep concern for Mimi's sake. No, she *would* find that gold and all would be well. "Yes. I'll still research Wildcat Bluff County for my book."

"Good. Lots of people are counting on it now."

"I wonder if—"

Cole's phone rang. "That'll be the sheriff. I need to open the gate for him. Remember our story."

"Got it."

"Better let me do all the talking."

Chapter 18

COLE STOOD BESIDE AUDREY AT THE BIG OAK OUTSIDE THE dump's chain link fence. They were both subdued after giving statements to one law enforcement agency after another at the ranch and the dump. Right now, they'd been sent to the sidelines while the professionals collected evidence below where the mustangs had been loaded and carried away.

"Look here." She pointed at a section of the tree trunk. "This is that wire I told you about. I took some more photos. Hopefully, they're better than the last ones. See if you can make out the initials."

He bent down and looked, touched the wire with a fingertip, then stood up. "It's a heart all right, but more than that I can't tell."

"Me, too."

"You'll find a lot of old barbwire eaten by growing trees along fence lines. It's one way to tell the location of original property boundaries and old farmhouses or barns. You'd be surprised what you can find inside a tree when you cut it down."

"Really?" she said.

"I always check before I get out the chainsaw to make sure I'm not going to cut into metal or something else."

"That's interesting."

"For me, it's just a fact of life. Trees don't live forever, so there's an ongoing process of removal and replanting," he said.

"I like the old trees with their deep shade in Hot Springs."

He patted the tree trunk. "Now this is a post oak. It's the second longest living of the oak family. It's probably about a hundred and fifty years old."

"Just think. This tree was here when Lady Mauve roamed the county and it's still here for us to enjoy."

"True." He glanced down at the ongoing activity. "You know, I wonder if we jumped the gun."

"What do you mean?"

"You may have been right in the first place."

"Now I really don't know what you mean," she said.

"By the time they're done down there, those horse thieves won't come within miles of this location again."

"Do you think they'll know that their staging area has been compromised?"

"Oh yeah. These are smart rustlers. They've been one step ahead of us all the way. That means they leave nothing to chance," he said.

"And if they won't come back…"

"How are we going to catch them?"

"Evidence?" she asked.

"What are the odds there's nothing down there except tracks that could belong to any one of hundreds of trucks in the county? Same with the semitrailer. Unshod horse hooves aren't much better."

"I thought this would solve the situation."

"We had to tell them, but it may just complicate the matter," he said.

"The horse thieves will set up another site."

"Worse…what if they're done and gone, along with the mustangs?"

"That idea makes me sick at my stomach," she said.

"You and me both."

"But why would they go to all that trouble at the ranch today?"

He pointed below. "That was before. This is now. No way all this activity is going unnoticed in the community."

"Or by the horse thieves."

"Right."

"What do we do now? How do we catch them?" she asked.

"First, let's wait and see if the evidence leads anywhere."

"Okay."

"To be on the safe side, I'll put up more game cameras around the ranch...particularly hidden ones around the house," he said.

"Good."

"And the cowboys will be on triple alert."

"What can I do to help?" she asked.

He looked at the sincerity in her lavender eyes and felt a vast sense of relief that they were both on the same side and same page now. He'd wanted it from the first, but her actions hadn't allowed it. Bootlegger gold—who'd have thought it? Those old myths never died, like the one about buried Confederate gold. Folks still searched for it back up in the mountains of Southeast Oklahoma. He figured the lure was not only to acquire quick riches but to solve a mystery as well.

He'd like to solve the mystery confronting him, too. If he could figure what they were doing with the mustangs, that might help. He hoped they weren't being sold in Europe for meat or some other nefarious purpose. Above all, he wanted to bring those horses home.

"Really, I'd like to help," she said.

"You got us this far. That's something. I'm not going to discount it. I just wish it'd netted us the horse thieves."

"At least maybe we won't have any more trouble with them on the ranch."

"That'd be a plus," he said.

"Do you think I should move back to the guesthouse?"

"What? No." He stepped closer to her. "You're safest in the house. We don't know what the rustlers might do or not do. Besides, I want you with me. Unless you really feel it's best for you to go back to the guesthouse. I'm not trying to corral you...much."

She smiled. "I like the new bedroom a lot. And we're strongest together."

"That's true," he said.

She touched the heart twined with two initials again. "I wish I knew who left this here."

"Doubt you ever will. But it doesn't really matter, does it?"

"How do you mean?"

"They knew what was in their hearts and shared it. That's what counts."

She smiled again. "You're right. Still…"

"It's enough for me." He clasped her hand and threaded their fingers together.

"Maybe I'm living too much in the past right now, what with the journal and being in Wildcat Bluff. I feel a deep connection with Lady Mauve and I want to get her story straight."

"I'm confident you will. Give it time."

She squeezed his hand. "Okay."

He glanced back at the activity below. It looked like the investigation was breaking up. "Sheriff's coming. Maybe they learned something that'll help us."

"If they'll share," she said.

"Yeah."

Sheriff Calhoun joined them, big and strong and competent-appearing in his tan uniform with his cowboy hat and boots.

"How's it going?" Cole asked.

"They're wrapping it up."

"Good. Maybe things will get back to normal at the dump," Cole said.

"And maybe you'll let somebody else take over your job here," Sheriff Calhoun said.

"Might as well. Doubt they'll ever be back."

"Yeah." Sheriff Calhoun looked at Audrey. "Can't thank you enough for being here, seeing what you saw, and reporting it."

"I want those horse thieves caught as much as everyone," she said.

"Did you find anything useful?" Cole asked.

"It'll all go to labs." Sheriff Calhoun shook his head. "With this many departments involved, we'll be lucky to hear back anytime soon."

"That's a disappointment," Cole said.

"For you and me both...but not a surprise." Sheriff Calhoun glanced around the dump again. "You got to admit, it was a clever operation."

"Agreed," Cole said. "Now I have to wonder when, where, and how they'll hit the GTT next."

"Maybe this'll drive them from the county." Sheriff Calhoun adjusted his utility belt as if preparing to leave.

"Hope not," Cole said. "I want those mustangs back."

"Don't count on it."

"I'm not giving up on getting those horses or catching those rustlers," Cole said.

"Fine attitude," Sheriff Calhoun said. "None of us are throwing in the towel yet."

"Good." Cole lowered his voice. "Any news you can share about Zane Ranch trying to take Fernando from Steele Trap?"

"Talk about a mess!" Sheriff Calhoun shook his head. "Did you know they're going after the twins now?"

"Oh no," Audrey said. "That's terrible. Storm must be beside herself with worry, bless her heart."

"Mad as a wet sitting hen, that's what." Sheriff Calhoun glanced from one to the other. "Between us, take care. It's more than about the horse thieves. Zane cowboys are going armed at all times. They're acting like they're in the middle of an old-time range war."

"Most cowboys wear a sidearm, just in case of trouble with wild varmints," Cole said.

"Rifles in saddle holsters, too? Bad attitudes like

stay-off-the-premises unless invited by the big boss?" Sheriff Calhoun said.

"That's not Wildcat Bluff County friendly," Cole said.

"Not by a long shot." Sheriff Calhoun tipped his hat to Audrey. "Anyway, that's just a friendly warning. Don't take chances till we get our current troubles straightened out."

"We'll be on the lookout," Cole said. "Audrey is staying in the house with me now. Max and Folgie are on compound patrol from here on out."

"Glad to hear it." Sheriff Calhoun tipped his hat again. "Regret you arrived here in the middle of difficulties. We'll get them fixed. Wildcat Bluff is a good place to live. If there's anything I can do, or my deputies, please don't hesitate to call our office."

"Thank you." Audrey shook the sheriff's hand. "I appreciate all y'all are doing to catch the rustlers."

"You bet." Sheriff Calhoun glanced at Cole. "Y'all might as well head home. No more questions for now. We'll take it from here."

"Sounds good," Cole said. "Thanks for your help."

"Anytime." And Sheriff Calhoun headed away.

"Let's get out of here." Cole clasped Audrey's hand. "You're bound to be tired. I'm tired. It's been one long day."

"That's a fact."

He walked with her hand in hand to his truck, thinking that if nothing else about the day had gone to plan, this felt absolutely right.

When he had them out on Wildcat Road, away from the dump and the misery it had caused through no fault of its own, he breathed a sigh of relief.

"Bad, wasn't it?" she said.

"I'm just so frustrated with the whole mess."

"Me, too."

"It'll be dark soon and I've lost another day's work," he said.

"And I didn't make any progress on…"

He chuckled. "Bootlegger gold."

"Not funny."

"Really, it is. If you'd been from around here, you'd never have gotten up a head of steam about it." He glanced over at her, then back at the highway. "I ought to be grateful for the legend."

"Why?"

"If you hadn't gotten that wild hair, you'd never have come here and I'd never have met you."

"Oh."

"Is that all you've got to say?" he asked.

"You're right. I'd never have met you."

"That counts for something, doesn't it?"

"It counts for a lot. It's just that…"

"What?" he asked.

"I need…I mean, I want that gold."

"Forget it."

"I can't."

"Are you telling me you're still going to look for it?" he asked.

"Yes."

"Oh hell. Can't you let it go?"

"I can make the search part of my book," she said.

"Are you really, truly writing a book?"

"Yes."

"No way to dissuade you?"

"No," she said.

"Jake the Farmer is probably your best bet, then," he said.

"Agreed."

"But not tonight."

"No. I'm all done in."

"Want to go home?" he asked.

"Yes. Is there anything to eat?"

"Sandwich didn't stay with you?"

She glanced at him with a smile. "I was a little distracted to eat much."

"Me, too." He chuckled, memories of the countertop coming back in a hot rush.

"I don't want either of us to have to cook tonight."

"Okay. Chuckwagon Café is always good. Bluebonnet in Sure-Shot. Fresh sarsaparilla and snacks at the honky-tonk."

"Too much trouble."

"I've got it. Wildcat Bluff Diner. It's got takeout," he said.

"Drive-thru?"

"Yes."

"Perfect."

"Dates back to the fifties. The Norwood family moved here and turned an old train dining car into a café. Great burgers, chicken-fried steak, fried catfish…and pizza," he said.

"Pizza. Now that sounds wonderful."

"You've got it."

"You know, I thought this day would never end."

"It's officially over…except for the pizza," he said.

He drove a ways, turned off the highway, and hit a single-lane dirt road. He left a trail of dust behind them as he barreled down it.

"Are you sure you're taking us to the pizza place? How would anybody find it out here?"

"It used to be busier in this area. Trading post. Community church. Farmers' market. Cattle auction. Horse racetrack."

"Back here?" she asked.

"Times change. People get TVs, computers, internet, streaming. Not so much face-to-face interaction like in the old days."

"Stuck indoors."

"Nothing like the great outdoors," he said.

"This is definitely the great outdoors."

"They used to grow a lot of cotton around here, too." He chuckled as she glanced out the windows, no doubt looking for buildings when all she could see were acres of pastures, farmland, and orchards.

"It's beautiful."

"I think so, too."

He kept driving until he dead-ended at a two-lane gravel road. Straight ahead sat the café, while to each side of it grouped gray, weathered-wood structures, corrals, fences, and a former church with its tall spire. The bright purple train car had WILDCAT BLUFF DINER painted in hot pink across one side, while a purple Jeep had been parked near the front door. A fancy white double-wide provided living quarters behind the diner.

"This is great." Audrey grinned at him, then leaned forward for a better look. "But can they actually do enough business to make staying open profitable?"

"They deliver…almost unheard of in the country. See that Jeep?"

"How could I miss it? Bright purple."

"Three of those suckers stay on the road most of the time," he said.

"American ingenuity."

"At its finest."

He pulled up to one end of the diner near the sliding glass order window. It slammed open and a woman poked her head out. She squinted at him through purple cat-eye glasses.

"Cole Murphy, as I live and breathe." She pushed back a strand of platinum-blond hair with a hand tipped by long purple acrylic fingernails. "Long time no see."

"Last week, I believe."

"Cole, you know good and well that every time between visits feels like forever."

"I know it." He chuckled as he put a hand over his heart. "Did you save anything for me to eat?"

"What you want, darlin'?" She leaned halfway out the window, eyebrows raised in alarm. "You've got a woman with you! Are you two-timin' me?"

"You know I'd never two-time your burgers and pizza."

She appeared a little mollified at those words.

"This is Audrey Oakes. She's in Wildcat Bluff to research a book about Lady Mauve and our county during the bootlegger days."

"Smart, then? Cole, I didn't know you liked them smart."

"Ernestine, nobody can compare to you."

"No truer words were ever spoken." She adjusted her glasses. "Audrey, good to meet you, I think. If you're going to come around here or phone in an order, you can call me Ernie. Most folks do, except cutie pie here."

Cole chuckled, enjoying her good-ol'-girl patter.

"Audrey here reminds me of somebody. Can't think who. Maybe one of those scream queens from the classic horror movies. Those are my faves." She stuck an arm out the window and pushed up her sleeve. "Look at my new tattoo. Bride of Frankenstein."

"Looks good," Cole said.

Ernie raised both eyebrows and gave him a coy look. "What is really stunning is the full-color painting of Fay Wray on my inner thigh. If you want to see it...on occasion I do make personal deliveries."

"Ernie, you're more woman than a cowboy like me could ever handle."

"No doubt that's true. Simple, I'm not."

"You're definitely as beautiful as your body art."

"I'm so glad you recognize my finer qualities. But I must give credit where credit is due. Edsel is an absolute genius...an artist without compare," Ernestine said.

"He's good, no doubt. Where's he working now?"

"If you can believe it, he set up shop in the old trading post."

"Hard to believe," Cole said.

"I asked him, 'Who the hell is ever gonna find you out in the sticks?' That's exactly what I asked him. But Edsel, he don't pay no never mind to nobody."

"How's his business?"

Ernie jerked down her sleeve. "Booming, of course. Guy's got the Midas touch."

"If you two keep it up, you might resurrect Ranger Corner," Cole said.

"That'll be the day." Ernestine adjusted her glasses again and took a closer look at Cole. "How's your mustang trouble coming along?"

He shook his head. "Got a big tip, but so far those horse thieves are outsmarting us all."

"It's tough for honest folk. Our minds just don't work crooked."

"That's the truth," Cole said.

"But here I am yammering and y'all look hungry enough to pass out on me. What'll it be?"

"Pizza," Cole said.

"Hawaiian pizza," Audrey said.

"Now don't get me lying." Ernestine twisted her mouth to one side in contemplation.

"She means Canadian bacon and pineapple," Cole said.

"Nothing doing." Ernestine shook her head. "I'm not putting together prissy food, not in Wildcat Bluff."

"What are we getting?" He knew if they wanted pizza, they'd take what Ernie decided they should eat. Fortunately, it was always good.

Ernestine looked thoughtful. "I could get creative."

"You're always creative," he said.

"Darn tootin'. Go drive the backroads or snuggle in the back seat for a half hour or so. It'll be ready." Earnestine slammed shut the window.

He backed up and drove away.

"Oh my," Audrey said. "She's quite the character."

"That's what you get in Wildcat Bluff. It was settled by independent cusses whose descendants still go their own way...unless there's a need in the community to pull together."

"Like Wildcat Bluff Fire-Rescue."

"Ernie's one of our volunteer firefighters," he said.

"I'm not sure if I trust her with my pizza, but I think I'd trust her fighting my fire if I had one."

"Oh, you'll trust her once you bite into the pizza she makes for you. She'll have been testing your mettle, taking stock of your character, and deciding on likes and dislikes the entire time we were there."

"Really?" she asked.

"You might not believe it, but she can judge a person in nothing flat."

"Ernie didn't say much to me. Maybe she didn't like me."

"Not true. She'd never have told you to make out in the back seat with me if she didn't like you."

"She didn't say that."

He grinned, turned around, and headed back toward the diner. "No? I thought for sure that's what she said."

"That's just what's on your mind."

"What's on yours?" he asked.

"Pizza."

Chapter 19

AUDREY SAT AT THE TABLE ON COLE'S BEAUTIFUL PATIO. HE'D chosen a chair beside her, not across from her, so he was close. A tiki torch cast warm yellow light over them while ground lights accented the trees. She could hear the soothing gurgle of water in the fountain, along with the accompanying serenade of frogs. Darkness wrapped them in a protective cocoon. Everything beyond their small area seemed far away and unimportant—certainly not as important as the open box of pizza between them.

He had already wolfed down two slices while she worked on her first piece. Max and Folgie were in the barn gnawing contentedly on ham bones that Ernie had sent them. They were all content after their big day. She leaned back in her chair, sipped sweet tea, and relaxed into the moment. She felt as if she'd come home, even if this wasn't her real home.

"Was that a sigh?" Cole asked.

"Yes. I feel happy…satisfied."

"It's the pizza, isn't it?"

"That's the most amazing pizza I've ever eaten. One piece will do it for me," she said.

"You got ham and pineapple on your half. I got all the meat and veggies on mine."

"And all of it piled deep with a really good cheese and tasty sauce."

"Local. Ernie buys as many of her ingredients locally as possible."

"That's smart. Fresh is always best."

"And she supports our community that way," he said.

"It's a delicious way to do it."

"Knew you'd like her pizza."

"And we'll have leftovers for tomorrow."

"I like cold pizza," he said.

"Or we can reheat it in the microwave."

"Either way suits me."

"Ernie added chocolate mints for dessert," she said.

"They're made at the Destiny Chocolatier. Local again."

"Reminds me of the Chuckwagon Café's pies." Audrey selected a mint from the small white box with a gold inscription. "There's a lot of talent in Wildcat Bluff."

"True. And there's a lot of support for it, too."

"I wonder if that's what Lady Mauve experienced here. And part of why everything worked so well for her."

"There's always been a rich, supportive community in Wildcat Bluff," he said.

"And she tapped into it, didn't she?"

"Could be. Maybe that's what you'll find out as you research your book." He selected a mint and popped it into his mouth.

She bit into her mint. "Delicious."

"Good to have a peaceful moment."

"Feels wonderful."

"No fires. No leaks. No vandalism. No—"

"Just the two us," she said.

"Yeah." He raised his glass of tea in a salute.

She clinked her glass with his, took a sip, and glanced around the area. "You know, as terrific as this is tonight, maybe we ought to go to bed. It's been a long day and who knows what tomorrow will bring."

"Bed sounds good. Yours or mine?"

She chuckled, shaking her head. "I'm headed for a bath and then my bed. You're on your own."

"That's flat-out cruel."

"Practical."

"Can I entice you to stay longer? Open a bottle of wine? More tea? Pizza?" He grinned. "Me?"

"You're the biggest enticement of all, but still…"

"Understand. I just wish we'd get a break and find time for ourselves."

"We deserve it, but…" She really wanted to stay or go upstairs to his bed, but she was determined to be responsible. She needed to call home. She wanted an update on Mimi and she wanted to share the new photos. Besides, now was not the time to be indulgent, no matter this cowboy's hot kisses.

"Yeah." He closed the pizza box.

She stood up and started to pick up the plates.

"Let me get it all." He rose to his feet. "You've done enough for the day. Go ahead and get a good night's rest."

"You're sure?"

"About now, I'm not sure about much of anything except…go before I change my mind and decide not to be practical or responsible," he said.

She knew he was right. It wouldn't take much to send them both over the edge and onto the nearest surface. She quickly turned away and walked back into the house. She didn't break stride until she entered her new bedroom and shut the door behind her. Only then did she let the feelings held at bay all day long swamp her.

She sat down on the bed, hands between her knees, and let the emotions come. She liked Cole. She really liked him. And he liked her. They meshed through thick and thin. He supported her. She supported him. And it seemed as natural as if they'd been doing it all their lives. Love was definitely in the air, but she wasn't sure if she should trust it. After all, Oakes women didn't have good history with men staying with them.

She grabbed her phone and sent the new photographs by text before she pulled up FaceTime.

"Audrey, how did your day go?" Vivian asked with a smile.

"Busy."

"My kind of day, too."

"How's Mimi?"

"You'll find this hard to believe, but she got in a wheelchair. Well, the nurses helped her, but still she was strong enough to do it. And she wanted to do it."

"That's wonderful news."

"I took her outside to the patio. We sat in the sun and talked about your photos of that wire heart. She's decided they're the two initials of sweethearts. And she's determined to figure out exactly which letters of the alphabet. And she's even more determined to get to Wildcat Bluff as quickly as possible. She's concerned about Jake's health. I'm sure she's getting stronger for him as much as for herself."

"As far as I can tell, Jake is stable, but at his age…"

"Exactly," Vivian said. "Wildcat Bluff is beginning to look like a miracle cure for Mimi. I'm anxious to get there, too."

"Do you think she might be strong enough to come in a few days or a week at most?"

"I hope so. We're trying."

"Good. I'm waiting," Audrey said. "I just sent you more pictures of the heart I took today. Perhaps the lighting is different and will show other angles."

"Mom will love them." Vivian's lavender eyes lit up. "Dear heart, as you know, you're doing wonders for your grandmother. She waits every day just to hear your new report. I haven't seen her so interested in life for years. We can hardly wait to reach you."

"Please make it soon."

"We will. I'm more sure of it every day."

"I regret to say I haven't made progress locating the gold. In fact, I just learned from Cole that the legend is common knowledge and not given much validity," Audrey said.

"Oh no!"

"But I'm not giving up. And I told him so."

"Will he help you?"

"I don't know if he can. I'm going to ask Jake. If anyone knows the location, he will," Audrey said.

"If he knew, don't you think he'd have gotten the gold before now?"

"Maybe not. Guess I didn't mention it, but he can't see."

"Really?" Vivian said.

"It happened long ago and doesn't appear to slow him down."

"In that case, maybe he's kept the location secret since he can't go there."

"Could be. Still, why would he share it with me?" Audrey asked.

"I don't know. Guess I'm just grasping at straws."

"Make that two of us. I haven't given up yet."

"Good." Vivian smiled mischievously. "On a lighter note, how are you getting along with that hunky cowboy firefighter?"

Audrey grinned back. "I'm certainly enjoying the view."

"Great."

"How about Gerald?"

Vivian sighed and fluttered her eyelashes. "He just gets better all the time. I'm anxious for you to meet him."

"I want to. He makes you happy, so that makes me happy."

"Thank you. I want you to know this kind of happiness, too. We both deserve it."

"And Mimi deserves a good, long, happy life," Audrey said.

"No matter how long she has now, you're making her very happy and I can't tell you how much that means to me."

"And to me."

"I don't want to cut this short, but Gerald's coming over in a bit and I need to get ready for him," Vivian said.

"Go ahead. I'll update you more tomorrow."

"Good night, dear heart."

"Night, Mom."

And then Audrey just sat still, feeling alone and a little blue. Gerald was there now, but would he stay with her mom? Maybe it didn't matter how long or how short a time. Happiness was what mattered in the end. She'd turned down her own chance on the patio. Had she made a mistake? If she went back out there, would Cole still welcome her with open arms or...?

She took a deep breath, set down her phone, and ran a fingertip across Lady Mauve's journal. She was made of sterner stuff, like her great-grandmother. Whatever she and Cole might or might not have, whether it would last or not last. A few minutes, hours, days, weeks shouldn't make a difference if it was the real thing.

For now, she needed a little space to catch her breath. She flipped the covers back on the bed to reveal purple sheets. Looked wonderful, but nothing would help her more than a good, long soak in a whirlpool bath. Besides, she wanted to wash the grime—as well as the anxieties—of the day away.

She walked into the bathroom and started water running in the tub. She set out a purple towel and washcloth. A basket on the countertop held an assortment of lavender bath salts, bubble bath, body lotion, shampoo, and soap. She read the little card attached by a purple ribbon to the basket, *Compliments of Morning's Glory*. She selected bath salts from the basket and poured lavender chunks into the running water. She remembered looking at that store's display window in Old Town with Cole. It'd be the perfect place to find unique gifts to send Mom and Mimi as a little touch of Wildcat Bluff. Even better...let them arrive soon and they'd all shop there together.

She could hardly wait to get into the fragrant water. She quickly undressed, chucking everything to one side of the bathroom and shutting the door. She eased down into the tub and hit the whirl-pool control. Soon she was massaged by swirling warm water with the delightful scent of lavender. She leaned back and relaxed into the comfort. It'd been a long time coming and she deserved every bit of it.

The only thing better was if somebody—that somebody who was upstairs—had joined her. But when did she get everything? Occasionally? Rarely? Never? Actually, when she thought about it, the way to get everything, or at least what she wanted in life, was to go after it.

She glanced up at the ceiling. He'd never say no. He'd been saying yes from the first moment she met him. How easy to get what she wanted now. And she did want him in so many different ways. But was it right? Was it wrong? Most important, was she totally overthinking the situation? She *did* deserve happiness. So did he.

That last thought galvanized her. She quickly finished her bath, feeling clean and refreshed, physically and mentally, as she stood up and let the water drain. She toweled dry and slipped on the purple terry robe she'd found hanging in the bathroom and opened the door. She knew steam and the scent of lavender came with her. She didn't care. She wasn't going to be in the bedroom long anyway.

She jerked open the door and gasped in surprise.

Cole stood there with his arm raised to knock. He looked just as surprised as she felt.

"You're here," she said.

"Yes."

"I didn't have to come upstairs," she said.

"Is that where you were headed, not to the kitchen for a snack?"

"I'm hungry." She looked him up and down. He'd taken a shower and changed to navy cotton T-shirt and jogging pants.

He grinned, brown eyes darkening to chocolate.

She grasped the soft fabric of his tee in her fist and tugged him toward her. She didn't have to pull hard because he was already moving in her direction. They met just inside the doorway. She walked backward toward the bed, never letting go of him. He never lost contact with her eyes.

When she hit the bed with the back of her legs, she tugged his tee upward slowly—ever so slowly—to reveal his muscular stomach, then his chest with the sprinkling of dark hair, then his broad shoulders. She stopped there and glanced up at his face. A smile quirked the corners of his lips.

"Like what you see?" he asked.

She returned his smile. "So far so good. I do believe I need to see more to make a final decision."

"Do you, now?" He grinned, letting her know he was totally into her game.

"Yes indeed." She tugged at his tee. "Surely you have no more need for this, do you?"

"No need at all." He pulled his T-shirt up and over his head, then tossed it to one side.

"Oh my." She inhaled sharply. "You're so beautiful."

"No. You're beautiful. I'd be happy with handsome."

"Handsome it is, then," she said.

"Thanks."

"Thanks to you, too." She wouldn't say it again, but he *was* beautiful with his sculpted arms and chest and shoulders leading up to his strong throat and finely chiseled face and downward to his muscular stomach with the indented bellybutton and a glimpse of dark hair just above the edge of his pants.

"What's under your robe?" he asked.

She smiled, so ready to play any game he wanted to play.

"A smile? Is that all?" he asked.

She gave him an even bigger smile, knowing the look in her eyes was egging him on.

"If you won't say, maybe I'd better find out."

"Are you saying you want more than a smile?"

"Oh yeah. I want a whole lot more than a smile," he said.

"Do you deserve it?"

"That's for you to decide."

She put a fingertip to her lips and bit down lightly on the nail, as if considering whether he'd been good or bad.

"I'm not sure I'm ready for this much suspense."

"Not ready?"

He grinned. "I'm ready. All you need to do is give the go-ahead."

She loosened the tie on her robe.

"Is that the go-ahead?" he asked, voice gone husky.

She let the robe slip off one shoulder to show a little more creamy flesh, watching his reaction of dilated eyes and quickened breath.

"I'm not sure how much longer I can play."

"Is there a time limit?" she asked.

"I'm strong, but only so strong where you're concerned."

"Really?" She teased him, but she teased herself as well, wanting to up the tension to almost unbearable heights.

"Yeah. Really."

She slid the robe off her other shoulder, so the fabric slipped down and caught on the upper slopes of her breasts. Who would make the next move? she wondered as she made eye contact with him again. He smoldered, as if the embers inside him would blaze at any moment. She wanted his heat. She wanted him to ignite her. She wanted them to go up in flames together.

She dropped her robe to the floor so she stood naked before him.

He drank her in as if dying of thirst, but not touching her with anything more than his heated gaze.

She held out her hand.

He clasped it.

And they caught fire.

She perched on the edge of the bed and tugged him toward her. He scooped her up in his arms and sat down with her body cradled on his lap. He planted fierce kisses across her face, down her neck, and back up to capture her mouth in a deep, lingering, passionate kiss. When he raised his head, she was breathless and his eyes had turned even darker.

He rubbed his palms up and down her arms, creating friction that caused chills, then heat, then chills, then... A deep desire spiraled up out of her inner core and turned into raging need when he cupped her breasts and kissed each tip into hard peaks. She turned in to him, wanting closer contact, wanting what only he could give her, wanting to quench their fire.

He kissed her lips again, then gently laid her back on the bed. He knelt over her, stopped, glanced around the room and back at her.

"What is it?" She didn't want him to stop...ever.

"Condom."

"Surely, we—"

"I'd never take a chance with you," he said.

"But..."

He scooped her up in his arms again, strode through the open doorway, walked into the hall, and started up the staircase.

She cuddled against his strong, warm chest as he quickly took the stairs and entered the master suite. A floor lamp in one corner cast soft light across the decidedly masculine room. The wall behind the king-size bed had been covered in natural gold-tinted leather. A cowboy-and-horse theme bedspread had been thrown back to reveal smooth beige sheets.

He carefully set her down on the bed. She snuggled up against a big pillow that smelled of him, all musk and citrus.

He jerked open the drawer of his nightstand, pulled out a condom, and cast the wrapper aside.

"Wouldn't it have been easier to bring that downstairs than carry me up here? Weight-wise?"

"You don't know how many times I've imagined you lying right there in my bed waiting for me," he said.

"How many?"

"Count the nights since I met you and you'll have the number." He appeared self-satisfied. "Now I have you exactly where I want you."

"And I'm where I want to be." She smiled at his words, well aware that she felt the same need to complete what they'd started downstairs.

"Did you think of me at night in your bed across the courtyard?" He slipped on the condom.

"What if I did?"

"What did you think?" He knelt between her legs.

She looked him up and down, then spread her legs wider.

"Tell me."

She reached up, thrust long fingers into his hair, and held him still so she could gaze into his eyes. "This. I thought about this very moment."

He gave a satisfied nod as he raised her hips with both hands, then kissed her as he thrust deep into her hot core.

She grasped his shoulders and pulled him closer, wanting, needing him to fulfill her.

He raised his head and looked into her eyes. "How does our reality compare to your fantasy?"

"No comparison...except it definitely whet my appetite for more, so much more." She thrust up with her hips, urging him to fulfill their erotic fantasies.

And he moved within her, slowly, gently at first, then with more power, more drive, faster and faster, until they both panted for breath, were bathed in sweat and arousal and unlimited possibilities and they spiraled up to their highest peak...clinging there together for the longest of moments.

And when they came back to earth, he gently, tenderly tugged her to his side. She snuggled against his chest, where she heard the strong beat of his heart match the rhythm of her very own.

Chapter 20

ANOTHER WEEK HAD PASSED WHEN AUDREY PARKED HER SUV on the circle drive at Oakes Farm. After window replacement, she was glad to have her own vehicle back, although Cole's Jeep had been fun. She'd enjoyed her days driving back roads, visiting small towns, and talking with folks as she'd gathered information for her book. She'd become more and more excited about seeing Lady Mauve's time come alive.

She'd made much more progress on the book than locating bootlegger gold, but she hadn't given up achieving that main goal. Best of all worlds, Mimi continued to improve as she gained strength and interest in life again. Her doctors and nurses were amazed at the change in her. Audrey and her mother were thrilled to be part of the transformation. If this kept up, they'd be coming to Wildcat Bluff in no time at all.

Audrey visited Jake every chance she got. They'd shared wonderful times together. Still, she sensed he was holding back. He'd told her tales of high drama as bootleggers outfoxed revenuers. He'd told her about his days making hooch and delivering it to the popular speakeasy on Hallelujah Ranch. He'd told her about having the best still with the best whiskey in all of Texas.

And yet he'd put off talking much about Lady Mauve because he'd said he wanted to set the backdrop for her vivid splash across Wildcat Bluff County. Maybe those days were too painful for him to recall. Maybe he hadn't known Lady Mauve quite so well after all. Maybe he simply enjoyed Audrey's company and so strung out his information. Today she trusted him enough to bring her great-grandmother's journal in hopes it would loosen his tongue.

Jake awaited her like he always did, on his swing with the soft green cushions. He was dressed Western in a pressed blue shirt and Wranglers. He appeared ready for company.

She felt a lift in her spirits at the sight of him. From the first time they'd met, he'd meant more to her than simply another person to interview. That feeling had only intensified over the past month since she'd been in Wildcat Bluff. Now she couldn't imagine life without him, but then she felt that way about the entire county... especially Cole Murphy. She'd come to Texas to save Mimi, but sometimes she wondered if she wasn't saving herself as well.

She'd never unpacked in the downstairs bedroom, no matter how lovely it'd been decorated for a visitor. Cole had carried her bags to his suite and she'd been there since the moment they'd come together in his big bed. They'd even settled into a comfortable and happy routine on his ranch that included so much more than their incredible lovemaking. They were sharing the small moments of life, loss as well as gain, as they supported each other.

Fortunately, they recently hadn't been plagued with horse thieves or fires or any other major trouble. It made them both feel a little uneasy, as if they were living on the edge of the next problem. But they handled that knowledge like they did everything else, one day at a time. Together.

Mimi was always on her mind, so she never forgot that overriding issue. She tried not to lose hope in finding the bootlegger gold, but her options were dwindling fast. Maybe today Jake's information would be a major turning point.

She was dawdling and knew it. She didn't want to upset the balance she'd managed to achieve in life. Today might do it. For that matter, almost any day might do it. She simply needed to get on with it. She picked up her purse with Lady Mauve's journal safely tucked inside and looped the strap over her shoulder. She'd brought lunch from Ernie's diner. She leaned down and carefully raised the pizza box, then stepped out of her SUV.

"I can smell it from here," Jake called. "That's Ernie's special supreme, isn't it?"

"You know it." She'd learned early on that all his senses had developed super status after his loss of eyesight.

"Hurry up. I'm hungry."

She chuckled as she made her way up the steps, careful not to drop her two important items—journal and pizza.

"Let's sit at the table. You're liable to be messy," he said, teasing her.

"Me? I thought that was you." She easily returned his banter.

"Never." He chuckled as he stood up.

She set the pizza box in the center of a vinyl red-and-white-checked tablecloth over a small round outdoor table with two chairs. He'd already placed white napkins, red paper plates, and blue plastic glasses of tea on the table. She set her purse on a rocking chair, then watched him step over to the table. She couldn't help but wonder if maybe he moved a little slower or more cautiously than when she'd first met him. She didn't want to think he might be losing ground. Most likely it was just her concern for his age.

He pulled back a chair for her in gentlemanly fashion.

"Thanks," she said as she sat down.

"Good to have you back." He selected the other chair and nodded at her with a smile.

"Good to be back." She returned his smile with a feeling of pleasure that she by now knew he could sense.

"How have things been at GTT Ranch?" He picked up a piece of pizza and took a bite.

"Quiet."

"That's good. Any news on the horse thieves? Law doing their job?"

"If there's news, Cole hasn't been told." She savored a delicious bite of pizza as she enjoyed her surroundings. She wished Mom and Mimi could be sitting here now, taking in the beautiful setting and delightful company. Soon now.

"No more missing mustangs?"

"No. Still, Cole worries about the others he's lost to the rustlers."

"It's a shame, but all kinds of losses happen in the country." Jake sipped tea, then gave her a rueful smile. "Reminds me of the time I kept losing hooch. For the life of me, I couldn't figure out how or why a line kept breaking and spilling whiskey out into a puddle on the ground."

"Did you catch the thief?"

He laughed, shaking his head. "Yeah, I did at that."

"Who?"

"Drunk bear."

"Bear!"

"Some yahoo bought a black bear, not full grown, from a circus wintered up at Hugo, Oklahoma. Brought it back to his ranch as a talking piece, but that bear was smart as a whip and never could be kept corralled. He considered all our ranches and farms his playground. You can't just let a bear, no matter how tame, go roaming around the countryside. It's not safe for him or anybody else."

"Understandable."

"Yeah."

"Do you mean that bear was drinking your whiskey?"

Jake chuckled. "Yep. He got a taste for it. He'd break a line, let the hooch spill out, and lap it up."

She laughed, too. "I'd like to have seen a drunk bear."

"Not too close, you wouldn't. But yeah, it was a pretty funny sight."

"What did y'all do about him?"

"Drunk, he was controllable, if a little on the wild side," he said.

"I can't even imagine."

"We got a posse together, collared the bear, and suggested the owner take him back to the circus where he belonged. Circus folk know how to handle the animals they train. Except for maybe a few spoilers, they feed animals, love them, and give them jobs. That's about what most of us want in life. Food. Love. Job."

She nodded, thinking that he wasn't far off the mark.

"Yeah. If you drill down deep enough, life gets pretty simple."

"Did the bear get back to his real home?"

"You bet. We were pretty persuasive," he said.

"I'm glad you intervened so the bear got safely home."

"He probably lived a good long life in the circus. Out of it, he wouldn't have had much chance at all."

Satisfied at the outcome of Jake's story, she took another bite of pizza. Delicious, as always.

He finished off his piece of pizza, then leaned back in his chair and cocked his head to one side as if listening to far distant music.

"What?"

"You won't know this, but you sound like her."

"Who?" she asked.

"Mauve."

Audrey felt her breath catch in her throat. Was this what she'd known might be coming, a change to her world? Was Jake finally ready to talk about Lady Mauve?

"I didn't want to let on too soon, not until you'd come to know me better and we'd become friends. Still, I knew the minute I heard your voice."

"I...I..."

"Mauve had a particular melodic quality to her voice coupled with a smooth, almost Southern accent. You have only a bit of the Texas in your voice, but the other cadence carried across the generations. I think you both would have made fine singers if you'd chosen that as a profession."

"You believe I'm related to Lady Mauve?"

"I know you are." He hesitated before he continued. "Also… Doris of the Buick Brigade called me. She said they are all in agreement that you're the spitting image of Mauve."

Audrey paused for a moment. Now or never. Like Jake, she'd waited until they'd become friends and trusted each other enough to reveal precious knowledge. "It's true."

"That's how you came to have the journal, isn't it?"

"Yes. I recently found it in Mauve's old dusty trunk while looking for interesting items to use as decoration for our store in Hot Springs."

"You can trust me, you know." He smiled gently, as if trying to tame a skittish horse or collar a drunken bear.

"I know that now, but in her journal, Mauve wrote not to trust anybody in Wildcat Bluff County."

"There is trust and then there is trust."

"What do you mean?" she asked.

"It's easy to trust others if you don't invite them into your world, but if you open that door, your trust must be complete."

"In the days of bootleggers, I suppose she would have invited few into her inner world."

"She invited me." Jake inhaled sharply, as if savoring the memory. "And I never betrayed her trust nor let her down. Until… Well, I never let her down, although she might not have realized it at the time."

"How so?"

"That's for another day, perhaps. Today, you brought her journal. I long to touch it again."

"I brought handy wipes so we don't smudge the cover."

"Good idea."

"Are you done with the pizza?" she asked.

"Yes. One piece does it for me."

"Me, too. I'll leave the rest so you can have it later."

"Are you sure? It'll take me days to clean it up," he said.

"I'm sure. Put it in the fridge and you've got easy meals."

"Thanks."

She closed the pizza box and stacked the plates. She got up and slipped the package of wipes out of her purse, pulled two from the package, handed him one, and used the other.

"Let's sit in the swing." He tossed his used wipe down on the table.

"I'd like that."

While he got comfortable on the swing, she put the handy wipe package back in her purse and pulled out the journal. She sat down beside him, holding her great-grandmother's last words on her lap.

He held out cupped hands.

She gently set the journal on his palms.

"Thank you so much for sharing your treasure. You can't imagine how much this means to me. This is as close to her as I'll ever get again." He clasped the journal, then gently stroked it front to back, opened the cover, felt inside, and did the same with the back. Finally, he closed it and simply sat there.

She sat quietly with him as she listened to birds sing in the treetops as a slight breeze ruffled tree leaves.

"Did you read it?"

"Yes," she said.

"And?"

"Maybe the most important thing she wrote, and that has always stayed with me, was about this county."

"Will you share her words with me?" he asked.

"'I left my heart in Wildcat Bluff County, Texas.'"

He bowed his head, brought the journal to his face, and tenderly kissed its cover.

She looked away to give him privacy. She had no doubt now. He'd loved Lady Mauve. He still loved her. But it must have been an agonizing unrequited love that lasted a long lifetime. No wonder he never married. He never got over his first great love.

Audrey's heart hurt for him, but there was nothing she could do, not after all these years, to ease that emotional pain...except to be here for him and share the moment.

"Thank you. I needed to know that," he said.

"You're so very welcome. I don't understand why she left Wildcat Bluff. She obviously loved it here."

"I doubt we'll ever know. Mauve was Mauve. Besides, we can't go back and change history. Choices were made. We live with the consequences," he said.

"But still..."

"Please tell me about your family. *Her* family. She must have met someone and fallen in love after she left here."

Audrey hesitated. Did she tell him everything, even the most important thing that she hadn't even told Cole?

"Is it so terrible that you can't share it?" He sounded agonized, as if he could hardly bear that thought.

"No. Not at all." She couldn't withhold from this man who had known her great-grandmother. It just wouldn't be right. Besides, she trusted him enough to allow him into her world.

"Good. That brings me comfort." He stroked the cover of the journal as if stroking Lady Mauve's hand.

"She had one daughter. Mimi. She's my grandmother. My mother is Vivian."

"All Oakes?"

"Yes."

"No men in your family? No other last names?" he asked.

"For some reason, we don't seem to form lasting bonds with men."

"And it started with your great-grandmother?" he asked, sounding urgent.

"I guess so. That's just the way it's always been."

"And you've made Hot Springs your family home all these years?" he asked.

"Our business is there, too, like I told you."

"I remember." He cocked his head toward her. "Did you never think to visit Wildcat Bluff before now?"

"We didn't know about it."

"How come?"

"I guess Lady Mauve hid her past, maybe for legal reasons, when she left this county," she said.

"But you finally found the journal."

"Yes."

"And here you are at Oakes Farm," he said.

"Yes."

"Serendipity or fate?"

"Neither." She looked off into the distance and took a deep breath. "Mimi isn't well."

"Oh no. Surely—" He clutched the journal with both hands.

"She needs expensive medical help. I came here to find the bootlegger gold that Mauve mentions in her journal."

"Everyone around here claims it's just a legend," he said. "No big deal."

"I know that now, but still she mentions it in the journal. I think it's important."

"There are many kinds of gold when you think of it as a value," he said.

"At one of the sites she mentions, I found this wire twisted into a heart with two initials. It's too weathered to make out the initials."

"Big post oak by the dump?"

"Yes. How did you know?"

"Folks used to meet there before the dump was built," he said.

"I sent photos of it to Mom and Mimi. They're trying to figure out the initials."

"Good for them." He smiled and tapped the journal with a fingertip. "Tell me about Mimi."

"Oh, she was a firecracker in her day. Now she's in a nursing home. She was getting weaker by the day until I started sending reports to her through Mom about Wildcat Bluff...and you."

"And now?" he asked with a smile.

"It's amazing. Mom says she's improving all the time."

"Love. It's the greatest gift in the world." He stroked the journal one more time, then handed it to Audrey. "I made that for her."

"You did?"

"I told her that she ought to record her thoughts. She lived on the cutting edge of a wild time that should never be forgotten."

"What did she say?"

"She laughed that wonderful laugh and said she was too busy living life to write about it. And that was true. Still, I hoped she would record at least a bit here and there," he said.

"She did."

"It's good to know she listened to me once...or at least twice."

"And I have the journal to prove it."

He stood up. "My dear, I need to give all of this some thought. Will you come back and read sections of her journal to me? I would very much like to hear her voice again through you."

"Of course I will." She got to her feet. "I didn't mean to tire you."

"You didn't. All your news energizes me. I'm a new man... hopefully, a better one."

"I don't know how you could be better."

"A man or a woman can always do better, be better." He held out his hand.

She didn't shake it. She simply held it for a long moment, joining them together. It felt right.

"Will you ask your mother and grandmother to visit me?"

"They're anxious to meet you. They plan to come to Wildcat Bluff as soon as Mimi is strong enough."

"That's wonderful news. I hope they make it sooner than later. At my age, I never know if I'll see the next dawn."

"You'll see lots more dawns."

"I may very well do it," he said. "I have plenty to live for now."

"So do we." She smiled. "I mean, you actually knew Mimi's mother."

"And she never met her father?"

"No. He left before she was born."

"That's sad," Jake said.

"We're Oakes women. We're strong. We make it on our own."

"It's good to be strong. It's good to make it on your own. I should know. That's my life."

"I understand," she said.

"But family…now that is something to hold with reverence in your heart of hearts."

"I'm grateful to my mother and grandmother." She felt a little mournful. He had all the friends in the world, but somehow family had eluded him.

"Tell Mimi and Vivian to visit soon," he said as if he relished saying their names out loud.

"I will. And I'll be back to see you tomorrow."

"I'll be here."

She picked up her purse and placed the journal safely inside it. "Audrey?"

"Yes?" She stopped and looked at him. He appeared so resilient, not like a full-grown tree that could be uprooted in a strong wind but like a sapling that would bend but never break.

"Do you know Nocona Jones in Wildcat Bluff?" he asked.

"I've never met her, but I understand the Steele family is using her to fight back against Zane Ranch trying to take Fernando."

"Yes, that's right. She's an excellent attorney."

"Why do you ask?"

"Oh. Just on my mind, what with the Steele problem and all," he said.

"I'm glad she's on their side and they can trust her."

"Yes. Remember that. She's trustworthy…just in case you ever need legal counsel."

"Thanks. I'll remember." Audrey felt touched by his concern. He was looking out for her. Maybe just in case she found the gold.

"Bye for now," he said.

"Till later."

She left him on his porch, feeling as if she shouldn't leave him, feeling as if he might not be there when she came back, feeling as if she'd left something important undone. But there was nothing she could do about it now. She still had Mimi to think about first. Jake had discouraged her about the bootlegger gold, but she had Lady Mauve's own words to fuel her continued quest.

She returned to her SUV, headed for Wildcat Road, GTT Ranch, and one fine cowboy.

Chapter 21

BACK AT GTT RANCH, AUDREY POURED A GLASS OF TEA OVER ice in the kitchen, then walked out onto the patio. She selected a chair under an old oak that provided shade and comfort. She tossed her cell phone onto a section of straggling grass that obviously struggled to survive in the shade. That's the way she felt at the moment—struggling to survive.

And all because she hadn't wanted to leave Jake, not after hearing his revelations…or maybe she'd picked up his struggle to survive without sight and without the love of his life and internalized it. Lady Mauve. How many men had she left in her wake when she'd abandoned Wildcat Bluff? Audrey had always been under the impression that it was the men who left Oakes women. Maybe it was the other way around, at least in her great-grandmother's case.

But it was so long ago. Who knew or cared anymore? She wished nobody did, but she knew better. Jake cared. She cared. Mom cared. Mimi cared. Maybe to protect their hearts, Oakes women somehow designed their lives to be without men, although Gerald was now giving her mother a new chance at love.

Audrey glanced up at Cole's bedroom window. Did she already have one foot out the door so she could get in the rejection first if it came to it? She hoped not, but she knew that underneath all the happiness lurked a little worm of doubt that Cole would continue to want her to stay with him. If she wasn't careful, that little worm could grow into a fire-breathing dragon and consume all the trust and happiness they were building between them.

She couldn't let that happen. He'd come to mean too much to her. Jake had come to mean too much to her. Life in Wildcat Bluff had come to mean too much to her. Acquaintances here had come to mean too much to her. She didn't want to abandon it all based on some outdated feelings that were no longer relevant in her life. When she went back to Hot Springs, she wanted to keep the connections here unlike the way her great-grandmother had left it all behind for her new life.

Audrey sat up straight in her chair, blinking in astonishment as she rethought Lady Mauve's poetic words. "*I left my heart in Wildcat Bluff County, Texas.*" Maybe her great-grandmother hadn't wanted to leave, but she'd been compelled to go for some unknown reason. Love. Had it had a hold on Lady Mauve that just wouldn't let go? If so, Audrey was beginning to understand exactly how that felt and how you never wanted to let it go.

She leaned back and sipped her iced tea. Complications. She had expected everything to be simple here, even to finding the gold. She hadn't counted on the intensity of emotion that assailed her around almost every corner, catching her repeatedly by surprise. Heat kept rising in her, so she enjoyed the cold liquid sliding down her throat. She needed to stay calm, cool, and collected to save her grandmother. She just didn't know quite how to do it.

For now, she would relax in the quiet and safety of the GTT compound. Cole was out doing ranch stuff. She'd talked with Jake and shown him the journal. That was enough for the day. At least, she didn't want to do any more right now. Jake's words about drunken bears and handmade journals filled her mind. She didn't want to replace them with anything else just yet.

She sipped more tea. Max and Folgie lay curled together near the fence, where they slept in warm sunlight. She felt a little sleepy, too. If anyone approached—friend or foe—they'd bark to warn her. A nap would feel good. She didn't have to solve all her problems in a day or a week or even a month. Some things took time to develop and this was turning out to be one of those times. She couldn't rush it, no matter how much she wanted to do so.

As she sat there relaxing, enjoying the quiet, convincing herself that she was doing the best she could do in the circumstances, she heard her mother's ringtone. She set down her tea and grabbed her phone.

"Mom, what is it?"

"No FaceTime today. I look a mess."

"You always look beautiful," Audrey said.

"It's been a long day, so just leave it be."

"Okay. Please tell me."

"Are you sitting down? If not, do," Vivian said.

"Is it that bad?"

"It's not good, but it could be worse."

"I'm in a chair," Audrey said.

"Okay. Now, Mimi is okay."

"Oh no." Audrey felt her heart sink. Just when she'd convinced herself that she was in control, not only of her life but her heart as well.

"She fell."

"Tell me she didn't break her hip or any other bone."

"She didn't," Vivian said.

"That's good news."

"Yes. We're at the hospital. She's stabilized."

"I'll come home. If I start out right away—"

"You'll do no such thing," Vivian said.

"But, Mom—"

"She's okay. They're keeping her overnight for observation and to keep tabs on her vitals like blood pressure and oxygen levels."

"You're sure she doesn't need me?" Audrey asked.

"She always needs you, but right now she needs you in Wildcat Bluff."

"Why? I can't help her here."

"You're helping her more than you realize," Vivian said.

"I don't understand."

"She fell because she feels so much like her old self in spirit. It's just that her body isn't quite there yet. She got up out of her wheelchair and her legs gave way."

"Oh no," Audrey said.

"She's bruised but not broken."

"Good."

"And the best news is her doctors are impressed that she is so much more active and interested in life. She's even participating in rehab now."

"But she hated it," Audrey said.

"Not now. She's stronger now. Doctors think it was probably low blood sugar that caused her fall."

"That's fixable."

"Fixed," Vivian said. "Now she's determined to get back to rehab so she can come to Wildcat Bluff sooner than later."

"That's what we all want, but we want her to be safe, too. What do her doctors say?"

Vivian chuckled. "Mimi doesn't care. She says she's the final decision maker in her life."

"I'm trying my best to find the gold, but—"

"Dear heart, every call you make, every photograph you take, every story you tell…that's the gold for your grandmother. She's completely engaged in Lady Mauve's world."

"It means that much to her?" Audrey asked.

"Yes. She wants to meet Jake in person. She plans to sit down with him and talk about her mother. He's the only one alive who can share memories with her."

"I saw him today. He's anxious for both of you to visit him."

"Wonderful. We want to visit him, too," Vivian said.

"Would it help if I talked with Mimi today?"

"Not right now. She'll want to speak with you later. I'll keep passing your stories to her."

"Whatever you think is best. I do miss her," Audrey said.

"We miss you, too."

"Mom, Jake held the journal in his hands today. He said he made it for Mauve in hopes she would record some of her thoughts. And she did."

"He loved her, didn't he?" Vivian asked.

"I think he still does."

"She had a powerful effect on people."

"Yes. And they never forgot her."

"I want to walk the land where my grandmother walked. I want to talk with the man who knew her," Vivian said. "We'll come as soon as we can."

"When do you think Mimi might be strong enough?"

"Soon, I think. She's raring to get there."

"Good. And I'll keep looking for the gold for Mimi's sake," Audrey said.

"Like I said, *you* are the gold."

"I'm afraid I won't be accepted as payment for medical bills." Audrey looked at Folgie and Max dozing in the sun. She wished they'd dig up the treasure and bring it to her. But she supposed that'd be too easy.

"At this rate, maybe there won't be any major medical bills," Vivian said in a serious tone.

"Thanks, Mom. No medical bills. I wish. You do know how to lift my spirits."

"I'm serious. She's that much better."

"Good."

"Guess it's hard to believe, but keep the faith," Vivian said.

"Always."

"Now...on a happier note, how is your cowboy firefighter?"

"Better than ever." Audrey sighed loudly. "Mom, do you think we two Oakes women really stand a chance at love...real, enduring love?"

"I think if there's even the slightest chance of it, we should grasp it with both hands and never let go."

"Gerald."

"He's a blessing in so many ways," Vivian said.

"I'm glad for you."

"And I am for you. Don't even think about rushing back to Hot Springs. I'm handling the business just fine on my own. Mimi has good care. And you have a wonderful place to live. Enjoy it," Vivian said.

"If I can just get a lead on that gold…"

"That sounds like Mimi. 'If I can just figure out those initials…'"

Audrey chuckled. "We're two of a kind, aren't we?"

"You definitely are."

"You'll give Mimi my love, won't you?"

"You know I will. For now, I'd better go. I'll spend the night in her room to keep her company. It's best to have someone you love and who loves you with you when you're in a hospital."

"Wish I were there with you."

"We'll be together soon…in Wildcat Bluff."

"Bye for now, Mom. Love you."

"Love you, too."

Audrey set down her phone. She looked at the dogs again. They were solid reality in a world that kept changing and morphing until she could scarcely keep up with it. Mimi. She'd felt well enough to get out of her wheelchair. She was determined to come to Wildcat Bluff. She wanted to meet Jake. Audrey had only meant to save her grandmother's life. She hadn't intended to turn it inside out or upside down. But maybe it was for the absolute best.

She reached to pick up her glass of tea but knocked it over, watching as liquid spilled across the grass and was absorbed into the dirt, making mud. Was that what she was doing—making mud out of the lives of her loved ones? Mimi could really hurt herself trying to do too much too fast in order to get to Wildcat Bluff. She might even destroy her chances for medical help. And Mom. Was she overdoing it at the store as she tried to balance work and care for Mimi?

Maybe Audrey should go home, where she could help her mother and care for her grandmother. Was she chasing so much pie in the sky? Was she giving herself way more credit than she was due by thinking she could actually find that gold and write a book, too?

She slumped down in her chair, feeling as if she'd taken a wrong turn somewhere. Perhaps she should just back up and start over with an entirely different plan. But she'd thought and thought before she came up with this one. There had been no alternative then…and there wasn't one now.

She felt as if life was closing in on her, leaving her with no good options. If she stayed, she might not make a difference. If she went home, she might not make much difference there except to hold Mimi's hand while she slowly ebbed away. That thought was intolerable.

She jumped to her feet, wanting to get away from her thoughts and her emotions. She walked down to the dogs and sat beside them, finding comfort in their calm presence.

Folgie raised his head and cocked it as if to inquire about her.

Max gave her the once over, then whined deep in his throat.

Both dogs got up at once. Folgie lay down on one side of her, lending furry warmth. Max stretched out on her other side, snuggling close.

She stroked both their heads, so glad of their presence. She wished Cole were there, but he didn't even know about Mimi's condition, so he couldn't help ease her emotional pain anyway. She sighed. Maybe she'd been holding back too much, too long, so she didn't feel comfortable sharing with anyone outside her immediate family. That'd seemed fine before she came to Wildcat Bluff. Now it didn't feel so right anymore, particularly not with Cole or Jake.

She lay back against the grass. Trust. She needed to trust that all would be well. She would do her best and that was all she could do. She felt the sun warm on her face and the dogs warm beside her. She could be content here, if not for…

"Audrey! What are you doing down there?" Cole slammed the sliding glass door behind him with a bang.

She didn't even get up. The dogs didn't either. They were all too content with the moment.

Cole knelt beside her. "Are you okay?"

She smiled up at him. "You're so handsome."

"Was it a rough day? Did you get into the whiskey?"

She chuckled, reached up, and stroked down one side of his face. "Do you really think we have a chance?"

"No question about it." He plopped down beside her. "Looks like you, Max, and Folgie have the best idea of the day."

"It's just so much… I wanted relief. Here I am. No matter what you say, I'm not moving one inch."

"Me either." He patted Folgie and Max, then lay back beside her. "My day wasn't a picnic either."

"Tell me."

"No. You tell me first."

"I'm not sure I want to go there," she said.

"Helps to get it out of your system with somebody you trust."

"Trust?"

"Yeah. Aren't we to that point?" He threaded their fingers together.

"Oakes women aren't noted for their longevity with men."

"You're breaking that rule, if it is one."

"Lady Mauve started it. Mimi came next. Mom after her. And now me."

"Take yourself off that list. You don't belong there." He sat up to look down at her, brown eyes filled with concern.

"I want off that list in the worst way."

He leaned over and pressed a soft kiss to her lips. "Do I need to carry you upstairs? We could forget about everything except each other."

"I'd love it…but I need to tell you something."

He fell back against the grass. "Another secret?"

"Not a secret. We just didn't get here yet."

"Tell me." He squeezed her hand.

"Mimi is my grandmother. Lady Mauve's daughter."

"She's still in your life?"

"Yes."

"That's wonderful," he said.

"She's not well. I need that gold for medical procedures to save her life."

"Oh hell." He sat upright. "Don't worry about it. I'll sell some cattle."

"What?" She sat up beside him. "You will not. This is my family's concern, not yours."

"You don't think I'm family?"

"We haven't known each other that long."

"Doesn't matter. We knew each other the moment we met." He plucked a handful of grass and tossed it away. "Why do you have to fight everything?"

"It's not that. It's… I'm desperate to save Mimi."

"I'll help you any way I can." He looked her over. "What happened today? Was it something with Jake?"

"Mom called. Mimi fell out of her wheelchair."

"Break something?"

"No. She's okay," Audrey said.

"Good."

"The thing is…she's getting stronger and she's determined to come to Wildcat Bluff to talk with Jake about her mother."

"That's great. Isn't it?" he asked.

"Yes."

"Why is she coming now?"

"Mom's been telling her about all I'm doing and experiencing here. She says it's given Mimi a reason to live, excitement about life again," she said.

"That's amazing. So the gold is really Wildcat Bluff."

"I don't know that for a fact. Mimi still needs medical help. I want her to have the best, the latest, even if it is experimental."

"We can drive to Hot Springs and bring them here. They wouldn't need to use the stairs in the house. The downstairs bedroom would suit them fine," he said.

"You'd do that? Invite them here?"

"Yes, of course." He stroked hair back from her face. "You mean everything to me. Don't you know that by now?"

She felt warmed by his words, warmer even than the sunlight bathing them. She kissed him, long and slow, then leaned back to see his expression.

He smiled, nodding in appreciation. "Okay. You do know. I won't press you for more. You're already under a lot of pressure. But this is just the beginning of our journey together. Whatever affects you affects me."

"But this is complicated."

"Just tell me what needs to be done and we'll do it…together."

"Jake invited Mom and Mimi to visit him," she said.

"Good. He's their only connection with Mauve. And they are his only connection with her. It's rare they'd get this opportunity to visit. If you don't want me to go and get them, when are they coming here?" he asked.

"Mimi is in rehab. Mom says she's getting stronger all the time."

"Soon, then."

"I hope so. I'm still going to find that gold. Mimi may yet need medical treatment," she said.

"You sound as determined as Lady Mauve must have been when she ran this county."

"I don't know about that, but I do want this county's story told. And I do want Jake and my family to meet."

"Did you learn anything new from him today?"

She laughed. "I heard about a bear drunk on Jake's whiskey."

"Now that's a story I want to hear."

"Later." She glanced up at his bedroom window. "Maybe when we're up there and…"

"Relaxing."

"Right. But tell me about your day. Anything on the mustangs?"

"I did get some news." He took a deep breath. "Feds don't think the horses have been moved out of the area."

"That's wonderful."

"It's a relief. Gives us a much better chance of rescuing them."

"What now?" she asked.

"I'm going to talk with other ranchers about late-night semis on the roads around here. Might be backcountry dirt roads. Somebody's got to have seen something. It might not have seemed significant at the time, but shine a different light on it and who knows what might be revealed?"

"If I can be of help, let me know. So far I've turned up nothing, but you never know."

"We make a good team," he said.

"Yes."

He glanced up at his bedroom window, then back at her with a question in his eyes.

She nodded, feeling as if her world had just turned right again. She helped him. He helped her. That's the way it was done in Wildcat Bluff.

As Cole stood up, his phone chirped an alert. He clicked it open and turned on speakerphone.

"Slade here. Storm's with me. Open your gate."

"What?"

"Remember that talk we had in the café?"

"Yes," Cole said.
"We're headed in with a load."
"I'll get the gate."

Chapter 22

COLE GRABBED AUDREY'S HAND AND HEADED FOR THE HOUSE. Folgie and Max cavorted around them as if it was playtime—which it most certainly was not.

"Are they bringing Fernando?" she asked.

"Sounds like it."

"That means the situation got worse."

"I'd guess so...or they want to be on the safe side." He slid open the patio doors and walked straight to the kitchen where he kept the gate remote control on top of the bar. He heard Audrey and the dogs behind him.

"What can I do?" she asked.

"Hang on. First things first."

He grabbed the remote, walked back out the open patio door, over to the fountain where he had a good line of sight, and pushed a button. When he saw the gate start to open, he hurried back.

Audrey, Max, and Folgie stood just inside the open door, as if they were his backup lieutenants waiting for instructions in an escalating war. Maybe that was about right. Between the mustangs and Fernando, something was rocking their normally peaceful county. It looked to be heating up. By the time all was said and done, he doubted anybody would be standing on the sidelines.

"What now?" she asked.

"It's up to Slade, or more likely Storm. She may be only nine years old, but this is her show."

"Do you want me to keep watch and let you know when they arrive?"

"No. They'll be here any minute." He slipped the remote control in his shirt pocket and snapped it shut.

"What then?"

He glanced at the dogs. "We don't need them underfoot or irritating Fernando."

"They'll start herding?"

"And trying to help."

"Do you want me to put them on the patio?"

"Yes. They can keep watch from there."

"Okay."

"And, Audrey, make sure you close the door, then come out front to the courtyard. Once we see what we're dealing with, we can go from there."

"Okay."

He quickly walked across the living room and out the front door, mind whirling with possibilities, primarily where to put Fernando. He was a huge bull, two thousand pounds at least. He was as tame as they come, but that only went so far in a tense situation. Primarily, they had to keep him out of sight. That was definitely possible on a four-thousand-acre ranch. But at the same time, they didn't want to involve any innocent bystanders—like the GTT cowboys—in a legal situation.

Cole walked out to the center of the courtyard between the house and the guesthouse. He didn't have to wait long. Soon the sparkling blue one-ton came through the open gate pulling a long blue trailer. He took the remote out of his pocket and closed the gate.

Slade pulled up beside him and lowered his window. He looked grim. Storm sat beside him. She looked even grimmer.

"Hoped it wouldn't come to this," Cole said.

"You aren't the only one." Slade pushed the brim of his cowboy hat up with a thumb. "Owe you for this one."

"No, you don't. Glad to help out."

"Just so you know"—Slade motioned with his head toward the trailer—"we've got Fernando, Daisy Sue, Little Fernando, and Margarita."

"You brought them all, then."

"Had to. Zane Ranch foreman claims the twins, too."

"In that case, you made the only choice you could make," Cole said.

"He's had spies out and about on our ranch. If he managed to get a court order and we had to comply, we might never see any of them again...no matter the final outcome."

Storm leaned toward the open window. "Don't believe a word coming out of Zane Ranch. Something's not right and we've got to prove it."

"That's what we're trying to do," Slade said. "In the meantime, we've got to keep them safe."

Audrey walked up to the group. "Just so y'all know, Folgie and Max are confined to the patio area. They won't bother Fernando."

"Thanks." Slade gave her a quick nod, then looked back at Cole. "Sydney is staying at the ranch, not working at the café while this is going down. If that outfit arrives looking for trouble, she'll give it to them or get them so confused they won't know which end is up."

"Good for her," Cole said.

Slade glanced around the area. "What do you have in mind?"

"It's up to you." Cole looked at Slade, then Storm. "I'm leery about putting them out in a pasture."

"What about your horse barn?" Storm asked.

"It may be our best bet. It's got five indoor stalls. Each one opens into a narrow fenced run, so they can safely stretch their legs outside."

"Are all the stalls empty?" Slade asked.

"Fortunately, yes." Cole nodded toward the long rock structure down from the guesthouse. It had a metal roof with a wide overhang that allowed horses to be outside in rainy weather and still stay dry. A fourth of the building was given over to tack, feed, and grooming supplies.

"I like it," Storm said. "It's pretty snazzy."

"Okay." Cole smiled at her. "Pretty snazzy, huh?"

Storm grinned back. "Only the best for Fernando and family."

"We brought feed and treats, so you won't be out anything. And we'll pay rent," Slade said.

"Nothing doing. No rent." Cole shook his head. "But they'd probably like familiar food."

"They're particular," Storm said.

"Let's get them installed before they get too restless." Cole patted the cab of the one-ton like he would a horse to get it to move forward.

"One thing," Slade said. "Can we lock up the whole shebang?"

"You bet. Keyless entry. I'll give you the code."

"I'm feeling better about this all the time," Slade said.

"Glad I could be of help." Cole patted the cab again.

Slade drove forward, passed the guesthouse, and pulled up in front of the horse barn.

Cole glanced at Audrey. "Not a word of this to anyone. Far as you know, I've got horses I'm training in there."

"Horses in training. Got it." She took a deep breath. "I'll tell you one thing."

"What?"

"Wildcat Bluff doesn't lack for excitement."

He just shook his head, clasped her hand, and walked toward the barn. When they reached it, he opened the extra-wide door and stepped back.

Storm and Slade got out of the front of the cab. A leathery-skinned, bred-in-the-bone toughness cowboy, with a sharp-eyed cow dog sporting a red bandanna around his neck, stepped down from the back.

"Good to see you." Cole held out his hand, and the cowboy shook it.

"Likewise," the cowboy said.

"Audrey, this is Oscar Leathers, foreman of Steele Trap Ranch, and his furry friend Tater."

"Hello," she said.

"Oscar, I don't believe you've met Audrey Oakes. She's staying at GTT while she researches a book about Lady Mauve's time here in Wildcat Bluff."

"You don't say." Oscar took off his cowboy hat—revealing a bald head—and placed it over his heart. "Mighty fine to meet you. Tater's glad to meet you, too."

Tater held up a paw.

Audrey shook it. "Good to meet both of you, too, although I wish the circumstances were better."

Oscar put his hat back on his head. "Sure enough. But this deal buys us time to set the matter right."

"Glad to help out," Cole said.

Slade walked up, dressed as usual in Western shirt, jeans, and boots. Storm sported FERNANDO THE WONDER BULL in rhinestones across the front of her pink T-shirt. She also wore turquoise cowgirl boots that were caked with dirt from lots of wear.

"Take your pick of the stalls," Cole said.

"Okay," Slade said.

"Thank you so much for helping us." Storm tried to smile, but she didn't quite make it.

Slade and Storm walked around to the side of the trailer, opened the door, and stepped up into it.

"How about the feed I brought?" Oscar asked. "That's my job today. Got to make sure those critters stay in the pink."

"There's hay you can use, if you want," Cole said. "Stack your feed where there's room."

"Suits me," Oscar said.

Slade looked out of the trailer, then lowered a short ramp. "Cole, you and Audrey better step back. Fernando's a little skittish over this whole move."

"Don't blame him." Cole clasped her hand and eased them out of the way but stopped close enough to watch the action. If anything went south, he wanted to be near enough to help.

After a moment, Storm glanced outside. She held a rope in one hand that was attached to the leather halter of a huge black Angus bull. "Is it okay to walk him straight into the barn?" she asked.

"Yes," Cole said. "It's safe. Take the center aisle and pick a stall. The largest one is on the end."

"Thanks." Storm tossed back a long strand of strawberry-blond hair, then glanced at the bull. "New home."

Fernando peered over her shoulder and snorted at the unaccustomed sight and smell.

Storm led him down the ramp, across the courtyard, and into the barn.

"No wonder he's got the hottest sperm. That is one fine bull," Cole said in admiration.

"You know it. And it's why we're where we are," Oscar said.

"Yeah," Cole said.

"But we're not the only ones with trouble." Oscar adjusted his hat as if all the problems had caused a high wind that might blow it away.

"I'm still missing all those mustangs," Cole said. "But we'll get those horse thieves."

"Didn't mean your particular trouble," Oscar said.

"There's more?" Cole asked.

"Yep."

Slade stuck his head outside the trailer, looked all around, and then led a black Angus cow down the ramp. He headed toward the barn with her.

"That Daisy Sue is a beauty, isn't she?" Cole said.

"Sure is." Oscar agreed. "Good thing nobody is trying to take her away."

"Glad of it." Cole looked from Daisy Sue to Oscar. "But tell me about the trouble."

"You haven't heard?"

"No. I've been too busy on the trail of those mustangs to pay much attention to anything else."

"It took a while to come to light," Oscar said. "You know how that goes."

"Right. Too big a range. Too few cowboys. Too many cattle to keep proper count."

"That's true for the big ranches," Oscar said. "The smaller outfits know exactly what they've got at all times. Cows go missing and they go on alert."

"Rustlers?" Cole thought about his own operation. He'd better make sure there was a head count tomorrow.

"Yep. They were smart at first, picking off stragglers or strays in the big herds. Guess they got greedy and started hitting the smaller ranches. That's when they got noticed, big time."

"All over the county?" Cole asked.

"Far as we can tell. We're still reaching out to ranchers. Sorry we didn't alert you sooner, but we've been caught up in this Fernando business and it's got us worried to the point of distraction."

"Think nothing of it," Cole said.

"Still…"

"That's okay. I'll check my own herds. And I'll help get the word out," Cole said.

"Thanks."

"Got to wonder if some big out-of-state outfit has moved in on us. They'll haul the cattle out fast," Cole said.

"Figure as much," Oscar said.

"Guess Sheriff Calhoun knows."

"He's on it, but so far these guys are smarter than smart. No trail left to follow," Oscar said.

"What's going on around here?" Cole asked. "First, my mustangs. Second, y'all's Fernando. Now, everybody's cattle."

"Do you wonder if they're connected somehow?" Audrey asked, joining in the conversation.

"No way," Oscar said. "They don't fit together. Wildcat Bluff's just got a run of bad luck."

"Yeah," Cole agreed.

"Guess that makes more sense," Audrey said.

"Sheriff Calhoun and Nocona Jones will sort it out." Oscar patted Tater's head. "We just got to make sure we keep Fernando and family safe."

"We will," Cole said. "I recently tightened my security system. Nothing is getting into this compound."

"That's what I like to hear," Oscar said.

Slade and Storm walked out of the barn, both looking satisfied with their actions.

"All okay?" Cole asked just to make sure the accommodations were up to their standards.

"Fernando approves," Storm said. "He's next to Daisy Sue, so he's happy. They can see each other outside. But they want their babies near them."

"They're yearlings now." Slade stopped beside Cole. "I don't know what we're going to do about the Wildcat Bluff County Spring Stock Show."

"It's coming up soon. Little Fernando and Margarita are entered to win what I'm sure will be blue ribbons. Only now…" Storm bit her lower lip in distress. "Now they've had to go into hiding to be safe, so how can they enter?"

"Zane Ranch." Oscar rubbed his chin while Tater growled low in his throat. "What's wrong with those folks?"

"Greed?" Audrey sighed. "Storm, I regret your trouble. Maybe it'll get resolved by the stock show."

Storm tossed her head. "It better. Fernando and Daisy Sue are proud parents and they want their babies to win…just like their legion of fans."

"Come on, let's get the twins," Slade said. "We're burning daylight and we won't get that matter resolved today."

Storm quickly went into the trailer with Slade right behind her.

"It'd be a real shame if the twins couldn't compete in the stock show," Cole said.

"That's not the only thing that'd be a real shame." Oscar stroked the top of Tater's head. "If Storm lost Fernando and the twins, it'd break her heart."

"We just can't let it happen," Audrey said.

"They're safe here now." Cole gave her what he hoped was a reassuring smile, but he had no idea how the issue could be resolved in Steele Trap Ranch's favor. But at least now there wouldn't be any midnight raids to spirit Fernando away.

A little later, Storm walked down the ramp, leading a big and muscular, sleek black young bull with smart dark eyes that quickly took in the new surroundings.

"Please meet Little Fernando," Storm said. "Isn't he just the most handsome young bull ever?"

"He's gorgeous." Audrey smiled at them. "He's bound to win a blue ribbon."

Cole looked over Little Fernando. He obviously had great bloodlines. He was a very valuable animal. No wonder Zane Ranch was trying to get their hands on him, too. But that wasn't what mattered to Storm or Fernando's fans. They loved him for nothing more than who he was to the world.

"Let me present Margarita." Slade led the young cow down the ramp to the ground.

"Isn't she the picture of her mother?" Storm asked. "And she's just the sweetest thing."

"She's gorgeous, too," Audrey said.

Cole felt a little sick at the prospect that this beautiful young cow could be taken away from those who loved her. Who knew what would happen to her on Zane Ranch? One way or another, he was going to keep these vulnerable animals safe on GTT Ranch.

"We'd better take them to Fernando and Daisy Sue," Storm said. "They fret when their babies are gone too long."

Cole watched as the yearlings disappeared into the barn. He glanced at Oscar.

"Yeah, I know. That's why we brought them to you," Oscar said. "It'd be a crying shame for something bad to happen to them."

"I'll do everything I can for them, but you know I don't have a good track record with the mustangs," Cole said.

"That's why these are in your barn. No pasture for them. Not till this is over and we've won."

"Right."

"Best let me get the feed in there," Oscar said.

"I'll help."

"No need. You're doing enough letting us borrow your barn."

"No point arguing with me," Cole said. "My mind's set. Get up there and toss the sacks down to me."

"Guess you got a little sass still left in you." Oscar chuckled as he stepped up into the trailer.

"I had a lot more before I lost my mustangs."

Oscar laughed as he tossed out a fifty-pound sack of feed.

Cole grunted as he caught it and set it on the ground. "Throw that a little harder next time, will you?"

Oscar laughed even more as he threw down the next sack.

Cole set it beside the other one. "What'd you do, put rocks in these sacks?"

"When did you get so weak?" Oscar tossed another sack.

"I'm conserving my strength." Cole set it down, too.

"One more and that's all you're getting today. If you need

more, holler." Oscar threw down the last sack, then hopped to the ground.

"Best not bring any more. Let me get the feed or use what I've got here. We don't want anybody getting suspicious."

"Good point."

Slade and Storm walked out of the barn, looking dejected over leaving the cattle inside.

"I'll take good care of them," Cole said.

"I know." Storm smiled at him. "But I'll miss them."

"Couldn't you come visit?" Audrey asked.

"Not without another reason to be here," Storm said.

"Maybe we can come up with something." Audrey gave her an encouraging smile.

"Yeah," Cole replied. "We'll give it some thought."

"Good." Slade picked up a feed sack, put it under an arm, and did the same with another sack.

Oscar hefted the others and followed Slade into the barn.

"They're certainly strong," Audrey said.

"Ranch work." Cole glanced at Storm. "Makes a cowboy or cowgirl strong, doesn't it?"

"Yes...but we'll never be as strong as a bull," Storm said. "And Fernando is the strongest bull in the whole wide world."

"And the most handsome," Audrey said with a twinkle in her lavender eyes.

"That's true." Storm rubbed the front of her tee with one hand. "See? It says right here, 'Fernando the Wonder Bull.' And that's a fact."

"I'd like to get one of those T-shirts," Audrey said.

Storm grinned in delight. "They're for sale on Fernando's website or I have some at the house. Even better, I'll make them available at the stock show." She shook her head. "I mean, I'll have them there if the twins get to go."

"Let's plan on all of us going to it," Audrey said.

"Okay." Storm gave a brisk nod. "It's a deal."

Cole decided then and there that somehow or other, Zane Ranch had to be made to back off their claim. He didn't know how he was going to do it any more than he knew how he was going to get the mustangs back. But right was right...and they were in the right.

Slade and Oscar walked back out, one tall and muscular, the other a little bow-legged from a life on horseback. Both had the same determined expression.

"Cole, can't thank you enough," Slade said. "You've made a little girl very happy."

"Glad I could be of help."

"We'll get out of your hair now." Slade put an arm around Storm's small shoulders.

"Oh yes, Granny sent you good eats by way of thank you." Storm ran around the truck, opened the door, reached inside, and came out with a big sack. She lugged it back and held it out to Audrey.

"Thanks." Audrey cradled the sack in her arms. "We can sure use some good food."

"Chuckwagon is the best," Cole said.

"What about Ernie's?" Slade chuckled. "Heard you made a run out that way for pizza."

"Can't I get away with anything in secret?" Cole asked, mock-complaining at the situation.

"Not in this county." Storm laughed.

"That's what I'm learning." Audrey patted the sack. "Thank Granny, and all of you, for the tasty treats."

"There's more where that came from. Just let us know." Slade opened his truck door. "Can't leave Fernando's caretakers to starve."

"When we win our fight, we'll be coming back for our loved ones just as fast as lightning." Storm ran around to her side of the truck.

"And they'll be waiting for you," Cole called after her.

Slade and Storm got back into the one-ton's cab. Oscar and Tater got into the back seat. And they took off.

Cole watched them go, then turned to Audrey.

"I know," she said. "We must find out what's going on in Wildcat Bluff."

"And save the day."

Chapter 23

AUDREY PATTED THE SACK OF CHUCKWAGON CAFÉ FOOD AGAIN.
"Is there a rivalry between Wildcat Bluff Diner and Chuckwagon Cafe?"

"No. Slade likes to josh about it, but he's supportive of Ernie and she's supportive of him."

"That's just the way it is in Wildcat Bluff, isn't it?"

"Yep…except in cases like what's going on right now," he said.

"Think they're outsiders?"

"Don't know for sure, but maybe so."

"Could be outsiders with insider help," she said.

"It'd make sense."

She hugged the sack of food closer. The warmth felt good, comforting even.

"Want to go check on our guests?" He gestured toward the barn.

"Yes, indeed." She walked beside him up to the door. "Just think how many fans would be thrilled at the opportunity to host our celebrities."

"Plenty. But I doubt they'd have a clue how to go about it."

"True. I sure wouldn't," she said.

"You have other gifts."

She glanced at him with a smile. "And what would those be?"

He grinned. "I'll let you show me later."

"Show?"

"Upstairs." He grinned even bigger, eyes lighting up with inner fire.

"Can't you keep your mind on business for one minute?" She laughed in delight at the happiness they were generating between them.

"Not with you around."

"Oh, Cole." She felt that happiness expand and fill her entire body.

"Come on. Let's check on our guests, then we've got some good food to eat."

"And then?"

"After a day like today, we deserve a little reward, don't we?" he asked.

"How little?"

"Maybe not so little." He pressed a kiss to the tip of her nose, then opened the door to the barn.

She stepped into the shadowy aisle that ran the length of the horse barn and caught the scent of hay, grain, and cattle. The four sacks of feed had been piled neatly to one side of the entry. One had been opened, used, and reclosed.

"I'll get those sacks put up later," Cole said. "What I'll do is rearrange a section so it's nothing but Steele Trap stuff."

"Think you'll need to buy more feed?"

"Depends on how long the situation lasts," he said.

"Hopefully, not long."

"Right. Our guests will be at the end in the last four stalls."

She walked with him down the length of the structure, noting the closed doors that led into stalls. Empty buckets for water and feed hung outside each stall. A water hose had been coiled and hung up on the wall. It dripped from the nozzle, creating a wet place on the cement.

"Looks like Storm set out feed and water before she left," Cole said. "That's the mark of a good, caring cowgirl."

"And a good guest. She saved you extra work."

"Appreciate it, too."

When they reached the occupied stalls, four heads poked out to investigate the newcomers.

"Hey, Fernando, Daisy Sue, Little Fernando, Margarita." Cole held his hand out to them, palm flat, so they could smell him.

She did the exact same thing and was rewarded with the feel of hot, moist breath as the animals took in her scent.

"It's important for them to remember us," Cole said. "They'll do it by scent even more than sight."

"They need to know we're friends, don't they?"

"Absolutely. One of the ways to do that is to feed them. Treats like oats are easiest. I have horse cookies. Not for the wild mustangs, but for the trained horses."

"That's great. Can we feed Fernando and the others?" she asked.

"Later. They've got food and water. For now, I just want them to settle into their new home."

"Okay. You're my guide."

"If I can, I'd like to get Fernando to trust my touch. I might need to lead him out of here by his halter. He's huge. No way I can do that if he doesn't let me," Cole said.

"They shouldn't need to be moved, should they?"

"No. But I'm not taking anything for granted...not after the mustangs."

"That's smart," she said.

"Okay. This does it for now. Let's let them get comfortable here. I'll check on them later and maybe give them treats."

"Will they be okay?"

"They'll miss Storm and Steele Trap Ranch. That's familiar territory. But they'll also trust she wouldn't leave them in a bad place," he said.

"That's a lot of trust."

"True. And we want to make sure their trust isn't broken here."

She looked into the intelligent eyes watching them. She smiled, liking their gentle composure. They were a calm, comforting, beautiful presence. She liked them. She could easily understand why this group had a huge online following of fans.

"I'll be back later." Cole reached out and gently stroked fingertips down Fernando's long nose.

Fernando tossed his head.

"Guess he's not quite ready to make friends," she said.

"We'll get there." Cole turned away from the stalls. "Ready to go?"

"Yes. We'd better eat what Granny sent before it gets cold."

"Let's do it."

She walked back down the aisle with him, out the door, and waited while he made sure the keyless entry was secure behind them.

"Here, let me carry the food. It's probably getting heavy by now," he said.

"It's okay."

"Come on, let me…"

"You just want to be in control of the food." She chuckled as she handed the bag to him.

"You know it." He laughed as he clutched the sack in one hand. With the other, he clasped her fingers.

As they walked hand in hand toward the house, she felt content…and hopeful that all would work out for the best.

Inside, they went straight to the kitchen. He set the sack on top of the bar, then started taking containers out of it.

"What did Granny send for us? Smells delicious." She selected paper plates, napkins, and silverware, then set them on the bar.

"Sure does." He started popping open containers. "Looks like she outdid herself."

"Good. I'm getting used to Wildcat Bluff food and don't know if I could ever live without it now."

"Glad to hear it, since you're never going to be without it."

She just chuckled as she peeked into one container after another. "Fried okra. Potato salad. Coleslaw. Red beans and rice. Lemon pie."

"But here's the important container."

"What?" She looked around his broad shoulder.

"Bet we've got two pounds of smoked meat. Turkey. Chicken. Sausage. Beef. And barbeque sauce."

"That'll last us for days!"

"Hah. You maybe. Not me," he said.

"True. I've seen you eat."

"Let's get to it."

"Go ahead and sit down while I get the tea," she said.

"Thanks."

Pretty quick, she had ice in glasses, tea poured, and food on her plate. She scarfed down a slice of sausage first, moaning in delight at the flavor.

"I'm going to have to do some more grilling," he said.

"We have plenty here."

"I want you happy with the food I cook for you, not Slade's."

"Oh my." She leaned back on her stool and looked at him. "Jealous?"

"Always." He grinned, then chomped down on a piece of beef with gusto. "And forever."

"You're just looking for trouble."

"Think you can give it to me?" he asked.

"I could…but would I?"

He grinned even bigger. "With a little persuasion, I bet you'll give me all the trouble I want."

She smiled back at him. "Might be. But are you cowboy enough to handle it?"

He set down his fork, going serious. "Are you questioning my cowboy credentials?"

"Just letting you know the honor of all cowboys everywhere is on the line here."

"And I need to uphold their romantic integrity?"

"Something like that."

He glanced around the kitchen again, as if measuring counter-top heights for optimal use, like he'd done before. He turned his gaze back to her, as if the cabinets weren't good enough, and held out his hand.

She clasped his long fingers, smiling in anticipation. She realized she'd just challenged him...and the cowboy in him couldn't possibly turn down a challenge.

He led her into the living room, where he pushed back furniture until a section of tile floor was exposed in the center.

She had no idea what he had in mind. Maybe she should've just been satisfied with a piece of pie. Slade's, of course... And that brought a smile to her lips thinking about how it would affect Cole if he knew what was on her mind. She licked her lips in anticipation. She had no doubt that whatever Cole came up with would be so much better.

He walked over to the fireplace, looked through several thumb drives, then inserted one in the small electronic device on top of the mantel. Music filled the room and Dolly Parton sang "I Will Always Love You."

Audrey went still as Cole's message drove deep into her heart. Love. Were they at that place? Had they been there from the first moment they met? Or had the feeling come on gradually over time? She didn't know. She didn't care. She just knew they were there...and she didn't want to be any other place.

He held out his arms.

She slipped into them.

He pulled her close.

And then he began to dance, leading her in the time-honored two-step that filled dance halls and honky-tonks throughout Texas most nights of the week. She put her head on his shoulder and he tugged her closer, molding their bodies together as if they were one. One slow dance after another, the songs changed but his message didn't. He held her as if he would never let her go...and she wanted to always remain in his arms.

After a time, he nuzzled her ear, nibbling, kissing, teasing with his hot breath. "How am I doing?"

"You're about to win the buckle."

"I could sure use another."

"Bet you don't have enough," she said.

"Not this one. What would it say?"

"Let's see...World's Best Cowboy Firefighter to the Rescue."

"What rescue?" he asked.

"Let's see...extinguishing flames."

"Thought I started them," he said.

"Let's see...All-Around Cowboy Hotness."

He chuckled. "I think we're getting somewhere."

"Where?"

"Wherever you want to go."

"Do I have to wait?" she asked.

"Never." He pressed kisses down her neck, lingering in that sensitive place between neck and shoulder.

She shivered at his touch, feeling her body ignite in response. No, she didn't want to wait. *It doesn't get any better than country music and cowboy kisses.*

She slipped her fingers into his thick hair and lowered his face until she could reach his lips. She kissed him long and deep and slow as they continued to dance in an ever tighter circle.

He stroked her back, pressing her into him, moving his hands lower and lower until he clasped her bottom and pulled her into his hardness.

She shivered again. He was definitely on the right path to winning that big buckle, the multicolor one with glass stones and gold filigree.

"Audrey, I feel like the buzzer sounded and my timing's good, but I'm hanging on for dear life."

"Do you need help?"

"Yes...*you.*"

"Time to win that big buckle, is it?" she asked.

"Time to win *you.*"

"I just threw out the timer."

"Good. It's not about time. It's all about *you,*" he said.

"Let's move to the sofa." She spread the soft cotton throw over the smooth leather sofa, and then lay back against it, raised her hands over her head, and gave him a come-hither look.

He stood there a long moment simply looking at her, brown eyes like melted chocolate. He finally sighed on a long exhale of breath. "I take that back about the timer."

"Really?"

"I may win the world record for fast."

"Really that ready?" she asked.

"Do I still get the buckle?"

"Really want it?"

"Yes."

"The *All-Around Cowboy Hotness* buckle isn't given for time, short or long. It's given for heat," she said.

"Good to know. I'm burning up."

"Short of a fire extinguisher or AC, I know of only one way to fix it."

"I hope it's the way I have in mind."

She held out her arms to him. "Come here...and win your buckle."

He gave her a hot smile as he scooped her up into his arms and sat down with her on his lap.

"Good start."

"It gets better...and this time I'm prepared. Condom in my pocket."

"Let's see."

He pulled it out and set it on the table.

"That's my cowboy."

"I can't wait…not upstairs, not anywhere else," he said.

She was so hot she couldn't wait another moment. She rose to her knees and straddled him. She unbuckled his belt, undid the button, and unzipped his jeans. He was more than ready. She reached down, released his long, hard length, and slipped on the condom.

He quickly jerked down her jeans and thong, then tossed them aside. He grasped her hips, positioned her above him, and drove in deep.

She gasped at the delicious sensation. She held on to his shoulders as she rode him, matching his rhythm with one of her own as he drove harder and faster and deeper. She moaned. He groaned. And they went over the edge together, kissing deeply and passionately as they rode the crest of the wave and then gently came to shore…in each other's arms.

He lay down on the sofa. She snuggled to his chest. They took deep breaths, relaxing together to the sounds of country love songs.

"Did I win my buckle?" he asked in a husky voice.

"And your spurs."

"Those too?" he asked.

"Yeah."

"I must be good."

"You're the best," she said.

"Just what I wanted to hear."

"Are you hungry?"

"Starved," he said.

"We've got lots of food…"

"Just waiting for us."

"But I'm so relaxed I'm not sure I can move."

"No need. I'll go clean up, fix a tray, and bring you tasty treats," he said.

"Thanks."

He kissed her lips, tucked a soft throw around her, and then left the room.

She yawned, stretched, and felt utterly content. For the moment, she didn't care about bootlegger gold or stolen mustangs or cattle in the horse barn. It might be selfish, but she only cared about being happy in Cole's home. She closed her eyes and let sleep overtake her.

"Audrey, wake up," Cole said.

She pulled up out of a deep sleep because he sounded urgent. She opened her eyes. He'd changed to a tee and sweatpants, but he didn't hold a tray of food. Instead, he held out his cell phone to her. She abruptly sat up.

"It's for you."

She felt a little confused, dazed even. "Is that my phone?"

"No, it's mine."

"Why is someone calling me on your phone?"

"It's Nocona Jones," he said.

"The attorney?"

"Yes. She didn't have your number, but she knew you were staying here," he said.

"Why is she calling me?"

"She didn't say, but she wouldn't call on a lark. It's bound to be important."

"But why me?" she asked.

"Don't know." He thrust the phone toward her.

She took it but felt wary. She needed to get the cobwebs out of her head for this call.

"Nocona's waiting," he said.

"Hello." She hit speakerphone just in case she needed Cole's help in whatever was coming out of the blue.

"Audrey Oakes?" a brisk feminine voice asked.

"Yes."

"You're the daughter of Vivian Oakes?"

"Yes," Audrey said.

"And you're the granddaughter of Mimi Oakes?"

"Yes."

"I've been asked to contact you in regards to your family."

"Oh." Audrey gasped. "Nothing's happened to them, has it?"

"Not at all. Excuse me. I didn't mean to alarm you."

"Good."

"I understand you have been in contact with Jake Oakes."

"I didn't know his last name was Oakes," Audrey said.

"He changed it to that some years ago."

"All right. It just seems odd considering my last name."

"You won't think so once you are made aware of the nature of my call."

Audrey looked at Cole and shrugged her shoulders, not able to imagine where this conversation was going from here.

He leaned forward, appearing concerned for her.

"All right." Audrey was glad when Cole sat down beside her and put a comforting arm around her shoulders. She leaned into him.

"Jake asked me to tell you that he decided after your last visit that time was of the essence. Otherwise, he would have told you this news himself," Nocona said.

"Oh no, he's sick." Audrey could hardly stand the thought.

"Not at all. He is as hale and hearty as ever. However, he is over a hundred years old, so he is aware of time limitations."

"We are all constrained by time," Audrey said.

"True…but Jake feels it more than most of us." Nocona cleared her throat. "Jake has informed me that he would like to take a paternity test to ascertain whether or not he is the father of your grandmother."

"What?" Audrey clutched Cole's hand, shivering all over.

"He thought you might not be too surprised by the news."

"Of course I'm surprised. I'm shocked. And if it's true, that'd make him my…"

"Great-grandfather," Nocona said. "And what a wonderful gift that would be to your family. And Jake."

"He's never been in our lives. Why now?"

"Jake didn't know you existed until you turned up on his doorstep. He's been thinking about it, wondering about the timing, considering the connections ever since he met you," Nocona said.

"He didn't mention it."

"Not directly, but I believe he let you know in other subtle ways."

Audrey sat up straight. "I like Jake. He's become a friend. And he's been very helpful in my research. But he's not part of my family. I can't imagine why he'd suddenly want to push his way into it."

"He's not trying to push his way into your family. He understands you are a close-knit family. What he wants to know is whether or not he had a child with Lady Mauve all those years ago."

"If she'd wanted him to know, I'm sure she would have told him. She didn't, so I sincerely doubt we're related to him," Audrey said.

"I regret you feel that way."

"How else could I feel? This is a total surprise." Audrey clutched Cole's hand harder. She felt as if she was losing her family. First, Mom with Gerald. Now, Mimi with Jake. It'd always been the three of them—all for one and one for all. But now...

"Jake would like to know if your grandmother would be willing to take a DNA test to establish relationship."

"She's in a nursing home," Audrey said. "She's not well. She doesn't need to be agitated or disturbed in any way."

"Audrey." Cole squeezed her hand. "If this is true, think what it would mean to Jake. He's lived so long on his memories of Lady Mauve. And your grandmother would surely like to know her father."

Audrey took a deep breath, feeling pushed in a direction she didn't want to go. Why couldn't she be glad about the prospect?

Again, it felt like she was losing, not gaining. Still, Cole was right. She shouldn't stand in the way of other people's happiness.

"Jake and I would like your permission to contact your grandmother through the nursing home and go from there," Nocona said.

Audrey took a deep breath. "I believe my grandmother should be eased into this situation. I prefer that she not have any sudden shocks."

"We absolutely agree."

"My mother is in Hot Springs. She could explain in person. She should be the one to handle our end of the paternity test," Audrey said.

"That is quite reasonable. Besides, she could be Jake's granddaughter."

"Perhaps."

"Nocona," Cole said, "do you want Audrey to contact her mother and ask her to call you to set up a test?"

"Cole, thank you. I understand this is quite shocking. Audrey, would that be acceptable to you?"

"Yes. I'll call her soon."

"Cole can give you my number here at the office and my cell for elsewhere. And please, take action now."

"Okay," Audrey said. "I'll do it."

"Thank you. I'll look forward to talking with her soon. Goodbye."

Audrey handed Cole's phone back to him. She sat there, feeling too stunned to move.

"Jake's a great guy. You'd be lucky to have him in your family," Cole said.

"I know. It's just the shock."

"Why don't you call your mom, and then we'll eat? I'll get your phone and be right back." He stood up and walked over to the bar.

She felt numb, not excited or upset, just numb. How had this happened? She'd come to Wildcat Bluff for bootlegger gold. And yet everything kept spiraling out of control.

"Here you go." Cole handed her the phone and sat down beside her.

She held the phone for a long moment, then gathered the courage to call her mother even though she knew it might change all their lives.

"Dear heart, what's up?" Vivian answered her cell.

"Mom, when great-grandmother Mauve came to Hot Springs, was she pregnant?"

Vivian inhaled sharply. "It's not something we talk about. Back then if a woman got pregnant out of wedlock, she was considered loose and it hurt her reputation."

Audrey sat up straight, holding the throw to her tightly with one hand...as if for comfort or defense. "Are you telling me Lady Mauve arrived in Hot Springs with a bun in the oven?"

"Well, yes, I guess that's one way to put it. We didn't tell you before because there was no need for you to know."

Audrey fell back against the sofa, feeling as if her world had been rocked anew.

"Why? Has something happened?" Vivian asked.

"Jake wants to take a paternity test."

"What?"

"And he changed his last name some years ago to Oakes," Audrey said.

"Are you saying that..."

"He believes he may be Mimi's dad."

"Really?" Vivian said. "But that would be absolutely remarkable. He would be my grandfather. Your great-grandfather. After all these years of not knowing, of wondering, and suddenly out of the blue..."

"We don't know it for a fact."

"But it sort of fits, doesn't it?" Vivian asked.

"Maybe."

"He wants to know for sure, doesn't he?"

"Yes. A local attorney just called me. She wants to contact Mimi about setting up a test. I told her that she should go through you. But what do you think?" Audrey asked.

"One way or another, we should all know the truth. I'm excited about the prospect, aren't you?"

"Not really. I've got so much on my plate already…"

"No matter what we find out, it won't change our lives much."

"I'm not so sure about that," Audrey said.

"Give me the number. I'll get this ball rolling. Mimi is going to be totally excited about the possibility of finding her father."

"I don't want her to be disappointed if it turns out Jake isn't related to us."

"She's a tough old bird. She'll be fine either way," Vivian said.

"Jake's attorney is Nocona Jones. I'll get her phone numbers from Cole and text them to you."

"Thanks," Vivian said. "And, Audrey, this is just one more exciting thing to come out of Wildcat Bluff. I'm beginning to feel an even deeper connection to the place."

"I wouldn't get too attached just yet. As soon as I find the gold—"

"I already told you. *You* are the gold," Vivian said.

"But you're my mom. Naturally you'd say that."

Vivian chuckled. "Send me those numbers. Mimi will want to get on this right away. She's waited a lifetime to find out about her father."

"Okay. Talk later. Love you."

"Love you, too." And Vivian was gone.

Audrey tossed her phone on the table, then looked at Cole. "What is this county doing to me?"

He smiled, tenderness warming his eyes. "Wildcat Bluff is bringing you home."

Chapter 24

A WEEK LATER, COLE STOOD IN FRONT OF FERNANDO'S STALL IN the barn. The big bull had accepted his change of locale and, even better, now considered Cole a friend—not on the order of Storm, but acceptable company. Cole stroked Fernando's long nose with the palm of his hand while Daisy Sue, Little Fernando, and Margarita ate hay in the outdoor runs, soaking up the sun.

Fernando's fans didn't know he was in hiding because Storm was posting old photos and updates about the twins' participation in the upcoming Wildcat Bluff County Spring Stock Show. Fernando's hideout had to be the best kept secret in the county, and it was increasingly necessary because Zane Ranch was upping the pressure to get the big bull and the twins transferred from Steele Trap to Zane. Any day those armed cowboys might decide to take matters into their own hands or be ordered to do it by the Zane head honcho.

Nocona Jones had her hands full with the matter, but she was holding her own if not gaining ground with Zane. She was making progress with Jake's paternity request, despite Audrey's concern about it. In fact, Audrey hadn't been back to see Jake since she'd received the news. She said she'd be uncomfortable until they got the results back and she knew one way or another if they were family. Cole understood she didn't want her grandmother upset, but on the other hand, he hoped they'd learn that Jake was related to her. For now, they were waiting for the test results to come back.

He planned to go out later and ride the ranch like he'd been doing every day, searching for some clue to the missing mustangs.

He was overlooking something important, he just knew it. He guessed Audrey felt the same way about the bootlegger gold. She was out there today, searching for another location mentioned in Lady Mauve's diary. Nothing could dissuade her that the legend was nothing more than a legend.

Bottom line, not much had changed. It felt like they were all stuck in molasses, struggling to get a leg up on their situations. So far it wasn't happening and he was frustrated as all get-out.

He patted Fernando's head again, then turned and walked down the aisle. Outside, he made sure the door was locked tight. He didn't like it, but he kept Folgie and Max in the patio area now, so they didn't disturb Fernando and the others. He preferred them outside on patrol, but for now this was the way it had to be.

As he strode up to the house, his phone alerted him to an incoming call. He pulled the cell out of his pocket and checked the caller. Ernie. Now that surprised him. He hadn't ordered food. Maybe Audrey had done it to surprise him.

"Hey, Ernie," he answered.

"Got a pizza here with your name on it," she said.

"Pizza? Did Audrey order it?"

"No. You did."

"I did?" he asked.

"Forgot, did you?"

"Guess so."

"Anyhow, best you get right over here and pick it up," Ernie said.

He hesitated, trying to process what she was telling him. If Audrey hadn't ordered a pizza and he hadn't ordered a pizza, then what was up?

"Don't want it to get cold, now do you?"

"No." He'd better go along with her. She wanted him at the diner and this was her way of getting him there, no other way to see it.

"You'll head my way now?" she asked.

"Yes. I'll see you in a bit."

"Right." And she clicked off.

He put his phone back in his pocket and stood there for a moment. He could put off checking out that back pasture. He doubted he'd find anything helpful, but he had to keep trying to find a clue to the mustangs. The horse thieves hadn't been back to the dump, but he hadn't expected it. He hadn't lost any more horses to them either, but that was about what he'd expected, too. One thing after another just didn't add up, and now Ernie's call didn't make sense either.

He'd go see her, find out what was going on, and pick up a pizza. At least the pizza would be worth the drive to Ranger Corner.

He glanced around the compound to make sure everything looked normal, then he jumped in his pickup. He sent a text to Audrey to let her know where he was going and that he'd bring pizza home for supper.

He hit Wildcat Road, where everything looked normal. That was a relief because too much in his life was spiraling into the not-normal realm. But he was rolling with it just like he was rolling with Ernie's request, or more like entreaty, to get to her soon. He pressed down on the accelerator.

Ranches flew by, green leaves, green grass, colts, and calves. Spring was a great time of year with everything coming on strong, changing day to day, and growing fast. Maybe that's what it was. He was caught up in springtime.

Audrey *was* springtime. She'd arrived with a nourishing rain that filled ponds and caused crops to grow. He'd never thought much about the birds and bees until now. Audrey had taught him love was the answer to the unfulfilled hunger that had ridden him hard until she had arrived at his ranch. She might not realize it yet, but she belonged with him on the GTT and in Wildcat Bluff. She just needed time to sort out her feelings…and he'd happily help her do it.

For now, he'd see about Ernie. He turned off the highway, hit the dirt road, and came upon the sadly neglected group of buildings. Unlike Old Town or Sure-Shot, Ranger Corner hadn't been maintained over the years. Folks had just left, like so many ghost towns, and never come back—except for the diner.

He pulled up in front of the train car and cut the engine. Ernie must have been watching for him because she popped out the door and down the steps with a big pizza box in hand. She looked left and right, as if making sure nobody was around to see her, before she opened his passenger door and sat down beside him.

She dropped the box on the floorboard and turned to him.

"Is there a pizza in that box or is it just a prop?"

"Sausage. Pepperoni. Tomatoes. Onions. And pineapple."

"Sounds good. How much do I owe you?" he asked.

"Nothing. It's on the house."

"What's going on? Are you in trouble? What?"

She adjusted her eyeglasses, then shrugged a shoulder and winced. "Feels like the Black Widow is biting me."

"New tattoo?"

"You know it."

"Painful?" he asked.

"Those needles hurt, but it's worth it. Now, some folks like the pain. Not me. I do it strictly for the final outcome."

"How many more scream queens are you going to do?"

"As long as I've got bare skin, I've got a place for another one. Those beauties deserve to be immortalized on me," she said.

"Better you than me."

"Squeamish, huh?"

"I prefer to be pain-free."

"Got you." She shook her head. "You got me totally off track."

"Scream queens will do that."

"Sure will." She grinned, then looked serious. "Thanks for getting right out here."

"No problem."

"Okay. Here's the deal. I wanted to tell you in person. Never know who's listening on phone calls in this day and age," she said.

"What deal?"

"Zane Ranch."

He sat up straight, suddenly all ears. "Nowadays that outfit is nothing but trouble."

"Tell me about it." She leaned toward him. "I mean, really, who gets attitude about pizza?"

"Don't they pay?"

"They pay, but those cowboys get real snarky if every little bit of a pizza isn't exactly to their specifications. Give me a break. Haven't they ever heard of artistic license?" she asked.

"Maybe not when it involves pizza."

"Probably not when it involves anything." She shook her head as if getting rid of cobwebs. "Anyway, I was out there last night, delivering four extra-large give-it-everything-you've-got pizzas to their cowboy bunkhouse."

"And what?"

"I just happened to be a little slow getting back to my vehicle."

"And? If you draw this out any longer, I'm going—"

"Hold your horses." She grinned at her own joke. "It's spring-time. Weather's nice. Windows were open."

"And you were listening."

"Once they'd decided I'd actually made the pizzas right, they forgot me."

"That's handy."

"Sure was." She took off her glasses, then put them back on. "Now I could be all wet, but I don't think so."

"Just spit it out."

"I think they've got your mustangs."

"Oh hell...you're kidding me," he said.

"No. Now, like I said, I could be wrong."

"Now that you've pointed a finger at them, I can believe it. There's something seriously wrong on that ranch. They've gone after Fernando and the twins. Now this news. But what makes you think so?" he asked.

"How do you get rodeo stock? I mean broncs that'll go wild under a saddle and rider."

He sat there a moment, letting her words sink in.

"Rodeo stock brings a pretty penny. You know it. I know it."

"No markings of any kind. Clean as a whistle. They could be sold one by one and distributed across the country," he said thoughtfully. "And nobody the wiser."

"Maybe even cash under the table."

"Is that what you heard?" he asked.

"Not exactly. I wasn't getting it all since I was outside, but I heard enough relevant words to draw a conclusion. Rodeo stock. Mustangs. GTT Ranch. County dump."

"Yeah. If put in the right context, those are definitely the right words."

"If you hadn't been telling me what was going on, I wouldn't have thought anything about it," she said.

"Glad I did."

"You know I'm out and about in the county, so I see and hear stuff nobody else does."

"Good thing, too," he said.

"This time for sure."

"But, Ernie, this is all hearsay. No proof whatsoever."

"That's your job."

"Sheriff Calhoun can't act on it either," Cole said.

"You can. You must. You find those mustangs on Zane Ranch and those cowboys are busted but good."

"Zane covers a lot of territory."

"Think like a cowboy. What pastures suit wild mustangs? Where is there water and grass to keep them in tiptop shape?" she asked.

"I'll check topographical maps. Maybe talk with some old-timers who might know that ranchland. If those mustangs are there, I'll find them…one way or another."

"Be careful. Those guys are like coiled rattlers. They're spoiling for a fight. I mean, give me a break. They almost got into it with me over pizza," she said.

"Don't they know you're armed and a sure shot?"

She smiled, looking smug. "I always pack a little something in my cowgirl boot to deal with trouble. I'm a fast draw, too."

"Don't doubt it for a minute."

"Seriously, Cole. You may want to talk with the sheriff before you go off half-cocked."

"What he doesn't know won't hurt any of us or him."

"True enough," she said.

"Now you've pointed me in this direction, will you keep your eyes and ears open for Zane?"

"You got it. I'll make all their deliveries myself."

"But be careful. It's not worth getting hurt over," he said.

"Are you kidding? My scream queens would never allow harm to come to my body." She grinned, chuckling, and opened the door. "Anyway, I best not be seen in your company while this operation is hot."

"Thanks. I owe you."

She looked him up and down with a coy expression. "And you know just how you can repay me."

"Way things stand now, I don't dare step out of line."

"So Audrey's the one, huh?"

He grinned, nodding but not saying.

"Lucky her." Ernie opened the door, stepped out, and hurried back into the diner.

He just sat there for a moment. Zane Ranch. He needed to take a closer look at the operation. It used to be an okay outfit. Something had shifted. But what? It'd require more than getting land stats. Had the place changed hands? New owners could make a world of difference. He hadn't paid much attention until now, not with the missing mustangs so much on his mind.

Zane had gone after Steele Trap. Maybe they'd gone after GTT, too. Cattle rustlers were working the local ranches. Was that Zane? For the first time, he began to see a pattern…and it wasn't a good one.

He put his truck in gear and headed out. Wildcat Bluff County didn't stand for this kind of nonsense. They had a tight-knit community that pulled together at the first sign of trouble. Well, they sure had trouble and it was time to pull together. If Zane was behind it, they'd just stirred up a hornet's nest.

He drove straight to the Chuckwagon Café in Old Town. He needed a confab with Granny and her personal posse a.k.a. her kids. He parked a few slots down from the front of the café because it was busy as usual. He sandwiched his one-ton in between other big trucks and hit the boardwalk.

Just as he started to open the front door, it swung out. He stepped back as three cowboys filed out of the café. He didn't know them. Dark hair. Dark eyes. Tanned skin. They could've been local cowboys in typical Western shirts, jeans, hats, and boots, but the smirks and swaggers belonged elsewhere, if anywhere at all.

When they saw him, they spread out and one of them bumped his shoulder, he figured on purpose. The guy stopped and made an exaggerated expression of surprise.

Cole got ready to fight. No other reason for the bump. No other reason for the stop. No other reason to crowd him on the boardwalk.

"Excuse me." The guy who'd bumped him gave a sharklike smile. "Don't believe we've met."

"No, we haven't," Cole said as he took stock of his surroundings. They were the only ones on the boardwalk, but there would be plenty of locals inside.

"I'm Sug Culley. I ramrod the Zane. Chap and Tony here work the ranch."

Cole just nodded, on high alert now that he knew who they were. But what did they want?

"Aren't you Cole Murphy? GTT Ranch?" Sug asked.

Cole gave another nod.

"Not real talkative, are you?" Sug asked.

"No reason to be," Cole said.

"Just being friendly." Sug's smile was more of a smirk. "Heard you have a little trouble keeping your mustangs on your range."

Cole returned the smile. Now they were getting somewhere. If he hadn't believed before Zane Ranch was the troublemaker, he was getting there fast. This guy couldn't resist driving the knife in and twisting it.

"Any luck getting them back?"

"Wish I could say I had, but I'm afraid those horses are long gone." Cole could play this game. Sug wanted info on the investigation, but he was never going to get anywhere near the truth.

"Right sorry to hear it," Sug said.

"Thanks." Cole did his best to look downcast. "Lots of trouble going on in Wildcat Bluff about now."

"That's what I hear," Sug said. "We may be new around here, but if we can be of any help, just let us know."

"That's right neighborly of you."

"We aim to be good neighbors," Sug said. "Ranchers gotta stick together."

"I hear you."

"Good to meet you." Sug tipped his hat, then headed down the boardwalk with his two friends behind him.

Cole noted no shaking of hands, not friendly at all. He jerked open the café door and stalked inside, holding down his anger by sheer force of will. Zane Ranch had an attitude all right. Sug had just about called him out for breathing the same air. Good neighbor, ha. Nothing but veiled threats.

He glanced around for Granny. They needed a one-on-one

pronto. He didn't see her, but she must have seen him because she came out of the back and motioned him over to her private table in the corner.

He jerked out a chair and sat down hard.

"Simmer down." She perched on a chair near him. "I saw it all on our camera that monitors the door."

"Sug Culley, huh?"

"Yep. He's the mover and shaker at Zane. Wouldn't want to get him cornered."

"More like he's the one doing the cornering around here," Cole said.

"Best that's what he thinks for now. As long as he believes he's the predator and we're the prey, he's off guard."

"I thought that was us."

Granny leaned closer. "He thinks by the time he's done, Zane is gonna own this county."

"Never happen."

"Right." She looked him over. "You're not here for food. What's happened? Are your guests enjoying their accommodations?"

"Yes, they are. This isn't about them."

"Better let me order you something, so our little confab looks on the up and up. What do you want?"

"I don't know. I'm so mad I'm not hungry. I swear he threatened me."

"Got you. I've been on that end of his sharp, oily tongue." She stood up. "How about breakfast?"

"It's the middle of the afternoon."

"Comfort food, that's the ticket. Be back in a jiff." And she headed for the kitchen.

He leaned back in his chair and took several deep breaths. It wouldn't do to let a lowlife like Sug Culley get to him. If Sug had hurt one hair on the mustangs, he was going to get steep payback.

By the time Granny came back with a tray of food, he was a

little more under control, but it only meant his anger had gone deep and he was simmering mad now…a mad that lived on. Sug was a fool for making enemies in Wildcat Bluff right and left. He'd only do that if he thought he had the upper hand. It was about time somebody, or a county, taught him a lesson he'd never forget.

Granny unloaded her tray with a quick dexterity developed over years of practice.

Cole picked up the cup of coffee first and took a big sip while he eyed the overflowing plate of fried steak, hash browns, and biscuits and gravy. He developed a sudden appetite and dived into the lot.

"Glad to see a cowboy with a yen for my cooking," Granny said with a smile. "Get that down your gullet and tell me what brought you here in an all-fire hurry."

He did exactly as she said to do, taking more pleasure in the food than usual with the sharp taste of adrenaline still in his mouth. When he'd cleaned his plate, he leaned back and picked up his coffee. He downed it and looked at her.

"Ready?" she asked.

"Ernie called me to pick up a pizza."

Granny raised an eyebrow.

"I didn't order it."

She raised both eyebrows.

"Zane cowboys tend to complain about her pizzas."

"They do lack manners. Wouldn't be a bit surprised if they were all raised in a barn."

"That's the least of it." Cole paused, glanced around, and leaned closer to her to make sure what he said stayed private. "From what she overheard there, she thinks they're the horse thieves."

Granny nodded.

"We put your trouble with my trouble with the county's cattle trouble together…"

"And came up with Zane Ranch."

"Yep. But you're not surprised at my news," he said.

"We've been getting there, putting this and that together. It's an ugly picture."

"The ugliest."

"Nocona's been looking into the ranch," Granny said.

"Guess it's about time somebody did."

"They weren't up-front with us, so we had to. They've kept you and the other ranchers in the dark."

"What did she find out?" he asked.

"All-hat-and-no-cattle guy out of Dallas got his hands on the ranch. He's having trouble hanging on to it. That's why he came after Fernando."

"Quick, easy bucks." Cole gave it a little more thought. "But how did he find out about Fernando's history?"

"Folks talk. Cowboys come and go. Word gets out. If you're looking for something to use, you can usually find it."

"Yeah. So the Dallas guy needs money. That explains the horse thieves and the cattle rustlers."

"Right."

"He's desperate, then. If we don't stop him, he'll keep escalating till he eats up our county," Cole said.

"That's the truth."

"Okay. I figure if we bring Sug Culley to heel, the others will fall into line," Cole said.

"All-hat-and-no-cattle has met his match in Wildcat Bluff."

Cole grinned at Granny and she grinned back.

A meeting of minds had been achieved.

Chapter 25

AUDREY SAT IN HER SUV IN FRONT OF THE COUNTY DUMP that was closed for the day. She'd just revisited the post oak and taken more photographs, not that she thought it would do much good. She still couldn't make out the initials. No, she'd started coming here more as a pilgrimage than anything. It was the one place she had found something from the past. Not bootlegger gold, of course, but at least it was something from Lady Mauve's time and it had helped Mimi reconnect with life.

She didn't want to give up on finding the gold, but she had to admit she was discouraged at the prospect. Cole's words that the gold was just a legend, nothing more, haunted her. Worse, none of the leads from Lady Mauve's journal had panned out. She didn't know where to go from here.

On the plus side, she'd gathered wonderful material for the book she now intended to write. All her stories had motivated Mimi. And then there was Cole Murphy. If she was the gold in her mother's life, Cole was surely the gold in her life. How could she even think of returning to Hot Springs and her old world after living with him? She hadn't expected to meet a wonderful man and fall in love. And yet she'd done exactly that.

Still, Mom and Mimi were in Hot Springs. She couldn't imagine life without them nearby. As far as Jake Oakes, she'd heard nothing on the paternity test, but she worried about it. She liked him. She didn't want a rift between them. Still, she didn't want anything to destabilize her grandmother's slow but steady improvement. Maybe her mother was right that Mimi might recover without experimental medical care. She knew people could heal on their own, but she would still like to find the gold as backup.

She'd done what she could do for the day. She ought to head back to GTT, but she lingered because she felt closer to her great-grandmother here and she felt a need for inspiration. If she left, she could go to Ernie's for pizza or the Chuckwagon for barbeque or the store for a couple of steaks. But she didn't move, waiting, watching... Something was building, something was coming her way.

When her phone chirped, she wasn't even surprised at the sound. She picked it up and hit speakerphone. No FaceTime today, so it would be all voice.

"Audrey!" Vivian sounded breathless.

"Yes?"

"We have news...great news!"

"Really?" Audrey sounded cautious and knew it, but she was concerned about her loved ones.

"Audrey!" Mimi sounded just as breathless.

"Mimi, how are you? It's so good to hear your voice."

"Yours, too, dear heart," Mimi said. "Are you sitting down?"

"Yes."

"Vivian, do you want to tell her?" Mimi asked.

"No, Mom. I'll let you run with it."

"Thank you."

"What news?" Audrey asked, wondering if this road led straight to Jake Oakes.

"We got the paternity results back," Mimi said.

"And?"

"He's my daddy!" Mimi said in a little girl's voice, breaking with emotion on the last word.

Audrey felt chills run up her spine. So it was true. If she'd felt protective of her grandmother before, now she felt doubly so. Jake was a good man, well liked, well respected, but he now had the power to hurt her loved ones…even her. He was the daddy none of them had ever had, and for the first time, she realized just how much they must have missed a father figure in their lives. Family friends helped, but it just wasn't the same. Blood ran thicker than water. And she'd felt that deep connection with Jake from the very first moment.

"Audrey, what do you have to say?" Vivian asked in a concerned voice. "He's your great-grandfather."

"I'm not sure what to say. I'm sort of stunned at the news."

"Be happy for us," Mimi said. "Oh, how I wish Mama were here to be with us all…a real, complete family at last."

"Did you talk with him?" Audrey asked.

"Yes!" Mimi said. "And his attorney requested you visit him right away."

"I'm not sure I want to."

"What? Whyever not?" Mimi sounded shocked.

"It's so sudden. And…and…"

"You're worried about our hearts, aren't you?" Vivian asked.

"I don't want any of us to get hurt."

"Audrey Oakes, I'm ashamed of you," Mimi said. "You have this amazing opportunity to be with your great-grandfather. You should be thanking your lucky stars instead of shunning them."

"It's not that. It's—"

"Mom, she doesn't trust him. She's never known a man to be there for us in her lifetime."

"That's right," Audrey replied.

"There's always a first time for everything," Mimi said.

"True." Vivian chuckled. "Might I mention Gerald, Cole, and now Jake. We've gone from no men to lots of fine men."

"Please open your heart to Jake," Mimi said. "If for no other reason than it would make me happy."

"I guess I could go see him again." Audrey didn't want to cause unhappiness in her family.

"Give him a chance," Vivian said. "I gave Gerald a chance and he is a great blessing in my life. Don't you feel the same about Cole?"

"Yes, I do." Audrey sighed. "You're both right, but still I'm going to be cautious."

"Caution is good," Vivian said.

"No, it's not!" Mimi snorted. "I'm done with being cautious. See where it got me? Nursing home hell. I'm out of here and never coming back."

"That's a lovely place," Audrey said. "They care about you."

"I'm throwing out my walker and snagging the first plane, train, or car going to Wildcat Bluff," Mimi said.

"What?" Audrey asked in shock.

"That's right. I'll be winging my way to my ancestral home."

"What your grandmother means, dear heart, is that we're driving over tomorrow," Vivian said.

"But Mimi can't leave the nursing home. She needs skilled care." Audrey was so alarmed, she dropped her phone, fumbled around on the floorboard, and picked it up again.

"Ha!" Mimi snorted. "I checked myself out today. Left my diaper on the bed and that place in my dust."

"Mom?" Audrey asked. "What did her doctors say? I doubt they'd agree to her just taking off to Texas."

"No doctors. I fired every last one of them." Mimi snorted again. "They had me one foot in the grave and the other on a slippery slope."

"They were taking care of you," Audrey said.

"They can take care of somebody else."

"Mom?" Audrey asked.

"Daddy needs me," Mimi said. "I'm coming to Wildcat Bluff to take care of him. I'm moving into his farmhouse tomorrow."

"What? At your age?" Audrey asked, feeling more worried by the moment.

"He says I'm a spring chicken."

"Well, I guess in comparison to him, you are," Audrey said. "But that's not the point. You fell. What if you do it again out in the middle of nowhere?"

"I don't have time to fall. Daddy and I are going to farm. It's spring. We've got to get in the garden."

"Mom?" Audrey tried again for help injecting reason into the conversation.

"She's happy," Vivian said. "She's going to make up for lost time with her father. And we get to do the same thing. He's my grandfather. I can hardly wait to meet him. You've already had that privilege. Now it's our turn."

Audrey took a deep breath, realizing she'd lost her argument from the get-go. Safe or not, Mimi was coming to Wildcat Bluff. She'd tried to be the voice of reason, but she'd lost that battle. Now she felt a building excitement that she'd be with her family soon. And Jake? She hardly knew what to think except he'd turned her life upside down.

"We have more news for you," Vivian said with pride in her voice.

"Good, I hope."

"The best." Vivian chuckled. "Gerald is bringing us. We've made reservations to stay in this darling B&B called Twin Oaks. He's anxious to meet you."

"I'd like to meet him, too. And I guess y'all will want to meet Cole."

"Absolutely!" Mimi said. "I've got a soft spot for cowboy hunks."

Audrey glanced around the interior of her vehicle, wondering where she'd mislaid the grandmother she'd always known. Who was this sassy stranger?

"We can hardly wait to get to Wildcat Bluff," Vivian said.

"What about the store? Our life there?"

"I have one word and one word only on the matter," Vivian said. "Cole."

"We haven't made any type of commitment to each other."

"It's simply a matter of time," Mimi said.

"If y'all take that attitude with him, you're never meeting him. You'll just embarrass me all over the place."

Mimi chuckled. "He'll need your grandfather's approval to join the family."

"What?" Audrey finally just gave it up and started to laugh. She felt as if she must've stepped into somebody's sitcom and didn't know her lines.

"Oh…and another thing," Vivian said. "Gerald is going to look at available ranches while we're there. Did I mention he recently sold his business? He's looking to reinvest in something new."

"Gerald? Ranches?" Audrey's breath caught in her throat.

"Didn't you listen? We're all moving to Wildcat Bluff."

"Wouldn't Mom just love it!" Mimi chirped.

"Lady Mauve." Audrey shook her head. "You know, I have a feeling she might not even be surprised at this turn of events."

"She was a thinker, a planner, a doer," Mimi said. "Organizer, too. I wouldn't be one bit surprised if she didn't have this planned down to the last detail."

"I'm not sure I'd go that far," Audrey said.

"Loosen up," Mimi said. "Life is too short to watch your back trail. Keep your eyes on where you're going."

"Guess I'm going to see Jake."

"Be kind to him," Vivian said. "He loves us so."

"He doesn't even know us…I mean, all of us."

"Of course he does," Mimi said. "We're blood of his blood."

"Oh yes, another thing," Vivian said. "His attorney is preparing a new will to include us."

"He's moving fast." Audrey looked at her phone to make sure she really was having this conversation.

"At his age, and my age for that matter, we need to get all our ducks in a row," Mimi said.

"Whatever he wants to do with his farm is fine with me," Audrey said. "Before we dive off the deep end, I think we'd better consider our own business in Hot Springs. It won't run itself."

"I left it in good hands," Vivian said. "We'll cross that bridge when we come to it."

"We could open a bookstore in Wildcat Bluff," Mimi said. "I like to read."

"Gifts, too," Vivian said.

"In that case, at least one place would carry my book…if I ever get it written."

"Of course you will, dear," Mimi said. "I'm sure our dearest Lady Mauve would have covered that base in her plans, too. She wants her story told and you're going to tell it."

"And we're going to sell it," Vivian said.

Audrey sighed…and then she had an idea. "Old Town in Wildcat Bluff has wonderful shops. We aren't needed there."

"Oh no." Mimi sounded disappointed at that news.

"But there's this place called Ranger Corner that's pretty much a ghost town. Old, interesting, weathered buildings that could use restoration. Right now there's a fabulous diner and a great tattoo artist."

"That's it?" Vivian asked.

"Lots of potential. And I think you and Mimi would fit right in," Audrey said.

"What's the traffic like?" Mimi asked.

"Zilch unless you want pizza or a tat."

"Not encouraging," Vivian said.

"But we'd be in on the ground floor," Mimi said. "Besides, I'm in need of a tat."

"Really?" Audrey didn't know why she was even surprised. "In that case, you're going to love Ernestine. She's immortalizing all the classic scream queens in tattoos across her body."

"Oh my, how exciting," Mimi said. "I bet she doesn't have Fay

Wray of *King Kong* fame. She's one of my all-time faves. Boy howdy, could that girl scream her lungs out."

"You'll be able to see her on Ernie's arm," Audrey said.

"Wow! Vivian, dearest, put a visit to Ranger Corner high on our to-do list."

"Got it, Mom."

"You two are sounding more like Lady Mauve every moment. I wonder what she'd do with Ranger Corner," Audrey said.

"Books are good," Mimi said, "but in honor of Mama's legacy, maybe a honky-tonk would be better."

"Not a bad idea," Vivian agreed.

Audrey chuckled. "What I'm beginning to think is that you two are just flat-out bored with civilization. You might as well scrawl 'GTT,' as in *Gone to Texas*, on your door and hightail it to the West like in the old days."

"I'm ready," Mimi said. "Wish I'd done that on my nursing home door. They'd have been scratching their heads over that one."

"It's enough that you told them to put your wheelchair where the sun don't shine," Vivian said.

"She didn't!" Audrey couldn't keep from laughing at the idea.

"Did so," Mimi said. "They got between me and the exit. They're lucky I didn't go at them with my walker."

"All right, you two," Audrey said. "You'd better go pack. I'm going to see Jake, where sanity prevails."

"Don't count on it," Mimi said. "It's overrated anyway. I've had some most interesting conversations with those on the fourth floor."

"I'm not even going there." Audrey finally understood life as she'd known it in Hot Springs was over. Lady Mauve had lured them all to the wild, wild West with her tell-only-a-little-bit journal and the promise of bootlegger gold. From here on out, it was all about Wildcat Bluff County.

"One more thing," Mimi said. "I finally figured out those two letters entwined in the wire heart."

"Really?" Audrey was amazed at that fact.

"Yes, indeed. M and J. Mauve and Jake." Mimi sounded proud of herself.

"Now that we know about them, it makes sense," Audrey said.

"You're right," Vivian said. "But now we really must go. So much to do. So little time."

"Right. I've got a tat in my future. See you soon," Mimi said.

And they were gone.

Audrey sat there for a moment, tried to shake off the disorienting experience but couldn't. She had a strong feeling that Lady Mauve's legacy was about to take on a whole new meaning...and life. No wonder she kept coming back to the post oak. Mauve and Jake had left a message about their love there.

She started her SUV's engine, left the dump, and headed down Wildcat Road. It was time to see Jake.

By the time she pulled to a stop in front of his farmhouse, she was ready to get his side of the story. As soon as she saw him sitting in his swing, she realized how much she'd missed him during the last week. He'd become a vital part of her life and she hadn't even realized it. But still...great-grandfather?

She walked up to the porch where he waited for her as if he knew she was coming to see him. She mounted the steps, but she didn't sit beside him. He had some explaining to do. She sat in a chair and faced him.

"You've heard." He raised his face, as if toward the sun, in her direction.

"Yes."

"You don't trust me."

"Not completely," she said.

"Wise. You want an explanation, don't you?"

"Yes. Please."

"I should have been in your lives all along. It's true."

"Why weren't you?" she asked.

"It's strictly my fault. Not Mauve's. I take full blame."

"Tell me."

"First, I want to make up as best I can for time lost, love lost, happiness lost…for all of us. And that includes my dear, beloved, departed Mauve."

"I'm concerned about Mimi," Audrey said. "She's giddy about living here with you."

"I feel the same way." A poignant expression crossed his face. "To live in the same house with my child born of Mauve's love and be with her every day is more than I ever could have hoped for in this life."

"She's not in the best of health," Audrey said.

"You'll be surprised how quickly she'll improve on Oakes Farm."

"I understand people can get well in the right environment, but still I'm concerned for her. She has to take three steps to get up to the porch and into the house."

"She'll make it fine." Jake smiled. "I'm still strong enough. And I'll help her be strong again."

"That's vital."

"But that's not your main question, is it?"

"No," she said.

"I haven't told Mimi or Vivian. I'll give you that honor, if it is one. I'd like you to tell them."

"All right."

"When Mauve first knew me, I wasn't blind. I can still see her vivid lavender eyes, the blackness of her hair, the porcelain luster of her skin. And her laugh was infectious. Everyone loved and admired her. Me…most of all." He stopped and cocked his head to one side. "Do all of you look like her?"

"Yes. Pretty much. Strong genes."

"Good. She was always prettier than me, although she begged to differ." He paused again. "I so wish I could see the three of you together. It'd be like seeing Mauve in all the stages of her life."

Audrey felt her heart begin to soften toward him again.

"We did so much together. Laughed. Loved. I made the best whiskey. She sold it. And they came from all over to revel in the luxury of her speakeasy and drink my special whiskey that was sold nowhere else."

"It must have been an amazing time."

"True enough. But all good things come to an end, or so they say. I'm not sure it's true because what Mauve and I shared endures forever...particularly now that I've been given a second chance with the family we created in love."

Audrey's heart softened a bit more.

"Nocona Jones brought my new will over today. I signed it."

"Please don't be hasty."

"Not hasty. I'm grateful to be able to give my legacy to my family. Oakes Farm does well and it will pass to the three of you," Jake said.

"Thank you, but—"

"No buts. This is what I want for my daughter, granddaughter, and great-granddaughter. What a treat to be able to say those words. And it will be an even bigger treat for the three of you to sit on the porch with me."

"They'll be here tomorrow," she said.

"I know. It doesn't seem possible and yet it seems exactly right."

"You still haven't answered my question."

"Unspoken and yet very much in the air." He lowered his head a moment, then raised it again. "Somebody sabotaged one of my stills. I didn't know it. All I knew was that it wasn't working right. I leaned over it, fiddled around, and it blew up in my face. Left me blind."

"Oh no. That's...that's..."

"Long past. It was just at the end of 1932 and Prohibition had been repealed, to go into effect in 1933. Mauve and I knew our bootlegger days were over, so we were making plans for our future. Together."

"But you didn't go forward with them," Audrey said.

"No. We were young. She had her whole life ahead of her. I didn't want her encumbered with a blind man. She deserved better."

"But she loved you."

"I figured she could love again. I knew I couldn't, but I did it for her."

"What?" Audrey asked.

"I sent her away. I told her I didn't love her. I was going to remain in Wildcat Bluff, but she needed to go out into the bigger world and make her mark there, like she had here. I insisted she never tell me where she went. And she didn't. So near and yet so far."

"She didn't want to go, did she?"

"No. She cried. She cajoled. She even got down on her knees and begged me not to forswear our love," Jake said with anguish in his voice.

"But you did."

"I did it for her." Tears leaked from his eyes and ran down his cheeks. "It was the biggest mistake of my life. She didn't tell me and I didn't know she was pregnant with the greatest gift of our love. Mimi."

"But she finally went."

"Yes."

"And that's why she wrote in the journal you made for her, 'I left my heart in Wildcat Bluff County, Texas,' isn't it?" Audrey asked.

"Yes. And she took my heart with her."

"That's so sad."

He raised his head…and smiled through his tears. "No more. Now our hearts are together again through our living love."

Audrey's heart softened completely. Jake wasn't just her friend. He was her beloved great-grandfather. She felt happiness rise up in her. Finally, her family was complete in a way it had never been without him.

"Can you forgive me, as I've never been able to forgive myself?"

"Love doesn't require forgiveness. Love is simply love."

"Thank you," he said.

"And Lady Mauve's love has come home to you...to all of us."

"Forever."

Chapter 26

COLE WAITED OUTSIDE THE BARN FOR SLADE, STORM, AND Oscar to show up. He'd asked them to come over. He had big news that, like Ernie, he wasn't taking a chance sharing over the phone. The day was turning out to be gold, from Ernie to Granny to his own discovery. He'd texted Audrey, but he hadn't heard back from her. He hoped she'd arrive any minute, too.

He'd left the gate open so they could just drive on through, but he still watched for them and kept an eye out for trouble. He checked the photos on his phone again as he paced back and forth. He wanted to get this show on the road.

He heard the deep growl of a one-ton engine. Finally. He looked up and saw Slade's blue pickup inside the compound. Right behind it came Audrey's much smaller SUV. He was glad she was safely home.

He stepped back to make way for the vehicles. Slade parked near the barn. Audrey parked at the house. Tater leaped out first, followed by Oscar, Storm, and Slade. Audrey hurried across the courtyard to join the group.

"What's up?" Slade asked, glancing around as if to make sure everything was still in place.

Cole grinned at them. "Let's go to the barn. I want you to see something."

"You look awful happy," Oscar said. "Must be good news."

"Yep. Did Granny tell y'all about our chat at the café?"

"Sure did," Slade said. "Ernie rivals the Buick Brigade for knowing everything going on in our county."

"Good thing, too." He opened the barn door. "I think we're finally getting a handle on this whole mess."

"Mess is right," Storm said. "The stock show is coming up soon. If I don't get to show Little Fernando and Margarita, Fernando and Daisy Sue will just be sick over it."

"We'll get there," he said. "Let's go see Fernando."

He led the group all the way down the center aisle until he reached the big bull. Daisy Sue, Little Fernando, and Margarita were outside soaking up the sun in their runs.

Fernando leaned his head out of his stall and snorted at them.

Storm threw her arms around his neck and kissed his nose. "How are you doing? I know you miss home, but you won't be in hiding forever."

Fernando snorted again.

"Okay, spill the beans," Slade said. "At this point I'm hoping for a miracle. Bottom line, Zane Ranch wants money and they appear willing to do anything to get it. At the least, we may have to split everything Fernando earns…and it's enough to excite those vultures."

"That's what you're here about," Cole said. "Backstory. Audrey and I picked up pizza at Ernie's. She showed us her new tattoo."

"It's beautiful work by a local artist," Audrey said.

"What do tats and pizzas have to do with Fernando?" Oscar took off his cowboy hat and scratched his bald head.

"Pizza, nothing. Tattoos, everything," Cole said.

"Come again?" Slade asked.

"Zane claims ownership of Fernando due to his ear tattoo," Cole said. "Those unique numbers and letters would be listed in the ranch's computer records, as well as with the American Angus Association. Right?"

"Yep. Old news," Slade said.

"Ernie's tats got me to thinking…what if Zane altered Fernando's tattoo and hacked records?"

"Who'd have the gumption to do something out-of-bounds like that?" Oscar asked.

"Better yet, who'd think of it in the first place? And have the know-how to carry it out," Slade said. "That's serious criminal activity."

"Somebody desperate for cash looks around for big, easy, quick money. And there's Fernando. Quite a few locals know he was a runaway. Somebody at Zane puts two and two together and comes up with a plan," Cole said.

"And somebody carries it out." Slade looked thoughtful.

"Right. Anyway, it was just an idea until I looked at Fernando's tattoo. I snapped some shots of it and played around in the edit function for more contrast. Take a look. I think it's been altered." Cole held out his phone.

Slade took it and flipped through the photographs. "Could be. But how?" He handed the phone to Storm.

She looked at the photos, shook her head, and held out the phone.

Oscar took it and scanned the pictures, then returned the cell to Cole. "I'll take a look at Fernando's ear. Dirty tricks turn up now and again."

"You ever hear of altering a tattoo?" Cole asked.

"Nothing new under the sun." Oscar walked over and stroked Fernando's long nose before he looked at the tattoo and rubbed a thumb over the punched code.

"What do you think?" Slade asked.

"We may have a winner," Oscar said. "Green ink looks well matched, but that's not hard to come by."

Slade examined the tattoo on Fernando's ear, then turned back to Cole with a raised eyebrow.

"I thought about the location of GTT to Steele Trap and decided to check my own files for Fernando's tattoo—owner's herd letters, individual animal identification number, and year letter," Cole said. "I got a close hit in my own files."

"How close?" Slade asked in a tense voice.

"Looks like somebody altered GTT herd letters to Zane herd letters on Fernando's tattoo. You can turn a P into a B easily enough. It wouldn't work with just any herd letters, but in this case not much needed to be adjusted to fit Zane."

"No other changes?" Slade asked.

"None."

"Hell of a note. Bet they were counting on the fact that tattoos aren't always perfect," Slade said. "If they could get Steele Trap to admit Fernando was a lost calf raised by us, nobody would look any deeper into the situation."

"And that's bound to be what happened," Oscar said, looking disgusted at the idea. "We weren't on our toes."

"But how could they alter the tattoo?" Audrey asked. "Fernando is huge. He'd need to be sedated or something."

"Tranquilizer," Oscar said. "He's been in a pasture. He's used to people. Pour out some feed and he wouldn't be leery of you. Use a dart gun. Our air guns will shoot thirty feet, easy. No problem getting to him."

"Fernando could've been hurt." Storm stroked down the bull's long nose.

"He's okay," Slade said. "Big strong animal like him isn't easy to hurt."

"It's illegal as all get-out." Oscar shook his head. "That's something else they were counting on."

"Right," Slade said. "We're honest. Gives them an edge."

"We don't know if Zane changed the AAA's records or just counted on nobody checking them," Cole said.

"We'll get Nocona Jones on it," Slade said. "I'm getting madder the deeper we get into our trouble with Zane Ranch."

"If we legally prove our position, Fernando and the twins are free and clear of Zane." Cole glanced around the group for affirmation.

"That's the best possible outcome," Slade said.

Storm walked over to Cole, put her hands on her hips, and looked up at him. "Fernando's GTT, not Zane?"

"That's what I think. Good stock, too. We need to get the documentation squared away to prove it," Cole said. "That done, his sperm will go for even bigger bucks."

Storm glanced from Cole to Fernando and back again. "What do you want for him and the twins?"

"Money?" Cole asked, shocked she'd go there.

"Yes. We'll do whatever we have to do to keep him at Steele Trap," Storm said. "Fernando has earned a bit of money. I'd set it aside for my college education. But you can have it all in exchange for him."

Cole knelt down so they were at eye level. "When's your birthday?"

"I already had it."

"How about May Day?" he asked.

"That's when the twins were born."

He smiled. "In that case, I'll give a gift of Fernando and the twins to you for May Day."

Storm's blue eyes widened in surprise. "Really?"

"That's generous," Slade said. "Storm doesn't have to use her own money. Steele Trap would be willing to buy them, make a trade or something."

Cole looked up at him. "This is Wildcat Bluff. We take care of our own...and that includes Fernando, Daisy Sue, Little Fernando, and Margarita. They're family. And they belong on Steele Trap."

"Thank you!" Tears filled Storm's eyes and she threw her arms around Cole in a big hug. "Fernando thanks you, too."

Cole hugged her back, then stood up. "That's settled. Now we get down to the dirty work. We've got to shut this outfit down on several fronts."

"They used to hang cattle rustlers and horse thieves," Oscar said. "I've got plenty of rope in the barn and I'm about ready to get it out."

"We have law and order in the land now. Let's use it," Cole said. "If my mustangs are on Zane land, I'm going to find them. Once I do, I'll get the feds on their case. They'll come down hard on those horse thieves...and most likely cattle rustlers."

"Sounds to me like they're a one-stop-shop outfit," Oscar said. "We bring them down and Wildcat Bluff is cleaned up."

"Right. But let's not breathe a word to anyone outside our circle. We need to come up with a sting to catch them by surprise," Cole said.

"Nocona Jones will handle the legal end of it," Slade said.

"Good," Cole replied. "She can work with the law, too."

"Sounds like a plan." Slade gave Cole a rueful smile. "And to think if you hadn't had a hankering for pizza, we'd still be in a pickle."

"Don't forget Ernie's beautiful tats," Audrey said.

"Fernando will give Ernestine a special T-shirt in honor of her help." Storm smiled around at the group. "I mean, when it's all said and done. And we win big time."

"She'll love it," Cole said. "Maybe she'll even make space for a Fernando tattoo."

Storm grinned big. "That'd be great."

"Scream queens and Fernando," Audrey said. "What a combination."

Oscar laughed. "Truth of the matter, Ernie just might do it."

Everyone chuckled with him, easing the tension in the barn.

"Cole, if it's okay with you, let's keep Fernando hidden here and out of harm's way till all is resolved in our favor," Slade said.

"They're welcome to stay as long as necessary," Cole said.

"Thanks." Slade shook Cole's hand.

"It's getting on toward dark." Cole glanced down the length of the barn at the gathering shadows. "I'm going mustang hunting later."

"Need help?" Oscar asked. "Tater's always ready for action."

"Thanks, but no. I want to slip in and out of Zane Ranch with nobody the wiser."

"Be careful," Slade said. "If we don't hear from you by morning, we'll send in the sheriff."

Cole chuckled. "Appreciate it, but I ought to be able to get the job done without getting caught by that mangy outfit."

"We'll leave you to it," Slade said. "Granny and Sydney will want to hear all about Fernando's GTT tattoo."

Storm gave Fernando a kiss on his nose, then hurried down the aisle ahead of the others.

"You've made a little girl happy. You know my niece means the world to me," Slade said. "I can't thank you enough."

"Glad to help out. If we play our cards right, we'll wrap up Zane, tie the outfit with a big bow, and present those rustlers to the authorities."

"I'd like nothing better than to see them in handcuffs," Slade said.

"We'll get it done."

Slade strode down the aisle with Oscar and Tater right behind him.

Cole smiled at Audrey, put an arm around her shoulders, and walked with her outside.

"I'll be in touch," Cole called as the Steele Trap crew piled into their one-ton and took off.

"That was a neat bit of detective work," Audrey said.

"I owe it all to Ernie."

She laughed as they walked to the house.

"Ready for pizza?" Cole asked.

"Yeah."

"Ernie sent it home with me."

"Good for her."

He opened the front door and they stepped inside.

"I've got news," she said.

"You, too?" He pulled the pizza box out of the fridge. "Cold okay? If you prefer, we can heat it in the microwave."

"I like cold pizza." She set paper plates on top of the bar, then poured tea into two glasses.

"Me, too." He popped open the top of the pizza box, then sat down at the bar.

"I'm starved." She joined him and selected a piece.

He picked out the biggest slice and bit into it.

"Sausage," she said.

"Good." He barely got the word out around a big mouthful.

"Yeah."

They ate silently for a while, drinking tea, chewing pizza.

Finally, she turned to him. "Mom, Mimi, and Gerald are coming here tomorrow."

"What?" He choked, coughed, and grabbed his glass of tea. He took a big swallow and turned to look at her. "Here? Tomorrow? Who's Gerald?"

"Surprise to me, too." She hesitated, glanced away, then back at him. "Cole, we just found out…"

He grinned and gave her a quick kiss. "Jake's your great-grandfather."

"Yes."

"That's wonderful news. He's a terrific guy."

"I know it. Still, it's hard to believe…and yet it feels so right. Plus he's welcoming us with open arms," she said.

"Sounds like him."

"Mimi is moving in with her father to take care of him."

"I thought she was sick," Cole said.

"Wildcat Bluff is having a healing effect on her."

"And she hasn't even arrived yet." He turned serious. "So you don't need bootlegger gold to pay for medical bills anymore?"

"I'm not sure, but I don't think so."

"I told you I'd sell cattle to pay for whatever she needs," he said.

"I'm coming to believe love is what she needs. Not medical intervention."

"And Jake has plenty of it to give."

"Yes," she said. "And so do we."

He nodded in agreement, thinking how love had come to them all.

"Something else."

"What?" He felt his stomach tighten. What if she went back to Hot Springs now that she no longer needed the gold?

"Mom and Gerald. They're thinking of moving here."

"Gerald?" Cole felt as if events were spinning so fast he'd be catching up for months.

"They met at the nursing home before his mother passed a few months ago. They've been an item since then," Audrey said.

"I don't understand," Cole said. "Move here? What about their work?"

"Gerald sold his business. Mom says she left ours in good hands."

Cole smiled. If Vivian was moving here, Audrey would be staying, too. "Where will they live when they get here? We've got room."

"They already have reservations at a B&B...Twin Oaks," she said.

"Nice place. But they're welcome here."

"Thanks. I think they'll be more comfortable on their own for now."

"Okay." He meant that it was okay in more ways than one, especially if Audrey stayed in Wildcat Bluff.

"Cole, this is a big deal for them. It's almost like coming home. And it's all about Lady Mauve and the heritage she left us."

"It's a big deal to me, too. As long as they're here, I suspect you'll be here. And I don't want you anywhere else."

"Thanks. I want to be here...with you."

"Good." He smiled, feeling a lightness of heart. "You look like you have something on your mind. What is it?"

"Lady Mauve's speakeasy. Do you suppose we could rent it, borrow it, or something to throw a welcome-home party for my family? It'd be you, Jake, Gerald, Mom, Mimi."

"And the ghost of Lady Mauve." He smiled tenderly at her.

"Without a doubt."

"Did you just include me in family?"

She returned his smile. "Sounded like I did, didn't it?"

"Yes…and that's the way I want it."

"Me, too." She squeezed his hand. "I don't know the speakeasy owners. Can you set it up? Short notice and all."

"I don't doubt for a minute y'all will be welcome there. I'll make a call later."

"Thanks. If that's not possible, we could meet at Jake's house," she said.

"Or here."

She nodded. "But wouldn't the speakeasy be perfect?"

"You know it. Go ahead and set in your mind that we'll make it happen."

"Wonderful."

"I've got more news for you, too. But we can share our day later. Right now I've got one thing on my mind," he said.

"Mustangs?"

"Right." He slapped the pizza box top down and stored it in the fridge. "I've got to find those horses while they're still on Zane, if they are."

"How?"

"I checked topographical maps earlier and found some old photos online. There's one prime pasture that would suit the mustangs. It's where I'd put them. The Zane outfit is smart. I'm counting on them to protect their investment by running the horses there."

"How do you get to that particular pasture?" she asked.

"Not easy…but not too hard either. I've got it mapped out in my head. Tonight's the night." He put his hands down flat on top of the bar and leaned toward her.

"Are you driving there?"

"I'll take the Jeep—four-wheel drive—and get in as close as I can without spooking the mustangs and alerting the Zane cowboys. I'll hike the rest of the way from there," he said.

"Sounds dangerous."

"I'll be trespassing, so I'll go armed. I'm out of here as soon as I change to dark clothes. Night vision goggles are already in the Jeep."

"And you plan to go alone?" she asked.

"Sure."

"No, you're not."

"I'm not?" he asked.

"If you get into trouble, you need somebody with a cool head to get you out of it."

"Would that be you?" He chuckled, loving her a little more every moment they were together.

"Yes." She grinned with a mischievous glint in her eyes. "Let's just say Lady Mauve rides again."

"It's her old stomping ground, so she's sure to know the way."

"And she wouldn't let anybody get away with stealing from her," Audrey said.

"You're absolutely right. Let's get into some dark clothes and get on our way."

"You got it." She stood up, picked up the debris of their meal, and tossed it in the trash.

As they headed up the stairs, he clasped her hand, holding tight until they separated in the bedroom to change clothes.

"One good thing about Zane." He pulled on navy sweat pants before he tugged on a long-sleeve tee.

"What?" She dressed in about the same clothes, except smaller.

"If they hadn't stolen the mustangs, you wouldn't have seen them, and they wouldn't have chased you onto my ranch."

"Are you saying we owe them for our introduction?" she asked.

"I'm saying Lady Mauve works in mysterious ways."

Audrey chuckled, shaking her head. "Come on. Let's go find our mustangs."

And he led her down the stairs, out the front door, and into his Jeep. He checked to make sure he had two sets of night vision goggles in back, along with several bottles of water and a couple of fire extinguishers.

As he drove out of the compound, watching to make sure the gate closed behind them, he felt the adrenaline kick in like when he was fighting a fire. It felt good. Come hell or high water, he was going to find those mustangs and bring them home.

He drove down Wildcat Road, turned onto a gravel lane, hit a twisty dirt path, and came up on Zane Ranch from the back. He pulled off the road and edged behind thick brambles. He cut the lights and the engine. He'd driven with the windows down. Now he listened for any sound that didn't fit. It was quiet except for normal nocturnal rustles and the scampering of small critters.

He reached into the back and picked up the two goggles. He handed one to her and slipped on the other, setting it up on his head where he could easily drop it over his eyes when he needed it later. Tonight the moon was fairly full, so they should be able to make their way once their eyes adjusted to the night.

"Ready?" he whispered, squeezing her hand.

She smiled in response, looking excited about their adventure.

"If right's right, those mustangs—every single one of them—will be waiting for me to find them."

"I so hope they're there," she said.

"Fingers crossed."

"And toes."

He shared a smile with her, then turned and got out. Now he had to focus. Nothing mattered but getting in, finding the mustangs, and getting out without being caught.

He led the way, no trail, nothing to mark the way except the lay of the land and what he had in his head. Clouds scudded across the dark sky, obscuring then revealing the light of the moon.

As they progressed, stepping over fallen trees, around thick bramble bushes, through grass high enough to brush knees, the land around them turned silent when insects, frogs, birds, armadillos, skunks, and other animals went to ground until the intruders passed on by.

He knew how to walk quietly in pastures and woods, but Audrey had no such skills. He'd be happy to teach her. She'd need the knowledge as a Wildcat Bluff resident. He smiled at that thought, almost forgetting the importance of his mission. And then he was back on target. Mustangs. His heart hammered harder, as if urging him forward.

He stopped and leaned near her ear. "We're close. Stay right behind me. If the mustangs are in this pasture, Zane might have a guard on duty. Be as quiet as possible…like a little mouse."

She nodded in agreement.

He eased out from behind the huge trunk of an ancient oak, taking slow, steady steps toward the fence ahead. He heard her match him step for step. Good. She was learning already.

When he reached the fence, he stood by a post so as to partly camouflage his body. He felt her heat behind him, then to one side. He looked out across a beautiful open pasture with tall grass, wildflowers, and shade trees.

And the clouds overhead parted so moonlight bathed the pasture in a silvery glow to highlight a herd of wild mustangs.

Chapter 27

OAKES FARM HADN'T SEEN THE LIKE...NOT SINCE 1933, Audrey figured, as she sat with Jake in the swing on his front porch.

They'd sat together like this on many occasions, but this time was different. He held her hand, bone structure so much alike, as her dearly beloved great-grandfather, where before they had simply been friends. The difference was remarkable. She wouldn't trade it for the world. She smiled as she looked back and forth between them. She wore Western, too—pearl-snap purple shirt, Wranglers, and black boots. She definitely fit right in with him.

Oakes Farm hadn't seen the like...not after Lady Mauve sat in this very swing with her young lover.

And then Mauve disappeared from Wildcat Bluff. She'd gone into the unknown to never return, while Jake sat in this swing year after year with his memories and his regrets and his loneliness.

Oakes Farm hadn't seen the like...not until a big red SUV with Arkansas plates turned into the drive and made its way to the front of the pristine white farmhouse. Two doors opened. Two passengers stepped out. Two women walked up to the porch steps. They wore Western for the occasion—lavender shirts with white piping, upscale jeans, and fancy cowgirl boots.

"They're here," Audrey said unnecessarily as she patted Jake's hand.

"Will they like me, do you think?" he asked in a low voice edged with repressed emotion.

"They'll love you. No, they already love you." She stood up.

He got to his feet, straightened his shoulders, and took the few steps to meet them. "Welcome to Oakes Farm."

"Oh, Daddy!" Mimi cried out, then took the steps fast and sure, like a young woman. She threw herself into his arms, tears cascading down her cheeks.

"Mimi...my little Mimi, all grown up." Jake's tears joined hers as he hugged her close.

"Yes. I've been grown a long time now."

"Not to me." He gently set her back. "Audrey tells me you look like your mother."

"My hair is silver, but my eyes are definitely the same as hers."

"Beautiful. Like amethyst. I remember so well."

"Thank you."

"Vivian, I'm so glad you're here, too." He held out his arms to her.

"I can't tell you... I have no words for how happy I am to be here with you." She walked over and embraced him, tears shining in her lavender eyes.

Audrey watched the scene unfold as if she weren't part of it, although she knew she was. It's just that she'd known Jake for some time, while they were only now meeting him. She stayed silent because she wanted them to have this special moment together. And yet she very much wanted a group hug.

Jake placed his hands on either side of Vivian's face. "Audrey tells me you look like your grandmother."

"Yes. Strong genes."

"Beautiful ones." He held her there for a long moment. "You definitely have her bone structure."

"I'm glad."

"So am I." He turned toward Audrey and beckoned her over. "My family." He spoke the words with deep reverence and pulled them into a group hug. "I never thought to see the like...not here at Oakes Farm or anywhere else in this life. I am grateful beyond measure."

"We're grateful, too," Audrey said. "Mom. Mimi. It's wonderful to see you in Wildcat Bluff."

"After all your stories, how could we resist coming here?" Vivian asked.

"They tried to keep me in the nursing home," Mimi said. "They even suggested I might need to move to the fourth floor, considering my delusions about Wildcat Bluff."

Jake chuckled. "Bless their hearts. How could they know? Unless you've been here, how could you even begin to believe its reality?"

Mimi joined his laughter. "It may be the best kept secret in the world."

"Maybe we'd better keep it that way," Vivian said.

"It takes a special person to live here." Audrey smiled at her family as they separated but didn't go far. "I doubt it'd suit everybody."

"Or they'd suit Wildcat Bluff," Jake said.

"True." Audrey glanced around the group as she gave them a big smile. "I don't mean to rush us, but I have a very special reunion planned for the Oakes family."

Jake chuckled. "You sound like Mauve. She always had an ace up her sleeve to surprise and delight everyone."

"I hope y'all are happy with my surprise," Audrey said. "If everyone will get into my SUV, I'll drive you to our party venue. Cole is picking up Gerald and meeting us there."

"I'm all in. I could use a good party." Mimi headed for the steps. "They tried for good times at the nursing home, but…"

"Mom, you had fun there," Vivian said.

"I'm going to have a whole lot more fun here."

Mimi was halfway to Audrey's vehicle before anybody could catch up with her.

When everyone was settled inside, with Jake riding shotgun, she headed toward Wildcat Road. She drove slowly and carefully so she didn't jostle her passengers.

"Audrey, I appreciate your caution," Mimi said, "but I believe I speak for us all when I say we'd like to get to our party sometime in this century."

Jake laughed, turning his head toward his daughter. "You remind me of Mauve. She was always in a hurry."

"I'm making up for lost time," Mimi said.

"Okay." Audrey sped up, smiling to herself. To hear Mimi well enough and strong enough to be cantankerous was an absolute delight.

Not long after, she slowed down and rattled over the cattle guard under a ranch sign.

"Hallelujah Ranch," Vivian read the sign. "I like the name."

Jake stiffened in his seat. "Hallelujah? Audrey, where are you taking us?"

"I thought we'd enjoy a trip down memory lane with Lady Mauve."

"It's been a long, long time. Last time I was there, I could see... and it was an amazing sight to behold."

"Are you okay about going there?" Audrey asked. "I thought you'd like it, but maybe not."

"Alone, I wouldn't go. But with my family, it's the right thing to do. Y'all will get a real sense of Mauve."

"You two are talking in riddles," Vivian said. "Where are we going?"

"You'll see when we get there," Audrey said. "I want it to be a surprise."

"I like surprises," Mimi said. "Bring it on."

Audrey hit a dirt road that wound back into the ranch where red Angus cattle grazed on green grass and wildflowers waved colorful heads in the breeze. She passed a small blue pond shaded by a weeping willow tree. Finally she stopped beside Cole's truck in front of Big Rock, a sandstone outcropping that rose high into the sky from the plains around it.

Mimi laughed. "You brought us all this way to party on top of a rock? Really, Audrey, couldn't you do better?"

Jake laughed, too. "Hold your horses, Daughter. Trust your mother to never have done anything halfway."

"Okay, my lips are zipped." And Mimi made a zip motion across her mouth.

Jake chuckled again. "Oh…how I've missed the wit and the attitude."

Mimi simply rolled her eyes.

Audrey caught it all in her rearview mirror. Gold was nothing compared to an invigorated grandmother.

Mimi popped out of the back seat and opened Jake's door. "Daddy, would you escort me?"

"I'd be honored." Jake chuckled as he stepped down and held out an elbow.

"Thanks." Mimi tucked her hand around his arm.

Vivian got out and joined them.

"Here, Granddaughter." Jake held out his other elbow.

"Thanks." Vivian made it three abreast.

Audrey felt her eyes fill with tears of happiness. She'd made this happen by coming to Wildcat Bluff. She thanked her lucky stars for all her many blessings. Now she'd just keep adding to them.

She got out and walked over to Big Rock. She motioned to her family, and they followed her. She stepped into the dark interior of the rock, knowing that to them she'd just disappeared from view, but she'd also activated a motion sensor that turned on a light in the area. She put her fingertips on a brick wall, then stepped to the side and disappeared from their view again. She popped back out so they could see her.

"Audrey, you're playing games, aren't you?" Jake called out, chuckling.

"I couldn't resist letting them see how the blind tiger worked back in its heyday."

"Nobody who wasn't in the know ever suspected this was the entrance to Mauve's domain," he said.

"No wonder." She gestured to Mimi and Vivian. "Come on in."

"Blind tiger?" Mimi asked. "I've heard that phrase before, I'm sure, but not for a long time."

"You'll see. Come on," Audrey said.

When they joined her, she gestured for them to turn left and go forward. When they did, she kept a cautious eye on Jake, but he appeared to know the structure like he did his own farmhouse. In that moment, she knew for sure he had been here many times before, so long ago.

She followed them and stepped into Lady Mauve's famous speakeasy. She smiled at Cole, who stood beside a tall lean blond man dressed casually in a blue knit shirt, charcoal trousers, and leather loafers. He was a good-looking guy and about her mother's age. He raised a hand in greeting. She figured he must be Gerald and she liked him on sight.

But he didn't hold her attention long. The speakeasy called to her. She noticed a row of plush scarlet sofas accented with small walnut tables on one side of the long room. Individual round tables with crimson upholstered chairs were grouped across the room. A grand piano rose majestically on its personal dais in one corner. Instead of a pianist tickling the ivories, 1920s jazz softly filled the speakeasy from a thumb drive inserted into a small music player.

A walnut horseshoe bar with a white marble top at the far end was the centerpiece of the room. Round walnut stools with red leather seats surrounded the outside of the bar. Behind the bar rose floor-to-ceiling shelves filled with sealed bottles of moonshine. Crystal glasses and a silver set gleamed on the white marble countertop beneath the liquor shelves. An Art Deco–design chandelier overhead cast soft light over the room, along with recessed lighting in the pressed-tin tile ceiling.

"Wow…just wow," Mimi said. "Mom really outdid herself."

"Lady Mauve's domain," Jake said. "We spent many a happy hour here. It's good to be back." He ran fingertips across a tabletop. "How does it look? I heard it was in perfect condition when found by Hallelujah's owner."

Cole stepped forward. "Y'all might not have heard about it in Arkansas, but the discovery of this speakeasy was big news in Texas."

"I'm not sure, but didn't it have something to do with a lonely hearts club?" Audrey asked.

"Yes," Cole said. "Violet Ashwood runs Cowboy Heart-to-Heart Corral from here. She moved most of her stuff out of the way and behind the bar so we could see the place as it was in Lady Mauve's day."

"So sweet of her," Vivian said.

"Generous," Mimi added.

"And the perfect place for our first family reunion," Jake said. "Audrey, you've got the Mauve touch."

"Thank you. I hope so."

"If I'd known we were coming to a speakeasy, I'd have bobbed my hair, put on my flapper dress and ankle-strap heels, and been ready to Charleston with my favorite beau." Mimi danced over to the piano, leaned back against it, and tossed her head. "Any takers?"

Everyone laughed, enjoying her antics.

"Oh dear… Gerald, I apologize," Vivian said. "I should have introduced you to Jake and Audrey right away."

"No problem." Gerald walked over to her. "You were caught by the magic of this speakeasy."

"That's the truth," Vivian said. "It's stunning, isn't it?"

"Yes, it is, but not as stunning as you," Gerald said.

"Thank you." She turned to Audrey. "This is my daughter and this is my grandfather. You've heard me speak often about them."

"So true. And always in glowing terms."

"Audrey. Jake. Please meet Gerald Carswell."

"It's an honor to meet you both." Gerald shook their hands, then stepped back. "I'm looking forward to many celebrations in Wildcat Bluff. I'm short of family myself, so this is a special treat."

"I'm glad you like it here," Audrey said.

"I do. In fact, I like it so much, I've been talking with Cole about finding my own little place in Wildcat Bluff."

Cole chuckled. "By little he means a sprawling ranch."

"I don't like to do things halfway," Gerald said. "If I'm going to do something, I'm going to do it right."

"You sound like Mauve," Jake said. "That was always her motto. Look around you. We spent many an hour creating this speakeasy together. She was the brains. I was the muscle. We got it done together."

"It's truly a work of art," Audrey said.

"Thank you." Jake smiled at her. "I'm so glad it's in use again. Mauve would have loved a lonely hearts club in a place where she encouraged lonely hearts to come together and heal their loneliness."

"Do you miss that time?" Gerald asked.

"I don't miss Prohibition or bootlegger runs, but I will always miss Mauve," Jake said. "Only now I have a part of her back in my very own daughter, granddaughter, and great-granddaughter."

"And that's why we're here to celebrate," Audrey said. "We have you in our lives and we couldn't be happier."

"Is it time?" Cole asked.

"Yes, it is." Audrey gave him a warm smile.

He walked behind the bar and picked up a silver tray with a bottle of champagne and seven crystal glasses. He set the tray on top of the bar.

"Everyone, let's join Cole and toast our reunion." She walked over to him and the others followed her.

Cole popped the cork, poured bubbly liquid into every single glass, then handed a glass to everyone. A single glass of bubbly was left on the tray.

"To our very first family reunion," Audrey said.

"May there be many, many more," Vivian said.

"Right here in wonderful Wildcat Bluff County," Mimi said.

They all clinked crystal glasses, then sipped champagne.

"There's one glass left. It belongs to Lady Mauve." Audrey picked it up. "Jake, will you do the honors for her?"

"It would give me great pleasure to think she is with us here on this very special day," Jake said.

Audrey set the glass in his hand, then glanced around the group. She raised her glass. "To Lady Mauve, long may her legacy live on."

And everyone clinked their glasses together again.

Chapter 28

AFTER A LITTLE OVER A WEEK OF SHOWING HER FAMILY around the area, Audrey arrived at the Wildcat Bluff Youth Spring Stock Show. Cole parked his truck among all the other pickups, most with trailers. Excitement filled the air. It was an all-day affair, but it wasn't a casual affair. Youngsters had worked long and hard to raise heifers and steers to enter the competition. Not only were reputations on the line, but trophies, buckles, and scholarships as well.

Audrey glanced over at Cole. He looked grim and determined. She knew how he felt. They weren't there for the show, the food, the competition. They were there for the sting. Zane Ranch was about it get its comeuppance.

Once they'd found the mustangs, things had moved fast. Cole had contacted Sheriff Calhoun, who had taken it from there and alerted the feds. U.S. Marshals. Bureau of Land Management officers. Game wardens. Maybe even a Texas Ranger. All would be represented at the show. Along with the sheriff, they would make sure justice came to Wildcat Bluff because nobody messed with a federal program to protect endangered mustangs.

Steele Trap Ranch provided the bait. Fernando and Daisy Sue, Little Fernando and Margarita were deemed irresistible lures to the all-hat-and-no-cattle who turned out to be Marvin Elwood, great-grandson of a famous East Texas wildcatter who brought in oil gushers that turned to gold. But that was a long time ago and the Elwood family hadn't fared so well in recent years.

Normally Elwood played it safe in his office penthouse in

downtown Dallas and kept his hands clean, no matter his under-handed dealings. Sug Culley usually did the dirty work for him on the ranch, but this time was different. Sug was no match for the feds when they confronted him about the mustangs—and Fernando's altered tattoo. They had all the evidence they needed to put Sug away for a long time, but they wanted his boss, Elwood. Sug rolled. He gave up Zane Ranch's horse thieving, cattle rustling, and Fernando stealing for the prospect of a lighter sentence. He now worked undercover for the feds, not Elwood.

News spread fast when it was announced on KWCB radio station and Fernando the Wonder Bull's website and social media that Fernando and family would appear at the stock show. They were a big draw. Sug persuaded Elwood that he should show up personally to take possession of Fernando and the twins. It would be covered in all the media and it would elevate him to stardom... and big bucks. Elwood bit.

To make the sting work, Storm had agreed to withdraw the twins from the stock show competition due to Zane Ranch's ownership claim. She'd also made a big deal out of her loss on social media to help lure Elwood to Wildcat Bluff. But Cole had let her know that once the feds had Elwood in handcuffs, he would give her proof of ownership for state-validated stock.

With everything and everyone in place, Audrey wished she felt more relaxed for the coming confrontation. Yet she didn't. Too much rode on the sting going down as planned. But what if it didn't? Fernando or Daisy Sue or the twins might get hurt, might bolt, or might be injured in some way. Fernando was huge, at least two thousand pounds. Little Fernando wasn't full grown, but he still weighed about seven hundred pounds. If it came to controlling them, halters and leads were no match for that much power.

"I wish you wouldn't worry," Cole said. "They're professionals. They've got it all worked out. We'll sit in the bleachers with your family and watch it all go down."

"I know. It's just that Zane Ranch has been so crafty up to this point that I can't help but wonder if they don't have another dirty trick to spring on us."

"Let's don't go there. It's all under control."

"You feel the same way I do. Go ahead and admit it," she said.

"I admit I won't rest easy until Marvin Elwood and the Zane Ranch rustlers are all behind bars."

"I wish the mustangs were already back on GTT land." She picked up her purse and hooked the strap over her shoulder.

"Me, too. But if we move them before Elwood is arrested, he might be alerted and back off."

"I know, but still…"

"Don't fret. We'll get them back," Cole said.

"I just want this all over and done with so I can fully enjoy Wildcat Bluff with my family."

"It'll happen. Today's the day to set everything right."

"Good."

"Come on. Let's go enjoy the stock show," he said.

"I've never seen one before, so it'll be a new experience."

She stepped down from the truck and he joined her. As they walked toward the show barn next to the rodeo arena, she realized she was beginning to feel right at home. She'd dressed Western like everybody else, and that was comfortable now, too. Of course, word had spread about Jake's unexpected relatives coming to live near him in the county. They were immediately accepted into the fold because of their family connections. She knew Mimi and Mom felt like she did—that they had finally come home. Cole was just the icing on the cake for her…and it was a thick, rich, delicious icing that was totally addictive.

Cole nodded or said hello to folks as they neared the barn because he had a lot of friends. She kept a smile on her face because she wanted to make a lot of friends. Bootlegger gold had brought her here, but friends and family would keep her here. They were more valuable than any amount of gold, particularly as it turned out to be nothing more than a tantalizing legend.

They entered the show barn with a line of other people. A buzz of voices filled the air, along with the scent of hay, feed, and cattle. On one side of the barn rose bleachers that were already half-full of spectators. On the other side stretched a line of pens made of continuous metal fence panels that held different breeds of heifers and steers groomed to perfection. The show ring dominated the center of the barn with a row of tables for the judges on the floor in front of the bleacher section.

"Mom texted me that she, Mimi, Jake, and Gerald are here. They found good seats near the judges on the bottom row. You're taller. Do you see them?"

"Yeah." He pointed and waved toward the bleachers. "Glad they made it. I'm even gladder they didn't try climbing up high."

"Me, too. I want them to stay safe." She was so happy to see her family sitting there all in a row. It hardly seemed real, but they were at the stock show together.

"Let's go see how Storm is doing," Cole said.

"I hope she's not too disappointed about having to withdraw the twins from competition."

"She'll have plenty more opportunities for them to win trophies. What's most important is keeping them, and Fernando, at Steele Trap."

"That's certainly true. I'm so glad you made that happen," Audrey said.

"I had a lot of help. I'll feel better when they're safely home."

"Just a few more hours and it'll all be done."

"Can't happen soon enough for me."

She walked with him over to the pens, where each animal had its own professional display and branding on the wall in back. The displays ranged from simple colorful banners to metal and wood cut-out signs. Heifers and steers stood or lay in their pens.

"Fine animals," he said. "You'll notice they're provided with cedar fiber bedding, probably six to ten inches deep to keep them comfortable and sound."

"I wondered what that was. Guess it's a good idea."

"Real good idea. These are valuable and loved animals, so they get the finest of care. You'll notice they've been bathed and their hair clipped all over."

"They're beautiful," she said.

As they continued down the row, she saw a variety of breeds that she'd never seen before this moment.

"If you're wondering, that's an Aberdeen. Red Angus is next. Hereford. You'd be surprised how many breeds get shown at a stock show."

"I want to learn about cattle. They're so interesting," she said.

"I'll be happy to teach you."

"Thanks."

As they moved onward, she glanced at the people. Lots of them obviously tended cattle in the pens, appearing as if part of a famous person's entourage. Other folks checked the animal in each pen, perhaps looking at competition or for possible acquisition. A few simply wandered by. She wondered which ones might be the undercover agents. She figured at least one or more would stay, even if unobserved, near Fernando.

When they reached the Steele Trap pens, she saw Granny, Slade, Sydney, and Storm. Fernando, Daisy Sue, Little Fernando, and Margarita had been groomed to perfection. Folks slowly walked by or stopped to admire them.

"Hey there," Storm called when she saw them. She rushed over, wearing her special long-sleeve tee with FERNANDO THE WONDER BULL emblazoned across the front. She hugged Cole.

"How's it going?" he asked.

"I'm about ready to show Fernando in the ring. Just us. Nobody else."

"I'll watch."

"Thanks," Storm said.

Slade walked over and shook Cole's hand. "Appreciate what you did for us…and the entire county, for that matter."

"Think nothing of it. Glad to help out."

"Listen," Slade said. "You've gone well beyond being a good neighbor on this deal. I talked with Storm, and she wants to give you a calf out of Fernando and Daisy Sue."

"That's not necessary."

"We'd like to do it anyway. Besides, it'd be good to continue the bloodline on GTT Ranch."

"Okay. I'd appreciate it," Cole said.

"That's wonderful. And generous." Audrey looked from one cowboy to the other. And she thought of Lady Mauve—no wonder she left her heart in Wildcat Bluff. There was no better or safer place to nurture a woman's heart, or a man's for that matter. She was so glad to be here.

"Uncle Slade. Cole. Audrey. I'm going to show Fernando now." Storm walked up with the huge black bull on a thick lead attached to his halter.

Audrey couldn't help but think how easily he could jerk the rope out of the little girl's hand. The big bull let her lead him out of choice. No other reason, not with a powerful animal like him.

Storm led Fernando to the in gate, then took him into the show ring. When they reached the center, the barn went silent as everyone stopped to watch Storm walk Fernando the Wonder Bull around the ring.

Audrey looked on in awe as she stood beside Cole and Slade.

"Impressive," Cole said.

"Girl or bull?" Slade asked.

"Both," Audrey said.

As Storm turned toward the out gate, a loud commotion sounded at the entry of the show barn. Soon a big man in a dark blue Western suit with a bolo tie, straw hat, and alligator cowboy boots strode up to Storm. He stopped. She stopped. Fernando stopped. The stranger was followed by a man holding up a cell phone to record the event.

"Storm Steele, this bull is mine. I'm Marvin Elwood, the rightful owner of Fernando, as well as his twins, Little Fernando and Margarita. My cowboys are backing up trailers as we speak to load them up and transport them to a fine place I have near Dallas." He glanced up and around the show ring with a big smile because phones had gone up everywhere to record what was going on.

"You're wrong." Storm raised her voice. "Fernando belongs to me…and you're going to jail!"

"Stupid little girl. You don't know anything." Elwood jerked the lead out of Storm's hands and turned to go. He pulled on the rope, but the big black bull didn't budge. Elwood glanced back, surprise written on his face.

"What an idiot," Slade said.

"Where are the cops?" Cole asked.

Audrey glanced around in concern. "This is where the law arrives to save the day, isn't it?"

"And catch the crook," Cole said.

"We'd better help." Slade hurried through the in gate with Cole and Audrey right behind him.

Storm grabbed the lead and tried to take it away, but Elwood pushed her away. She stumbled into Fernando, then righted herself.

"I said this bull belongs to me!" Elwood jerked on the lead as he looked around the barn. "Where are my cowboys?"

Fernando bellowed in outrage, pawed the floor, and lowered his head.

And from the cattle pens, two yearlings busted through their fence panels and charged across the show ring, echoing Fernando's bellow of outrage.

"Little Fernando! Margarita! Stay back," Storm called to them.

"I don't care what you pay me, I'm out of here," the guy video-ing the event said as he turned and ran away.

Elwood pointed at the enraged yearlings. "They're mine, too! And I'm taking them today."

"No, they're not." Storm stalked toward him.

Slade ran up, lifted her into his arms, and carried her to Cole and Audrey on the sidelines.

Little Fernando slammed into Elwood's front. Margarita charged his back. He spun around and straight into Fernando. The big bull lowered his head, caught Elwood between the shoulders, and tossed him into the air. He came down hard, groaning as he tried to crawl away, but he couldn't make it. He collapsed onto the show ring floor.

"Come here. I have oats. Come here." Storm held out her hands as she called to Fernando from where she stood in front of Slade, Cole, and Audrey.

Fernando raised his head, looked at her, then back at the downed man. He snorted, then turned and walked toward her, followed by Little Fernando and Margarita.

Sheriff Calhoun and three other law officers ran up to the fallen man while Storm and Slade led Fernando and the twins back toward the pens.

"You're under arrest," Sheriff Calhoun said. "Horse thieving. Cattle rustling. And tampering with legal documents."

Elwood groaned. "Just get me out of here."

"Happy to oblige," Sheriff Calhoun said. "Wildcat Bluff Fire-Rescue is on its way. I'd say you're going to have a lengthy stay in the hospital before you have a lengthy stay behind bars."

Elwood groaned again. "Lawyer. I want to call my lawyer."

"All in good time." Sheriff Calhoun stood up. "Here you go. EMTs are better than you deserve."

Two muscular cowboys wearing firefighter gear ran into the

show ring. One brought a gurney. The other carried a medical bag. They quickly strapped Elwood to the gurney, then wheeled him outside.

Sheriff Calhoun walked over to Cole and Audrey. "We got it done. No more trouble from Zane Ranch. Thanks for your help."

"Anytime," Cole said.

Sheriff Calhoun turned to go, then looked back with a smile. "Oh yeah, the mustangs are back on GTT Ranch where they belong." He walked to the other law officers and they left the show barn.

"We really did it, didn't we?" Audrey said.

"More like Fernando and gang did it." Cole chuckled.

She laughed, too. She glanced across the show ring at her family. Mimi gave her a thumbs-up while the others waved at her. She waved back.

"Audrey, as much as I love your family and as much as I love the Steele family and Fernando..." Cole said.

"Yes?"

"Do you suppose we could go home now? We've hardly had a moment alone in the last week."

"I recall night times in your big bed."

"I'd hope so." He smiled. "I want to check on the mustangs. I want...I just want to be with you—only you—now that this is all over."

She squeezed his hand. "And I only want to be with you. Let's go."

"You're sure?"

"Yes." She waved at her family in the bleachers, then tugged him away from all the activity and out of the show barn.

"Might even be cold pizza in the fridge," he said when they reached his pickup.

She leaned into him. "I don't want pizza. I want you."

"In that case, get in the truck and let's get out of here."

She laughed as she swung up into the passenger seat and settled onto the soft leather seat.

He joined her in the cab, revved the engine, left the parking lot, and hit Wildcat Road with a heavy foot on the accelerator.

After a bit, she gestured at the land around them. "Mom says Gerald says Marvin Elwood can't hang on to his property."

"Don't doubt it for a minute. Lawyers will take what little he has left."

"Mom says Gerald is going to bid on Zane Ranch."

"Really? That's a big spread," Cole said.

"Yeah."

"He'll need help."

"Yeah."

"Guess that's what family is for." Cole glanced over at her. "You are going to marry me, aren't you?"

She looked into his warm brown eyes. "Is that a proposal?"

"Yep."

"Not very romantic."

"Hang on. I'll show you romantic." And he stepped on the gas, letting his truck roar down the road toward his destination.

She just sat back, thinking about marrying him, thinking about life on GTT Ranch, thinking about Wildcat Bluff. Life couldn't get much better than settling down here with the love of her life.

He turned under the GTT Ranch sign, rattled across the cattle guard, cut off on a dirt road, and followed it across a pasture. He stopped the truck at a fence and opened his door.

"This is romantic?"

"Come on. We aren't there yet."

She got out, figuring she'd just about follow this man anywhere.

They walked hand in hand across the pasture. Birds chirped in the treetops. Wildflowers scented the air. Bees buzzed as they flitted from flower to flower.

Cole stopped and pointed. "Now that's romantic."

And in the distance she could see the mustangs. They'd finally come home…just like she had.

Acknowledgments

Lots of appreciation goes to Hot Springs, Arkansas, with its rich historical heritage that inspired its connection to Wildcat Bluff, Texas. Hot Springs is always a treat with its hot springs and vintage hotels where visitors still enjoy spas with medicinal waters. Bathhouse Row attractions include historical museums such as the Gangster Museum of America with information and artifacts about the Roaring Twenties, Prohibition, revenuers, bootleggers, and speakeasies. Hot Springs National Park was established in 1921. Oaklawn Racing of thoroughbreds, Woodland Gardens, and the *Belle of Hot Springs* riverboat are nearby fun.

As always, I owe a debt of gratitude to Christina Gee of Gee Cattle Ranch. She helped me figure out how Fernando's past brought a big problem to Steele Trap Ranch and how it could be resolved to everyone's satisfaction. Not only did we have fun coming up with this plot element, but we did it over delicious snacks at a little outdoor eatery enclosed in a wooden corral— naturally off the beaten track.

I turned to Rod Williams when I needed to work out the logistics of how the horse thieves were transporting mustangs out of the county dump. We brainstormed over a long phone call, and I can't thank him enough for getting me past that book snag.

Logan Williams tromped through high grass on the ranch with me, discussing this and that until he came up with the county dump as an interesting element for my novels. I'm much appreciative for his idea.

At a peewee rodeo, I hung out with Gee Cattle Ranch cowboys

and cowgirls to watch barrel racing come alive in a small-town dusty arena. We were there to watch Laren Gee—long blond hair the same color as her horse blowing in the breeze—ride to another big win. She definitely inspired my own cowgirl Storm Steele, so this is a shout-out to Laren.

About the Author

Kim Redford is the bestselling author of Western romance novels. She grew up in Texas with cowboys, cowgirls, horses, cattle, and rodeos. She divides her time between homes in Texas and Oklahoma, where she's a rescue cat wrangler and horseback rider—when she takes a break from her keyboard. Visit her at kimredford.com.